PRAISE FOR

BLOOD GUILT

'Fast-moving action and a lot of twists make this debut novel a most enjoyable read.'
— Marcel Berlins, *The Times*

ANGEL OF DEATH

'The nature of justice and its moral ambiguities are studied in this fast-paced novel.'
— *Left Lion Magazine*

JUSTICE FOR THE DAMNED

'A violent novel that would make a cool British gangster flick.'
— *Crime Thriller Hound*

SPIDER'S WEB

'*Spider's Web* is a fast-paced, thoroughly researched, and heartbreaking novel.'
— *CrimeSquad*

THE LOST ONES

ALSO BY BEN CHEETHAM

Blood Guilt

Angel of Death

Justice for the Damned

Spider's Web

THE
LOST
ONES
BEN CHEETHAM

THOMAS & MERCER

This is a work of fiction. Names, characters, organizations, places, events, and incidents are either products of the author's imagination or are used fictitiously.

Published by Thomas & Mercer, Seattle

www.apub.com

ISBN-13: 9781503940079
ISBN-10: 1503940071

Cover design © blacksheep-uk.com

Printed in the United States of America

For Clare

DAY 1
10.32 A.M.

OPERATOR: Caller, you're through to the police. How can I help?

CALLER: It's my daughter. She's gone and we think we've found blood.

OPERATOR: What do you mean by 'gone'?

CALLER: She's disappeared. We can't find her anywhere.

OPERATOR: How old is your daughter?

CALLER: Nine.

OPERATOR: What's her name?

CALLER: Erin Jackson.

OPERATOR: And what's your name?

CALLER: Amanda.

OPERATOR: OK, Amanda, I need you to tell me what happened. How long has Erin been missing?

CALLER: I'm not sure. Maybe forty minutes. She was playing down by the stream.

OPERATOR: You said 'we'. Who else is with you?

CALLER: A man and a woman. I don't know their names.

OPERATOR: Can you tell me where you are?

CALLER: Harwood Forest. About fifteen minutes' walk along the track behind Newbiggin Farm.

OPERATOR: Could your daughter have wandered into the forest and got lost?

CALLER: I . . . I don't know. Maybe. Oh, God, it's so red. It's got to be blood!

OPERATOR: I need you to stay calm and remain on the line, Amanda. Officers are on the way. They'll be with you as soon as possible.

CALLER: Please hurry. Please hurry—

DAY 1

FOUR AND A HALF HOURS EARLIER...

Tom Jackson stared at his sleeping wife. One of Amanda's slender arms rested on the pillow above her shoulder-length auburn hair. The other was extended towards Tom. His clammy fingers lay against her soft, warm upturned palm. His eyes traced the long line of her neck, her strong jaw, her half-moon lips, the straight slope of her nose. In the muted metallic gleam seeping through the curtains, she possessed a kind of timeless beauty. Like an image sculpted from marble.

He found his mind flashing back through the years to the first time he'd seen her. She'd been sleeping then, too. Cradled by the roots and shadows of Harwood Forest, she'd looked like something from a fairy tale. He'd watched her from behind a tree, feeling slightly guilty for doing so, but too spellbound to take his eyes off her. He'd jerked back out of sight when she stirred and opened her eyes. After a breathless moment, he'd risked another peek and seen her cycling away along one of the sandy tracks that crisscrossed the forest. His heart had tightened. Who was this girl? Was she from Middlebury? Would he ever see her again? He wasn't religious, but he'd prayed that he would do. His prayer had been answered five years later when, once again by chance, he spotted her in a local pub. That was the night he'd fallen in love with her.

Amanda moved her head and the light picked out lines at the corners of her mouth and eyes, creases in her cheeks. Her face had always been like that – a slight shift in the light or her mood could add or erase years from it. Sometimes she barely seemed to have aged a day in the twenty-one years they'd been together. At other times Tom was struck by how old she looked.

Amanda's eyes moved beneath their closed lids. Tom wondered what she was dreaming about. Was she seeing what he saw in his good dreams or in his bad ones? Security and prosperity or uncertainty and hardship? Her peaceful face suggested the former. Of late his dreams – when he managed to sleep at all – were almost always a mundane echo of his waking fears. He saw court appearances, bailiffs, eviction. Worst of all, he saw himself having to go cap in hand to his in-laws.

Heaving a sigh, he slid out of bed. Amanda stirred but didn't open her eyes as he shrugged on his dressing gown. He quietly opened and closed the door behind him. Then he stood motionless for a moment in the silence of the morning. His gaze moved around the landing – four doors, a mirror, a framed landscape painting, a steep set of stairs leading up to the attic. It wasn't a bad little house. But he wanted so much more. Wanted it so badly he felt it like an ache in his chest.

Tom caught sight of himself in the mirror – rumpled short black hair, darkly stubbled chin, once-broken nose. He patted his stomach. He was still in reasonably good shape, although he was a little thinner on top and thicker in the middle than he'd been back when he acquired the bump on his nose.

'Daddy.'

The sleepy little voice came from an open door opposite. Tom padded into a bedroom with pink walls and a cloud-painted ceiling.

A spray of faintly luminous stars arched over a bed crowded with stuffed toys. A sign hanging on the wall read, 'Star light, star bright, watch over our sweet Erin tonight.' A young girl was sitting up in the bed, flushed with sleep, rubbing her eyes and squinting at Tom. Erin had her mum's tousled autumnal hair and her dad's dark-chocolate eyes. Her cute button nose and dimpled cheeks were all her own.

'Shh, go back to sleep, sweetie,' murmured Tom.

'What time is it?'

'It's early.'

'Why are you up, Daddy?'

Because today is the day that will decide our future, thought Tom. But he would never have said such a thing to Erin or her older brother Jake. He tried his best to keep his worries from them. Not that he always succeeded, especially where Erin was concerned. She had an almost uncanny ability to pluck his thoughts out of his head – something else she'd inherited from her mother.

'Is it because you had a bad dream?' asked Erin.

'No. I had a good dream. I dreamt about you and Jake and your mum. That we were all happy.'

A faint frown disturbed the smooth surface of Erin's face. 'But we're happy already, aren't we, Daddy?'

Tom smiled. 'Yes. Very. Now lie back down.'

As Erin returned her head to the pillows, he pulled the duvet up over her shoulders and kissed her forehead. He retreated slowly, watching her slide back into sleep. Perfect. That was the only word for her. She deserved the world and he was determined to give it to her. His thoughts returned to what awaited him in the coming hours, dragging another deep sigh from his lungs.

He headed downstairs, made a coffee and took it into the small room he used as his home office. He approached a bookshelf lined with ambitious-sounding books such as *Adventures in Making*

Millions and *Becoming the Ultimate Entrepreneur*, and more prosaically entitled ones such as *Open-Cast Mining and Quarrying* and *Hydraulic Excavator Applications*. He plucked out a book entitled *Believe and Succeed* and flicked through its dog-eared pages until he found the highlighted quote: 'Do not fear. Fear is useless. Believe in yourself and there is nothing you will not be able to achieve.' He murmured the words, clenching his fist as if to catch hold of them.

He sat down at the desk. His gaze lingered on a blown-up photo Blu-tacked to the wall. At the photo's centre was a crescent of grey-gold rock cut into the flank of a grassy hill. Meadows and thickets of trees dotted with an occasional house spread out from the base of the hill. The edge of a larger tract of woodland encroached onto the right-hand side of the scene. But it was what occupied the upper centre of the photo that drew and held Tom's attention. To his eyes there was something strangely alien about the circle of five standing stones that crowned the rounded summit of the hill. The regularly spaced stones marked the edge of a disc of rough grass. They were in turn haloed by an earthen circle highlighted by the long shadows of a low sun. According to folklore, the stones were the Five Women, a coven of witches turned to stone for dancing on the Sabbath. Pagans gathered there every summer solstice to celebrate the longest day of the year. As a teenager, Tom had got drunk and watched white-robed druids silhouetted against the setting sun weave in and out of the stones to the beat of drums. He and his mates had performed a mocking jig of their own as the druids chanted, 'We are a circle within a circle, with no beginning and never ending . . .' Back then he'd thought all that crap was hilarious. A big joke. Now it made his head pound to think about it.

Turning his attention to his laptop, Tom opened a file entitled 'Speech to planning committee'. He scanned through the file, adding a word or two here, deleting one there. He'd been working on it for weeks, obsessively honing and fine-tuning. Three minutes. That was all the time he had to deliver the speech that would make or break his ambitions. He was determined to use every available second to maximum effect. He started a stopwatch and began to recite, 'Mr Chair, members of the committee . . .' When he reached the end, he hit the stopwatch again and checked his timing: 2 minutes 58 seconds. About as close to perfect as he was going to get. Just let those planning jobsworths dare reject his proposal.

There was a soft knock at the door. Amanda poked her head into the room. Her hair was tied in a loose ponytail. Her strikingly green, almost oriental, eyes gave Tom an appraising look. 'You couldn't sleep,' she stated.

'I got a couple of hours.'

'How are you feeling?'

Tom pushed out his lower lip, cocking his head slightly. 'Nervous . . . Ready.'

Amanda nodded, satisfied by his answer. 'Have you had breakfast yet?'

'No.'

'I'll make you some.' Tom started to say he wasn't hungry. But, as she was so good at doing, Amanda read his thoughts and responded before he could speak. 'You need to eat something.' With a wry glimmer of a smile, she added, 'Breakfast is the most important meal of the day, you know.'

Tom smiled back at the line he'd heard her use so many times on the kids. 'OK, but give me at least half an hour. I need a shower before I can face food.'

On the way to the bathroom, Tom detoured into the master bedroom, opened the wardrobe and rummaged through the pockets of his suits. It wasn't a shower he needed so much as . . . He found what he was looking for – a packet of cigarettes. He continued to the bathroom, locked the door and opened the window wide. He perched on the windowsill, blowing smoke outside. He hadn't had a cigarette in weeks. He'd promised to give them up for good. But today was the exception to that promise. Today he needed every psychological and physiological crutch he could get. He flushed the stub down the toilet, brushed his teeth and rinsed with mouthwash. Like a knight preparing for battle, he took his time over getting ready, shaving his thick stubble and styling his hair meticulously, carefully choosing a suit and matching shirt and tie. Everything had to be just so. There must be no chink in the armour.

Finally satisfied, Tom returned downstairs. Amanda was at the cooker. Erin was munching cereal at the kitchen table in her pink princess dressing gown. She gave him the same serious, appraising look as her mother had done. With a twinge of sadness, he suddenly found himself thinking, *She's growing up, in a few years I'll lose her, like I lost Jake.* 'You look really nice, Daddy,' she said.

'Thanks, sweetie.'

Amanda set down two plates of scrambled eggs and bacon. They ate a few forkfuls in silence, then Tom asked, 'So, what are you two doing today? Any plans?'

'We were thinking of going for a walk in Harwood Forest,' replied Amanda.

Tom glanced out of the window. The sun was already bright in a clear blue sky. 'Looks like it's going to be hot. What about Jake? Is he going with you?'

Amanda raised her eyebrows as if to say, *What do you think?*

'Jake never goes anywhere with us any more,' said Erin. 'He just stays in his room all day. I don't know what he does in there all that time by himself.'

Tom and Amanda exchanged a knowing glance as Erin continued, 'I wish he would come with us, like he used to.'

'Tell you what, sweetheart, I'll talk to him,' said Tom.

'He won't listen to you, Daddy.'

'I wouldn't be too sure about that. I can be very persuasive when I want to be.'

Tom pushed back his chair and stood. Amanda followed him into the hallway. 'Erin's right, Tom. You're just going to annoy him if you wake him up.'

'It's the second week of the summer holidays. We're in the middle of a heatwave and he's barely set foot outside his room.'

'He's fifteen, Tom.'

'Exactly. When I was his age I was working ten-hour days on the farm during the holidays. By seventeen I was living on my own. If Jake had to fend for himself, he wouldn't last a week.'

Amanda listened with an air of having heard it all before. 'Times have changed. Kids grow up more slowly these days.'

Tom shook his head dismissively. 'I don't buy that. We're too easy on him, that's what it is. But, do you know what, I wouldn't give a toss if he lay in his pit till midday every day so long as he got out there and enjoyed himself when he was up.'

'He does go out sometimes with Lauren.'

'Yeah, another weirdo. She's even more miserable than he is. I swear if that girl smiled, her face would crack into—'

'Are you calling your son a weirdo?'

Tom caught the sharp note in Amanda's voice and softened his own. 'No, of course not. He's a good kid. He just needs a kick up the arse sometimes.' He turned and started up the stairs.

'Just because you're stressed, don't take it out on Jake,' Amanda said to his back.

Is that why I'm doing this, to take my mind off the way I'm feeling? wondered Tom as he made his way to the attic. Maybe it was, in part, he conceded, but it still needed doing. He'd let things slide with Jake for too long. For months they'd rarely seen each other, and barely spoken when they had. He realised a good part of that was his fault. He'd buried himself in working on the quarry proposal and everything else that went along with it. But on the few occasions he'd tried to connect with Jake, he'd come up against a brick wall. It was almost as if they were strangers. As if all the years of playing, laughing and talking had been swept away by a wave of adolescent hormones.

A sign on the attic door read JAKE'S ROOM. Underneath it someone had scrawled in black marker, 'Keep the fuck out!' Tom entered Jake's bedroom without knocking. Sunlight filtered through black curtains, gloomily illuminating a chaotic scene. The floorboards were strewn with books, magazines, screwed-up clothes, plates of partly eaten sandwiches and pizza. The walls were papered with posters of death metal and goth bands Tom had mostly never heard of – although he'd heard their music thumping through the floor often enough. One wall was dominated by a poster of a pentagram with a lustrous black snake coiled around it. Multi-coloured candles in various stages of melting were clustered around a laptop on a desk. A book lay open on a bedside table. Tom gave a little shake of his head at the chapter title: 'Occultism and Witchcraft'. He'd never thought a son of his would be into all that nonsense. He recalled what he'd said to Amanda a few weeks back when the pentagram poster first appeared – *You know something, Jake's the kind of kid I would have ripped the shit out of when I was in school.* Amanda hadn't spoken to him for two days after that.

Tom swished open the curtains. A pale, skinny boy splayed face down across a bed pulled a duvet over his long black hair and groaned in a recently broken voice, 'What are you doing?'

'What do you think I'm doing? I'm waking you up.'

'Why?'

'Because it's a gorgeous day and you're not going to waste it festering in here.' Tom stooped to tug the cover off his son's head. A silver stud in Jake's nose glinted in the sunlight. Tom felt a barb of irritation. Amanda had let Jake have the stud put in on his fifteenth birthday. Tom hadn't been consulted. They'd argued for days afterwards and the issue was still a sore topic. Blinking, Jake pressed his hands to his eyes. 'Help, I'm melting. I'm melting,' teased Tom, pulling his son's hands apart.

'Go away!' yelled Jake, wrenching free. 'This is my room. You can't just come in here whenever you fucking want.'

'Oh, yes I can, because this is *my* house. And don't you dare talk to—' Hearing the anger in his voice, Tom pulled himself up short. His gaze moved over Jake's face, taking in the scattering of spots, the faint shadow of stubble, the smudge of something that looked suspiciously like mascara. He continued evenly, 'Look, Jake, I didn't come up here for an argument. I came up here because . . . Well, because I'm worried about you. You don't seem happy. I can't remember the last time I saw you smile or heard you laugh. You just sit in here by yourself with all this' – Tom glanced at the pentagram and the open book – 'stuff. What is it you find so interesting about witches and magic?'

Avoiding his dad's eyes, Jake shrugged.

The taciturn response sparked another little flare of irritation, but Tom suppressed it. 'I know we haven't spent much time together recently, but I promise you that's going to change after today.' *And not only that,* he found himself adding in his mind, *but everything. One way or another, everything is going to change today.* 'We're all going to spend more time together. Start doing things as a family again.'

Jake stared at some indeterminate spot on the wall, his expression indifferent.

Holding in a sigh, Tom glanced at his watch. Time was running short and he still needed to print out his speech. 'I've got to go now. We'll talk more later. Oh, your mother and sister are going walking in Harwood Forest. Erin really wants you to go with them.' Wrinkling his nose, Jake opened his mouth to speak. But

Tom continued quickly, 'Before you say you don't want to, just hear me out. I'm not going to force you to go. I'm asking you to as a favour to me. It would mean the world to Erin. And, who knows, you might even enjoy yourself.'

Tom waited for a reply, but Jake's expression made it clear one wouldn't be forthcoming any time soon. He lightly brushed the dark curtains of hair away from Jake's face. 'Whatever you decide to do, try to enjoy yourself. I know you think I'm being a hard-arse, but I just want you to make the most of your holiday.' Jake shook his hair back down over his eyes. This time Tom's sigh escaped. 'See you later.'

He headed for the stairs. Once the attic door was closed behind him, all thoughts of Jake were driven from his mind by what lay ahead of him. He hurried down to his office and set the speech printing.

Amanda came in. 'What did he say?'

'Hmm? What did who say?' Tom replied absently, without looking up from his work.

'Jake. Who do you bloody think?'

The edge in Amanda's voice got Tom's attention. She'd changed into cut-off jeans and a vest top that hugged her curves. Even without make-up, her skin glowed from days spent walking and horse riding with Erin. He felt a faint stirring in his groin. 'Sorry, darling, I was miles away.'

'So what's new?' Amanda muttered under her breath.

Tom accepted the prickly comment, knowing he deserved it. Jake wasn't the only one he'd neglected in recent months. 'He didn't say much, but I think I got through to him. I'm sure he'll be going with you.'

Amanda arched an eyebrow, unconvinced. Moving close to her, Tom stated the obvious. 'You're dressed.'

'I decided to throw on some clothes and head straight out.

Don't worry, I'll be all showered and sweet-smelling by the time you're home.'

'Don't bother.' Tom nuzzled Amanda's neck, murmuring, 'I like you sweaty.'

She gave a little shudder. 'Isn't it about time you got going?'

'I can spare a few minutes.' Tom slid his hand up the inside of Amanda's thigh. She gently but firmly pushed it away. He drew back, his eyebrows pinching together.

Amanda returned his frown. 'Don't look at me like that, Tom. What do you expect when one minute it's like I don't exist and the next you're all over me? I don't know where I am with you these days.'

His eyes fell away from hers. He turned back to his desk and inserted his speech into a plastic folder. There was a slight tremor in his hand. Sighing, Amanda took hold of it and squeezed. 'You'll be fine.'

Tom's eyes worriedly met hers. 'I've sunk every penny we've got and more into this. If they turn us down, the bank won't release the business loan and then . . .' He couldn't bring himself to say what then.

'They're not going to turn you down. And, even if they do, we'll get by. I could get a job.'

Tom shook his head. 'You know how I feel about that. I want you to stay at home while the kids are young.'

'They're not that young any more, Tom.'

'Erin is. And, anyway, it's not only about the kids. You gave up a lot to be with me.'

'No, I didn't. Perhaps when the quarry's up and running you'll finally understand that.'

'Do you really think we'll get planning permission?'

'I'm certain of it. They know what's best for Middlebury.'

'You're right.' Tom drew in a steadying breath. 'You're always right.' He kissed Amanda's cheek. 'I love you.'

She smiled, a trace of something that might have been sadness in her eyes. 'You haven't said that in a long time.'

'I know. I should say it more. You're everything to me. You and the kids. I don't know where I'd be without you.'

'You'd probably be out enjoying yourself every night, like you used to when we first met,' Amanda teased.

'Funny, I was just thinking earlier about when we first met.'

A wry note came into Amanda's voice. 'You mean when you saved me from the unwanted attentions of that bloke in the Black Bull. You remember, the one who later turned out to be your best mate.'

'No, I was thinking about the forest.'

'Ah, you mean when you spied on me taking a nap.'

'I didn't spy—' Tom started to protest. He smiled. 'Actually, I suppose I did. But what else could I do? You were the most beautiful thing I'd ever seen. I was only fourteen, but I remember thinking to myself that you were the girl I wanted to be with for ever. And then you rode away and I was heartbroken.'

'Aw, poor baby.' Amanda briefly kissed Tom on the lips.

'I love you,' he said again, whispering in her ear.

She drew away, her eyes levelled at his chest. He waited for her to say, *I love you too.* But she said nothing. A little stung by her silence, he tucked the folder under his arm, went into the hallway and put on some shoes. At the sound of the front door opening, Erin came running from the living room. 'Daddy, you haven't said goodbye!'

He bent to wrap his arms around her and plant a kiss on her apple-red cheek. 'Bye, gorgeous. Have a lovely day.'

She wriggled free, frowning. 'Have you been smoking, Daddy?'

'I . . .' Tom began hesitantly, caught off guard. Erin had badgered him more than anyone to give up smoking. She was like him – as tenacious as a dog with a bone when she wanted something. 'No.'

'Honest?'

'Honest.' Tom felt a vague prickle of guilt at the white lie as he turned to Amanda. 'Wish me luck.'

'You don't need luck, Tom. You've done everything possible to prepare. The rest will take care of itself.'

He held her words in his mind and tried to believe them as he headed for his Volvo. Waving to his wife and daughter, he reversed onto a leafy road lined by scattered houses. Some, like his own, were modest places separated from the road by low stone walls and neat little gardens. Others were much bigger, set well back behind tall hedges. He eyed his house – small porch, single garage, two bay windows beneath a peaked slate roof. It had been a happy place to bring up his family, but the thought that this might be *it*, that this might be as far as he ever got, made him press down harder than necessary on the accelerator.

A short drive brought him to a humpback bridge whose trio of stone arches crossed a shallow river. Large houses with terraced gardens lined the far bank. His gaze lingered on one whose decorative battlements mimicked those of the church's bell tower rising in the background. He'd fantasised about living in that house since he was a boy. He knew the ageing owner was amenable to selling up to a local family for the right price. He sometimes pictured himself triumphantly taking possession of the house. That would be the moment he'd know he'd truly made it.

Houses and buildings were spread across the gentle hillside to the north of the river. They were built of the same grey-gold sandstone as the level-topped, heathery hills to the north-west. The eastern and southern horizons were dominated by oak woodland, pine plantations and rolling green fields.

Tom crossed the bridge into town, passing rows of pretty terraced cottages – many of which served as holiday homes for wealthy out-of-towners – and hotels and B&Bs that were busy all year round with tourists who came to sightsee, hike, cycle and climb in the surrounding countryside. The broad high street was the usual mixture of pubs, cafes, banks and local shops that characterised Northumberland's smaller, remoter market towns. Nothing much had changed about it since Tom was a child. And he saw that as both a good and a bad thing – good because it was important to preserve the traditional way of life; bad because as well as preservation there had to be progress. Without progress people stagnated and didn't improve their lives. It was all about balance. The people of Middlebury would have to decide – was their town little more than an open-air museum, or was it a place of opportunity and growth?

At its midpoint, the high street opened out into a cobbled square with a stone war-memorial cross in one corner. On market days, as it had been since the twelfth century, the square was crowded with traders and shoppers. Today, although there were no stalls, there was a large crowd. Not of shoppers, but of protesters. The crowd was gathered in front of the Town Hall – a broad stone building with an arched doorway and a pinnacled clock tower – watched over at a slight distance by a couple of constables and a passing trickle of curious locals and tourists.

The protesters were divided into three distinct groups. There were the eco-activists. Or what Tom's business partner, Eddie Reed, referred to as 'those bloody hippies'. Since setting up camp several months ago on the site Tom and Eddie hoped to develop, the activists had become a familiar sight around town with their colourful clothing, dyed and dreadlocked hair, tattoos, piercings and 'Save Maglin Hill and the Five Women' banners. They were a pain in the neck. It was going to cost thousands to clear out their camp. But Tom wasn't overly worried about them. One way or another – either of their own volition or with a police boot up their arses – they would be leaving town after today.

The second group was smaller and also prompted little more than irritation. Seventeen men and women wearing black hooded capes over flowing white robes were formed into a circle with joined hands. At the centre of the circle was a grey-haired woman crowned with a circlet of leaves and carrying a long staff. The staff was raised and her head was thrown back as if she was proclaiming something to her obscure gods. Her chanting voice was all but drowned out by the deep, rhythmic drumming coming from the eco-activists. Tom didn't recognise any of the druids. They turned up twice a year on the summer and winter solstices, did their thing, then buggered off back to wherever they'd come from. They contributed nothing to the local economy, apart from the consumption of an inordinate amount of cider in the pubs. So as far as he was concerned, their voices counted for nothing.

The third group was smaller still. Its members ranged from young children to OAPs. Each was carrying a home-made placard bearing the blood-red slogan 'Stop the Quarry'. Except for one young girl whose sign read, 'The meek shall inherit the earth'. A small grimace passed across Tom's face. The girl was a classmate of Erin's. He recognised her fellow protesters too. Some of them he'd known all his life. Two or three who lived near Maglin Hill had already voiced opposition to his plans. But the others had remained silent until today. They were people he'd considered friends. Now he knew different. And he knew too that life in Middlebury would never be the same for him and his family. These weren't the kind of people who chose their allegiances lightly. If he went against them, they wouldn't forgive or forget. They would hold their grudges as tight and close as he held his.

A reporter from the local news was interviewing several protesters in front of a video camera. The sight was too much for Tom. He sped out the other side of the square as if he was being pursued by an angry mob. All he could think was, *If they're the meek, what does that make me?*

DAY 1
9.13 A.M.

Tom sat in his car, staring at the small dormant quarry that fifty years ago had been blasted into the lower part of the hillside. Nestled against the crumbling sandstone cliff was a ramshackle collection of blue plastic tents and tepees. A treehouse constructed from scraps of wood was perched high in the boughs of a solitary old oak near the quarry's entrance.

A footpath climbed to an exposed nipple of grass capped by the stone circle. At that distance of three hundred or so metres, the standing stones might indeed have been tall, top-heavy women. The Five Women commanded sweeping views, taking in the brooding crags, lonely heather and grass mosaics, peaty bogs and tarns of the Simonside Hills to the north-west. Blanketing the southern flanks of these hills was the immense man-made expanse of Harwood Forest, where Tom had spent many hours walking without ever encountering another soul. It was a landscape he loved. It cut him up that anyone who knew him would think he'd hurt it unnecessarily. The quarrying operation would pump fresh blood into the area, provide strength for new growth. But, like any operation, it would leave a scar, a permanent reminder of the cost of progress.

'What the hell are you doing here?' Tom wondered out loud. His phone rang for the fifth time in the space of as many minutes. He didn't need to look at it to know who was calling. Bracing himself for an earful, he put it to his ear. 'Morning, Eddie.'

'Where the bloody hell are you?' retorted a gruff voice. 'You were supposed to be here a quarter of an hour ago.'

'I needed some time to . . .' Tom's voice faded lamely.

'The meeting's about to start. So get your head on straight and get your arse over here.'

'I'm on my way.' Tom hung up and murmured forcefully to himself, 'Stop being a dickhead. No fear. Believe and succeed.'

He headed back to town. When he arrived at the market square, the druids had finished whatever ritual it was they'd been performing. Likewise, the eco-activists had ceased their drumming. But they started up again with thunderous intensity on seeing Tom, accompanying the rapid-fire booms with chants of 'Say no to the quarry!' and 'Middlebury Stone wants to destroy our environment for profit!' The local protestors simply stared at him with a silence more scathing than any words.

The reporter shoved a microphone in his face. 'Can we get your thoughts on this protest, Mr Jackson?'

Ignoring the question, Tom hastened up the steps into the Town Hall. A stocky man with thinning short brown hair and a neatly trimmed beard was waiting agitatedly by a door marked COUNCIL CHAMBER.

'Sorry I'm late, Eddie. I—' began Tom.

Eddie cut him off with a swipe of his hand. He prodded the folder under Tom's arm. 'Is that your speech?'

'Yes.'

'Let's bloody well hope you haven't missed your chance to give it.'

Eddie took hold of Tom's arm and pulled him towards the door. Beyond it was a lofty-ceilinged, oak-panelled room. Five churchlike pews were packed with planning applicants, objectors and other interested parties. They were faced by two long desks and a lectern fitted with microphones. The planning committee was seated along one of the desks. Local councillors occupied the other.

All eyes turned towards the two men. A portly, bespectacled man with a broad red face and a thatch of silver hair was addressing the room. A little laminated sign identified him as COUNCILLOR BROOKS. He raised an admonishing eyebrow as Tom and Eddie found a seat, before continuing, 'As I was saying, I now ask Mr Carl Wright to step forwards and speak.'

A tall thin man with a goatee beard and a limp blond ponytail approached the lectern. His wiry arms were laced with colourful tattoos and his earlobes were stretched around CND-symbol hoop earrings. He was wearing heavy boots, camo trousers and a faded T-shirt that matched his nickname of 'Greenie'. Tom and Eddie had spoken to him only once, when Greenie had informed them that he would rather die than let any harm come to Maglin Hill. Eddie had replied that that could easily be arranged. That was on the day Greenie had set up camp with his little army of eco-warriors. A scuffle had broken out between Eddie and Greenie. The police had been called. They'd advised Tom and Eddie to stay away from the camp until the planning permissions were settled.

'You have three minutes, Mr Wright,' Councillor Brooks informed Greenie.

'Ladies and Gentlemen,' Greenie began in a mellow voice that didn't match his sharp, sunken features, 'the quarry on Maglin Hill has been dormant for fifty years for good reason. It is situated within an area of outstanding natural beauty less than three hundred metres from an ancient monument. People come from all over the world to walk and worship in this tranquil, sacred setting. How can they do that with the noise of cranes and bulldozers in the background?'

With a practised ease that accentuated Tom's anxiety, Greenie talked about the devastating effect the quarry would have on the diverse wildlife that found sanctuary on Maglin Hill. And how Middlebury Stone's plans to extract fifty thousand tonnes of sandstone a year for the next five years would not only irrevocably ruin the immediate landscape, but also impact on the wider area through noise, dust and traffic pollution. As his allotted time drew to an end, he made a final passionate plea. 'I beg you all, in our modern world there are so few places left like Maglin Hill where we can truly connect with our ancient landscape. Please don't allow it to be destroyed for the sake of senseless profit-mongering.'

'Thank you, Mr Wright,' said Councillor Brooks. As Greenie returned to his seat, the councillor turned his gaze on Tom. 'I now ask Tom Jackson to speak.'

Fighting down an urge to flee, Tom made his way to the front of the room.

'Three minutes,' the councillor reminded him.

Tom looked at the room and wished he hadn't when he saw all the eyes staring expectantly back.

'Ladies and—' Tom's words caught on a nervous swallow. He cleared his throat and continued, 'Middlebury's economy has suffered in recent years, just as the national economy has suffered. Jobs are needed that will bring long-term benefits to our area. Middlebury Stone's proposal for the extraction of sandstone from the existing Maglin Hill quarry will be worth millions to the local economy. And it's not only jobs that are needed. We need new houses too. Middlebury is traditionally a quarrying area. For hundreds of years quarrying has been a part of our way of life. Without stone we can't build new houses that preserve the unique character of our area. We are, of course, acutely aware of people's concerns, and we fully support the recommended conditions for planning approval that address those concerns.'

Tom's voice grew in confidence. He'd been building towards this moment for so many months. Now he felt a sense of release as the words flowed from him. He described how screening and landscaping would minimise the visual impact of the quarry. And how stone saws would be used only within a shed, so noise levels would not exceed acceptable limits. He conceded that there would be increased traffic, but pointed out that the comings and goings of lorries would be restricted to daytime hours. Nearing the end of his speech, he felt sufficiently at ease to deviate from his notes.

He met the gaze of each councillor. 'Members of the committee, the previous speaker appealed to your hearts, I'm appealing to your common sense. I wouldn't be standing here if I didn't believe the economic benefits of our proposal far outweighed the environmental impact.'

Relief washed through Tom as he returned to his seat, but it was tempered by the knowledge of what was to come next. Eddie patted his shoulder, whispering, 'You nailed it.'

Tom tried to ignore the hammering of his heart as Councillor Brooks said, 'The committee now has the opportunity to debate the application before we go to a vote.'

An elderly woman whose desk sign identified her as COUNCILLOR HALL was the first to speak. 'It's difficult,' she began. 'I have sympathy for the environmentalists, but the fact is this area is in need of jobs. With that in mind, I think this is something that will be good for Middlebury.'

Another councillor spoke up. 'As Councillor Hall said, it's difficult. We're damned if we do and damned if we don't. However, I'm going to move for rejection of this application.'

Tom clenched his teeth as the councillor continued, 'I believe the negative consequences of approving it will outweigh the positive. The potential impact on the sensitive landscape of Maglin Hill is unacceptable. As too is the impact the development will have on tourism.'

'Does anybody else have anything to add?' asked Councillor Brooks. His enquiry was greeted with silence. 'In that case, let's move to the vote. The planners' recommendation is approval. All those in favour.' Ten councillors raised their hands. 'All those against.' One hand was raised. 'Abstentions.' Councillor Brooks put up his own hand. 'That is approved.'

A huge grin split Eddie's beard. Tom leaned his head back and let out a breath that came from the bottom of his lungs. It had hurt when Amanda didn't say, *I love you*. But it was nothing compared to how he would have felt if he hadn't heard those other three words. *That is approved.* They seemed to echo in his head like a validation, not only of all the family time he'd sacrificed in recent months, but of everything he'd ever done.

Carl 'Greenie' Wright sprang to his feet, yelling, 'Fix! It's a fix!' He thrust a finger at Councillor Brooks. 'You're Tom Jackson's father-in-law. How can you make an impartial decision?'

'I strive to always be impartial,' the councillor responded calmly. 'But in this case I accepted that might not be possible. And so I abstained.'

'You shouldn't have been involved at all.'

'I'm Leader of the Council.'

'Exactly!'

'We've listened to you speak, Mr Wright, and we've made our decision. That decision is fair and final.'

Greenie screwed up his face contemptuously. 'You people wouldn't know fair if it bit you on your fat arses.'

'I think perhaps it's time you left. Or do I have to summon the police to remove you?'

'You won't get away with this, I promise you that.'

'Yeah, go on, piss off,' Eddie said quietly but vehemently as Greenie strode towards the door. 'And keep going until you're out of our county.'

Greenie glared at him. 'This isn't your county. It belongs to all of us and we'll do whatever's necessary to protect it from you and your kind.'

Eddie laughed and said to Tom, 'Some people just can't accept losing.'

'Oh, we've not lost,' said Greenie. 'This is only the beginning.'

'We'll see about that,' Eddie threw after him.

'Why did you have to provoke him like that?' said Tom. 'Now we're never going to get him out of the way without a fight.'

'It was always going to come down to a fight. The guy's a fanatic.'

With the drama over, Councillor Brooks brought the proceedings to a close. As the room emptied, he approached Tom and Eddie. The serious mask had dropped away, revealing a broad smile. 'Congratulations.'

Tom shook his father-in-law's hand. 'Thanks, Henry.'

'Yeah, thanks for all your help, Mr Brooks,' Eddie said with a slightly deferential air.

'What help?' Henry Brooks's eyes sparkled with a decidedly mischievous light. 'I dare say that's more excitement than this lot have seen in a very long time. They'll be talking about this meeting for years.'

Outside, the drumming started up again, accompanied by angry chants of 'Shame on Middlebury Council!' and 'Fix!'

'Perhaps they're heating up a big pot to boil us in,' Tom joked gloomily.

Eddie laughed. 'Nah, we've no worries on that score. They're all veggies.'

A policeman entered the council chamber. 'It's Constable Foster, our friendly town bobby,' Eddie said in a tone that suggested the police weren't his favourite people.

'How's it going out there, Mike?' enquired Henry.

'It's getting a bit rowdy, Mr Brooks. They could turn nasty if provoked. I think it would be best if you left by the back door.'

Eddie scowled. 'I'm not sneaking away like I've done something to be ashamed of. This is our fucking town not theirs. Excuse the language, Mr Brooks, but it makes me so mad.'

'Well, it's up to you,' said Constable Foster, 'but I can't guarantee your safety.'

'It's not us you should be worried about.'

'I'm warning you, Eddie, if I see you taking any potshots I'll have no choice but to arrest you.'

Eddie spread his hands. 'I won't lay a finger on them if they don't lay a finger on me.'

As Constable Foster returned outside, Eddie rubbed his hands together in anticipation. 'Right, let's go face the music.'

'Maybe we should leave by the back door,' Tom suggested.

Eddie wrinkled his nose as if he'd smelt something sour. 'Tom Jackson wussing out of a fight. I never thought I'd see the day.'

'I'm not wussing out of anything,' bristled Tom. He brought his voice back under control. 'We've won. Why risk messing everything up?'

'I'll tell you why, I'd rather have lost than let those arseholes think I'm scared of them. So are you coming or what?'

With a sigh, Tom nodded. Eddie's grin returned. 'Thanks again, Mr Brooks. And don't worry, this quarry is going to be a huge success.'

'Oh, I'm not worried about that.' Henry gave Tom a glance. 'I know you're going to do this town proud.'

Tom resisted the urge to lower his head under the weight of expectation in his father-in-law's eyes. Eddie headed for the door. Tom made to follow, but Henry said, 'Tom, can I have a word alone?'

'I'll wait in the hallway,' said Eddie.

'Your friend's got a real temper on him,' Henry observed as the door swung shut.

'Eddie's always been the same.' Tom tried to keep his tone light. 'I used to call him Mr Hothead when we were kids.'

'You're not a child any more. You're a married man with children of your own.'

I've been a father for fifteen years and I've never dodged my responsibilities, Tom felt like retorting. But as he always did at such moments – of which there had been more than he cared to remember – he held his silence for Amanda and the kids' sake.

Henry's voice dropped almost to a whisper. 'I called in a lot of favours to make this happen. Don't give me cause to regret it, Tom.'

Tom reflected that it was just like Henry to try to claim all the credit. The descendant of a long line of local landowners, Henry Brooks was a powerful man within the small community. Undoubtedly his influence had played a part in the application's success. But Tom knew, or at least told himself, that his own hard work had been the deciding factor. Besides, he'd never asked for any favours from Henry on this or any other occasion. So he was damned if he was going to fawn with gratitude.

Henry's voice returned to its usual loud, overly cheerful volume. 'So what are my daughter and two gorgeous grandchildren up to today?'

'They're out walking in Harwood Forest. I was about to phone and give them the good news.'

'Well, don't let me stop you.'

Tom took out his phone and dialled Amanda. He got through to voicemail. 'I think she's out of signal.'

'If you and Amanda want to go out and celebrate tonight, Cathy and I would be happy to look after the kids.'

'Thanks, but I think Jake's old enough to babysit his sister.'

Disappointment flickered in Henry's eyes, but he said, 'You're right. And the responsibility will do him good.'

Tom felt a little bad – not for snubbing Henry's offer, but for depriving Jake and Erin of time with their grandparents. Regardless of his resentment at his father-in-law's interfering manner, there could be no doubting the old man's devotion to his grandchildren. Rarely a week went by when Henry and Cathy didn't come calling with presents for the kids. More than once, Tom had asked Amanda to tell her parents to stop spoiling them. To which she always replied, 'They're grandparents. That's their job.' But to Tom it wasn't quite that simple or innocent. Rightly or wrongly, he'd come to regard the presents as a subtle dig at him, a constant reminder of what they could and he couldn't easily afford.

But starting today all that was going to change.

'You'd better get going. Eddie's waiting,' said Henry.

'Aren't you coming?'

The twinkle returned to Henry's eyes. 'Not that way, I'm not. I have absolutely no problem with using the back door.'

Both men left the council chamber. The drumming and chanting reverberated like a battering-ram against the front door. 'Good luck,' said Henry, continuing towards the rear of the building.

'OK, let's have some fun,' said Eddie.

'No fucking around,' warned Tom. 'Let's just get to our cars.'

Taking a deep breath, Tom reached for the door handle. As the door opened, the noise swelled to a fever pitch. 'Shame! Fix! No quarry! No to Middlebury Stone!' The environmentalists, pagans and locals had mingled into a little sea of irate faces. Greenie stepped from the crowd, his voice booming through a megaphone, 'Here they come! The men who want to rape our land for profit!'

Tom descended the steps with his head lowered. Eddie smiled and waved as if he was accepting an award. The crowd held its ranks as if it wasn't going to let them pass. Constable Foster pushed a path through it with the two men at his heels. Tom found his way blocked by Greenie. The self-proclaimed eco-warrior thrust the megaphone in his face, shouting loud enough to make his ears ring, 'We will never give up!'

Tom stepped around Greenie, who stuck out a sly foot. As Tom tripped over it, he caught hold of Greenie's wrists. Both men went down heavily and scuffled on the ground. There was a tearing sound as Constable Foster dragged them apart.

As if displaying a trophy from a defeated enemy, Greenie held aloft the pocket he'd ripped off Tom's jacket. The crowd cheered.

'You saw what he did,' Tom said as Constable Foster guided him away. 'He tripped me. That's assault.'

'All I saw was you pulling Mr Wright to the ground. I can try to find out if anyone saw anything.'

Tom swiped the offer away. It was hardly likely any of the protestors would back him up. Boos and jeers followed him to his car. Eddie chuckled and shook his head at Tom. 'I thought you said no fucking around.'

'That Greenie's a piece of work. The police are going to have real problems shifting him from the quarry.'

'Then let's not depend on the police. I know some Geordies who'd be more than happy to send him scarpering.'

'No. We have to do this right.'

'So you keep saying, Tom, but—'

'This isn't up for discussion, Eddie. Everything has to be done legal and proper or we could lose—'

'Oh, Jesus, what now?' interrupted Eddie, looking past Tom.

The leader of the druids was approaching. Tom half expected her to take a swing at him with her staff, but she planted it on the cobbles and held out a sheet of black paper. He warily accepted it.

'Bloody weirdo,' Eddie said loud enough for the woman to hear as she solemnly returned to her companions.

There was spidery silver writing on the paper: 'Thomas Jackson & Edward Reed'. Underneath was a short verse.

We worship,
The Gods of Light,
We practise,
Peace not might,
We know whatever we do to thee,
Will come back to us times three,
By this Law that holds universally true,
We take the consequences of our actions,
And so must you.

Eddie recited the last two lines and asked, 'What does that sound like to you?'

'A warning.'

'My thoughts exactly.'

Eddie made to rip up the sheet, but Tom said, 'Don't. I want to show it to Amanda.'

'That's not a good idea. This'll freak her right out.'

'You're probably right, but there's another reason we should hold onto this. If they try anything funny, we've got evidence that they threatened us.'

'They're not going to try anything funny. They haven't got the balls.' Eddie pointed to the environmental activists. 'They're our biggest problem. I'm going to head over to the office, get cracking with organising the eviction. All legal and proper, of course.' The words came with a sardonic upward tilt of his lips. 'You coming?'

'Maybe later.' Tom indicated his torn jacket. 'I need to get changed.'

As Eddie headed for his car, he turned to shake a triumphant fist at Tom.

Tom shook a fist back, but with little conviction. He didn't feel particularly triumphant. He felt strangely flat and drained. His gaze returned to the sheet of paper. He quickly folded it into his pocket and reached for the car door.

DAY 1

9.47 A.M.

Seth Wheeler lay beneath a cream cloth canopy on a four-poster bed. Parallel to the bed was a floor-to-ceiling window with a dressing table in front of it. A wall-mounted flat-screen television was tuned into the local radio station. An open door led to a spacious en suite. The room was bigger than Seth needed and cost more than he could afford. But after reading an article in the previous day's *Middlebury Gazette* headlined 'Demonstrations Set for Controversial Planning Meeting', he'd wanted a window overlooking the market square. The net curtains were pulled aside so he had only to turn his head to get a direct view of the Town Hall. Right then there was nothing kicking off in the square, so he was leafing through a well-thumbed scrapbook.

Faded newspaper articles were pasted into the book's crowded pages. The margins were crammed with doodlings of flowers, dogs, cats, birds, stick figures, houses, suns, moons and stars. The newspaper headlines jarred incongruously with the childish scrawls. 'Town in Shock after Double Murder' ran one dated Wednesday, 26 July 1972. Seth's pale, ice-chip eyes skimmed over the ensuing article, although he'd read it so many times in the past few days he could have recited it from memory.

> The picturesque Northumbrian town of Middlebury is reeling after the murder of two of its residents. Police called to a house in the early hours of Monday discovered the bludgeoned bodies of Elijah Ingham, 46, and his wife Joanna, 38. The couples' daughters, Rachel, 12, and Mary, 8, were asleep at the time of the brutal attack. Rachel found the bodies and raised the alarm. The daughters have since been put into the care of a local foster family. Police do not have any suspects for the attack, although they have reason to believe it may have been a robbery gone wrong. Residents of Middlebury have been speaking of their shock. One neighbour said, 'Everyone just feels sick to their stomachs. You hear about this kind of thing, but it always happens in other places. It's almost impossible to believe something like this could have happened in our little town.'

Seth's mouth tightened derisively. Barely a week went by without some idiot on the news saying that same thing or a variation of it. *He seemed like such a nice man . . . This is a lovely neighbourhood . . . She was a quiet girl . . . No one around here would ever have thought . . .* If life had taught him one thing, it was that regardless of who and where they are, underneath, everyone was the same seething mass of hate, fear and greed. To believe otherwise was either stupidity or wilful ignorance, which amounted to the same thing.

His gaze slid over other headlines: 'Police Appeal for Information on Middlebury Murders'; 'Detectives Still Baffled by Couple's Savage Slaying'; 'Middlebury Vicar Claims Satanists Responsible for Murders'. Seth lingered on the last headline. It was a particular favourite of his, right up there with classics like 'Aliens Abducted My Hamster'. 'Reverend William Douglas is convinced Satanists targeted Elijah and Joanna Ingham because of their born-again Christian beliefs,' began the article.

> Parishioners were left stunned after he made the astonishing claim during Sunday Service. Police have this week released further details of the murders, including the gruesome revelation that someone drew on the walls of the Ingham house in the victims' blood. The drawings, which consist of seemingly random swirls and shapes, look like the work of someone high on the drugs that have become so problematic these days. Reverend Douglas, however, believes they convey a sinister message. During his sermon he claimed one drawing was 'the all-seeing eye of Lucifer'. Another scrawl was 'a Thaumaturgic triangle'. A symbol that is supposedly used for summoning demons. The reverend also claimed that the recent series of animal mutilations in fields near the Five Women stone circle is further evidence of bizarre satanic rituals. Police have been quick to state that they have no evidence of occult involvement.

Seth's attention was drawn to the window as the drumming and chanting started up again with redoubled intensity. The crowd sounded proper pissed off. It seemed things were about to heat up nicely. The noise peaked as two men emerged from the Town Hall. There was a scuffle between one of them and a protester. They fell over and Seth sprang to his feet, standing on tiptoe to try to catch a glimpse of the wrestling figures. A constable jumped in to part them.

Seth rubbed his hands together gleefully. This was what he'd paid to see!

The man was escorted through the crowd and rejoined his companion. One of the pagans approached them and gave them something. What was it? A petition? Some kind of cursed object?

'Shit,' Seth swore softly. The two men had their backs to him. Half the enjoyment was in seeing their faces.

No matter. The morning's entertainment had made the extra outlay on the room more than worthwhile. And anyway, he reflected, soon money wouldn't be an issue. Soon he would be wealthy enough to stay in any hotel in the world. The men got in their cars and drove away. Seth returned to the scrapbook.

DAY 1
9.48 A.M.

Amanda and Erin walked side by side along a sun-dappled gravel road walled in by dense, drooping pines. The forest's gloomy floor was carpeted with rusty pine needles and smears of livid green moss. The pines opened out into a large clearing sprinkled with gorse bushes. The clearing was split into three branches, each of which followed a slender channel of water. To the west was Newbiggin Burn. To the north was Blanch Burn. At its centre the streams converged to form the River Font, which flowed south-east towards Fontburn Reservoir. The road sloped down to cross the river on a low stone bridge a few metres beyond the V-shaped confluence.

Amanda took in the view, which brought back so many happy memories. As a child she'd loved to come here for picnics with her parents. As a twenty-one-year-old she'd made love with Tom for the first time on the riverbank. And as a parent herself, she'd watched her own children splash around and build dams in the streams.

'Come on, Mum. Keep up,' said Erin, breaking into a sort of skip-run.

Amanda started after her, but hesitated as her phone rang. A flutter rose from her stomach. The planning permission verdict must be in. Which way had it gone? Part of her hoped she'd been wrong and the planners had rejected the proposal. Maybe then she'd get back the man she loved. The man who wanted to make money, but not at the expense of his family's happiness. She knew how the desire for wealth and the respect that came with it could twist perceptions. How it could make people think they were doing the best for their loved ones, when in reality they were only serving their own interests.

A deep frown formed as Amanda looked at the phone.

'Is it Dad?' Erin called to her.

'No.'

'Who is it then?'

'It's no one. Go play by the streams. I'll be along in a minute.'

Erin skipped away. Amanda put the phone to her ear, turning towards the trees as if fearing Erin might read her lips. 'I told you not to phone me.' Her voice was quiet and carefully emotionless.

'I'm sorry,' a man's voice replied. 'I tried not to. I really did. But you're all I think about. Can I see you?'

'No.'

'I only want to talk.'

'I've already heard all you've got to say. Hearing it again won't change my mind.'

'I didn't put myself across very well last time we spoke. I'm not good with words like you are. All I'm asking for is one more chance to convince you that we're meant to be together.'

'We're not meant to be together. We were a mistake,' Amanda stated flatly.

'Please just hear me out and if you say no after that I promise I won't contact you again.'

Amanda sighed at the wobble in the man's voice. 'I'm not meeting up. Say what you've got to say now and do it quickly.'

There was a pause as if the man was gathering himself up for one final effort. Then he began, 'I was thinking the other day how a flower doesn't know it's a flower. It just is one. Sometimes love can be like that.'

'I know how I feel about you.'

'But do you, though? You didn't realise you were attracted to me until a few months ago. Isn't that true?'

'Well yes but—' Amanda admitted hesitantly.

'So couldn't it also be true that you love me but you don't know it yet?' the man interrupted in a tone of eager triumph.

'No. It. Could. Not.' Amanda spoke each word like a sentence.

'I've loved you for years,' the caller continued as if he hadn't heard her. 'You've only loved me for a few months. It takes time for love to grow and blossom. That's the best kind of love because it lasts a lifetime.'

'Enough!' snapped Amanda, losing her composure.

Desperation flooded the voice. 'What I'm trying to say is it doesn't matter how long it takes for you to realise you're a flower . . . No, I mean your love for me is a flower . . . Because we've got the rest of our lives for us to realise it . . . Or rather for you to realise it, because I already know . . . But you don't know because . . .'

A kernel of sympathy opened inside Amanda as she listened to the man tying himself in knots. She hardened herself against it. She'd already tried the soft route and it clearly hadn't worked. 'No,' she hissed. 'No. No. No! Do you hear me? Am I getting through your thick skull? My answer is no. I'd rather chuck myself off a cliff than spend the rest of my life with you.'

There was a silence, as if she'd slapped the caller with her words. She added coldly, 'Flowers bloom and then they die', and hung up before he could say anything else.

Amanda stared at the phone, tensed for it to ring again. Ten seconds passed. Half a minute. She closed her eyes, silently praying, *Please God let this be the end of it.* As she turned to make her way down to the bridge, another frown touched her forehead. Her gaze travelled along all three water channels. Erin was nowhere to be seen.

'Erin!' she shouted, scanning bushes and clumps of bracken. 'Come out. I'm not in the mood for hide-and-seek.'

The clearing was silent, except for the chatter of birdsong. A thought quickened Amanda's footsteps: *What if Erin's fallen in the water?* She peered over the bridge's wooden handrails. Orange-brown water gurgled along a streambed littered with pale-golden stones. She drew a little breath of relief. Erin wasn't in the water. But then where the hell was she? Her gaze moved to the dark lines of pine trees. Surely she hadn't gone into them. Amanda had always drummed it into her, *Don't wander off into the forest. All the trees look the same. It's easy to get lost.*

She called Erin's name for several minutes, but the only reply she got was the echo of her own increasingly anxious voice. Her heart was beating hard now. This wasn't like Erin at all. Something was badly wrong. Her gaze landed on two figures on the gravel road at the top end of the clearing. She ran towards them. It was a middle-aged man and woman walking a cocker spaniel.

'Have you seen a little girl?' Amanda asked breathlessly.

'No,' they replied.

'I've lost my daughter Erin. She's only nine. Will you help me look for her?'

'Of course,' said the man. 'Where did you lose her?'

Amanda pointed vaguely in the direction of the bridge.

'How long's she been gone?' asked the woman.

'I'm not sure. Twenty minutes at most.'

The man indicated the stream running adjacent to the gravel road. 'We'll search along Blanch Burn.'

'Thank you.'

Amanda ran back towards the bridge, glancing from side to side to side, wondering which branch of the clearing to search.

Newbiggin Burn led into the heart of the forest. Erin had no possible reason for going that way. The River Font looped out of the forest, meeting the reservoir not far from where they were parked. Beyond that it snaked its way towards Middlebury through fields of grazing sheep. Could Erin have decided to head back to the car or even into town? But why? Why would she do that? One stomach-clenching possibility occurred to Amanda. Had Erin overheard her on the phone? Surely she'd been too far away. But what if she'd come back up the slope? *I'd rather chuck myself off a cliff than spend the rest of my life with you.* Picturing Erin repeating those words to Tom, she ran alongside the River Font with a frantic look in her eyes.

'Erin! Erin!'

After a few hundred metres, the clearing flared towards a patchwork of fields and moorland. Amanda pulled up sharply as someone called, 'Hey!' She turned and saw the man gesturing to her. 'I've found something.'

She dashed over to him. 'What is it?'

'I'm not sure.'

Something about the way he said it made Amanda's heart beat even faster. He led her to the lower end of Blanch Burn. They splashed through the stream. Amanda tripped and fell face first. Gasping at the cold water, she scrambled upright. She waved off the man's attempts to help her and continued to the far bank. He pointed to a stone the size of a rugby ball half embedded in the peaty earth. Something dark and wet-looking was streaked over it and the grass beside it. Amanda touched her fingers to it and looked at them. Her fingertips glistened red.

'I think it's blood,' said the man.

'Blood,' Amanda echoed as if unsure of the word's meaning.

'You should call the police,' put in the woman.

Amanda took out her phone, but hesitated. All it would take was for the police to check her phone records and her whole world would come crashing down. But what other choice did she have? She'd made her bed. Now it was time to lie in it. She dialled 999 and asked to be put through to the police. 'It's my daughter,' she shakily told the operator. 'She's gone and we think we've found blood.'

DAY 1
10.18 A.M.

Tom didn't head for home. He headed for the western edge of Middlebury. Half a mile or so beyond the town, he turned onto a winding lane bordered by sheep-grazed fields and conifer plantations. He left the lane behind for a rutted farm track that terminated after a short distance at a wooden gate. A dry-stone wall enclosed a muddy yard and a small house clad in flaking pebble-dash. A dilapidated barn, its roof sagging and missing slates, was attached to the house.

As always, the sight of the house where he grew up brought back a rush of bittersweet memories. Tom saw himself sitting in the kitchen with his father, whose dour, rugged face seemed to have been constructed from the same stone as the house. He saw his mother setting the table, her features worn hollow from long nights of lambing. He saw his brooding, shy brother whittling wood on the stone-flagged floor by the fire. He shook his head. Christ, they were like scenes from another life.

His mind looped forwards to his parents near the end of their lives, his father crippled with arthritis, his mother's breath rattling from a succession of chest infections. He'd pleaded with them to give up the farm and move into sheltered accommodation, but they were as immovable as the Simonside Hills. He'd wanted to shake some sense into them. They'd worked their fingers to the bone and what did they have to show for it? Nothing! What little money they'd made had mostly gone on rent, lining the landowner's pockets. They'd even had the gall to suggest that as the eldest son he should take over the farm. It had been all he could do not to laugh in their faces. He'd rather have drowned himself in a vat of sheep piss than follow in their relentless, cheerless footsteps. Besides, he'd never had any talent for farming. The sheep had always been nervous around him, perhaps sensing his resentment at having to spend his time tending them when his schoolmates were out chasing girls.

Luckily for him and his parents, there was Graham. His brother was a born farmer – steady, tireless, more at ease with animals than with people. Tom could still vividly recall the day his father had signed over the tenancy to Graham. It was bright and bitterly cold. Lambing season was fast approaching, and they weren't ready for it. His mother was in hospital, quietly succumbing to pneumonia. His father's knuckles were so swollen he could barely hold a pen. As Graham signed the tenancy agreement, his face – rosy-cheeked, still in its teens – had expressed neither happiness nor anxiety. He'd accepted his poisoned chalice as if there had never been any choice in the matter.

Even now, over two decades later, Tom still felt a stab of something – guilt? shame? relief? – whenever he thought about that moment.

With a hint of hesitancy, he opened the car door. He hadn't come to see his brother. He'd come to remind himself of how far he'd made it – if not in distance then in almost every other way – from where he started. But now he was here he should say hello to Graham. He crunched through the sun-baked mud past a rusty tractor and rapped on the front door. Silence. Somewhere off in the distance the bleats of sheep, sounding, as they always did to him, strangely pained. He made as if to knock again, but his hand dropped back to his side. He'd knocked once. That was enough. Moving more quickly, he returned to the car. His head twisted at the sound of an engine in the lane. Graham's mud-spattered blue Land Rover pulled into view with a sheep trailer attached.

The brothers locked gazes, their unreadable faces momentarily reflecting each other. Tom smiled thinly, raising his hand in greeting. Graham's lips remained straight. He got out of the Land Rover, a wiry black and white border collie at his heels. The dog eyeballed Tom as taciturnly as its master.

'Hello, Bob,' said Tom, putting out his hand to the dog.

The dog rolled its eyes up at Graham. At a twitch of his master's chin, Bob trotted forward and Tom ruffled his thick fur. Tom straightened as his brother approached. They shared the same dark features and broad shoulders, but Graham was a couple of inches taller. Black hairs curled over the open top buttons of his short-sleeved chequered shirt. His arms hung at his sides with the kind of looseness that spoke of powerful, compact muscles. He was three years younger than Tom, but innumerable sleepless, weather-lashed nights had left him with a face that looked at least that much older.

'What are you doing here?' There was no animosity in Graham's voice, but neither was it welcoming.

'I just wanted to see the old place.' Tom shifted a little awkwardly under his brother's unchanging gaze. 'How's things?'

'What things?'

Tom held back an irritated sigh. His brother was a master of playing the stone face, bouncing questions back at him when he full well knew their meaning. 'You know, *things*. The farm. Life in general.'

'The farm's the farm. It ticks over. Life in general's the same.'

It was one of Graham's typical conversation-shutting-down responses. Tom briefly considered sharing his triumph with his brother, but he knew his news would be greeted with indifference. 'I'd better get going. I've got work to do.' With a nod goodbye, he started towards his car.

'For a moment there, I thought maybe you'd come to see me,' said Graham. His tone was as flat as ever, but Tom felt the accusation in the words. It had been a year, maybe even two, since he'd last visited the farm. He turned back towards his brother. They stared at each other a few more beats. An apology teetered on Tom's lips. Holding it in, he ducked into the car.

Graham reversed the Land Rover to a spot where the lane widened like a bulb. Tom kept his gaze straight ahead as he passed his brother. He heaved a sigh as the Land Rover receded from view. It was always the same. He always came away from encounters with Graham feeling that he'd somehow let him down. He knew the feeling was undeserved – Graham was just as guilty as him of not bothering to keep in contact – yet it gnawed at him anyway.

Tom wound down his window and inhaled as if to clean out an unpleasant smell. This was a happy day. He was determined not to let anything ruin it. By the time he arrived at his house, Graham's parting words had faded to a shadow at the back of his mind. Amanda's VW Golf was missing from the drive. Obviously she was still out walking with the kids. He bounced into the house and headed for the kitchen. He removed several bottles of champagne from a wine rack. Amanda had put them in the fridge the previous night, but he'd returned them to the rack. Chilling the bubbly before they had anything to celebrate seemed a bit too much like tempting fate.

He kept one bottle out of the fridge. It wasn't even eleven, but to hell with it. He more than deserved, and needed, a drink. He popped the cork, took a swig from the bottle, then filled a champagne flute. He reached for a phone on the work surface and tried Amanda. Again, he only got through to voicemail. Was she still out of signal? Or was she on the phone to someone else? A crease appeared between his eyebrows. Henry better not have called her or there was going to be trouble. This was his day, his big news to give. Washing away the thought with another mouthful of bubbly, he headed upstairs to the bathroom. He unbuttoned his shirt and checked his shoulder in the mirror. There was a red mark where he'd gone down hard on the Town Hall steps. He flexed his shoulder and winced as something pulled tight. No matter, a hot shower and a couple more glasses of champagne would sort that out.

He started to unbuckle his belt, but hesitated as the heavy strains of rock music thumped through the floor overhead. His frown returning, he quickly ascended to the attic. Jake was straddling the window ledge, smoking a cigarette. Caught out, he guiltily jerked his gaze to Tom.

'Put that out,' snapped Tom.

Recovering himself, Jake eyed his dad defiantly. 'Why should I? You smoke in the bathroom.'

Tom opened his mouth to deny the accusation, but thought better of it. The bathroom window was directly below Jake's window. Smoke doubtless wafted into his bedroom. 'That's different. If I want to smoke in my house—'

Rolling his eyes, Jake interrupted, 'Do I have to hear the *this-is-my-house* speech again already?'

'Yes, you do! And you'll keep hearing it until you learn to respect what I say. Now put it out.'

Provokingly slowly, Jake stubbed the cigarette out on the window ledge and flicked it into the garden.

Tom pressed his lips together, then said in a voice of forced calm, 'You can go pick that up when we're finished speaking. But first, what are you doing here? I thought we decided you were going out with your mum and Erin.'

'No, Dad, that's what you decided. I tried to tell you I didn't want—'

Tom held up a silencing hand, cocking his ear towards a sound that was scarcely audible through the grinding music. 'Turn that down, will you.'

Jake hopped from the window ledge and switched off the music. Someone was persistently, almost forcefully, knocking at the front door.

'Who the hell's that?' Tom wondered out loud. It crossed his mind that it could be Carl 'Greenie' Wright come to take another pop at him. He shot Jake a glance. 'I'm not done with you.' If he'd had eyes in the back of his head, he was pretty sure he would have seen his son giving him the finger as he turned to go downstairs.

His movements grew cautious as he neared the front door. If it was Greenie, he had no intention of resuming their confrontation. He crouched on the stairs where he could see the door without being seen. It wasn't the eco-warrior, it was Constable Foster and a female colleague. Unsure whether to be relieved or more worried, he quickly buttoned up his shirt and opened the door.

'Whatever it is, I'm innocent,' he joked.

Unsmiling, Constable Foster indicated his colleague. 'Tom, this is Constable Hutton. Can we come in and talk?'

'Sure.' Tom stepped aside and closed the door behind them. 'So what's this about?' He fully expected to be told they were there about the quarry. It wouldn't have surprised him one bit if Eddie had gone against his wishes, gathered together a few of the lads and launched an attack on the encampment.

'At approximately half past ten we received an emergency call from your wife,' said Constable Hutton.

'My wife?' echoed Tom. He added quickly, 'Is she OK?'

'She called to report your daughter missing.'

Tom's mouth fell open. *Missing*. The word hit him like an icy blast, threatening to snatch his breath away.

'What do you mean, Erin's missing?' The voice belonged to Jake. Tom twisted to see him descending the stairs.

'Go back to your room.' Tom's voice was hollowed out by shock.

'We need to speak to Jake too,' said Constable Foster.

Jake repeated his question and Constable Hutton answered, 'All we can tell you right now is that Erin was reported missing in Harwood Forest.'

Panic touched Tom's voice. 'Does that mean someone might have taken her?'

'It means we're still trying to figure out what the exact situation is,' said Constable Foster.

'When was the last time you saw your daughter, Mr Jackson?' asked Constable Hutton.

'I kissed her goodbye when I left the house. That was just before nine.'

'Have you spoken to her since then?'

'No.'

Constable Hutton looked at Jake. 'What about you?'

'I haven't seen or spoken to Erin since yesterday.'

'Do you mind if we have a look around?' asked Constable Foster.

'What for?' said Tom. 'Erin's not here.'

'She might have made her own way home.'

'Why would she run off from her mother? And besides, the forest's over two miles away.'

'I know it's unlikely. Still, it pays to be certain.'

Tom gestured for them to go ahead.

'Could you please take me to your daughter's bedroom,' said Constable Hutton.

As Tom led her upstairs, Constable Foster said, 'I'll have a look around down here.'

Constable Hutton's gaze swept intently over Erin's pink bedroom. 'Erin, are you here?' she called out.

Silence.

Tom leaned against the door frame, his head reeling. He watched the constable peer under the bed and into the wardrobe, hardly able to believe what was happening. The whole situation seemed both unreal yet all too horribly real, like one of his lucid nightmares. 'Dad, Dad,' Jake was saying.

Tom replied without looking at him, 'Not now, Jake.'

'But Dad—'

'I said not—' Tom started to snap, jerking towards his son. His anger died as quickly as it had flared when he saw Jake's pale, worried face. His voice softened. 'What is it?'

'I just wondered if I should I go out and look for Erin?'

Constable Hutton answered before Tom could. 'When we're done here, we're going to join the search at Harwood Forest. I assume you'll be coming with us, Mr Jackson.'

'Of course.'

'Then Jake needs to stay here in case Erin returns home.'

Constable Hutton searched the remaining first-floor rooms, before climbing the attic stairs. 'My bedroom's up there,' said Jake, squirming at the idea of someone snooping through his things. 'I've been in it all morning.'

The constable gave him a sympathetic glance. 'I believe you, Jake, but we have to search the entire house.'

Jake stood fidgeting while Constable Hutton checked out his bedroom. His cheeks reddened as she moved aside scrunched-up boxer shorts and dirty crockery to look under his bed. Her gaze lingered briefly on the pentagram before she left the room.

'All clear down here,' called Constable Foster as they descended to the hallway.

'Same up here,' replied Constable Hutton.

'Tom, can you think of anywhere outside the house where Erin might be? Does she have a favourite place to go?'

Tom's forehead knotted. His head was aching so badly it was difficult to process even such a simple question. 'The newsagent's. They stock her favourite magazine. And of course she likes the park. We don't allow her to go very far. We only recently started letting her out on her own.'

'What about her friends?' asked Constable Hutton.

'I . . . I'm not sure,' Tom said as if admitting something slightly shameful. 'Amanda deals with that kind of thing.'

'She's best friends with Emily Fogerty,' put in Jake.

'I know the Fogertys,' said Constable Foster. 'I'll give them a call.'

'Are you riding with us or would you rather follow in your own car?' Constable Hutton asked Tom.

'I'll follow you. I might need my car later.' Tom laid his hand on Jake's shoulder. 'Are you OK staying here on your own?'

Jake nodded.

'I'll call as soon as we find your sister,' added Tom, trying to sound as if it was a foregone conclusion that they would. He gave Jake's shoulder a squeeze and hurried to his car.

DAY 1
11.26 A.M.

On the way out of town, they stopped by the newsagent and the park. Erin hadn't been into the newsagent. Nor was she at the park. Tom felt a squeeze in his chest at the sight of the swings, slide and climbing frame he'd spent so many hours watching Erin play on. He could almost hear her sweet laughter echoing in his ears. For the second time that day, he found himself climbing gently away from the western edge of Middlebury. He snatched out his phone at the ping of a text. 'You're a fucking star!' read the message. It was from Eddie. It took Tom a second to register what his business partner was referring to. All that already seemed so distant.

A quarter of a mile or so before the turn for Graham's farm, they followed a sign for FONTBURN RESERVOIR. The cars rumbled over a cattle grid onto a single-lane road that arrowed through fields of rough grass and wetland scrub dotted with scattered farms. A couple of hundred metres to the right of the road a thin line of birch and oak followed the River Font. They passed a flock of sheep – white-faced Cheviots that got their name from the rounded hills straddling the border between Northumberland and the Scottish Borders. The flock, Tom knew, belonged to Graham – which meant his brother had most likely been out this way earlier. Tom wondered whether Graham had seen Amanda and Erin on their way to the forest. He hadn't mentioned it, but then again there hadn't been much room in their conversation for chit-chat.

The road swung around a wooded corner, emerging at the eastern shore of Fontburn Reservoir by a stone valve tower that rose from deep-looking water like the tallest turret of a drowned castle. They crossed the dam, which sloped steeply away on their left into the water and on their right into a broad grassy depression. At the base of the depression was a water-treatment plant shadowed by the towering stone arches of a disused railway aqueduct. At the far side of the dam a tarmac drive split leftwards from the road, terminating after a short distance at a car park popular with the fly and bait anglers who were scattered along the sandy shoreline. As a child, Tom had spent many hours on that shoreline himself. On rare days off, his dad had loved to fish the reservoir for the rainbow and blue trout that teemed in its cold depths. Whenever a fish bit, his dad's usually grim face used to come alive with excitement. Those were some of the few memories from childhood that Tom cherished.

Tom braked and honked his horn. The police car stopped too and Constable Foster wound down his window. 'That's Amanda's car over there,' Tom called to him, pointing towards the car park.

'We know,' replied the constable. 'We've got someone keeping an eye on it.'

About fifty metres beyond the turn, the road split again at a small pine plantation. They took the narrow left-hand fork, which steadily climbed the flank of the river valley. As they crested a slope, the dark-green swathe of Harwood Forest came into view. Rank after rank of pines, a vast army of trees marching against the craggy fortress of the Simonside Hills. The cars rumbled over another cattle grid, descending towards a stone farmhouse connected to a long string of slate-roofed barns.

Shortly before the farm, three police cars were parked at the roadside. They pulled in behind them and got out into the blue-skied July day. Tom followed the constables along a footpath that sloped down through a field of grazing sheep, passing the farm on its left.

'Did you manage to contact the Fogertys?' asked Tom.

Constable Foster nodded. 'They haven't seen Erin today.'

Beyond the farm, the terrain was strewn with thickets of bracken and clumps of marsh grass. They crossed the shallow River Font by a wooden footbridge. The path looped towards the forest. Five more minutes' fast walking found them on a grey gravel road shadowed by tall pines. After a quarter of a mile, they came to a huge clearing.

To the north a couple of constables in hi-vis jackets were poking around in long grass and bracken. There was another constable just inside the treeline to the east. A Land Rover was parked on the bridge at the clearing's centre. Amanda was beside it with a park ranger and a fourth policeman. Breaking into a jog, Tom called to her. She whirled towards his voice. Her eyes were swollen from crying.

He wrapped his arms around her. Her clothes were wet through. 'What happened?'

'I . . . Erin was playing . . .' The words were gasped out, stumbling over each other.

'Where?'

Amanda pointed towards Blanch Burn. 'She was playing and . . . and then she was gone.'

'What do you mean gone?'

'I don't know.' Amanda's voice was shrill, close to breaking. 'I wasn't . . . Oh, God, Tom, I wasn't watching her, I wasn't watching—' The words snagged in her throat as tears overwhelmed her.

Tom held her close, stroking her hair. 'It's OK, shh. It's going to be all right.'

She shook her head, pulling away from him. 'No, it's not.'

'Yes, it is. We're going to find her.'

'You don't understand. Martin found—'

'Who's Martin?'

'He was out walking with his wife. They helped me look for Erin and he . . .' Amanda clutched Tom's shirt as if to stop herself from falling over. 'He found blood.'

His stomach lurched. 'Show me where.'

Amanda drew him towards the far side of the bridge. Their way was blocked by a policeman wearing a flat-topped cap. 'I'm Sergeant Phil Dyer. I'm coordinating the search,' he said, extending his hand.

Tom briefly shook it. 'Why wasn't I told about the blood?'

'Because we didn't want to panic you.'

'You have no right to keep something like that from me.'

'We have every right, Mr Jackson.'

'I want to see where this blood was found.'

'I'm sorry, but we can't let you near that area. There's nothing to see anyway. The blood was on a stone that's been removed for analysis.'

'There was blood on the grass too,' said Amanda. 'I thought maybe she'd slipped and hit her head.'

Tom stared into the narrow channel the stream had cut through the turf. His head was full of an image of Erin lying at its edge, her face pouring blood. How had she got there? Had she slipped? Had she been pushed? Both possibilities were gut-wrenching – the latter so much so that he could barely bring himself to consider it. 'How many people have you got searching?'

'There are currently six constables and myself, plus three park rangers,' said Sergeant Dyer.

Tom frowned. 'Ten of you. My daughter's missing, maybe even . . .' he forced himself to say the word stabbing at his mind, 'abducted—'

'Now, hang on,' interjected the sergeant. 'Let's not start bandying around words like that. There's no evidence a crime has been committed. We can't even be sure the blood belongs to your daughter. The carcass of a sheep that looks like it was recently killed by an animal was found nearby. The blood may well have come from that. Chances are, Mr Jackson, your daughter has simply wandered off into the forest.'

'Erin wouldn't do that. We've been bringing her out here since she was a baby. She knows not to wander off.'

'Sometimes children do things they shouldn't do.'

'Of course, but—' Realising the conversation was going nowhere, Tom broke off and took out his phone.

'What are you doing?' asked Sergeant Dyer.

'We need more people out here.'

'I agree, but we can't have members of the public searching the forest willy-nilly. Any search needs to be properly coordinated by myself.'

'Then you'd better get coordinating, Sergeant, because in about an hour there's going to be half of Middlebury out here.' Tom looked at Amanda. 'Call your dad. I'm going to call Eddie.'

They were forced to walk a few metres up the slope to find a signal. Eddie answered the call and said, 'I was just about to ring you. I've been on to the bank about—'

'Forget the bank, Eddie,' broke in Tom. 'Something awful has happened. Erin's missing.'

'What? What do you mean?'

'What I said. She's gone and we don't know where.' Tom rapidly recounted what he did know.

'Fucking hell, Tom,' breathed Eddie. 'What do you want me to do?'

'Spread the word. We need as many people as possible to help with the search.'

'Will do.'

Tom hung up. Amanda was still on the phone. 'OK, Daddy,' she said, tears streaming down her cheeks. 'I love you too.'

So she can say I love you to him but not me. Tom flung the unbidden thought aside, silently admonishing himself, *Save your self-pity for after Erin's found.* 'What did he say?' he asked as she lowered the phone.

'He's going to get someone he knows at Radio Northumberland to put the word out for volunteers.'

'That's a good idea,' said Sergeant Dyer. 'Have the volunteers meet at the Town Hall. I'll send some of my constables to help organise them.'

As Amanda and Tom got back on their phones, Sergeant Dyer reeled off instructions to Constables Foster and Hutton. With a shuddering exhalation, Amanda suddenly slumped over and braced her hands against her thighs. Tom darted out a hand to support her. Although the sun was beating down, she was shivering as if it was December.

'You should go home and change into dry clothes,' he said.

She shook her head fervently. 'Erin needs me here.'

'And Jake needs you at home.'

Amanda's face contracted at the mention of her son. 'Does he know what's happened?'

'Yes and he's scared.'

She gave a reluctant nod. 'OK, I'll go. But I'm coming back once I'm sure Jake's all right.'

'I'll see you soon.'

They silently held each other's gaze, Tom trying not to show the turmoil churning inside him, Amanda's eyes glassy with tears and fear.

'Constable Hutton will take you to your house,' said Sergeant Dyer. 'I think it's best if we leave your car at the reservoir for now in case Erin shows up there.'

Hanging her head, Amanda started up the slope towards the treeline. As he watched her trudge away, Tom felt something else he knew he shouldn't – a stirring of relief that it wasn't him who'd lost Erin. If anything bad happened to her he couldn't have lived with himself for letting her out of his sight. Once again, he discarded the thought, telling himself with as much conviction as he could muster, *But nothing bad has happened to her. There'll be some perfectly simple innocent explanation for all this.*

He turned his attention to the seemingly endless trees. Cupping his hands to his mouth, he shouted, 'Erin! Erin!' Her name echoed back at him. Then silence.

DAY 1

12.28 P.M.

Seth was drifting on the edge of sleep to the sound of Radio Northumberland. Occasionally his face twitched as an acid tongue spat insults at him from his unconscious: *You're an idiot, a retard, a moron.*

The suddenly serious DJ's voice pried its way into his sleep. 'And now I have an urgent message for the residents of Middlebury and the surrounding area. Earlier this morning nine-year-old Erin Jackson went missing in Harwood Forest. Her granddad, Councillor Henry Brooks, is appealing for volunteers to search for her. Anyone who can help should go to Middlebury Town Hall right away. This is a terrible situation and all our prayers are with Erin and her family.'

Seth sat up, rubbing his unshaven chin thoughtfully. He went into the bathroom, lathered his face, shaved and styled his floppy-fringed blond hair into a neat side-parting. He dressed in brown cords, a short-sleeved green-and-blue chequered shirt and sturdy boots – all brand new. He scrutinised himself in a mirror. He looked like just another one of the area's farmer boys – that is if you ignored the paleness of his complexion and the slightness of his build.

The acidic voice stabbed at him again: *Surely even you can't be stupid enough to do what you're thinking about.*

Ignoring it, he returned to the bedroom.

Don't you dare leave this room!

Seth's hand hesitated on the door handle. He pushed the voice away with a shake of his head. 'You can't tell me what to do any more.' He left the room, making sure to hang the DO NOT DISTURB sign on the door. He didn't want any cleaners poking their noses through his belongings.

The voice echoed after him along the hallway: *Idiot, retard, moron!*

In the hushed hotel bar, the staff were gathered at a window overlooking the square. As Seth stepped outside he saw what they were gawping at – a line of people was filing into the Town Hall. Many were those young or old enough to have spare time on their hands. Others had clearly dropped whatever work they were doing to help. *How very heart-warming*, he thought sarcastically. It was almost enough to give you faith in humanity. Almost. He joined the queue. The faces ahead of him were grave, but there was an undercurrent of excitement, an infectious sense of normal duty being suspended. He carefully adjusted his own expression to match theirs.

'Excuse me.'

The voice was female and had a soft Northumbrian accent. Seth turned to a young woman of maybe twenty whose rosy cheeks and bright eyes were characteristic of the local girls. He awarded her a snap rating of five out of ten on the sliding scale of attractiveness he applied to all girls around his age. In other words, she wasn't bad. A tad on the plain side, but a bit of make-up could easily bump her score up.

'Has there been any more information?' she asked.

'All I know is what was said on the radio. Do you know the Jacksons?'

'I know of them. What about you?'

'No.'

The girl gave Seth an open appraising look. 'You're not from around here,' she stated.

Faintly irritated that she'd seen through his camouflage so easily, he asked, 'How can you tell?'

'Your accent. Where are you from?'

'London.' The answer was specific enough to be accepted without question, but vague enough to pose no threat.

'What are you doing up here?'

'I'm on holiday.'

The girl's eyebrows lifted. 'My dad's obviously got it wrong.'

'About what?'

'He says Londoners don't give a stuff about anyone but themselves.'

Why should Londoners be any different from anyone else? Seth resisted the urge to shoot back. 'No, he's not wrong. Most only care about number one.'

'But not you.'

Seth gave a self-effacing shrug. 'I just thought about how I'd feel if it was my daughter.'

'You don't look old enough to have kids.'

'I don't have any, but . . . You know what I mean.'

The girl nodded, looking at Seth in that same direct way. He shifted a little uncertainly. He was used to passing unnoticed, as anonymous as a commuter on the tube. The sensation of being seen threw him off balance. At the same time, he liked the feel of her eyes on him. 'I'm Holly,' she said, extending her hand.

'Seth.' The reply popped out before he had time to consider whether it would have been wiser to give a false name. He took her hand. It was pleasantly warm and there was a roughness to it that hinted at manual labour.

'I'm from Netherwitton.'

'Where's that?'

'It's a village about three miles away. We've got a farm—' Holly broke off as they entered the Town Hall and a respectful hush settled over the line. They edged into a room jam-packed with serious, eager faces. Two constables and a sixty-something man with a vigorously ruddy face topped by swept-back silver hair occupied a small stage. The man was pacing back and forth as if looking for something he'd lost. An OS map of Harwood Forest was pinned to a board behind him along with a blown-up photo of a pretty young girl beaming a gap-toothed smile.

The man stopped pacing and began urgently, 'Thank you, everybody, for coming. I can't tell you what it means to see so many familiar faces. For those of you who don't know me, I'm Henry Brooks. Erin Jackson's grandfather. Time is of the essence, so I'm going to hand you over now to Constable Mike Foster.'

Constable Foster addressed the gathering. 'As you know, Erin went missing in Harwood Forest this morning. Erin is nine years old, approximately four foot two and of slim build. She has shoulder-length reddish-brown hair and brown eyes. She's wearing a white T-shirt with a pink butterfly design on it, denim shorts and brown walking boots. She also has a silver heart bracelet on her left wrist.'

Constable Foster pointed to a small island of white surrounded by a sea of green on the map. 'Erin was last seen by her mother in this area of the forest at roughly 10 a.m. There's no indication of abduction, but we do have reason to believe Erin may be injured. Right now we're working on the theory that she's lost in the forest. As you can see, Harwood Forest is huge and to complicate matters there are the Simonside Hills to the north. It's a dauntingly large area. So we've divided it into grids of two hundred and fifty square metres. And we will divide you into teams of ten. Each team will be assigned a grid to search. If you find anything – and this point is extremely important – you will not touch it. You will immediately alert a police officer. My colleague and I will now take your names. After that, please make your way around the back of the Town Hall where buses are waiting to take you to the search area.'

As the crowd milled forward, Holly said, 'I wonder how she got injured.'

'They didn't say she *was* injured,' corrected Seth. 'They said *may be*.'

'It's odd though, don't you think? How does a nine-year-old girl go missing like that out in the middle of nowhere?'

Seth's voice dropped. 'Are you suggesting the mum might be in on it?'

Holly looked at him in horror. 'No, I'm not! And you wouldn't either if you were from around here. You'd know that the Jacksons are a well-respected family.'

Seth held in a disdainful breath. *Well-respected.* Respect was like love, something people used to hide their dirty secrets. The difference was, respect gave you control over people. Love gave people control over you.

Seth saw a reassessing look in Holly's eyes. She took a step away from him. It was only a small step but he felt as if a big gap had opened up between them. 'I'm sorry,' he found himself saying. 'I didn't mean anything by it.'

'No need to apologise to me.' Holly's tone wasn't unfriendly, but neither was it quite so warm as before. 'It's not my mum you're bad-mouthing.'

'It was a horrible thing to suggest. It's just you hear about that kind of thing happening, don't you?'

'Not around here.'

Not around here. There were those idiotic words again. The girl was clearly not worth his time. And yet the way she'd looked at him outside. Like . . . well, like he was something worth looking at. He couldn't shake the thought of it. He inwardly scowled at himself for letting out a glimpse of his mind. From now on he would identify the signals and play his role accordingly.

When they reached the stage, Seth provided Constable Foster with a false surname and home address. Henry Brooks was handing out gratitude and copies of the photo of Erin. Seth extended his hand to him, saying resolutely, 'I'm going to do everything I can to find your granddaughter, Mr Brooks.'

'Thank you . . .' Henry looked askance at him.

'Seth.'

'Thank you, Seth.'

Seth headed for the door, noting that Holly was looking at him in *that* way again. He basked in the warm glow of her gaze as the flow of the crowd carried them outside to a bus. 'Do you mind if I sit by you?' asked Holly.

'Not at all.'

As Holly sat down, her thigh brushed Seth's. She didn't seem to notice. But he did. The sun slanting through the window accentuated her cheekbones and softened her golden-brown eyes. He gave her a sly reassessing look of his own. *No not a five,* he thought. *A six or maybe even a seven.*

'So who are you on holiday with?' she asked.

'No one.'

Holly treated Seth to a curious glance.

'Why are you looking at me like that?'

'You're a bit . . . odd.'

Seth suppressed a frown. *Odd.* He hated that word. He didn't want to be odd. He wanted to be – or at least, appear to be – as normal as possible.

'I don't mean that as an insult,' Holly added. 'I like odd. Some people say we're all a bit odd around here.'

The engine grumbled into life and the bus chugged away from the Town Hall. Seth's gaze fell to the photo of Erin. He traced the outline of her face with his finger. 'Such a pretty thing.'

'She is,' agreed Holly. 'Surely no one could hurt her.'

Seth looked into her eyes. 'I hope you're right,' he said, knowing she wasn't.

DAY 1
12.47 P.M.

When the police car pulled up at the house, Amanda sprang out and ran to open the front door. 'Erin,' she shouted into the heart-rendingly empty hallway. The replying silence weighed down her features.

There was a thudding of feet on the stairs. Jake descended into view. Amanda looked at him, then quickly glanced away from the apprehension in his eyes 'What happened, Mum?' he asked. 'How did you lose her?'

She winced as if he'd raked his nails across her cheek. 'I wasn't . . .' Her voice was tiny, crushed. Pressing the back of her hand to her mouth, she ran upstairs and threw herself onto her bed.

There was a knock at the bedroom door. She sucked in her tears. It wasn't fair, falling apart like this in front of Jake. He was already going through enough. In as steady a voice as she could muster, she said, 'I'm getting changed. I'll be out in a minute.'

'It's me, darling,' replied the soft, well-spoken voice of her mum. 'Can I come in?'

Amanda's lips quivered in hesitation. She wanted to cry out yes, but she could no more bear to look into her mum's eyes than into Jake's. The door opened and a well-preserved sixty-something woman swept into the room. Cathy Brooks had the same strong features and exotic green eyes as Amanda, but her hair was shorter and dyed a stately platinum blond. Light linen trousers and a pale-blue blouse fluttered around her still slim and shapely figure as she hurried to her daughter's side.

'Oh, Mum,' sobbed Amanda, losing control again. 'It's my fault!'

'Hush now.' Cathy wrapped her arms around her daughter. 'You're not to blame.'

'But I am. I should have been watching her.'

'We can't keep our eyes on them all the time.'

Amanda looked at her mum, her eyes swimming. 'Something awful has happened to her. I know it. I just know—'

'Don't talk like that,' Cathy broke in. 'In a few hours at most they'll find Erin safe and we'll be laughing off this whole awful episode.'

'I won't be laughing,' Amanda said vehemently. 'And I'll never let her out of my sight again.'

Jake entered the room, looking at his mum sheepishly from under his long hair. 'Sorry for what I said downstairs. I wasn't thinking.'

Amanda wiped her eyes and motioned him to her. 'You've got nothing to apologise for, sweetheart.' She dredged up a small smile, brushing Jake's hair back from his cheek with a tear-dampened hand.

'I want to go to the forest and help search.'

'No.' The word was out before Jake had even finished speaking.

Jake threw his hands wide. 'Why not? What use am I here?'

'Your mother's got enough to worry about without having to worry about you too,' put in Cathy.

'She doesn't have to worry about me, Grandma. I'm old enough to look after myself.'

Amanda's voice was suddenly weary. 'Please, Jake, just do as I say.'

His face scrunching unhappily, Jake sloped from the room. His feet thudded up the attic stairs. He closed his bedroom door just hard enough to convey his frustration. 'Maybe you should let him go,' suggested Cathy. 'After all, he'll be with his dad and granddad. What harm could possibly come to him?'

'He's staying put and I don't want to hear another word about it,' snapped Amanda.

Cathy held up a placating hand. 'OK, darling. Not another word, I promise.'

Amanda dragged off her wet clothes as if they were made of lead and pulled on dry ones.

'Mrs Jackson,' a voice called from downstairs.

Amanda hurried to the landing. A man in a drab grey suit with matching crew-cut hair and a long lean face was at the front door. 'I'm Detective Inspector Glenn Shields,' he informed her. 'Would it be possible for us to have a chat?'

Anxiety crackled in Amanda's voice. 'Why? Has something else happened?'

'No. I just need to ask some questions.'

Amanda descended the stairs, closely followed by Cathy. She motioned Inspector Shields to an armchair in the living room, and sat down beside her mother on the sofa. 'It might be best if we talk alone,' said the inspector.

'Why?' Amanda replied a little more quickly than she'd meant to. 'I've nothing to hide.'

'I'm not suggesting you have, Mrs Jackson. I simply find it's easier to talk openly that way.'

'My mum can hear whatever I have to say.'

Inspector Shields made a *have it your own way* gesture. He flipped open a notepad. 'Can you begin by telling me exactly what happened this morning?'

'I've already been through that with another officer.'

'And the longer this goes on the more times you'll have to go through it. I understand it must be uncomfortable, but we have to be thorough. It's easy to miss small details that can make a big difference. Please try to be as specific as possible about times.'

'We left the house at about ten past nine.'

'By "we" you mean you and Erin?'

'Uh-huh.'

'And what time did your husband leave?'

'Ten or fifteen minutes earlier. But why is that important?'

'As I said, it's all about nailing down the details. And it had been a normal morning, no arguments or anything like that?'

Amanda shook her head. 'No, nothing. Tom was a bit tense because of this business with the quarry.'

'Yes, I've read about that. I understand there's quite a lot of opposition to his plans. Can I ask you, Mrs Jackson, have there been any threats made against you by environmental activists or anyone else?'

'The activists have threatened to sabotage our business. But they've not made any threats of personal harm.' A fresh wave of anxiety rolled through Amanda. 'You don't think they might have something to do with this, do you?'

'We have no reason at all to think that, Mrs Jackson. Now, getting back to the events of this morning, you left the house at about ten past nine . . .' Inspector Shields tailed off to let Amanda continue.

'It's about ten minutes' drive to the reservoir car park, so I suppose we arrived there at twenty past nine. From there we walked along the road towards Newbiggin Farm. It took us maybe half an hour to get to the forest clearing where . . . where Erin—' Amanda's voice caught on the thought of what had happened next. Cathy gave her hand a steadying squeeze.

'So it was about ten to ten when you arrived at the clearing,' stated Inspector Shields, his voice flat, all business.

A little of his calmness seemed to seep into Amanda, who took a breath and continued, 'I suppose it must have been. I wasn't keeping track of time. Erin went to play by the streams, while I sat down at the side of the road.'

'Roughly how far would you say Erin was from you at this point?'

'Twenty or thirty metres.'

'And what were you doing while Erin was playing?'

Amanda hesitated a breath's space. The truth trembled on her tongue, but she couldn't bring herself to speak it. *This has nothing to do with the phone call*, she told herself. *All you'll do by telling him about it is make a bad situation even worse.* 'Nothing, really. I was just looking at the trees and thinking.'

Inspector Shields looked up from his notepad. 'Thinking about what?'

'Things . . . Things like whether we were going to get planning for the quarry. Or whether we'd end up losing—' Despite her earlier words, Amanda broke off with a glance at her mum as if unsure whether to continue in front of her.

'Go on,' prompted the inspector.

Amanda heaved a sigh. 'It's been a tough few months. We've put everything into the quarry. And if planning hadn't been granted, that's what we would have lost – everything. We still might if we can't get the quarry up and running in the next few weeks.'

'Oh, Amanda,' said Cathy, shocked. 'I didn't realise money was that tight. You should have come to us. You know we'd never let that happen.'

'And you know Tom would never take your money.'

'Pride!' Cathy's lips curled on the word. 'What good is pride if you lose your home?'

Mother and daughter stared at each other, their faces set into a look of old battles no one could win.

'So how long were you sitting there . . . thinking before you realised Erin was gone?' asked Inspector Shields.

'I'm not sure.' Amanda's tone was faintly defensive. She didn't like the suggestive pause in the question. 'About ten minutes.'

'Ten minutes. She could have put a fair distance between herself and you in that time.'

Amanda's eyebrows knitted together. 'Yes, but why would she want to?'

'That's the million-dollar question, isn't it? Can you think of any reason Erin might have for running away?'

'No,' Amanda said with as much conviction as she could summon up. 'Erin's a happy little girl.'

'Does she have a boyfriend?'

Amanda looked at the inspector incredulously. 'She's nine.'

'It happens. Especially these days with the Internet.'

'Christ, what are you suggesting? That she might have gone off with some sicko she's met online?'

'It's too early to suggest anything. I'm simply trying to build up a picture of your daughter. Does Erin have a mobile phone?'

'No.'

'What about access to computers and tablets?'

'She has a laptop and an iPad. But we monitor her usage of them. And before you ask, we don't allow her on social media.'

'Would it be OK if I took them to the station for the techies to look at?'

'Of course, whatever you think's necessary.' Amanda retrieved the laptop and iPad – both in pink cases – from a shelf.

'Depending on how things pan out, we may need to take a look at all devices in the house with online access.'

'You can look at them now if you like.'

'I don't think we're quite at that stage yet.'

Amanda wondered with a queasy feeling when they would be at *that stage*. The inspector's gaze returned to his notepad. 'So, after you realised Erin was gone, what did you do?'

'What do you think I did? I went looking for her. I saw a couple out walking. They helped me.'

'Martin and Rowen Saxton of Rothbury. Mr Saxton found the blood. Is that correct?'

'Yes.'

Inspector Shields skimmed back through his notes. 'I think that covers everything for now. I need to speak to your son Jake too.'

'I'll fetch him,' offered Cathy, rising.

Amanda stared at her lap, wringing her hands. 'You must think I'm a terrible mother.'

'I'm not here to make those kinds of judgements, Mrs Jackson,' said Inspector Shields.

Amanda clenched her fist and pounded it into her palm. 'I should have been watching her! I'll never forgive myself for—' She broke off, darting a look at Inspector Shields. *For what?* the inspector's eyes seemed to impersonally enquire. She blinked back down to her lap.

Cathy returned, looking flustered. 'Jake's not in his bedroom.'

Amanda jerked to her feet. 'Well, where is he then?' She rushed to the shoe rack by the front door. 'His boots are gone.'

'He must have snuck out.'

Amanda stuck her head out of the door, then dashed to the kitchen window. There was no sign of Jake at the front or back of the house. She slapped her palm against the work surface. 'I bloody well told him to stay put.' Her voice swayed between anger and upset. She lowered her head briefly, tears threatening to spill over. Then she snatched up a phone and scrolled through the contacts to 'Jake's mobile'. Her call went through to voicemail.

'Get your arse back here right away!' she barked. 'Do you hear me, Jake? Right away!'

'Go easy, Amanda,' said Cathy. 'He loves his sister and just wants to help.'

'If he wants to help he should do as he's told.' She slammed the phone into its cradle. 'Why can't he ever do as he's fucking told?'

'I'll go look for him. He can't have got far.'

'And I'll tell my officers to keep an eye out for him,' said Inspector Shields. He handed Amanda his card. 'Please don't hesitate to call me if you remember anything you think might be relevant. And try not to worry too much. In most cases of this type, the missing person turns up safe within a few hours.'

Amanda hauled in a shaky breath. 'Thank you.'

'Oh, and one more thing. Now you've gone public, you may well get a few journalists sniffing around. Please don't talk to them without clearing it with me first. From this point on, it's extremely important that I have control over what information we release to the media. OK?'

Amanda nodded. She nodded again when her mum asked, 'Will you be all right on your own?' But as soon as she was alone, Amanda collapsed once more into a puddle of self-loathing.

DAY 1

1.20 P.M.

Tom tried his brother's number again, and once again he got through to voicemail. He left a message. 'I know you're pissed off at me, Graham, but this isn't about us. Erin's missing. She disappeared in the forest. We don't know if she's—' *Alive or dead.* Those were the words in his mind, but he couldn't bring himself to say them. 'Please call me. I really need your help, little brother.'

He hung up and resumed pushing aside fronds of bracken with a stick. To either side of him, evenly spaced figures wearing the red-and-black jackets of the Northumberland National Park Mountain Rescue Team were engaged in the same task. He held back a rising sense of frustration. In the hour or so since Amanda had left, fifteen members of mountain rescue and half a dozen more park rangers had joined the search. But things still seemed to be moving infuriatingly slowly. They were working their way through dense bracken sandwiched between the bubbling Newbiggin Burn and towering pines eight or nine hundred metres west of where Erin had last been seen. It was all he could do to stop himself from running into the trees shouting for her. The thought of her lost in there, possibly injured and certainly frightened, was like a hand twisting his insides. But at the same time he had to believe that she was simply lost. The alternatives were too awful to contemplate.

Tom's phone rang and he snatched it out, expecting to see 'Graham', but another name flashed up. He put the phone to his ear. 'Where are you, Eddie?'

'I'm at the bridge.' Eddie's voice was barely audible. The signal was poor to non-existent that deep into the forest. 'They're dividing us into search teams. I thought you might want to come along with us.'

'See you in a minute.'

Shouting where he was going to his fellow searchers, Tom jogged back alongside the meandering stream. When the bridge came into view, his heart lifted. There were at least fifty people clustered to the south side of it. Many of them were friends and acquaintances of his. Others were strangers. Sergeant Dyer was addressing them from the centre of the bridge. 'Each team will walk their allotted search area in a line. Try to stay within sight of each other. We don't want anyone getting lost. And take it slowly. Pay particular attention to the forest floor. Erin might have dropped something that could tell us in which direction she went.'

As Tom moved among the volunteers, he exchanged grateful glances and nods with those he knew. Eddie was with Henry at the front. He'd swapped his suit for his usual outfit of jeans and a T-shirt. Henry was leaning on a sturdy wooden walking stick. He had a compass and map around his neck. A wide-brimmed hat shadowed his flushed, determined face.

'This is only the first busload,' said Eddie, gripping Tom's hand. 'There are more on the way. Don't you worry, mate, we're going to find her in no time.'

Tom felt tears forming. He blinked them back. 'Cheers, Eddie.'

Henry laid a supportive hand on Tom's shoulder. Tom almost flinched. His father-in-law had never shown him that kind of affection before. For the sake of Amanda and the children, they were generally friendly enough with each other. But there always remained a certain distance between them, an awareness that they were too different ever to be close. It struck him as somehow sad that it should take something like this to move them to see beyond their differences.

'Any questions?' asked Sergeant Dyer.

'Do you have any clue which way Erin might have gone?' asked a blond-haired young man.

'A small quantity of blood has been found on the west side of Blanch Burn,' said the sergeant. 'We don't as yet have any confirmation that it belongs to Erin. But if it does, it would seem to suggest she was moving northwards. Which is why we're concentrating our efforts on areas to the west and north of here. A specialist search team with tracking dogs is en route and should be here within the next hour. So it's important that you don't go trampling over the ground adjacent to Blanch Burn and obscuring any potential scent trail. OK, you all know what you need to do. So let's get to it.'

A ripple of talk went through the volunteers as they began breaking up into groups of ten and heading off in the direction of their search grids. 'Right,' Henry said purposefully. 'Everyone on my team, follow me.'

My team. Tom felt a rise of irritation. This was the Henry he knew. The Henry who always had to be in charge. His habit of overriding Tom's authority, especially where the children were concerned, had been a constant source of simmering tension over the years. Tom bit his tongue. Now was hardly the time for raking over old scores.

Henry strode along the gravel road, which ran parallel to Blanch Burn for fifty or so metres before veering towards an impenetrable-looking pine plantation. He was followed by Eddie and several local lads who were signed up to work at the quarry. The only members of the team Tom didn't know were a dark-haired young woman and the man who'd asked Sergeant Dyer a question. They had the look of farmers' kids, although the man was too pale to have spent much time outdoors.

Sergeant Dyer accosted Tom. 'There's a Detective Inspector Glenn Shields who wants to talk to you. He'd appreciate it if you'd meet him by Newbiggin Farm.'

'I'm done wasting time on talking.'

'It's your choice, Mr Jackson, but I assure you that you wouldn't be wasting your time. What you say to Inspector Shields could yield vital clues as to your daughter's whereabouts.'

'You can tell the inspector that I haven't got the first clue where Erin might be or why this is happening. Now, unless there's anything else, Sergeant, I'm going to look for my daughter.'

Tom hurried after the search team. Eddie was straggling along fiddling with his phone. 'What are you doing?' asked Tom.

'Trying to sort out when we're going to kick those eco-pricks out of the quarry.'

The knot that seemed to have lodged itself between Tom's eyebrows tightened. 'How can you be thinking about that now?'

'Because one of us needs to. I'm sorry, Tom, but if we don't get the quarry going asap the whole thing will go tits up. And you're not the only one who stands to lose everything if that happens.'

Tom sighed. 'You're right. You do what needs to be done. But don't expect any help from me until this is over.'

'Don't worry, mate. I've got it all in hand.' Eddie scratched his beard thoughtfully. 'Talking about those eco-pricks, have you considered that they might have something to do with all this?'

'No way are they that crazy.'

'Well, what about those druids or whatever the hell they are? They're definitely crazy enough.'

Tom shook his head dubiously.

'But what about that poem thing they—'

'No,' Tom broke in sharply enough to draw glances from the people ahead of them. 'Erin's lost and that's all this is.'

'OK, Tom.' Eddie's gruff voice was uncharacteristically gentle. 'She's lost and we're going to find her.'

As the gravel road delved into the trees, a hush fell over the search party that reflected the silence of the forest. After roughly half a mile, the road swung left. Among the trees, police and park rangers could be glimpsed, strung out in a long line. The road curved north-west. They walked briskly for several minutes more, then Henry consulted his map. 'This is our search area. There needs to be five of us on either side of the road, spaced out at intervals of twenty-five metres. Myself, Tom, Eddie and—' He pointed at the blond-haired young man. 'What's your name again?'

'Seth.'

Henry's gaze moved to Seth's female companion. 'And I'm sorry, I don't know your name either.'

'Holly,' she replied.

'Us five will take the left-hand side of the road. The rest of you will take the right. We'll keep going until we reach the moors. You all know what to do if you find anything.'

They fanned out into the trees, their boots crunching a springy layer of pine needles. The bare lower limbs of each tree bristled like a sea urchin's spines. The thickly needled upper branches doused the forest floor in cool, pine-scented shadows pierced by occasional shafts of sunlight. A familiar sense of the outside world receding, of entering a place somehow beyond the normal flow of things settled over Tom. It was a feeling that had drawn him to the forest since he was a boy. For the short time he was there his worries would dissolve like the mist that often rolled down from the Simonside Hills. But now it served only to nudge him closer towards the brink of panic.

DAY 1
1.21 P.M.

Hearing an approaching vehicle, Jake ducked behind a bush. He peered through the leaves and saw his grandma at the steering wheel of her Mini. Her face, normally so full of smiles, was lined with worry. Guilt prodded at him as he recalled her earlier words, *Your mother's got enough to worry about without having to worry about you too.* He knew his mum would be freaking out, but what else could he do? It just wasn't fair that they expected him to sit at home twiddling his fingers while Erin was lost or some shit worse. She could be an annoying brat, especially when she was playing up to her daddy's-little-princess status – which was most of the time. But she was his sister and the thought of anything bad happening to her gave him a horrible cold feeling in his stomach.

His phone buzzed a text message alert. As expected, the text was from Lauren. It read 'I'm at the park.' He texted back, 'See you in 2 mins. Just hiding from my gran.' The Mini loitered at the end of the street, before turning from view. Jake hurried on his way. Shooting glances in the direction his grandmother had taken, he went through a wrought-iron gate and cut across a bowling green towards a play park. A tell-tale thread of smoke was curling out of a little wooden house attached to a slide. He clambered up a ladder into the house. A girl was sitting cross-legged on its floor, smoking a cigarette. Her shoulder-length hair was dyed raven black and cut into a lopsided fringe. Her blue eyes were encircled in thick black eyeliner. Although it was hot, she was wearing a camo jacket and torn skinny jeans tucked into Doc Martens. A silver tongue-stud showed as she said, 'This is totally messed up, Jake. What are we going to do?'

He hunkered down beside her, hugging his scrawny legs to his chest. 'I dunno. But we've got to do something.' She passed him the cigarette. He inhaled, struggling not to cough as the smoke stung his lungs. 'We could go to the forest.'

'It's miles away. And that's where your gran will be expecting you to go. She'll find you and take you home before we even get there.'

'But what else can we do?'

Lauren took the cigarette back and puffed on it thoughtfully. 'Your sister disappeared by the river, right?'

'Yeah, so?'

'So she might have followed it back to town.'

'Actually, you could be right. I always told her to follow the river or a stream if she got lost.'

Lauren brought up a Google map of the area on her phone. 'Look at where the river meets town. Do you know what one of the first places it passes is?'

Jake shrugged again.

'It's the Ingham house. Y'know, where those murders happened way back in the seventies.'

Jake knew the Ingham house. All the local kids did. It was a big decaying place, the kind where you'd expect the door to be answered by a seven-foot-tall butler. Supposedly it was haunted by Elijah and Joanna Ingham. Local legend had it that on the anniversary of their murders, bloodcurdling screams could be heard coming from the house. Knocking and running from its door was something of a rite of passage for teenagers. Some kids went further. They broke in and took souvenirs – scraps of purportedly blood-stained wood and plaster. And they weren't the only ones. Over the years, thieves had stripped the house of its lead and copper. An unknown arsonist had attempted to burn it down. And most recently, police had been called there on several occasions to kick out ghost hunters who were spending the night. There'd been a long-standing campaign by neighbours for the council to purchase and tear it down. But its owner, Mary Ingham, the younger surviving daughter, had refused all offers.

Jake looked at Lauren narrowly. She'd been pestering him for months to go with her to the house and perform a seance to contact the spirits of the Inghams. As fascinated as he was by the occult – and as eager as he was to please her – he had no intention of messing with that shit.

'What are you looking at me like that for?' Lauren pouted. 'I'm not suggesting this because I want to go to the house. I really do think Erin could be there. I read this article about a little boy who went missing in London. Turned out he'd found his way into an empty house and got trapped in there. They didn't find him until a fortnight later, by which time he'd starved to death.'

'Erin wouldn't do something like that.'

'How do you know? No one knows why the boy did it. Maybe he just thought it would be a laugh. Or maybe someone forced him to go.'

The cold feeling in Jake's stomach intensified. What if some sicko had Erin? The Ingham house would be a good place to hide her. He couldn't really bring himself to believe that would ever happen. Not in Middlebury, which had to be just about the safest – or in other words most boring – town in the entire country. But still, he'd snuck out because he had to do something, and right then he didn't have any better ideas. 'OK, but we're only going to look around. We're not having a seance or anything.'

Pulling her *as if I'd do something like that* face, Lauren flicked the cigarette away and peered out of the wooden house. 'All clear. Follow me. I know the best way to get there without being seen.'

They darted across a playing field, hopped over a wall and slunk along an alley behind a row of terraced houses. Some worn stone steps led them down to a footpath that meandered through trees on the southern bank of the River Font. The river gurgled gently by on its way to the town centre. On the far bank, sheep and an occasional horse grazed daisy-freckled meadows. Through the trees on their left, widely spaced big old houses were visible.

Lauren pointed out a path that branched off the main one and climbed towards an overgrown hawthorn hedge. Beyond the hedge was a house almost completely swallowed up by ivy. Windows pocked with broken panes peered out through the foliage. A gaping hole exposed the fire-blackened bones of the roof. Birds' nests squatted on tall chimneys at each end of the dilapidated structure. More nests dotted a gnarled, strangely human-looking old oak that overshadowed its right-hand side. Rooks wheeled and cawed in the sky above. Jake felt a slight prickling of his skin. Even in the bright sunshine, the house looked creepy as anything.

Dodging nettles and brambles, they approached the hedge. The path ended at an arched, solid wood gate secured with a chain and padlock. A coil of rusty barbed wire crowned the arch. Curls of green paint clung to the wood. The gate was embossed with a carving of a crucifix with flared ends. Someone had attempted to scratch it out and crudely etched an inverted pentagram over it.

Lauren traced the pentagram's hornlike upright points. 'I bet this was done by Satanists.'

'What Satanists?'

'The ones who broke in here.'

'They were ghost hunters.'

Lauren treated Jake to one of her patented *don't be so naive* looks. 'That's just what they want us to believe. I mean, yeah, ghost hunters did come here. They've got a website full of stuff about glowing orbs and weird noises. But they weren't the only ones.'

'How can you possibly know that?'

'Katie Pattison lives across the street from here. And she said the people the police took out of this place a few weeks ago were butt naked. That doesn't sound like ghost hunters to me. More like Satanists performing a Black Mass.'

'Pfft. Katie's full of shit. Even if they were naked, they were probably wasted and having an orgy or something.'

'Believe what you like.' Lauren squinted through the gate's keyhole. 'But something truly evil once happened in there. This is consecrated ground for Satanists.'

Jake frowned at the quiver of excitement he heard. 'You're loving this, aren't you?'

Lauren returned his frown. 'No. I like Erin a lot. She's a cool little kid and I don't want anything bad to happen to her.'

Her voice was sincere and a little hurt. Jake blinked apologetically. He gestured at the gate. 'How are we going to get through that?'

'We're not.' Lauren motioned for him to follow. They skirted along the hedge to a spot where it thinned out. The gap had been filled in with wire fencing, which someone had pulled up at the bottom. They dropped to their stomachs and crawled into a large garden choked with tangles of grass and splotched with dandelions shimmering in the midday sun. A half-collapsed wooden summer house had been mostly reclaimed by nature in one corner. Butterflies and bees drowsily fluttered and hummed around shaggy purple buddleia bushes that partially screened the neighbouring gardens from view. Jake and Lauren pushed their way through the grass and weeds, staying low in case a neighbour happened to be looking out of an upstairs window.

At the centre of the Ingham house, crumbling steps led to patio doors boarded up with steel plates. TRESPASSERS WILL BE PROSECUTED signs were pasted to each plate. Some joker had spray-painted a grinning devil on one alongside, 'Welcome to Hell'.

Jake rapped his knuckles against a plate, producing a hollow sound. 'What now?'

'Shh,' hissed Lauren. 'What if Erin really is in there? What if someone's in there with her? They'll hear you.'

'If we can't get in, how could Erin or anyone else?'

Lauren pushed her fingers under the steel plate's edge and prised it free.

'Hey, how did you know that was loose?' asked Jake.

'The same way I knew about the Satanists.'

'No way would Katie go in there.'

'Not everyone's as much of a pussy as you.'

'Don't call me that.'

Lauren pulled the steel plate further away from the wall, exposing a mouldy French-door frame edged with jagged glass teeth. 'Coming?' she asked, sliding halfway through the narrow aperture.

'Hang on a second.' Jake stooped to grab a chunk of paving stone heavy enough to bash someone's skull in. 'Just in case,' he said, hefting it meaningfully.

Lauren arched an eyebrow as if to say, *Yeah, right.*

She disappeared from view. Jake squeezed after her, grimacing as a blade of glass scratched his wrist. The plate clattered back into place and for a moment he was blind. As his vision adjusted to the gloom, he saw that they were in a big, high-ceilinged room. Pinpricks of light pierced ventilation holes in the steel plates, dimly illuminating mildewed plaster that had peeled off – or perhaps been chipped away by souvenir hunters – in many places. The walls were scrawled with graffiti that ranged from the usual 'Gaz Woz Ere' to imitations of the long since faded symbols that had been drawn with Elijah and Joanna Ingham's blood. Dry leaves, empty beer cans and cider bottles were strewn over the floorboards. The air was thick with the smell of dust and rot.

Lauren pointed to a rubble-filled fireplace surrounded by a ragged brick outline where someone had torn out the hearth and mantelpiece. 'Elijah Ingham was sitting right there in his armchair,' she said in a voice of hushed awe. 'His killer crept up behind him and blam! They smashed his skull in. The police reckoned he died instantly, but the killer kept on hitting him until his brains were splattered all over.'

'Nice,' Jake muttered.

Lauren nodded, seemingly not catching the sarcasm. 'His wife, Joanna, was found beside him.' The floorboards creaked as she padded towards a doorless doorway. 'But that's not where she was first attacked. A trail of her blood led from the kitchen where she'd been making cocoa.'

Jake followed Lauren into a long hallway that ran alongside a flight of stairs missing its banister. Hazy sunlight filtered through holes in the ceiling, lighting up chandeliers of cobwebs. Tattered furls of wallpaper dangled like streamers at an Addams' family party. There were holes in the plaster where pipes, radiators and light fittings had been unceremoniously removed. Leaves crackled underfoot as they peered into more deserted rooms. Lauren paused at a room with a fireplace big enough to walk into. 'This was the kitchen. Joanna must have seen her murderer because she was killed by repeated blows to her face and the front of her skull.'

'I wonder why she was moved to the other room?' said Jake.

'Yeah, I've always wondered about that, too. Maybe she didn't die straight away and crawled there by herself.'

'Or maybe the killer thought she'd like to be with her husband.'

Lauren pushed her lips out contemplatively. 'You could be on to something there. They might have wanted her to see her husband one last time, although not for the reason you think.'

'Who's they?'

'Who do you think? The Satanists.'

'The police thought it was a robbery gone wrong.'

'Don't start with the naive thing again, Jake.'

'I'm not. If it was Satanists, why didn't they kill the two daughters?'

'The same reason they wanted Joanna to see her dead husband. The more pain they can cause, the more their master will reward them. If they'd killed them, Rachel and Mary's suffering would have been over in a moment. By letting them live, it carries on for the rest of their lives. Just think about Crazy Mary.'

Crazy Mary was the local kids' nickname for Mary Ingham. She lived on the small council estate across the other side of Middlebury. Jake had only seen her twice. The first time had been from the back seat of his dad's car. She'd been picking berries from a hedge. She'd looked like some kind of tramp, with her long frayed skirt, tatty army-surplus coat, scraggly grey-brown hair and grubby, gaunt face. 'Who's that, Dad?' he'd asked.

'That's Crazy Mary,' his dad had replied.

'You shouldn't call her that,' his mum had reproached. 'God only knows what that poor woman must have gone through.'

Jake had asked his mum what she meant, but she'd diverted the conversation to some other topic. His dad had given him a *we'll-talk-later* look. They hadn't talked about it later, though. And Jake had forgotten about Crazy Mary until Lauren's obsession with the Ingham murders kicked in. Even then, he hadn't made the connection between Crazy Mary and Mary Ingham until Lauren and he had seen her pulling a two-wheeled shopping cart through the town centre early one morning.

'That's *her*,' Lauren had whispered. 'Mary Ingham. They say the only thing she ever buys is cat food. She's got about fifty cats living in her house. She never speaks a word, not since *it* happened.'

Mary had walked with a jerky shuffling gait, as if her feet were too heavy to lift. Her eyes had never left the ground. 'Do you think she's really crazy?' Jake had asked.

'Totally batshit. Wouldn't you be if someone killed your parents and decorated your house in their blood?'

Jake had thought about that question and others that stemmed from it a lot since then. How would it feel to discover your parents' murdered bodies? How would it feel to know their killer or killers were still out there somewhere? Would you ever be able to sleep comfortably in your bed again? The look he'd seen in Crazy Mary's eyes seemed to suggest not.

Lauren craned her neck to peer up the kitchen chimney. 'Anyway, what's with going all Scully on me? I thought you believed.'

'I never said that.'

'Then why is there a pentagram on your bedroom wall? And why have you been reading all those books?'

Jake gave a lame little shrug. The truth was, he'd put the poster up because Lauren liked it, and he'd read the books for the same reason. Any sense of belief he had was half formed at best, born more of a desire to please her than anything else. But now that Erin was missing, he found he didn't want to even vaguely believe such things – Black Mass, human sacrifice, the devil – might really exist. 'Look, can we just do this and get out of here?'

'All right, chill.' Lauren approached a doorway at the far side of the kitchen. She sparked her lighter into life. Steep stone stairs led down into inky darkness. 'Whatever you do, don't go into the basement,' she intoned in a faux-ominous voice.

Jake peered over her shoulder. The blackness seemed to stare right back, daring him to enter it. 'Let's search upstairs. If Erin's here, I think that's where she'll most likely be.'

Lauren flicked him a knowing glance. But she turned and headed out of the kitchen, her silent acceptance of his suggestion betraying her own unease. An orchestra of creaks and squeaks accompanied their footsteps as they ascended the stairs. Halfway up, Jake crunched through a rotten floorboard. He yelped as something bit into his leg. He twisted his foot free and pulled up the leg of his jeans. A splinter protruded from his calf. Gritting his teeth, he plucked it out.

'You all right?' asked Lauren.

He nodded, looking uncertainly towards the landing. 'I'm not sure about this, Lauren. This place is a death trap.'

'That's exactly why we've got to make sure Erin's not up there.'

Lauren took hold of Jake's hand and urged him onwards. He didn't resist. He would have done pretty much anything for her. The only thing he'd ever really said no to her about was the seance. He'd read enough to know those things were bad news. The dead were never happy to be dead, even when their life had come to a natural end. So surely the spirits of murder victims would be pissed off beyond all belief. If Elijah and Joanna Ingham were lingering in this dump, he wasn't about to disturb them.

The walls and floor at the top of the stairs were scorched from the arson fire. Jake glimpsed blue sky through a hole in the sagging, water-stained ceiling. A landing lined with doorways stretched out to each side of the stairs. Another, narrower flight of stairs continued on up to the attic. They edged around the burnt floorboards into a room with a gutted fireplace and a bay window. Glimpses of outside showed through a straggle of ivy, somehow seeming very distant. An old mattress covered in dubious stains sagged against one wall. Jake pointed to a used condom on the floor beside it. 'I didn't realise Satanists practised safe sex.'

Lauren flicked him the finger, mouthing a sarcastic, *Ha ha.*

They peered into a smaller, empty room across the hallway. 'If that was the parents' bedroom, this must have been Mary's,' said Lauren.

'Why?'

'Because she was the youngest. The same way Erin sleeps in the room closest to your parents.'

Jake thought about Erin's room – the pink wallpaper, the mound of stuffed toys on her bed. He thought about the way he teased her because she insisted on sleeping with the door open and the landing light on. He told himself that if . . . no, not if, *when* she was found alive he would never tease her about that again.

They moved on to the adjoining room. 'Do you reckon this was Rachel's?' asked Jake.

'I dunno, but someone's a fan of *The Exorcist*.' Lauren pointed at a scrawl of graffiti: 'Rachel Ingham Sucks Cocks in Hell'.

'That's sick.'

'I think it's pretty funny, actually.'

'You would. Do you reckon Rachel Ingham's dead?'

'No one knows for sure. She lived with a foster family for three years after the murders. Then one day she just disappeared. The police said she ran away.'

'But you think it was Satanists.' There was a teasing edge to Jake's voice.

Lauren shot him a narrow look. 'Maybe. Or maybe she really did run away. I think about running away from this shithole of a town all the time. Going down to London. Finding some interesting people to be friends with.'

Jake felt a sharp little tug inside. Not at the side-swiped insult – Lauren's bitchiness was part of what attracted him to her – but at the mention of London. It wasn't the first time she'd spoken about running away. It was probably just empty talk, but you never quite knew with her. She was the only one of his admittedly few female friends he really cared about, the only one he wanted to be more than just friends with. 'Let's look in the attic,' he said, diverting the conversation.

As Lauren turned, there was a crack of snapping wood and her leg plunged through the floor. Jake's hands darted out, catching her as she keeled sideways. 'Thanks,' she gasped. 'I thought I was going to fall right through.'

'Are you hurt?'

'I don't think so.'

Jake lifted Lauren out of the hole and poked his head into it. The downstairs floor was visible through a mess of plaster and broken laths. 'Wow, that was lucky. You could've been killed.'

An object wedged in the aperture between the floorboards and the ceiling caught his eye. 'Hey, give me your lighter.'

'What for?'

'There's something in here.'

Jake sparked the lighter. A square of silver with what appeared to be a keyhole at its centre gleamed in the flickering flame. The floorboards groaned threateningly as he reached further into the hole.

'Careful, Jake,' warned Lauren, edging away.

'I can almost reach it.' The lock was attached to a dusty red rectangular object. A box? No, not a box. 'I think it's a—' He broke off with an 'Ouch!' dropping the lighter as its flame licked his fingers. 'Shit, I've lost the lighter.'

'We'll find it. How are we going to search the basement without—' Lauren's eyes flitted towards the ceiling. Her voice sank to a whisper. 'What was that?'

'What was what?'

'I thought I heard something.'

'Don't screw with me, Lauren.'

'I'm not. There it is again!'

This time Jake heard it too – a muffled tapping, scuffling noise from above. He got to his feet, suddenly aware of his heart beating. 'Maybe it's mice.'

'Or maybe it's someone tapping on the floor. Come on. Let's check it out.'

As quietly as possible, they returned to the stairs. The noise grew louder as they climbed towards a doorway slashed with sunlight. Jake's fingers tightened on the lump of stone. The sun hit him in the face as he peered into the attic. His blinking eyes travelled over soot- and weather-stained brick walls, roof tiles collapsed in by flames and prised apart by ivy, cobwebby arched windows, teetering chimney stacks, drifts of leaves and twigs. 'There's nothing—' he started to say, but fell silent as the noise came again. *Scratch, scratch, tap, tap . . .*

Lauren pointed to the far end of the attic, mouthing, 'It's coming from over there.'

They edged forward, testing to make sure the creaking floorboards would bear their weight. In the angle where the roof met the floor, there was a bundle of filthy white rags – just about big enough, Jake noted, to cover Erin. Exchanging a nervous glance with Lauren, he bent to lift a tattered edge of material. Something burst out from beneath it. All Jake saw was a flash of black, before whatever it was slammed into his face. He felt sharp points digging into his forehead and scalp. A sound like a child's scream vibrated in his ears, painfully high pitched. He cried out too, reflexively closing his eyes and swinging the stone. There was a soft crunch as it knocked loose his attacker. The screaming stopped. He opened his eyes. Black feathers were swirling towards the floorboards where a rook lay motionless.

'Fuck,' he gasped, regaining his balance.

'Ditto,' said Lauren. 'My heart's beating so fast I think it's going to burst out of my chest.' She pointed at Jake's face. 'You're bleeding.'

'Is it bad?'

'Just scratches. You'll live. Might even have improved your looks.'

Jake wiped a dribble of blood from his eye, one corner of his mouth hitching up. 'Girls dig scars, right?'

Lauren prodded the rook with her boot. It didn't move. 'It's dead. Nice shot, killer.'

Jake grimaced. He hated the thought of killing anything. As a little boy it had made him feel sick to watch his schoolmates pulling apart daddy-long-legs for fun. Lauren pushed aside the rags, revealing two grey-black balls of fluff curled together on a bed of twigs. 'Poor little babies. We can't leave them like this.'

'Why not?'

'Why do you think? Because they'll starve to death.'

'So what do you suggest?'

'Well, either we can take them and look after them ourselves or we can put them out of their misery.'

'What? You mean kill them? No way.'

'It's crueller to leave them alive. You don't have to do anything, Jake. I'll do it. A quick twist of their necks. It'll be over in a second.'

Jake thought of Erin. Perhaps she was crying for help somewhere with no one to hear or care about her. He put down the stone, gently laid the rags back over the chicks and gathered up the bundle.

'You really wouldn't make much of a Satanist,' Lauren commented with a smiling shake of her head.

'Who said I wanted to be a Satanist? Screw them dickheads. Let's check out the basement. Then maybe we can leave this dump.'

They descended to the landing. 'Hold this a minute,' said Jake, extending the bundle to Lauren.

'What for?'

'We need the lighter, remember?' But Jake wasn't thinking about the lighter so much as the red rectangular object lodged under the floorboards. He started towards the bedroom. A voice brought him to a stop.

'Hey! What are you doing in here?'

His gaze jerked to the foot of the main stairway. A female constable was standing in the open front door. He recognised her from earlier. She was the one who'd told his dad about Erin. What was her name? Hutton or something.

'I . . . Nothing,' he stammered, wondering if she recognised him.

'Come down here, both of you.'

Jake and Lauren did as told. Constable Hutton indicated the rags. 'What's that?'

Lauren peeled them back to show her the chicks. 'Their mother's dead. We're going to look after them.'

'This is private property. You're trespassing.'

Jake's eyes dropped contritely. Lauren treated the constable to a look of casual defiance. 'So arrest us.'

'I don't want to arrest you. I'm more concerned that someone might get hurt. This house is dangerous.'

'Why? Because it's a church of Satan?'

'No.' There was a faintly amused glint in Constable Hutton's eyes. 'Because it's ready to fall down around our ears. Is anyone else in here?'

'No,' said Jake.

'And how did you get in?'

'We climbed through an upstairs window,' lied Lauren.

Another constable appeared at the door. 'Who are these two?'

'It's Jake Jackson and . . .' Constable Hutton looked askance at Lauren, who compressed her lips into a silent line, 'a friend of his.'

'How did you know I was here?' asked Jake.

'We didn't. We're here for the same reason I'm guessing you are – to look for your sister. But now we've found you I think we'd best take you home.'

'You don't have to go with them,' said Lauren.

Jake sighed resignedly. 'I'd better.'

They headed outside, descending steps flanked by ivy-wrapped pillars. A cracked concrete driveway made its way between a jungle of grass, weeds and bushes to a tall, rusty gate. Constable Hutton opened the back door of a police car.

'You can forget it if you think I'm getting in that,' said Lauren.

'If I find you on this property again I will arrest you,' warned the constable.

Lauren raised her eyebrows as if to say, *Try it, I dare you*. She turned to Jake. 'What do you want to do about our babies?'

A faint heat rose into his face. Lauren's words made him think about what it took to make babies and how often he'd fantasised about doing that thing – the sex part, not the baby part – with her. 'I'll look after them. After all, it was me who killed their mum.'

He took back the bundle and, cradling it against his chest, ducked into the car. Constable Hutton waited until Lauren was out of the gate before starting the engine. As they pulled away, Jake looked over his shoulder at the decaying house. He half expected to see a pair of ghostly figures staring back at him from one of the upstairs windows. But there was nothing. He felt a sudden perverse reluctance to leave. As much as he disliked the place, its atmosphere of creepy unreality was preferable to the reality of what was happening out here.

'What happened to your head?' asked Constable Hutton, proffering a tissue.

Jake explained about the rook, dabbing the scratches gingerly.

'That's what parents do,' said the constable. 'They protect their children at all costs. So don't be too hard on yours for wanting to make sure no harm comes to you.'

A mixture of guilt and irritation jabbed at Jake. The last thing he wanted to do was make things harder for his parents, but he couldn't just sit by and do nothing. Why couldn't they understand that?

'What made you think your sister might be in that house?' asked Constable Hutton.

'I didn't think she was, not really. It was Lauren's idea.'

'I take it Lauren's the girl you were with.'

'Yes. Why did you think Erin might be there?'

'It's just procedure. We're checking out all empty properties, sheds and outhouses in the area on the off-chance Erin might be hiding in them.'

'Why would Erin be hiding?'

'I don't know. You tell me, Jake. Is there any reason for her to be hiding?'

Noticing the constable watching him in the rear-view mirror, he answered quickly, 'No.'

'You can feel free to speak to me, Jake. I won't repeat any of this to your parents.'

'There's no reason for Erin to be hiding,' Jake stated, annoyed. His parents might treat him like a useless little kid, but that didn't mean he was about to talk to this copper behind their backs, even if there was anything to tell – which there wasn't.

They pulled up outside his house. A balding, overweight man was taking photos of it from the street. 'Who's that?' asked Jake.

'A journalist.'

The man turned his camera on them when they got out of the car. As Jake stepped through the front door, his mum rushed into the hallway. Her eyes bulged at him, like they always did when she was really angry. 'Where did you find him?' she asked, her voice ominously flat.

'The Ingham house.'

Amanda's eyes grew even bigger. She pointed at the bundle of rags. 'What's that? And how did you get those scratches?'

Jake avoided her gaze and said nothing, worried she might not allow the chicks in the house.

She heaved an exasperated breath. 'Thank you, Constable Hutton. I'll let you get back to what you were doing before you were side-tracked.' She closed the door hard enough to rattle the glass and turned her intense green gaze on Jake again. 'Well, what have you got to say for yourself?'

'I told you, I have to—'

'All you have to do is what I tell you,' Amanda cut in, gesturing for him to follow her into the kitchen.

'I was only trying to help.'

Amanda took a tube of antiseptic out of a tin and rubbed the ointment on Jake's forehead. 'By breaking into an empty house? How's that helping?'

'The police think it's worth searching. Erin could have been taken there by someone.'

'And what if she had been? What if that someone had tried to hurt you?'

'I'd have hurt them back, worse.'

Amanda let out a harsh laugh as if she'd never heard anything so ridiculous. 'You couldn't fight your way out of a wet paper bag.'

Reddening, Jake opened his mouth to make a retort. Before he could do so, the front door opened and Cathy stepped through it. 'There's a reporter from the *Gazette* out there. I told him you're not interested—' She broke off, then continued in a relieved tone, 'Jake, you're back!'

'Tell him, Mum,' Amanda said sharply. 'Tell him how worried we've been.'

'It's all right, Amanda,' Cathy said, turning on her peacemaker's voice. 'He's home now. No harm done.'

'It's not all right, Mum. I'm not just going to let this pass. He's got to learn that everything he does has consequences.' Amanda thrust her palm out at Jake. 'For starters you can hand over your phone.' Reluctantly, he gave it to her and she added, 'You're also grounded.'

'For how long?'

'Until I say so. Now go to your room. I don't want to see you down here again today. Do I make myself clear?'

Jake ruckled his face at the injustice of it. 'This house is a prison,' he muttered as he headed for the stairs.

'What was that?' snapped Amanda.

'Nothing.'

'Don't push me, Jake. I can think up plenty more ways to punish you.'

Jake placed the bundle of rags on his bed. He flopped down beside it and lay staring at the ceiling. *Bitch*, he thought bitterly. *What right does she have to treat me like this?* He'd be sixteen soon. Old enough to get a job and his own place. Then she'd never be able to tell him what to do again. Perhaps he'd go down to London. That would really show her. His thoughts returned to Erin. What if he never saw her again? He vainly tried to recall the last thing he'd said to her. Going on recent form, he'd most likely either teased her about something or told her to go away.

With a grimace of self-disgust, he stood up suddenly, strode over to the pentagram poster and tore it down. He scooped up the half-melted candles from his desk and flung them into a bin along with the poster. He was done with all the bullshit. From now on he wasn't going to try to be anyone but himself. And if that wasn't good enough for his parents or Lauren, well then screw them.

He flipped open his laptop and Googled 'What do rooks eat?' A link to the RSPB website gave the answer – earthworms, insects, grains. He peered under the rags. The chicks were motionless. He laid his hand on them and felt their hearts flickering as fragilely as a candle flame.

'I'm going to take care of you,' he murmured, switching on his desk lamp and angling it towards them. 'You're going to be OK.'

DAY 1

1.28 P.M.

Seth inhaled the pleasantly cool air. He'd never been a countryside type. His natural habitat was the bustle of the inner city, where it was easy to blend into the crowd. Wide open, empty spaces made him nervous. But here among the trees he felt at ease. Here you could choose to be seen or unseen. Here he could imagine lying down in the shadows with Holly, peeling off her clothes, sliding his lips over her smooth skin. He glanced across at her twenty-five metres away to his right. She was advancing at a snail's pace, her gaze fixed on the ground. As if sensing his eyes on her, she looked at him and smiled. He was struck once again by how wrong he'd got it on first seeing her. She wasn't plain at all. She was like one of those paintings whose beauty could be properly appreciated only from a distance. His instinct was to drop his gaze, pretend he hadn't been watching her. He resisted the urge, mimicking her smile.

Holly's smile faded. A frown grazing her forehead, she resumed scanning the forest floor. Seth frowned too, wondering if he'd done something wrong. His brain gave a squeeze of realisation as it occurred to him: *You're not supposed to be enjoying yourself. You're here to find a missing little girl.*

His gaze moved beyond Holly. To her right was the thuggish-looking bloke who seemed to be best mates with Tom Jackson. He held no interest for Seth. Unlike Tom, who came next in the line, just barely visible among the tangle of tree trunks and branches. Seth had directed numerous furtive looks at Tom during the walk to their search grid. It was a habit of his – reading people. More than that, it was a survival tactic. After all, if he didn't read others, how could he read himself? How could he know how to react, what to feel? Fear and uncertainty were written across Tom's face. Also there, but less evident, he detected something else, something tightly coiled and ready to explode. It gave him a tingle of excitement, like standing too close to a lit firework.

The search party emerged from the ranks of pines onto a gravel road, beyond which the trees were sparser, less mature. From somewhere overhead came a *whump-whump-whump*. Squinting at the cloudless sky, Seth spotted a blue-and-yellow police helicopter circling a few miles to the west.

'Do you think they've found something?' Holly called to him.

'I guess we'll find out soon enough.'

'Let's keep moving!' The shout came from Henry Brooks.

Seth glanced towards the florid-faced figure at the centre of the search line. He found it curious that it wasn't Tom Jackson handing out the orders. The two men obviously came from very different backgrounds. Tom was well-spoken, but his accent was rough around the edges. Henry, on the other hand, spoke what Seth called proper posh. It seemed obvious, too, where the balance of power lay between them. More than once he'd caught a superior note in Henry's voice as he spoke to Tom. Henry Brooks was clearly someone used to being obeyed. Seth found himself wondering what it would be like to be him, to have people listen – really listen, not just pretend to – when you spoke.

Another hundred metres of painstaking searching brought them to the edge of the forest. A sprawling swathe of purple-flowering moorland climbed towards a hump of a hill maybe a mile away. Sandstone crags scarred the hillside, glittering in the midday sun. A marker stuck up on the summit.

'Everyone stop here,' called Henry Brooks. 'This is the edge of our search area. I'm radioing Sergeant Dyer for further instructions.'

'That's Tosson Hill,' said Holly, approaching Seth. 'The highest of the Simonside Hills.'

Seth only half heard her. His gaze had moved to a stream that threaded its way into the trees a stone's throw to the west. At the meeting of stream and forest there was a shallow bowl of marshy-looking grass. Something in the bowl caught his eye – a conical pyramid of branches with a scrap of tarp slung over the side facing the stream. 'What's that?'

'Looks like a bivvy.'

'A what?'

'A bivouac. A shelter made from branches and whatever else you can find lying around. It was probably built by kids. I built one once on a school trip here.'

'Let's take a closer look.'

'Do you think we should tell the others first?'

'Nah. Like you said, it was probably just built by kids.'

They waded through the heather to the crude structure. Branches stripped of needles rested against each other like interlacing fingers. They were overlaid with smaller bushy branches. A circle with a capital 'A' inside it was daubed in red paint on the tarp. The grass in front of the bivouac was flattened and there was a mound of ash inside a circle of stones. A couple of sooty tins were half buried in the ashes. A pair of wet blue jeans was spread across a flat rock on the bank of the babbling stream.

Holly pointed at the 'A'. 'I wonder what that means.'

'It's an anarchist symbol. I've seen them at anti-capitalist demonstrations in London.'

'Are you an anti-capitalist?'

'No.' Seth had once tried to impress a girl by telling her how he went along to such demonstrations not because he gave a toss about their causes, but because he got a buzz from being around the trouble that inevitably broke out. After that she'd stopped returning his calls. He wasn't about to make that mistake again. Squatting down, he held his hand over the ashes. 'They're still warm.'

A frown troubled Holly's face. 'I'm going to fetch the others.'

'I'll wait here.'

As she hastened back to the search party, Seth scanned the trees. There was no one to be seen, but that didn't mean there was no one there. He took out his lock-knife and flipped it open. He used the blade to lift aside the tarp. Inside the shelter was a green sleeping-bag on a thick mattress of marsh grass. Empty cans of Special Brew were piled beside a frayed army rucksack. His nose wrinkled at a smell of old sweat, wood smoke and patchouli oil.

He glanced up at the sound of Henry Brooks calling out, 'Remember what Sergeant Dyer said, Tom. Don't touch anything.'

Tom was sprinting towards the bivouac as if he'd been told Erin was inside it. His father-in-law and the others trailed behind. Seth quickly pocketed his knife. Tom pulled up abruptly at the sight of the anarchist symbol, the colour draining from his face. With a sudden movement, he tore the tarp down and ducked into the bivouac. He hauled out the rucksack and began unbuckling it.

Henry was next to reach the lip of the grassy hollow. 'What are you doing?' he puffed, his face as red as Tom's was pale. 'Put that down.'

Ignoring him, Tom pulled a rainbow-coloured jumper from the bag and flung it aside. Next he dug out a sheath of flyers. 'Look at these!' He thrust the flyers towards Henry. FUCK THE QUARRY was printed across the top of them. 'It's those hippies. They've taken Erin.' His fraught eyes moved to Eddie. 'You remember what Greenie said, they'll do whatever's necessary to protect the quarry.'

Henry snatched away the flyers and stuffed them back into the rucksack. 'If you're right, you could be contaminating vital evidence.'

'Oi!'

The shout came from a hulking figure carrying a bundle of sticks on the far side of the stream. The man was bare-chested, bare-footed and wearing a tatty kilt. He had a long black beard and his hair was shaved into a mohawk with dreadlocks at the back. He dropped all the sticks, except for one, and charged towards the bivouac, yelling in a thick Scottish accent, 'Get your hands off my stuff.'

'Where's my daughter?' demanded Tom as the man splashed through the stream.

Seth retreated towards where Holly was standing just outside the hollow. He had no intention of getting his skull crushed by some Braveheart wannabe. Eddie came barrelling past him, fists clenched for a fight.

'I dunno what you're talking about,' retorted the man, raising the stick threateningly. 'But if you've nicked anything, I'm gonna brae ya.'

'Liar!' Tom squared up to the taller man. 'I know who you are. I've seen you at the protest camp.'

The man's eyes widened in sudden recognition. 'It's you! You're the scumbag who wants to rape our beautiful mother earth.'

'I won't ask you again. What have you done with my daughter?'

'His daughter went missing this morning,' put in Eddie, coming up alongside Tom.

The man looked between them in surprise. 'First I've heard of it.' His gaze fixed unsympathetically on Tom. 'Maybe losing something you love will make you think about what you're taking from us.'

Tom's jaw slackened. Briefly, he looked too stunned to react. Then a word exploded from him. 'Bastard!'

He hurled himself forwards. His head connected with the man's chest. The pair of them toppled over and tumbled into the stream. Tom ended up on top. He clamped his hands to the man's head and thrust it under the water. The back of it struck a stone. The man gave a spluttering roar and lashed out with the stick, grazing Tom's forehead. Before he could take another swing, Eddie tore it from his grasp. Tom dunked the man again.

'Easy, Tom, he's had enough,' said Eddie, grabbing the man's flailing arms.

Tom shot his friend a glare that said, *Stay out of this!* Then, blinking and catching control of himself, he released the man, whose bearded face broke the surface with a choking gasp. Taking an arm and a leg each, Tom and Eddie hauled him up the bank. He wriggled and twisted like a fish trying to escape a net. 'Give us a hand. will you?' Eddie called to his fellow searchers.

Several – Seth not included – started forwards, but Henry held up a hand to stay them. 'No one else is to come down here.'

Tom and Eddie flipped the dripping-wet man onto his belly and twisted his arms up behind his back. 'Stay still or I'll break it,' Eddie warned, applying pressure with his thick, powerful fingers.

'Fuck you,' spat the man. 'You earth-raping corporate scum.'

Eddie laughed gruffly. 'Did you hear that Tom? Corporate scum, us? If only, eh?'

'Where's Erin?' Tom breathlessly demanded to know again. 'Tell me or do you want to go back in the water?'

'No one's going back in the water,' Henry said firmly. 'Sergeant Dyer is on his way.' Dabbing sweat from his forehead with a hanky, he turned his attention to the restrained man. 'So you might as well stop trying to escape.'

'I'm nae trying to,' groaned the man, 'cos I've done nae wrong.'

'We'll see about that, wee laddie,' mocked Eddie.

'Arseholes! Let me go, you arseholes!' The man made one final furious attempt to break free, then lay still, except for his heaving chest.

'What's your name?' asked Tom.

'Piss off,' muttered the man.

'And what are you doing out here, Mr Piss Off?' said Eddie.

'You think you're hilarious, don't you, pal? You won't be laughing a few weeks from now when someone puts a match to your quarry and everything in it.'

Scowling, Eddie leaned heavily on the man. 'You'll struggle to light a match with a broken arm, *pal*.'

'Eddie,' cautioned Henry as the man gasped with pain.

Eddie eased off the pressure. 'Sorry, Mr Brooks. He keeps provoking me.'

'I know, but let's all try to remain calm. Sergeant Dyer will be here any minute now.'

At the top of the slope, Seth's heart was beating pleasurably. Throughout the scuffle, his gaze had remained riveted on Tom. The look on Tom's face as he hurled himself at the man! Such intensity. Such raw emotion. It was exhilarating to see. 'Wow,' he murmured to himself.

'That was really horrible,' said Holly.

'Yeah, horrible.'

Henry climbed the slope. 'Well spotted, Seth.'

Seth accepted the praise with what he judged to be a suitably grave nod. 'Thank you, Mr Brooks.'

'Holly here was telling me how you're giving up your holiday time to help us.'

'It's nothing. I'm happy to be here.' *Happy, is that the right word?* wondered Seth. Henry's reply seemed to confirm that it was.

'It's not nothing to me, Seth. I just want you to know how much I appreciate what you're doing. One thing, though. If you see anything else, please tell me rather than investigating by yourself.'

'Will do, Mr Brooks. I'm sorry.'

'No need to apologise, Seth. I remember what it was like to be your age. There was no one more impulsive than me when I was in my twenties.' Henry gave a little shake of his head as if at some memory. He wafted his hat in front of his face and addressed the group in general. 'Phew, it's hot. There's no need for you all to stand here getting sunburnt. Why don't you wait in the shade?'

The group headed for the trees. Seth followed slowly, reluctant to let Tom out of his sight. The fight had left him greedy for more. Like an avaricious sponge, he wanted to soak up every emotion on offer. He settled down on the pine-needle-flecked grass. Holly passed him a bottle of water and he swallowed a mouthful. As he returned the bottle, her fingers touched his. A little jolt travelled up his arm and down into his groin. He found himself thinking once again about lying down with her in some hidden place. As if she'd read his thoughts, her usually direct gaze slid shyly away and landed on Sergeant Dyer, who was approaching along the treeline with four constables. Seth's gaze was drawn to the lean, broad-shouldered man following a short distance behind them. Even at that distance the family resemblance to Tom was obvious, but his features were harder edged, grimmer. A border collie trotted at his heels.

Seth rose and returned to the lip of the grassy hollow – he had no intention of missing a moment of whatever drama was to come. 'The police are here.'

Tom and Eddie none too gently pulled the activist upright. The instant Sergeant Dyer arrived, the man jerked his chin at Tom and yelled, 'He assaulted me.' He twisted his head to display the proof. 'Look, I'm bleeding.'

'What's your name?' asked the sergeant.

'Craig Ferguson.'

'I thought you said it was Piss Off,' taunted Eddie.

Craig glared at him. 'Prick.'

'Enough of that,' warned Sergeant Dyer. 'Let go of him.' Tom and Eddie did so and the sergeant continued in his firm, even voice, 'Now, Mr Ferguson, if you'd like to tell me what happened.'

'I was attacked for no reason. That's what happened.'

'No reason, my arse,' scowled Eddie.

Craig stabbed a finger at Tom then Eddie. 'He would have killed me, if this comedian hadn't stopped him.'

'Oh, come now,' put in Henry, 'I hardly think that's likely. The fact is, Sergeant Dyer, this man made a provocative comment about Erin and Tom reacted in a way which, under the circumstances, is entirely understandable.'

'Did you hit Mr Ferguson?' the sergeant asked Tom.

'I tackled him to the ground.'

'In that case you're going to have to accompany me to the station.'

Taken aback, Tom exclaimed, 'What for?'

'Surely that's not necessary, Sergeant,' said Henry.

'I'm afraid it is, Mr Brooks.'

'No way am I leaving the search,' Tom said heatedly.

'This man is accusing you of assault, Mr Jackson. And you yourself admit you hit him. You're both going to have to give a statement.'

'The only way you're going to get me away from here is by dragging me.'

'Then that's what we'll do if you force us to.'

'That won't be necessary,' said Henry, laying a firm hand on Tom's shoulder. 'Will it, Tom?'

Tom shrugged off his father-in-law. 'You know something, Henry, I've just about had enough of your—' Catching sight of his brother, his voice faltered. 'Graham, you came,' he said, as if he unsure whether to be surprised or pleased.

'Of course.' Graham's tone suggested there was no need for him to be either of those things. 'Go with the sergeant, Tom. I'll take your place here.'

The brothers looked at each other for a moment as if exchanging silent words. Tom heaved a sigh. 'OK. Come on, let's get this over with.'

'Do you want me to call our solicitor?' offered Eddie.

Tom shook his head. Sergeant Dyer made a pushing motion at the other members of the search party, who'd gathered again on the slope behind the bivouac. 'Could everybody please move back. Scene-of-crime officers are on their way. This area is strictly off-limits until they've completed their sweep.'

'What about my gear?' Craig demanded to know as the sergeant shepherded him away.

'It'll be returned to you later.'

Seth watched Sergeant Dyer and his constables escort Tom and Craig away. Tom and Henry exchanged a parting glance. What was that in Tom's eyes? An apology? Anger? A confused combination of both? Tom obviously wasn't happy with bowing down to his father-in-law. Seth's heart had given a leap when, for a split second, it seemed Tom would tear into the old man. He struggled to conceal his disappointment as he lost sight of Tom. He glanced at Graham. It hardly seemed a fair swap – an open book for what, on first impression, appeared to be a closed one.

'It doesn't seem fair,' Holly said as if echoing his thoughts. 'That Ferguson bloke got what he asked for.'

'I know,' said Seth, consoling himself with the thought, *Oh well, at least I've still got Henry.* It would be interesting to see how he reacted to Tom very publicly slighting his authority.

Henry signalled for the group to gather round. He pointed at an Ordnance Survey map. 'This is our new search grid.' His voice was calm, his features as unruffled as a windless lake.

He's a consummate performer, thought Seth, *just like me.*

DAY 1
2.40 P.M.

The search was building fast. As Tom hurried along, sodden shoes squelching, everywhere he looked lines of searchers were advancing between shadow-laced pines, silent as ghosts. Furious with himself for losing control, Tom avoided their enquiring glances. Further to the south-west now, the helicopter swept low over swaying treetops. Back at the clearing where Erin had seemingly been swallowed by the earth, two cars with red-and-yellow Battenberg markings and SEARCH DOGS on their bonnets had joined the growing assembly of emergency service vehicles. German shepherds and labradors had their noses thrust into the grass, trying to snuffle out Erin's scent. It gave him a light-headed feeling to see it, to know it was all for his beautiful baby.

When the grey outline of Newbiggin Farm came into view at the forest fringe, Sergeant Dyer stopped. 'I have to stay and coordinate the search,' he explained. 'Detective Inspector Shields is waiting at the station to take your statement.'

'Who exactly is this Inspector Shields?'

'He's been brought in from Newcastle. He has a lot of experience with missing children cases. Plus he used to live in this area. So you're in good hands.'

The rest of them climbed past placidly grazing sheep to the lane, which was becoming as clogged as a city road at rush hour. As Craig was led towards an ambulance, he shot Tom what seemed to be a triumphant glance. Tom resisted an impulse to charge at him again. Instead, he settled for firing only words back. 'The quarry's going to be a success no matter what you people do.'

He instantly felt even angrier with himself. What did the quarry matter? He'd put a match to it himself if doing so brought Erin back.

Tom was escorted to a police car. As it accelerated away, he stared back at the forest, overcome by an irrational sense that he was somehow abandoning Erin. A constable moved aside a strip of blue-and-white tape at the end of the lane. Beyond the cordon, a crew from a regional news show had set up alongside their satellite van at the roadside. They aimed their camera at the car as it passed.

A second cordon was strung across the entrance to Fontburn Reservoir car park. The car park was empty now, except for Amanda's Golf and a couple of police vehicles. A few fishermen were still dotted along the shoreline. On the way into town, the car passed groups of hikers, council workers digging up the road. Scenes of normality that seemed like a slap in the face.

The police station was on the edge of the town centre. Next to it was Middlebury Hospital in whose maternity ward Erin had come into the world. A lump formed in Tom's throat as his mind reeled back to that moment – crumpled grey-blue face slimy with blood, eyes squeezed tight against the unfamiliar glare of the outside world. She'd been a fortnight overdue. They'd joked that she hadn't wanted to leave her mummy's tummy. And she'd gone on as she'd begun, a quiet, loving child rarely far from either of her parents' side.

The station was a bland brick building whose personnel were more used to dealing with minor domestic incidents, shoplifters and occasional lairy tourists than with missing children. In his youth, Tom had spent the night in its cells on more than one occasion after getting into drunken fights. The station had been as quiet as a graveyard on those nights. Today it buzzed with activity. The car park was overflowing. There were Land Rovers and vans marked with the liveries of search-and-rescue teams from as far afield as Penrith, Tayside and Cleveland. A team was being briefed in the reception area. Tom followed a constable to a blank-walled interview room.

The constable motioned for him to take a seat at a table. Tom remained standing. 'Where's this Inspector Shields?'

'I'll find out.'

As seconds ticked by like minutes, Tom ground his teeth. All he could think was, *How could you be so stupid? You shouldn't be here.*

A tall grey-haired man entered. 'I'm DI Glenn Shields,' he said, regarding Tom with keen pale eyes.

'Tom Jackson. Can we do this as fast as possible? I want to get back out there.'

'Of course, Mr Jackson. Take a seat.'

This time, Tom sat down. His legs jigged restlessly beneath the table as Inspector Shields seated himself opposite and opened a statement pad. 'I need your date of birth, address, any contact numbers and marital status.'

Tom fired off the required information.

'Tell me what happened with Mr Ferguson.'

Once again, Tom rapidly recounted what Inspector Shields wanted to know.

'That seems fairly straightforward,' said Inspector Shields. 'You were provoked and reacted violently.'

'I reacted like any father would have done,' corrected Tom. 'So are you going to arrest Craig Ferguson?'

'He's done nothing wrong.'

'Nothing wrong? He's one of those eco-activist nutjobs. Have you heard of Carl 'Greenie' Wright? He's their leader. He threatened to do whatever's necessary to stop us from developing the quarry. And an hour later I find out my daughter's missing. That's a pretty big coincidence, don't you think?'

'Yes, I agree it would seem so. And yes, I know of Mr Wright. In fact I was on the phone to him when you arrived here. He tells me Mr Ferguson was expelled from their camp two days ago because his views are considered too extreme.'

'What do you mean, "too extreme"?'

'Apparently he advocates violent protest. But that's not to say I think he's got anything to do with your daughter's disappearance. If he did take Erin, why hang around? Why not run?'

'These people are fanatics, Inspector. Don't you see? He's offering himself up as a martyr to his cause.'

Inspector Shields pursed his thin lips and nodded. 'That's plausible, I suppose. But if that were the case, why would Mr Ferguson deny taking your daughter? Surely he'd want you to know what he's done. Otherwise, what would be the point?'

'Perhaps there were others with him. He might be trying to give them time to get Erin somewhere out of our reach.'

'That's highly unlikely, Mr Jackson. The vast majority of child abduction cases involve a single perpetrator acting alone. What's more, there's no real evidence that this is an abduction case.'

'Then what is it?' Tom retorted desperately. 'Just what in Christ's name is going on?'

'That's what we're all trying to find out. I'm not ruling out any possibilities at this point, including that Craig Ferguson is involved in this, alone or with accomplices. The most important thing is not to jump to conclusions.'

Tom thrust his head into his hands. 'I feel like I'm going to scream.'

Inspector Shields smiled sympathetically. 'Please don't. You'll get me in trouble.'

Tom managed to summon up a faint smile of his own at the dry remark. 'So what happens now? Can I go?'

'First, I need you to sign and date this.'

Inspector Shields slid the statement across the table. Tom quickly signed and returned it. 'There are a few more questions I need to ask,' said the inspector, taking out another notepad. 'You may already have been asked some of these questions today, but please try to answer them as fully and precisely as possible anyway. What time did you leave the house this morning?'

'About five to nine.'

'Did you go directly to the Town Hall?'

'No. I went to Maglin Hill first.' Tom looked narrowly at Inspector Shields. 'Why are you so interested in where I went?'

'These questions are asked as a matter of routine. You're not under any kind of suspicion. Why did you go to Maglin Hill?'

Tom sighed. 'I'm not entirely sure. I suppose I was trying to work out whether it's worth all the strife.'

'Strife.' Inspector Shields repeated the word as if it was significant. 'When I spoke to your wife earlier, I got the impression that things have been somewhat strained between you recently.'

The lines between Tom's eyebrows sharpened. 'Really? What did she say to make you think that?'

The inspector sidestepped the question with another of his own. 'Are you saying I got the wrong impression?'

'Absolutely. Things have never been better between us,' Tom said with perhaps a touch too much conviction. 'When I said strife, I was referring to the quarry and everything that goes with it, not my marriage.'

'But surely it's all part of the same thing. If you're stressed because of money troubles—'

'Did Amanda tell you we've got money troubles?'

Rather than answering Tom's question, the inspector continued, 'It seems clear to me that if someone's stressed about money, work or whatever, it's going to have a knock-on effect on their family relationships.'

'Well, it doesn't seem clear to me. I'd never allow that to that happen. Work is work. Family is family.'

Inspector Shields nodded. 'I myself try my best never to bring my work home. But sometimes stress just spills over.'

Tom silently sucked his upper lip. He spread his hands in an *anything else?* gesture.

'So I'm assuming you can think of no reason Erin might have run away?' asked the inspector.

'None at all.'

'And apart from the environmental activists, is there anyone else you can think of with a possible motive to be involved in this?'

Tom's mind returned to the market square and his meeting with the old Druidess. He fished the square of black paper out of his pocket and unfolded it on the table. He explained where it had come from as Inspector Shields read the spidery writing.

'Apart from yourself and the woman who gave it to you, has anyone handled this?' asked Inspector Shields.

'Only my business partner Eddie Reed.'

'Do you know the woman's name?'

'No. I'd never seen her before.'

'I'd like to hold onto this, if it's OK with you.' Tom nodded and Inspector Shields continued, 'Your son's interested in this kind of thing, isn't he?'

'What do you mean?'

'Paganism, witchcraft, the occult.'

Tom rolled his eyes. 'It's just a phase he's going through. Why? What's that got to do with anything?'

'We picked Jake up at the Ingham house about an hour ago. He was looking for Erin. Why do you think he thought he might find her there?'

'He's a teenager,' Tom said, as if that was all the explanation necessary. 'You used to live around here so you must know about that house.'

A shadow of something – some memory or perhaps regret – passed over Inspector Shields's face. 'Only too well. I'd just started as a constable in seventy-two. I was one of the first on the scene.'

'Look, I can see what you're getting at. The rumours about that house and devil worshippers and all the rest of that nonsense. But I'm telling you, Inspector, you're barking up the wrong tree.'

'I'm sure you're right, Mr Jackson.' Inspector Shields pushed his chair back and stood up. 'Depending on how things go with Mr Ferguson – and I'd say it's a good bet he's not going to back down – you may well find yourself back here in the near future facing assault charges.'

Tom showed what he thought of the prospect with a flick of his hand. 'I need a lift back to the forest.'

'I'll arrange it.' The inspector looked Tom up and down – damp trousers, grass-stained shirt missing several buttons, grazed forehead. 'I'd suggest you take a moment to go home, clean yourself up and get your act together. Because if there's another incident like the one with Mr Ferguson, I'm going to lock you up. And then you'll be no use whatsoever to your daughter. Is that clear?'

Tom exhaled a steadying breath. 'Crystal.'

DAY 1
4.14 P.M.

'They're still there,' Amanda said irritably, looking out of the living-room window. The *Gazette* reporter had moved on, but he'd soon been replaced by a little clutch of other figures taking photos and notes. 'I don't know what they think they're going to see here. They should be at the forest.' She swished the curtains shut. 'That's where I should be too.'

'Then why don't you go?'

'I need to keep an eye on Jake.'

'I told you, I'll stay with him.'

Amanda briefly considered her mum's offer, then shook her head.

'I know you're worried about him, Amanda, but you needn't be,' continued Cathy. 'He's not going anywhere. I'll make sure of that. I'll sit on a chair on the landing if that's what it takes.'

Amanda chewed her lips uncertainly. In what had become a familiar ritual over the past few hours, she glared at the phone as if she hated it, before snatching it up and punching in a number.

'You won't get through to him,' said Cathy. 'There's no signal in—'

Amanda cut her off with a 'Shh. It's ringing.' When the call went through to voicemail, her eyes flashed. 'Why the bloody hell isn't Tom answering?'

At the sound of an engine, she twitched aside the curtains. A police car pulled up and Tom got out, shaking his head as the reporters tried to accost him. Amanda exchanged an anxious glance with her mum. Like someone approaching a crumbling cliff edge, she moved into the hallway. 'Have they found something?' she asked as Tom opened the door.

He shook his head. 'I've just come for a change of clothes.'

Her head swimming with a bewildering blend of relief and disappointment, Amanda missed the flat, almost cold note in Tom's voice. She took in his dishevelled appearance. 'What happened to you?'

He rattled off his answer as she followed him up to their bedroom. 'Oh my god,' she gasped. 'Those bastards have got our baby.'

'Inspector Shields doesn't seem to think so.' Tom unbuttoned his shirt.

'But why else would that man—'

'I don't know,' interrupted Tom, pinching his forehead. 'I don't understand anything about what's happening. All I know is I'm powerless to stop it.'

'No, you're not. You could go to the camp, tell them you're not going ahead with the quarry.'

Tom was momentarily gobsmacked. Then he said, 'I can't do that. It's not only up to me. Eddie—'

'To hell with Eddie.'

'He's my best mate.'

Amanda yanked Tom's hand away from his forehead. 'Erin's your daughter!'

'Say I do what you want, you realise what it would mean, don't you? It would mean they've won. And we'd lose everything.'

'Everything except the most important thing.' Amanda clutched Tom's hand to her heart. 'Please, Tom. If you love me, do this.'

He stared into his wife's eyes. He stroked her hair and rested his hand against her cheek. 'I do love you, Amanda.'

'So you'll do it?'

He nodded. Tears spilling over her long lashes, she kissed his palm. 'Thank you, thank you.'

Tom peered out the window at the police and journalists. 'We don't want them following us.'

'We can sneak out the back. Get my mum to meet us in her car on Mill Lane.'

Tom gently pushed Amanda away and continued undressing. He left his clothes where they fell, hauling on jeans and a polo shirt. She waited restlessly on the landing as he washed the dried blood from his forehead. They hurried downstairs, Amanda calling out, 'Mum, we need your car.'

'Are you going to the forest?' asked Cathy.

'No . . . Yes.'

Cathy's eyes narrowed. 'What's going on?'

Amanda headed past her towards the back door. 'Meet us in your car on Mill Lane in five minutes.'

'Why are you sneaking out the back?'

'Please, Mum, there's no time to explain.'

Amanda turned to stare desperately at her mum. Sighing, Cathy nodded. Amanda and Tom crossed the back garden and opened a gate. Beyond it was a narrow lane. They waited furtively for Cathy. After a couple of minutes, she appeared in her Mini.

Cathy placed the ignition key in her daughter's palm, but kept hold of it. 'You're not going to do anything you're not supposed to, are you?'

'Just give her the keys,' snapped Tom.

Cathy gave him a look as if she was sizing up a cheap cut of meat.

'Please, Mum,' Amanda said again, quivering with urgency.

Cathy released the key. They accelerated away from her, keeping an eye on the rear-view mirror for pursuing vehicles. Amanda took the same route to Maglin Hill as Tom had that morning – a lifetime ago it seemed now. As they crossed the humpback bridge, Tom's eyes were drawn to the big house on the river's far bank. 'It'll never be ours now,' he muttered.

'It's just a house, Tom.'

'Yeah. Just a house.' He let out a sharp breath. 'Even after all these years your mother still looks at me like I'm something she scraped off the bottom of her shoe.'

Amanda knew better than to open that can of worms. 'We can get through this.'

'Can we?'

Her heart gave a hard thump at the spikiness of the question. She darted Tom a searching look. Did he know about the phone call? 'What's that supposed to mean?'

'You tell me. You're the one going around saying our marriage is on the rocks.'

He doesn't know, she realised with a rush of relief. 'I never said any such thing.'

'"I got the impression from your wife that things have been strained between you." That's what Inspector Shields said.'

'I honestly don't know what made him think that. I said it's been a tough few months, what with everything that's been going on with the quarry. I didn't mention anything to do with us. But let's face it, Tom, things have been difficult between us. You've been so caught up with—'

'I don't want to get into this now,' he cut in.

'Then why bring it up?'

'I'm sorry, I shouldn't have. It's that bloody Inspector Shields. He says we're not under suspicion but—'

'He makes you feel the exact opposite,' Amanda finished her husband's sentence. 'He was the same with me.'

'It's ridiculous. What does he think? That we'd hurt our own child?' Tom shook his head in disgust. 'We need to put up a united front. I don't want that man wasting his time investigating us.'

'You're right, Tom. I'm sorry.'

'It wasn't your fault. It's this situation. It's just so . . .' His voice thickened. 'I don't even know what to call it. It's like some sort of crazy nightmare.'

Amanda laid a soft hand on Tom's shoulder. He heaved a shuddering breath, a frightened look in his eyes. 'Do you really think we're going to get through this?'

Amanda countered his fear with a fiercely determined, 'Yes.'

The road climbed out of town between sun-splashed fields. Maglin Hill reared from the sea of green like the hull of a capsized ship. They turned onto the gravel track to the dormant quarry. A makeshift roadblock of tyres and tree trunks had been set up at the quarry's entrance. A white sheet was strung across it with MIDDLEBURY STONE WANTS TO DESTROY YOUR HERITAGE FOR PROFIT and SHAME ON THEM! emblazoned on it.

Several activists were chopping veg and tipping it into a big pan suspended over a fire. Others were setting out plates and cutlery on a trestle table in the shade of a quarry wall pocked with blasting holes. A pack of dogs as wiry and scruffy as their owners were sniffing around for scraps. Amanda was struck by how well organised it all looked. Despite the planning decision going against them, the activists appeared upbeat, chatting, smiling and laughing like they were one big happy family. Laughing! A muscle twitched in her cheek. How could they laugh when her daughter was missing?

A woman popped up from the treehouse and began clanging a cowbell. The dogs accompanied it with a chorus of barks, running out to circle the Mini. With the well-drilled efficiency of a ragtag army, the protesters dropped whatever they were doing and assembled at the roadblock. Amanda's gaze swept over their dreadlocked, tattooed, pierced ranks and fixed on Greenie's fox-like face. He was stripped to the waist, displaying a red 'A' circled by flames tattooed on the left side of his caved-in chest.

'Tom,' Amanda said in a cautioning voice as she noticed his fingers curling into fists.

'Wait here.'

'Uh-uh, forget it.'

'I'm not going to do anything stupid.'

'I know because I'm going to make sure of it.' Amanda laced her fingers into Tom's and squeezed. Her eyes shone with a brittle intensity that seemed to say, *Together we can do this.*

He squeezed back, then they let go of each other and got out. The dogs sniffed at their ankles and eyeballed them warily. Greenie raised his hands, palms outward. 'That's as far as you go.'

Amanda sensed Tom tensing at being told where he could go on his own land. Before he could make any kind of retort, she said quickly, 'We need to talk.'

'I've got nothing to say to you.'

'Well, we have something to say to you which you're going to want to hear,' said Tom.

'Then say it and go. You're not welcome here.'

Tom glanced at the hostile faces to either side of Greenie. 'Can we talk alone?'

Greenie's shrewd little eyes narrowed as if he suspected a trap. 'We have no secrets here.'

'Please, Mr Wright,' said Amanda, a tremor in her voice. 'I promise it'll be worth your while.'

Some of the hardness left Greenie's face. He considered her words and said, 'OK, but I can't allow you into the camp.' He gestured for Tom and Amanda to follow him along a footpath that skirted around the tents.

'Detective Shields said—' began Tom.

Greenie held up a silencing hand and pointed to the stone-crowned summit of Maglin Hill.

Tom blew an impatient breath. 'We haven't got time for—'

He broke off again as Amanda caught hold of his hand and gave it a sharp squeeze. The path flattened out at the summit, passing through a gap in the grassy bank that encircled the standing stones. As always, Tom found himself vaguely surprised by the sheer size of the monoliths. The nearest to the gap, a flat-faced block with deep vertical channels cut into it, loomed almost three metres tall. Greenie ran his hands over the channels. 'No one knows what made these. Just like no one knows who put the stones here or why. That's what I love best about them – the mystery. Each of us is free to see them in our own way. I see them as a family.' He reverently rested his forehead against the weathered stone. 'This one's the mother.' His gaze moved over the other stones. 'Those are her daughters.'

Three of the daughters were slightly shorter than their mother, equally broad at the top, but tapering in at the waist. The fourth was half a metre or so taller and slim from top to bottom. A diagonal channel ran from left to right down her inner face, which was dotted with bowl-shaped indents. 'She's the youngest and prettiest,' said Greenie. 'I call her Wren because you often see wrens bathing in the hollows on her head. The mother is Wardia. Her name means guardian. She'll do anything for her children.'

'So will we,' said Amanda.

Greenie turned to her, his eyes sympathetic. 'I was sorry to hear about your daughter.'

'Were you?' Tom asked sharply.

The guarded look came back. 'I've a daughter of my own. I can't imagine how you must feel. I'm amazed you're here. I thought you'd be looking for her.'

'We are.'

Greenie's nut-brown forehead contracted. 'I'm going to tell you what I told that copper. Craig Ferguson's got nothing to do with this camp.'

'Bullshit.'

'You can think what you like, but that's the way it is. And I'll tell you this 'n' all, Craig's got nothing to do with your daughter going missing. He's an out-there dude with some pretty heavy beliefs, I'll admit that. But snatching a kid . . . Nah, no way.'

'We won't go ahead with the quarry.' Amanda's words rushed out like a breath that had been held too long.

Greenie blinked, seemingly stunned.

'Tell him, Tom,' she continued. When Tom didn't speak at once, she added in a voice both sharp and pleading, 'Go on, tell him.'

'You win,' Tom said tightly, as if the words were being dragged out of him. 'All we want is Erin. All we want is our daughter back where she belongs.'

Greenie spread his palms. 'Whoa, you've got it wrong. Very, very wrong.'

'Look, we don't expect you to admit to what's going on here. How about you just say, *I win, you lose.*'

'No, I don't want to.'

'Please say it,' said Amanda, half demanding, half begging. 'Then we can all go home and get on with our lives.'

'No.'

Amanda's eyes suddenly blazed. 'Say it!'

Greenie retreated towards the centre of the stone circle. 'I've got nothing else to say to you.'

'We're not wearing wires.' To prove her point, Amanda pulled down her vest top. 'Nothing you say here will ever be repeated. And if you don't believe us about the quarry, we'll make it official. We'll have a solicitor draw up a document stating we'll never reopen it.'

'Piss off out of here.'

Amanda eyeballed Greenie, unmoving. Tom took hold of her arm and tried to draw her out of the stone circle, but she elbowed him away. She faced Greenie for several tense breaths. He shrugged as if to say, *Fine, I'll go then*. Giving Amanda and Tom a wide berth, he headed for the earthwork's entrance.

'Don't you walk away from me!' The words tore from Amanda's throat. She lashed out at Greenie, her fingers hooked like claws. Tom caught hold of her arms, pinning them to her sides. 'Let go,' she spat, driving her heel into his shin. He grimaced, but didn't loosen his grip. Directing her fury back at Greenie, she yelled, 'Give us back our daughter or you'll regret it! Do you hear me?'

Darting her a nervous glance, Greenie quickened his pace and disappeared down the slope. She struggled for another moment like a restrained wild animal, then went limp. 'Christ, Amanda,' Tom breathed. 'You're the one supposed to be keeping me out of trouble. If I let go, do you promise you won't go after him?'

She gave a resigned nod. 'Why did you stop me?' she demanded as he released her. 'We could have made him tell us where Erin is.'

'Oh, believe me, I'm going to make him tell us,' Tom said darkly. 'But not when he can cry out for help.'

Something like hunger twisted Amanda's beauty into ugliness. 'What are you going to do?'

Tom echoed Greenie's earlier words to him. 'Whatever's necessary. First I need to speak to Eddie.'

They headed back down the hill. The activists were gathered around Greenie, talking in lowered voices. Amanda scowled at the sight. 'Shame on us?' she burst out. 'More like shame on you!'

'Ignore the earth rapists,' said Greenie.

Amanda's eyes flared so bright that Tom thought he was going to have to grab her again. But she jerked her gaze away from the camp and stormed to the car, muttering, 'Whatever's necessary.'

DAY 1
4.41 P.M.

Sitting astride his window ledge, Jake lit a cigarette. He wrinkled his nose. He'd tried to force himself to like smoking for the same reason he'd spent the past few months reading up on black magic – Lauren. He would have pretended he enjoyed eating shit if he thought it impressed her. But he was past that now – or at least he told himself he was. He stubbed out the cigarette and deposited it in a mound of others that dammed the gutter above his window.

Erin was only nine, but she'd seen through his bullshit. She'd pinched her nose at his unwashed long hair, saying, 'Yuck, you smell like sweaty old socks. I liked you better before you started hanging around with Lauren.'

'Get lost, you little turd,' he'd retorted, instantly regretting it as a wounded look flashed over her face. He'd added more softly, 'You don't understand.'

'Understand what?'

'What it's like to be a teenager.'

Erin had made the scrunched-up hamster face she pulled when something perplexed her. 'If being a teenager means smelling like you, I never ever want to be one.'

A sharp pang rose from Jake's stomach as he found himself wondering whether her words would come true. Pushing the feeling back down with a hard swallow, he lowered himself to the carpet and looked at the chicks. He'd collected dead flies from a spider web in the corner of the ceiling and placed them by their beaks. But the chicks hadn't eaten them. They lay deathly still, eyes closed. Resting his hands lightly on their fluffy feathers, he was relieved to feel the pitter-patter of their hearts. *They're just sleeping*, he told himself. *When they wake up, they'll eat the flies.*

He looked out the window in the direction of the forest. *Maybe Erin's just sleeping too*, he thought. *Maybe she's curled up beneath the trees, dreaming of finding her way back to Mum.* His forehead rippled. This wasn't a fucking fairy tale. Wherever Erin was, she wasn't asleep.

His gaze moved from the horizon back to the Ingham house. He couldn't see it. But he could feel it somehow, away beyond the slate rooftops and the tree-lined river. He imagined it watching him back, like an invisible, malevolent presence. He thought about the red rectangular object beneath the floorboards. Surely it was a book. What's more, a book with a lock on it. He could think of only one type of book that had a lock – a diary. And if, as he suspected, the bedroom had been Rachel Ingham's, then surely it was her diary. He itched with curiosity to find out if he was right. He shook his head. What did it matter what the object was? It couldn't help find Erin.

He flopped onto his bed and closed his eyes. But he opened them again quickly, disturbed by what he saw in the confines of his mind – Erin crying, Erin in pain. His thoughts inexorably drifted back to the Ingham house. This time he didn't stop them from doing so. It was strangely soothing to think of the object beneath the floor, to lose himself in wondering what answers it might contain, what mysteries it might reveal.

At the shrill ring of FaceTime, he reached for his iPad. It was Lauren. He accepted the call and her anaemic face appeared on the screen. She was lying amid an incongruously pink duvet, smoking a cigarette. On the wall behind her was a poster of a beautiful red-haired woman in a black hooded robe, holding a staff topped with some sort of animal skull.

'I've been trying to call your moby,' said Lauren.

'My mum took it away.'

'Fuck. Did she go mad?'

'Big time. I'm grounded too.'

'How long for?' When Jake shrugged, Lauren went on, 'This is such bullshit. You were only trying to help. What are you going to do?'

Jake shrugged again. 'What can I do? I'm basically a prisoner.'

'I know what I'd do. I'd tell my mum to go screw herself.'

Jake opened his mouth to say, *Maybe that's what I'll do.* But he shut it again without speaking, sharply reminding himself that he was done with trying to impress Lauren.

'Any news about Erin?' she asked.

'No.'

Lauren took a frowning drag on her cigarette and tapped ash into a mug. 'We've got to do something.'

Irritation edged Jake's voice. 'Like what?'

'I dunno.' Lauren flicked up her middle finger at him. 'What you getting shitty with me for?'

He heaved a sigh. 'Sorry. I just feel so helpless.'

'Aww.' Lauren brushed her fingers suggestively down the screen. 'I wish I was there with you. I bet I could make you feel better.'

Jake felt himself turning red. Did she mean what he thought she meant? For a mad second, he teetered on the brink of doing what he'd been working up the nerve to do for months – telling her how he felt about her. But then Erin's face came into his mind again, bringing a sting of self-reproach with it. How could he care about crap like that at a time like this? 'I've got to go.'

Lauren looked surprised. 'Why?'

'I just have to. I'll talk to you later.'

Before Lauren could say anything else, Jake disconnected the call. He stared at the ceiling, his face puckered with uncertainty. As if he'd come to a decision, he sprang up and approached his desk. He rifled through the drawers until he found what he was looking for – a pair of scissors. He moved to a mirror, put the scissors to his hair and hesitated. *Yuck, you smell like sweaty old socks.* Erin's words echoed from his memory again. He started cutting.

DAY 1
5.45 P.M.

Amanda scanned the lines of emergency service vehicles, her eyes wide and dazed as if she couldn't process what she was seeing. Tom knew what she was thinking, because it was the same thing he'd thought: *All this for Erin!* It was both terrifying and reassuring to see the scale of the search.

A constable met them in front of Newbiggin Farm and escorted them to the forest clearing. Sergeant Dyer was waiting, grave-faced, on the little bridge that spanned the River Font. 'There's been a development,' he said ominously.

Tom felt Amanda's hand seek out his as the sergeant went on, 'The dogs have picked up your daughter's scent to the west of here.'

'West,' Tom echoed. That meant Erin had headed – or been taken – into the heart of the forest.

'Show us,' said Amanda, a breathless edge to her voice.

They crossed Blanch Burn and followed a trail of flattened bracken to the treeline. An avenue of scrubby grass wound its way through lofty conifers. They walked silently, Tom and Amanda tensely holding hands. In among the trees, the afternoon air was stiflingly warm. But the sweat on Tom's back was cold. Somewhere off in the distance he caught the barking of dogs. He exchanged an anxious glance with Amanda. What did it mean? Had they found something?

After five or six hundred metres, they emerged into another huge clearing fringed with orderly rows of sapling pines. To the north-west the ground climbed gently through patchy heather towards a solitary stone house maybe five hundred metres away. The house's front windows overlooked a well-tended lawn with a lonely oak at its centre. A gravel track followed the western edge of the clearing, forming a T-junction with another road that disappeared westwards behind trees before curving back north-east past the house. Tom knew the house was owned by the forest authority, but he had no idea who currently lived there.

'Who lives there?' Amanda beat him to the question.

'A forest ranger, his wife and two kids,' answered Sergeant Dyer. 'They've not seen Erin or anything out of the ordinary.'

The sergeant led them a short distance along the gravel track, then they plunged back into the pines. Constables were meticulously sifting through the undergrowth to the north. The barking echoed among the trees again, much closer now. Amanda's fingers flinched against Tom's, her nails digging into the back of his hand. He glanced at her. Her eyes were bright and moist, her lips pale and trembling. It was strange to see her so overwhelmed by emotion. He was the emotional one in their relationship. She was usually so calm and collected.

After several minutes, they emerged into yet another clearing. This one was roughly oval in shape with a circumference of two hundred or so metres. It was dotted with clumps of marsh grass. A drainage ditch ran along its nearside, emptying into Newbiggin Burn at its lower end. At the upper end of the clearing was a pool of peat-coloured water fringed with rushes. The pool was about twenty metres in diameter and at its centre was a little grassy island. Constables were prodding the water with long sticks that struggled to find the bottom even at arm's length from the pool's edge. Two tracking dogs were sniffing about on the pool's far side. More dogs were pulling their handlers around the clearing.

A man wearing a jacket with a National Search and Rescue Dog Association badge on it approached Sergeant Dyer and informed him, 'The dogs lost the scent at the near edge of the pool.'

'What does that mean?' asked Amanda, staring at the pool as if it frightened her.

'The ground here's boggy. It's difficult for the dogs to keep the scent. We're hoping they'll pick the trail up again on the far side of the clearing.'

'What if Erin didn't make it to the far side?' Withdrawing her hand from Tom's, Amanda took several faltering steps towards the black water.

'Please, Mrs Jackson, stay back from the pool,' said Sergeant Dyer. 'Can I ask, have you ever been to this spot before, either by yourselves or with Erin?'

'No,' said Amanda.

'I'm not sure,' mumbled Tom, his eyes fixed on the pool as if trying to penetrate its murk. An image of Erin's lifeless body floating in its cold depths clawed at his mind. 'I may have been. I went all over the forest when I was boy. I've definitely not brought Erin here, though.'

Amanda's tears spilled over again. 'What if she fell in? What if she was thrown?'

'I know it's difficult, Mrs Jackson, but try not to assume the worst,' said the sergeant.

Amanda flashed from fear to anger. 'How the hell am I supposed to assume anything else?'

Sergeant Dyer took the retort calmly. 'Perhaps it would be best if you join your father in the search.'

'He's right,' said Tom. 'There's no point us standing around here.'

Amanda stabbed a finger at the pool. 'Nothing's shifting me from this spot until I know my baby's not in there.'

'Then I'm staying put too.'

'No, you go.'

'But what if . . .' Tom shuddered. 'What if they find something?'

Amanda fought to steady her voice. 'Go. Let my dad know what's going on.' She paused a breath, before adding meaningfully, 'And Eddie.'

Tom looked at Amanda a moment longer, drawing strength from her eyes. He turned to Sergeant Dyer. 'Where can I find them?'

The sergeant unfolded an OS map. He pointed at a densely forested area about half a mile south-west of Craig Ferguson's campsite and a mile north of their location. 'They should be somewhere around here. I'll have someone take you to them.'

'No need, I know the way.'

'If you don't mind, Mr Jackson, I'd rather one of my officers went with you.'

Tom frowned. It was phrased as if he had a choice in the matter, but Sergeant Dyer's expression made it clear he didn't. His gaze returned to Amanda and he briefly took her hand again. 'I'll see you soon.'

With a constable shadowing him, Tom returned to the gravel track. He followed it past the ranger's house, all the while thinking and trying not to think about the pool. There were numerous such small but deep tarns dotted around the forest and moors. Local myth had it that some were inhabited by water spirits. A story his father had once told him rose into his mind. A fellow farmer had been swimming in one of the pools when he felt something grip his ankle. At first the farmer thought he was entangled in reeds, but then he found himself being pulled underwater. He fought desperately to break free. Just when his strength was about to give out, he succeeded in doing so. He clambered out of the pool and collapsed. To his horror, a slimy hand emerged from the dark water. It pointed a finger at him, before disappearing back beneath the surface. The story had scared Tom so much that he'd never dared swim in the pools. Years later it had occurred to him that this was perhaps precisely the desired effect. After all, every few years someone – usually a teenage boy – drowned swimming in them.

The track curved north-west, rising towards the moors. A cool breeze blew down from the hills, bringing ribbons of cloud with it. Tom spotted his search group fanned out like a skirmish line among the trees.

'Tom!' Eddie broke rank and hurried towards him. Henry instructed the other searchers to hold up before following.

'How did it go at the station?' Eddie asked.

'They don't seem to think the guy's involved.'

A scowl split Eddie's beard. 'Bollocks, he isn't.'

'Are they going to charge you?' asked Henry.

'Probably. Listen, forget about that, something else has happened.' Tom told them about the dogs tracking Erin's scent to the pool.

The ever-optimistic light in Henry's eyes faltered. Deep furrows scored his forehead. He shook his head and, with the same fierceness Amanda had inherited from him, said, 'They won't find anything. Not a bloody chance of it. Erin knows better than to go near those tarns.'

She knows better than to wander off in the forest alone too, Tom thought grimly.

They rejoined the other searchers. Graham nodded a silent hello, po-faced as ever. Irritation flickered in Tom that his brother hadn't thought it necessary to accompany Eddie and Henry for an update. But the feeling was gone almost as soon as it came, extinguished by a deluge of other concerns.

'Back to it everybody!' called out Henry.

Tom took up a position near the centre of the line with the constable on his right. They continued their laborious advance, prodding the undergrowth, peering into hollows, pushing aside low-hanging branches. They came to a clearing with mossy boulders strung along its edge. Tom passed to the left of the boulders, the constable to the right. The instant the constable was out of view, Tom motioned Eddie over and in a lowered voice told him about the encounter with Greenie.

Eddie's eyes widened. 'How could you offer to give up the quarry without talking to me first?'

'There was no time. Besides, you can relax, he told us to piss off.'

Eddie's surprise gave way to an expression that made him look like a wounded bear. 'I'd make the same offer in a heartbeat if I thought it would work, but there's only one language lunatics like him respond to.' He raised his fist.

'You're right.' Tom's tone was apologetic. 'If we could find some way to get him alone, then maybe . . .' He trailed off uneasily at the thought of what came after 'maybe'.

'And how the hell are we supposed to do that? I'll tell you what we need to do: we need to tear that camp to the ground.'

'You know how I feel about that. I don't want innocent people getting hurt.'

'There are no innocent people at the camp.' Eddie gripped Tom's arm. 'Face it, this is our best chance.'

Uncertainty lined Tom's face. Then the mantra vibrated forcefully through his mind again – *Whatever's necessary.* 'OK, Eddie, but it's got to happen by tonight or tomorrow at the latest.'

'That's seriously short notice. It'll cost extra.'

Tom spoke through his teeth. 'Sod the money. I'll borrow whatever we need from Henry.'

'I'll get on the blower to the Geordies.' Eddie took out his phone. 'No signal.'

'You can usually get one on the moors.'

As Eddie headed for the edge of the forest, Henry approached Tom and asked, 'Where's he going?'

'He's doing something for me.' Tom grimaced as if he was swallowing bitter medicine. 'We need to talk, Henry. I need some money.'

Henry's bushy eyebrows lifted high. 'What for?'

Tom darted a glance at the constable who'd emerged from behind the boulders and was looking in their direction. 'I'll explain later. I'm not sure how much I need yet, but it has to be available for tomorrow.'

'No problem, Tom. If you need a loan for the business, I'm happy to help.'

Tom resisted the urge to retort incredulously, *How could you think this is about the business?* He turned away from his father-in-law, struggling to stomach the thought of taking his money. It wasn't simply that it would give Henry a hold over him. It was the knowledge that, although this was about Erin, the money would also help get the quarry up and running. And that was something about which he'd wanted to be able to say, *I did this alone. Me!*

The searchers adjusted their positions to account for Eddie's absence. Thicker clouds were rolling in, blown on a high wind. The sun passed behind them, re-emerged, passed behind them . . . disappearing for a little longer each time, until finally it was lost for good. Evening crept relentlessly on, bringing a chill with it. The searchers pulled on jumpers and jackets. Tom refused the offer of a spare jacket. Erin was wearing only shorts and a T-shirt. He wanted to know how cold she felt. Behind the clouds, the setting sun turned the sky orange. And still nothing – no clues, no word as to how the search of the pool was going or whether the dogs had rediscovered the scent. As the gloom deepened with what seemed terrible rapidity, Tom felt the trees closing in claustrophobically.

They took a rest and passed bottles of water around. Tom shook his head when somebody offered him one. 'You should drink something,' said Henry. 'You'll get dehydrated.'

'Erin's got nothing to drink,' Tom replied resolutely.

Henry made as if to say something else, but thought better of it. The stubbornness of the Jacksons was well known in Middlebury.

Eddie returned and drew Tom aside. 'They're coming tomorrow. It's gonna cost fifteen thousand, cash up front.'

Tom caught a quiver of excitement. It crossed his mind that Eddie was enjoying all this. He knew the thought was undeserved. It wasn't *all this* Eddie was enjoying, it was the prospect of a good scrap. Eddie had been itching to get his hands on the activists for months. Now he had his chance.

Tom sidled over to Henry and told him how much he needed. 'I'll have the cash ready first thing,' said Henry. 'What exactly do you need it for?' Tom told him and Henry asked dubiously, 'Are you sure that's wise? If someone gets hurt, you could end up in serious trouble.'

'What other choice do I have?'

'Try talking to the police again. Maybe you can convince them to do something.'

Tom considered the suggestion, then swatted it away. 'I'm going to find out for myself if those bastards have got anything to do with this.'

'All right,' said Henry. 'But if anyone asks where the money came from, you don't mention my name.'

God forbid your precious name might be tarnished, Tom retorted silently. They searched on, the pace slowing maddeningly as starless darkness limited their vision to the ground in front of their feet. Torches were handed out, their beams bringing to life distorted faces in the tree trunks. Pale tendrils of mist licked the ground.

'Everyone gather round,' called Henry.

'What are we stopping for?' Tom demanded to know, although the answer was heartbreakingly obvious.

'A fog bank is descending from the hills. The constable here informs me that the search is to be postponed until it passes.'

Aghast, Tom rounded on the policeman. 'You can't do this!'

'Sorry, Mr Jackson,' said the constable. 'It's not up to me. It's Sergeant Dyer's call.'

'Then I want to talk to him.'

'OK, but it won't make any difference.'

The constable got on his radio. Sergeant Dyer's voice came through the speaker, 'Tell Mr Jackson that this entire area is forecast to be covered in thick fog within the next half an hour. It won't do his daughter any good if others end up getting lost and we need to search for them too.'

Henry doggedly tried to find a positive to latch on to. 'The fog usually doesn't last more than an hour or two at this time of year.'

Tom clutched his pounding head. The thought of stopping the search for even five minutes was too much to bear. He wanted to yell into the radio, *I won't let you do this!* But he knew Sergeant Dyer was right. The trees were already merging like shadows into the fog. He slashed his hands in front of his face as if trying to tear the whiteness to shreds. 'How is this possible?' His voice was somewhere between anger and desperation. 'It was a clear day two hours ago.'

'You know the weather around here, Tom. It can change like that.' Eddie clicked his fingers. 'Look, if you want to continue searching then I'm with you. But it seems to me that we could miss more than we see in this.'

Tom resisted an impulse to throw his head back and shout *Fuck you!* at the sky. If growing up on a farm had taught him anything, it was that the only sensible response to nature's indifference was to be indifferent right back. All his childhood he'd watched the elements mould his father's face into a mask as rugged as the hills. Never once had he heard him complain. Blizzards, lashing rain, gales, scorching sun, his father had endured them all with the same passive silence.

As the search party made their way out of the forest, they were joined by other groups, like a defeated army in retreat. Every footstep tormented Tom. He kept calling for Erin, but the only reply was the echo of his own voice. The fog pursued them like a silent assassin, erasing the forest until it was as if it had never existed.

Beyond Newbiggin Farm, volunteers were filing onto buses. Dogs were being loaded into search and rescue vehicles. Sergeant Dyer was issuing instructions to a cluster of emergency service personnel: '. . . and my team will remain here. The rest of you will return to the station and await further instructions.'

Amanda was sitting in the open door of the Mini, staring at the ground. Her face looked crumpled in, a hollow-eyed glimpse of her as an old woman. She jerked her head up and rose to her feet as Henry approached. He enveloped her in a hug. A sob broke from her as she pressed her face into his shoulder. Tom hung back from the pair and asked Eddie, 'What are you going to do?'

'I hate to say it, mate, but this fog looks set in. Might as well go home and grab something to eat. You should do the same. You look done in.'

Eddie patted Tom's shoulder and headed for his car. Tom's gaze moved to Graham, who was standing statue-like a short distance away. Tom mustered up a nod of thanks. As if he'd been given permission to leave, Graham tugged at Bob's lead and turned towards his Land Rover. Tom watched him with a sad frown. What had happened to them? he wondered. How had they become so distant? They'd never been best mates. They had too little in common. But they had at least used to talk occasionally, exchange a few words about their lives. Now it was almost like they were strangers.

Another sob from Amanda wrenched Tom's thoughts back to Erin. Keeping a proprietorial arm around his daughter, Henry said to Tom, 'I'm taking Amanda home. She's in no fit state to be here. Are you coming?'

Amanda's tear-swollen eyes pleaded with Tom to say yes. He looked at the whiteness where the forest used to be.

'What can you do here?' continued Henry. 'Better to gather your strength and come back at it fresh when the fog clears.'

It crushed Tom to accept it, but his father-in-law was right. He handed the Mini's keys to Henry and asked Amanda, 'Are you coming with me?'

She looked uncertainly from him to her dad, then nodded.

'Are you sure?' asked Henry.

Tom turned away to hide his irritation. What would it take to make Henry accept that Amanda needed to be a wife first and a daughter second? he wondered, already knowing the answer: a different husband.

'Yes.' Amanda removed herself from Henry's arm. She slumped into the passenger seat of Tom's Volvo, squeezing her eyes shut as if to block out some horrific image. His face as desolate as the fog, Tom started the engine. He wondered when they would return to the forest. If Erin turned up somewhere else before the fog cleared, would they ever be able to bring themselves to return? The answer to that question was painfully clear: it depended on the state she turned up in.

DAY 1
10.33 P.M.

Seth watched Tom, Amanda and Henry. Such drama, such pain. He wanted to soak it all up, store it like water to be rationed out whenever he needed to feel something. 'It makes me want to cry,' said Holly. He tore his gaze from the sad scene and looked at her. Her eyes were filmed with tears. One spilled over. Unthinkingly, he reached to brush it away. He started slightly as Holly curled her fingers into his. A thrill of something almost like fear went through him. His fingers were limp in hers. As if fearing she'd made a mistake, she started to pull her hand away. But he caught it in a tight grip that surprised him as much as it did her. A faint wince passed over her face. He quickly relaxed his grip.

They climbed hand in hand onto the bus. As it chugged towards Middlebury, Seth's mind whirled with questions. *How long am I supposed to hold her hand for? What does this mean? Are we an item?*

Holly untangled her hand from his. He darted her a look, wondering if it was because of something he'd done or not done. But she was simply reaching for her water. His eyes traced her movements as she took a mouthful then rested her hand on his again. Her palm was warm and dry. His was clammy.

'Beds have been set up in the Town Hall for those of you from outside the area who want to continue helping when the search restarts,' announced a woman at the front of the bus. 'The Black Bull, the Bridge End and the Old Oak are also laying on food.'

'I'm staying at the Black Bull,' Seth told Holly. 'Do you want to come for something to eat with me?'

'Sure,' she said casually, as if it meant nothing.

The bus dropped them in the market square. A reporter thrust a microphone in their faces as they disembarked. Putting his head down, Seth made for the Black Bull. The lounge tables were laden with sandwiches, pies, cold meats, cheeses, baked potatoes and salads. There were urns of tea and coffee.

Alcohol wasn't normally Seth's thing – he liked to keep a clear-headed control of whatever situation he found himself in – but right then he felt the need for a beer. He wondered if he should offer Holly a drink. In many ways he considered himself a master game-player. But this was a game whose rules he'd never been taught. 'Do you want a pint or something?'

'A pint would be good, thanks.'

The barman waved Seth's money away. 'On the house.'

Seth accepted the drinks with a nod, unsure how else to respond. He wasn't used to being given anything for free.

The lounge was rapidly filling with volunteers. Seth headed for a two-seat table. They sipped their drinks, not making eye contact. After a few minutes, Holly said, 'The way you asked that sergeant about Erin, I thought you were this super-confident guy. But you're actually quite shy, aren't you?'

Again Seth felt that fear-like thrill. Part of him wanted this girl to see him, see who he really was. Another part wanted to get up and walk away before that could happen. Every action, every word was like the flip of a card. Right now he was winning. But he could lose big on the next deal. He gave a non-committal shrug. 'I'm not really used to being around lots of people.'

'But you're from London.'

'It's easy to be alone in a big city.'

Holly sipped her pint thoughtfully. 'Do you enjoy being alone?'

'What's there to enjoy about it?' Seth regretted the words the instant they were out, realising they revealed more than he wanted to about himself. He steeled himself for the inevitable return question.

'Then why come on holiday by yourself?'

'I enjoy my own company out in the countryside where there aren't many other people,' he lied smoothly. 'In London it's different . . .' How could he explain what it was like to grow up in a loveless environment, surrounded by 8 million people who didn't know your name? Did he even want to try? 'I suppose it's a bit like that saying about being lonely in a crowd.'

'It's impossible to be lonely in our house. I'm the eldest of six. I've got two brothers and three sisters. I know I should be grateful, but sometimes I just feel like being alone. I've been saving for a deposit on a flat.' As if admitting to some secret desire, Holly added, 'What I really want is a farm of my own.'

'If that's what you want, I'm sure you'll get it.'

'What makes you say that?'

'I saw how you were today. You're not someone who gives up easily. That's one thing I'm good at. I can tell all sorts about people just from looking at them.'

'So what else can you tell about me?'

'You're an honest person.' In his mind Seth added, *You've never known real pain, real emptiness, real need.* In what he hoped was a playful tone, he continued, 'You're attracted to slim blond men with London accents.'

Holly laughed, an incongruous sound in the subdued atmosphere. 'Wow, you're amazing. You ought to be a fortune-teller. You'd make a packet. OK, my turn. Let's see what I can tell about you.'

She leaned forwards, resting her elbows on the table and her chin on her hands. Her probing gaze was too much for Seth. He took a mouthful of his pint. The lager tasted teeth-achingly sharp. The lights suddenly seemed to have become painfully bright. 'We've already established you're a bit of a loner—' began Holly, but she broke off as Seth pressed a hand to his forehead. 'Have you got a headache?'

A nod was all he could manage in reply.

'You've probably had too much sun. You should drink some water and lie down.'

With an effort, Seth asked, 'What about you?'

'Netherwitton's like four miles in the wrong direction from the forest. So I was thinking I might sleep at the Town Hall. Or . . .' Holly wavered off, looking at Seth from under her eyelashes.

'Good idea.'

'Oh, OK. I'll meet you here when the search restarts then.'

Holly blinked awkwardly away from Seth's gaze. *Am I missing something? Have I said something wrong?* he wondered. But his brain was in no condition to provide answers. Everything felt out of focus, like the moors wobbling in the midday sun. He stood up. 'Goodnight.'

'Night,' replied Holly, smiling but not looking at him.

Fighting a rubberiness in his legs, Seth dodged through the crowded lounge. He glanced at Holly from the doorway. One of the men from their search team was talking to her. Seth felt a twisting in his stomach that had nothing to do with his aversion to speaking about himself. He took a step back towards the table, but a carping voice rose from a dark corner of his mind: *What are you doing, idiot? Now's not the time to take up with some little whore.*

'She's not a whore,' Seth muttered under his breath.

They're all whores.

'You should know, Grandma.'

A cackle of shrill laughter echoed through his mind. He wrenched his gaze away from Holly. Grandma was right about one thing: now wasn't the time to get hung up on a girl. Now was the time to focus on what he was in Middlebury to do.

The DO NOT DISTURB sign was still on the doorknob. He gazed around his room intently. Satisfied everything was as he'd left it, he retrieved a bundle of time-yellowed envelopes from his bag. He selected one with a black heart scrawled on it and removed a letter. Then he fished a cheap pay-as-you-go phone and a white plastic box roughly the size and shape of a cigarette packet from the bag. The box had a shallow circular indent flanked by a volume control dial and red, green and blue buttons. He pressed a button marked ROBOT, placed the box over the phone's mouthpiece and dialled. After several rings, a man answered, 'Hello?'

Seth spoke into the indent. A speaker on the back of the box emitted a distorted machinelike version of his voice. 'Don't hang up or you'll regret it.'

Puzzled and uneasy, the man asked, 'What is this? Who are you?'

'I know what you did and I can prove it.'

'I don't . . .' The voice stumbled over itself. 'I don't know what you're—'

'Shut up and listen.' Seth began to read the letter aloud. 'I love everything about you. I love the way the sun makes your hair shine. I love the deep pools of your eyes. I love your lips, your hands, your feet, your fingers, your toes. Sometimes I wonder if you are real or if you are an angel come down from heaven.'

Silence followed these words, so deathly Seth wondered if he'd been hung up on. He caught the sound of tense breathing. 'If that's not enough to convince you I'm for real, then how about this?' He picked out another letter. 'My beloved, why do you not reply to my letters? I have already proven I will do anything for you. What else must I do to convince you we are soulmates? I will burn down this whole town if that's what it takes.'

Seth broke off. More silence. 'Still not convinced. Let's have one more try.' He read from a third letter. 'I have met another woman. She means nothing to me, but if you will not have me I will give her the life I could have given you. She will live like a queen. Whatever she wants, she will have.'

A sick-sounding, 'What do you want?' came over the line.

Seth had already pondered that question long and hard. 'A million pounds.'

'You must be mad!'

'One million or the letters will be all over the Internet by this time next week.'

There was another heavy silence. The man spoke again, curiosity competing with shock for ascendancy. 'Has *she* put you up to this?' He said 'she' with a sort of bitter longing, like a reformed alcoholic thinking about reaching for the bottle.

A telling tightness came into Seth's voice that the box didn't entirely filter out. 'You've got twenty-four hours to get the money together.'

'Or is it you? Are you her?'

'I'll be in contact again tomorrow. Any funny business and I'll make your life a living hell.'

'Wait! I'm going to need more—'

Seth hung up and turned off the phone. He flopped onto the bed, his heart racing. The wheel was in motion. There was no stopping it now. It was a strange feeling. Like the touch of Holly's hand, it left him both fearful and aroused. It occurred to him suddenly what he'd missed when Holly said, *I might sleep at the Town Hall. Or . . .* Or! She'd been angling for an invite to his room, perhaps just to sleep, maybe for something more. The realisation sent a surge of blood to his groin. He unbuttoned his trousers and began to masturbate.

Afterwards he fell into a fitful doze. His dreams were a jumble of Erin Jackson and Holly. He was saying something, but his voice was robotic and garbled. The more he tried to make himself understood, the blanker their faces became. With shrugs of incomprehension, they walked away from him.

DAY 1
10.44 P.M.

Tom pulled into the driveway, but didn't turn off the engine. The street was empty. The journalists seemed to have gone home for the moment too. He stared at Erin's bedroom window. It was well past her bedtime. Whenever he returned home late from work – which had been more often than not recently – if Erin was awake she would call to him from her bed, 'Daddy, I need a kiss goodnight!' And he would go to her, kiss her cheek and say, *I love you. Now go to sleep.*

At Amanda's touch on his wrist, he flinched and said, 'I don't know if I can face seeing her empty room.'

'I feel the same way, Tom, but we've got another child who needs us.'

He reluctantly removed the ignition key. As if he was wearing stone boots, he approached the front door. Cathy emerged from the house, looking at them hopefully. Her face sank when she saw their expressions. 'Nothing?'

Amanda shook her head.

'But I heard that search dogs had—'

'Please, Mum, I'm too tired to talk about it right now. How's Jake?'

'He hasn't been out of his room since you left. I took him up something to eat.' Cathy's gaze moved beyond her daughter as the Mini pulled into view. Henry got out and trudged towards them.

'Oh, Henry, you look completely exhausted,' said Cathy.

Henry mustered up a small smile. 'I'm fine, darling. I just need something to eat.'

Cathy rolled her eyes apologetically. 'I should have thought to make something. I'll do it now.'

She turned to go back into the house, but Amanda said, 'It's OK, Mum. You and Dad head home. He'll get a better rest there than here.'

Cathy's perfectly plucked eyebrows drew together. 'But, darling, we wouldn't dream of leaving you alone at a time like this.'

Amanda pointedly took Tom's hand in hers. 'I'm not alone. I know you only want to help, but I think we could all do with a moment to catch our breath.'

'You're right, darling,' said Henry. He leaned in to kiss Amanda's cheek, adding, 'Although hopefully we won't get much chance for a rest.' He afforded Tom a glance and a nod before returning to the Mini.

Cathy kissed Amanda too and dispensed a look that said, *Stay strong.* She gave Tom the briefest of pecks.

Tom followed Amanda into the house and closed the door. Silence. He'd been briefly distracted by his relief at Henry and Cathy's departure. But the silence brought it all crashing down on him again like a tonne of concrete. He dropped heavily onto the bottom step of the stairs. 'I love her so much,' he cried, hugging his arms across himself.

Amanda laid her hand on the top of his head. He grasped it and pulled it down to cover his eyes, sobs shaking his shoulders.

'Jake will hear you,' said Amanda.

'What do I have to do to get her back?' Tom yelled as if talking to someone only he could see. 'Just tell me and I'll do it.'

'Please, Tom. I don't want Jake upset any more than he already is.'

'Jake.' Tom said his son's name in a voice like a warning. He clutched the banister and hauled himself upright.

'What are you doing?' Amanda asked worriedly as he started up the stairs.

Tom made no reply. She caught hold of his arm, but he shrugged her off and stalked towards the attic.

DAY 1
10.45 P.M.

Jake Googled 'Ingham murders Middlebury paranormal activity'. A page of links came up. The top one was for the Northumberland Society for Paranormal Investigation. Underneath the website's name was 'The Ingham Case. The evidence for paranormal activity at a house in Middlebury where an infamous double murder took place.' He clicked the link and was taken to a page with a picture of the dilapidated Ingham house at its top. Underneath was a grainy photo of the Ingham family outside the house as it had been in the seventies – grim grey walls, well-kept garden. Elijah and Joanna Ingham were standing behind their daughters. Elijah was dressed in a navy-blue suit and matching tie. He had a sharp, stern face with a moustache and whiskers, like some Victorian throwback. Joanna was equally unsmiling with bobbed brown hair and a long floral dress that at least added a splash of colour. The sisters were wearing identical pastel-green knee-length dresses, long white socks and shiny black shoes. Their shoulder-length mousey hair was clipped to one side. They reminded Jake of the spooky twin sisters from one of his favourite films – *The Shining* – although Rachel was a head taller than Mary. She was plumper too with pale round cheeks and almost cartoonishly big doe eyes. In contrast, Mary had neat little features and a definite gleam of mischief in her eyes. The photo was dated May 1972. Almost three months before the murders.

A legal disclaimer beneath the photos read, 'Please note: this report was submitted to us anonymously. We are unable to verify its authenticity. No members of this society took part in the investigation described below.' Then came 'External temp and weather conditions: 16°C, dry and overcast with a light wind from the north-west.' This was followed by a table giving internal temperatures. 'Basement: 10°C. Ground floor: 13°C. First floor: 13°C. Attic: 15°C.' Finally there was a description of the investigation. 'We arrived after dark due to being unable to obtain permission from the owner of the property. Entrance was gained through a broken window at the rear of the house. EMF readings were taken, which displayed abnormally high levels of static electricity in the ground-floor rear living room and the kitchen. In all other areas the readings were normal.'

Jake opened up a separate tab and Googled 'EMF readings'. A website explained what he was already vaguely aware of – EMF stood for electromagnetic fields. The theory was that ghosts emitted an electromagnetic field that could be detected by EMF meters. He returned to the paranormal society website and the scientifically dry report.

> Night vision cameras were set up in the living room, kitchen, basement and on the first-floor landing. At 10.45 p.m. (approximately the time the murders of Elijah and Joanna Ingham are believed to have taken place) we held a seance in an attempt to contact any spirits in the house. During the seance, we were able to document several instances of paranormal phenomena. Spikes were recorded in ground-

> floor EMF readings and some electrical items showed signs of interference: wristwatches stopped working; mobile-phone signals were interrupted. However, our specialist equipment continued to work normally. At the same time, the ground-floor temperature dropped to 11°C. There was also an unexplained bang from the attic.

Jake glanced at the chicks, thinking maybe the noise wasn't all that difficult to explain. The two tiny balls of fluff still hadn't moved since he'd brought them home. Every ten or twenty minutes, he'd been feeling for their heartbeats. The last time he'd checked both were alive. But their grip on life seemed as tenuous and uncertain as Erin's fate. His gaze returned to the text.

> At 11.23 p.m., ten minutes after we finished the seance, two team members standing where Elijah and Joanna Ingham were killed experienced odd prickling sensations in their heads (Elijah and Joanna Ingham died from strikes to their heads). Approximately five minutes later a small pulsating ball of white light materialised in the living room. The ball travelled along the hallway and up the stairs to the first-floor landing. It entered the second room on the right (Rachel Ingham's bedroom) before dropping out of sight in the centre of the floor. At the same moment a loud scream that could be identified as neither male nor female echoed throughout the house.

Jake thought of the childlike scream the rook had made.

> This phenomenon was recorded by two of our cameras that were later confiscated by the police. Unfortunately, when the cameras were returned to us they showed signs

> of having been deliberately damaged to such an extent that we were unable to access the recordings.

It was all too convenient that such compelling evidence had been damaged, reflected Jake. But, at the same time, it was undeniably curious that the ball of light had disappeared where the rectangular red object was lodged under the floorboards. What could it mean? Could it be some kind of sign? Had the light been trying to point the ghost hunters towards something?

Jake jerked upright at a sobbing shout from downstairs. He couldn't make out the words, but the pain was plain to hear. *Erin!* he thought with a plummeting sensation. *They've found her and she's dead!*

He started towards the door but hesitated. What if he was right? Did he really want to know? He suddenly felt like diving under the duvet. He shook his head forcefully. He wasn't a little kid any more. He was almost sixteen. If he was right, his parents would need him. It was time to suck up his fear and be there for them. He hurried downstairs, stopping abruptly at the sight of his dad ascending towards him. His dad's face seemed more stricken by rage than grief. His mum wasn't far behind. Her lips moved as if mouthing a silent warning.

Tom paused a beat at Jake's new hairstyle – chopped short above the ears and clumsily combed into a parting – before demanding to know, 'Why didn't you go walking with your mum and sister?'

'What . . . I . . .' stammered Jake. He'd never seen such anger in his dad's eyes.

'I want an answer! Why didn't you go?'

Jake shied away with a shrug. 'I didn't feel like it.'

'You *didn't feel like it*,' Tom echoed contemptuously.

Jake looked to his mum for help. 'Where's Erin?'

Before Amanda could reply, Tom exploded, 'She'd be here with us if you'd done as you were bloody well told!'

Jake blinked as tears threatened his eyes. Was his dad right? Was this his fault?

'That's not true,' exclaimed Amanda.

'How do you know?' Tom shot back at her.

'I suppose I can't know for sure. How can anyone know something like that?'

'I'll tell you what I *do* know.' He stabbed an accusatory finger at her. 'You should have been keeping an eye on Erin. Just what did you think you were doing looking at the scenery while God knows what happened to our daughter?'

Amanda stiffened as if she'd been hit. 'I could just as easily say that if you'd paid more attention to your family this wouldn't be happening.'

'Everything I've ever done is for the good of this family.'

Amanda gave him a *who are you kidding* look. 'And money. Let's not forget the great god money.'

A scowl twisted Tom's lips. 'It's so easy for you, isn't it? All your life, all you've ever had to do is go crying to Mummy and Daddy if you need anything. It's because of parasites like them that my mother was dead at fifty.'

'Oh, listen to the working-class hero.' Amanda's voice was thick with sarcasm. 'You know what, Tom. No matter how much money you make, you'll never be anything but a pathetic little man.'

Tom's eyes swelled as if they would pop out of their sockets. He raised his hand to slap Amanda.

'Leave her alone!' cried Jake, grabbing his dad's wrist.

Tom whipped his arm backwards, catching Jake a hard knuckle-slap across the jaw. Jake staggered against the wall. There was a moment of stunned silence in which father and son stared at each other as if neither could believe what had happened. Then, pushing past his parents, Jake ran downstairs. Tom shook his head like someone waking from a dream and called after him, 'Jake, I'm sorry!'

Jake snatched up his boots and sprinted out of the front door. As he reached the pavement, his dad called again, 'I'm sorry, Jake! Please, I didn't mean any of it.'

Glancing over his shoulder, he saw his dad in the doorway. Jake shoved up his middle finger and darted across the road.

DAY 1
10.57 P.M.

'Leave him be,' Amanda said sharply, coming up behind Tom. 'You'll just make things worse.'

He turned to her, his eyes glistening. 'I'm so sorry.'

Amanda slammed the door. 'Oh, shut up, Tom. I don't want to hear it.'

'Please, Amanda.' He followed as she stalked into the living room. 'I don't know what came over me. That wasn't me.'

'Wasn't it?' Amanda snatched up a gin bottle and poured herself a large measure.

'You know it wasn't. It's this situation. I feel like I'm going out of my mind.'

'You and me both,' muttered Amanda.

Tom tentatively laid his hand on her back. She whirled to glare at him. He retreated from the venom in her voice as she said, 'I don't know what's worse. The fact that you tried to blame Jake for this nightmare or that you hit him. I'll tell you this, though, if you raise your hand to any of us again, I'll leave you. Do you understand?'

'It'll never happen again. I promise.'

Amanda stared at him as if trying to decide whether to believe him. She dropped wearily into an armchair. Tom lowered himself onto the sofa. They sat unspeaking, the silence broken only by the taunting tick of the mantelpiece clock. Amanda finished her drink and rose to pour herself another.

'Do you think that's a good—' Tom started to say.

She cut him off with a cold glance.

More silence. The clock ticked remorselessly on. With every passing second, Tom could almost physically feel Erin getting further away from him. When she was a toddler it had been as if she was attached to him by an invisible cord. Outside the house, she'd never stray more than ten metres from his side. Over the years, the cord had naturally grown longer. But now it was as if it were being unnaturally stretched towards the point where it would tear loose, taking his heart with it.

Tom pressed a hand to his chest as if swearing an oath. 'All I want is to give my family what they deserve.'

'And what's that? A bigger house? I love this house.'

'So did I when we moved in. But that was over fifteen years ago.' Tom made an onwards motion. 'I need to keep moving forwards.'

'Why? Was it really so bad where you came from?'

Tom thought of the damp, drab farmhouse. He thought of early mornings out in the fields, shoulders hunched against biting wind and rain. And he thought of long nights spent pulling lambs from their mothers' wombs, nostrils stinging from the hot sour smell of urine and blood. But most of all, he thought of the way the years had worn his parents down to shadows of themselves. 'It was for me.'

'Then why stay in Middlebury? Why didn't you leave when you had the chance? And don't you dare say it was for me, because I would have gone anywhere in the world with you.'

'Maybe it was because you're right,' Tom said bitterly. 'Maybe I'm just a pathetic little man.'

Shaking her head sadly, Amanda rose and left the room. This time he didn't follow. Tiredness washed over him as he leaned his head against the sofa. The clock hammered in his ears. He jumped up, yanked out its battery and returned to the sofa. His gaze slowly travelled the room where Amanda had told him she was pregnant – on both occasions – where the children had taken their first steps, where they'd all spent countless evenings watching TV, playing games or just chatting. This house was supposed to be his family's cocoon. The place where no harm ever came to them. He closed his eyes which were awash with shame.

DAY 1
10.59 P.M.

Jake kept running until he was sure his dad wasn't following. He stopped to pull on his boots. His jaw was throbbing. He ran a finger around the inside of his mouth. Its tip glistened with blood. Tears pushed up behind his eyes again as he replayed the moment his dad had hit him. It seemed almost surreal. His dad had a bitch of a temper. He'd shout, once or twice he'd even thrown stuff around. But hit him? No, never – at least not until now. And that wasn't the worst of it. He could forgive the slap. Put it down to the stress of the situation. But he wasn't sure if he could ever forgive the bastard for trying to blame him for Erin's disappearance.

Jake started walking, not thinking about where he was going, his eyes haunted by doubt. He knew his dad was wrong and his mum was right. And yet something else his mum had said earlier in the day kept echoing at him. *He's got to learn that everything he does has consequences.* The words filled him with a kind of paralysing dread. They made him want to find some lonely place beyond which his actions wouldn't spread like ripples of destructive energy.

He stopped suddenly. Seeing where he was, he realised he'd been aware of where he was heading all along. Beyond the ivy-clad garden wall and rusty gate, the Ingham house loomed like a solid shadow against the night sky. He stared uneasily at it, before checking out the gate. It was padlocked. He would have to go over. After a quick glance to make sure no one was around, he climbed past a STAY OUT! TRESPASSERS WILL BE PROSECUTED! sign. He hooked his leg over the gate, pulled the rest of himself after it and dropped to the ground. Keeping low, he darted towards the house. Beyond the orange pools of the streetlamps he slowed to a walk, both because he didn't want to fall in the darkness and because fear dragged at his limbs. He tried the front door – he didn't want to go through the murder room unless he absolutely had to – and discovered with a sinking sensation that it was locked. He headed around the back. An edge of the moon appeared from behind the clouds, palely lighting his way. Pushing aside clinging brambles, he emerged adjacent to the boarded-up French doors. He tried the steel plate, half hoping the police had secured it. They hadn't.

He stood motionless, his forehead pinched tight. His mum's words came back to him again – *He's got to learn that everything he does has consequences* – motivating him to slide through the gap. The house's interior was dark as the bottom of a well. His ears strained for any sound, catching only a whisper of wind. Goosebumps prickled on his arms. Was it colder in here? Or was he just imagining it? He took a slow breath, forcing himself to think calmly. *Of course it was colder. It was night-time.*

Stretching his hands out blindly, he crossed the room. He half expected a ball of light to materialise and lead him upstairs, but the darkness remained undisturbed. His fingers came into contact with the far wall. Keeping one hand against the coarse, cracked plaster, he made his way into the hall, every nerve in his body alert for any unexplained sound or odd sensation. A shaft of moonlight found its way through the ceiling, pooling against a wall. Was this the light the ghost hunters saw? The moonbeam could hardly be described as a ball of pulsating white light. But then again, from what he'd seen on television, ghost hunters weren't the most rational bunch. They were more likely to be motivated by hysterical fear or grief than hard facts. And he knew from his books on the occult that people like them – people who interpreted everything to suit their own needs – were easily tricked and led astray.

Houses like this one were good at tricking you. They made normal things seem strange. All you had to do was allow yourself to think of bludgeoned skulls, blood spattering and flowing, lives being snuffed out. *Actions. Consequences.* Jake thought about Crazy Mary picking berries from a hedge. He thought about her older sister, Rachel. Gone, disappeared. Like Erin. No, not like Erin. The police believed Rachel had run away from her foster home. And perhaps they were right. It was easy to understand why she might have wanted to put as much distance as possible between herself and this place. He knew of nothing that might have made Erin run away. But *something* had happened to her. Maybe the earth had simply opened up and swallowed her. He pictured her enclosed by cloying, constricting earth, like a mouse being slowly digested by a snake. The image somehow seemed more real to him than the possibility that Elijah and Joanna Ingham's spirits were trapped in this house.

The stairs creaked threateningly as Jake ascended them. He was suddenly conscious that his hands were sweaty, although the air was cool. A shadow seemed to pass across his vision. Heart palpitating, he almost turned and fled. Then he lifted his eyes to the hole in the roof. The moon had disappeared behind a cloud. That was all it was. He took another slow breath, telling himself to forget what wasn't there and stay focused on what was. The object beneath the floorboards. That was something tangible, something that could be seen and touched.

Back pressed to the wall, Jake edged along the landing. Rachel Ingham's room was a black hole. The floorboards shifted like cracked ribs beneath his probing feet. He dropped to his stomach and snaked his way to the hole. He reached into it, groping through dust and cobwebs, soft decayed timber and crumbling plaster. His fingers landed on something slim and smooth – the lighter. He sparked it to life. Its flame flickeringly revealed the red object. He adjusted his position so that he could stretch his other hand into the hole. The object was tantalisingly out of reach. Spreading his legs to anchor himself to the floor, he wormed his head and shoulders into the hole. His fingertips brushed the object, inching it towards him. It had the texture of slightly rough leather. He hissed a triumphant 'yes' as he managed to get hold of it between his thumb and middle finger.

Suddenly there was a loud crack and it was like the hole was swallowing him. Crying out, he grasped frantically for something to hold onto, but everything he touched disintegrated. For a gasping instant – long enough for him to think, *This is really going to hurt* – he seemed to hang suspended in the darkness. Then he slammed right arm and shoulder first into the floor of the room below. A bolt of pain shot up his wrist. He lay on his back, dust settling over him, mouth opening and closing like a fish out of water. *I can't breathe!* his brain screamed. But then air flooded back into his lungs and, coughing and spitting plaster, he jerked into a sitting position.

A whimper escaped his dusty throat as he tried to move his injured arm. Something didn't feel right – a deep, heavy pain. He could barely turn his wrist or flex his fingers. He tentatively tried moving other parts of his body. His right shoulder hurt like a bitch, but everything else seemed to be OK. The hairs on his neck prickled at what felt like a cool breath. He stretched out his hand and felt the right-angled opening of a brick fireplace. Reasoning that he must have fallen into the rear room, he continued to feel about himself. After a minute or two of searching, he found what he was looking for. The book. He was sure that was what it was now. It had a spine along one side. Three of its edges overlapped pages he could push his fingernails between. Clasping it to himself like a hard-won prize, he clambered to his feet.

Now that he had what he'd come for, he wanted to get out of the house as fast as possible. But the floor seemed to shift precariously beneath his feet, forcing him to lean against the chimney breast. He flinched as something hit the floorboards nearby with an echoing thud. He guessed it was only another chunk of plaster, but it seemed to him as if the house was shouting, *Go on, get out of here while you still can!*

He staggered in what he judged to be the direction of the French doors and was relieved to discover that he was right. Shouldering aside the metal plate, he squeezed outside. He started to head for the front of the house, but it occurred to him that he wouldn't be able to climb over the gate with his arm. He made his way through the overgrown garden to the hawthorn hedge. The moon showed itself again, providing enough light to find the gap in the hedge. He dropped to his knees, but putting even the slightest weight on his injured arm set sparks of agony dancing in front of his eyes. He turned onto his back and pushed himself under the wire.

In a haze of pain, he stumbled through the woods alongside the murmuring river. It was only when he reached the stone steps that the thought came to him, *What now?* He needed to see a doctor – that much was obvious. He also knew that if he turned up alone at Middlebury Hospital the first thing they'd do would be to contact his parents. He couldn't stand the thought of seeing his dad's face, let alone having to explain how he'd hurt himself. An idea came to him. His grandparents could take him to the hospital. Maybe they'd even let him stay with them afterwards.

As he walked, he examined the book by the light of the lamp-posts. There was no writing on its scuffed red cover. It was held shut by a rust-speckled lock and leather strap. He unsuccessfully tried to prise his fingers under the clasp. The edges of the pages were grey with dust and age. He reluctantly accepted that he would have to wait a while longer to find out what they revealed. He felt certain the book must hold some secrets. Why else would its owner have taken such care to hide it?

He stopped at a double gate wrought into curling iron branches and leaves. The gate was set between imposing posts topped by stone balls. Yews clipped into spirals, cascades and pyramids lined a long gravel driveway illuminated by ornate lamp posts. At the end of the drive, a handsome wood-beamed stone house faced onto a lush, well-tended garden. The house's only neighbours were trees whose dark outlines swayed gently in the breeze. Gold lettering on the gate announced RITTON HALL. His granddad had told him the hall's history many times. It had been built in the fifteenth century by the Ritton family, who lived there until great-great-granddad Brooks purchased it in 1901. At that time, the house had fallen into disrepair. Great-great-granddad Brooks had almost bankrupted himself restoring it to its Tudor glory.

A light glowed behind the curtains of the leaded living-room windows. His grandma's Mini and granddad's Range Rover were parked in the drive. He pressed an intercom button. His granddad's voice came through the speaker, harsh and wary. 'Who is it?'

'It's me, Granddad.'

A rise of surprise came into Henry's voice. 'Jake, what are doing here?'

'I need to see you.'

An electric motor whirred into action and the gates swung inwards. Jake crunched along the driveway. He was almost at the house when it occurred to him that the book could prompt some awkward questions. It might even be taken away from him before he'd had a chance to read it. He thrust it down the back of his jeans as the front door opened. Henry stepped out, his eyes widening at the sight of Jake. 'My God, look at the state of you. Is that blood?'

'Where?'

'On your forehead. And why are you covered in dust? What happened?'

'I fell.'

'Fell where? How?'

'I just fell,' Jake said with an evasive shrug.

'Yes, so you said, but—' Henry broke off as Jake's gaze dropped awkwardly to the ground. He sighed. 'Come inside, let's have a look at you and see what the damage is.'

Jake followed his granddad into a high-ceilinged hallway with dark oak-panelling and a broad staircase whose balustrade replicated the shapes of the topiary. His grandma appeared at the top of the stairs in her dressing gown. 'Who is—' she started to say, but put her hand to her mouth. 'Jake,' she exclaimed through her fingers, hurrying downstairs. 'You're hurt.'

'I had an accident, Grandma.'

'What kind of accident?'

Henry raised a hand to silence his wife. He carefully parted Jake's blood-sticky hair. 'The bad news is you've got a nasty cut and bump like half a cricket ball. The good news is it's stopped bleeding.'

'My right wrist hurts.'

Henry felt Jake's wrist. Jake yelped and pulled his arm back. 'Can you flex your fingers?' asked Henry.

'Not much.'

'Shall I get the first-aid box?' asked Cathy.

'I think this is going to take more than plasters and painkillers to fix,' said Henry.

'Do you think it's broken?' asked Jake.

'I'd say that's a strong possibility.'

'Oh, you poor darling.' Cathy took Jake's uninjured arm in both her hands. 'What have you been doing?'

'Let's save the questions for later, shall we?' Henry reached for his jacket. 'We'd better get ourselves to A&E.'

'I'll put some clothes on.'

'No need, darling. You stay here and get some rest.'

Cathy looked worriedly at her husband. 'If anyone should be resting, Henry, it's you.'

'I'd rather keep busy.' Henry kissed her cheek. 'I'll call you if it's anything serious.'

He started towards the front door. Jake hesitated to follow, giving his grandma a look of wide-eyed appeal. 'Don't call Mum and Dad.'

'But they need to know,' said Cathy.

'Please, Grandma.'

'Your grandma's not going to call anyone for now,' said Henry. 'You just concentrate on keeping your arm as still as possible.'

They headed outside, Jake cradling his arm. Henry helped him into the Ranger Rover. The book dug uncomfortably into Jake's back. He soon forgot about it as they accelerated away. Every bump in the road sent shudders of pain through his arm. As the sleepy streets swept by, he kept glancing at his granddad as if working up to asking something.

'Go on,' prompted Henry. 'Say what's on your mind.'

'I was wondering whether I could stay at your house.'

Henry raised a knowing eyebrow. 'Has something happened at home?'

Jake was silent for a few moments. Then he said, 'Sometimes I think my dad hates me.'

'Hate's a strong word. What's your dad done to make you so mad at him?' Jake told his granddad about the clash on the stairs. 'Well, I can understand why that would make you feel like you do,' said Henry. Choosing his words carefully, he went on, 'Now you listen to me, Jake. I think you know your dad and I don't always see eye to eye. Tom's an impulsive man. He often acts without thinking. And I'm sure that's all this is. Of course, that's no excuse for hitting you.' He let his words sink in, then rested a reassuringly heavy hand on Jake's shoulder. 'You can come and stay so long as your parents say it's OK.'

'Thanks, Granddad.'

'But I have to say, I think it would be best if you stayed at home. For your mum's sake. You might not think it, but she needs you.'

Jake stared at the passing buildings – houses, little shops, pubs. A sense of disorientation came over him, an eerie feeling of the familiar suddenly becoming unfamiliar. It faded as his granddad continued in a lighter tone, 'You know, Jake, you remind me of myself when I was your age. Nobody could tell me what to do. My parents were at their wits' end. Father and I were constantly at each other's throats.'

Jake glanced doubtfully at his granddad. It was difficult to imagine him as a rebellious teenager. 'What happened?'

'I grew up,' Henry replied, as if it was the most obvious answer in the world. 'Shall I tell you what a big part of growing up is? It's knowing when to listen to your heart and when to listen to your head. My heart was always telling me to do things that landed me in trouble. Then one day my head said enough is enough. It's time to buckle down and focus on what's really important – career, money, marriage, family. I know it's not fashionable to concern yourself with such things these days. But believe me, Jake, without them no one will ever take you seriously.'

They turned past a WELCOME TO MIDDLEBURY HOSPITAL sign, following a red arrow for ACCIDENT AND EMERGENCY. As they parked outside a boxy two-storey building, Jake asked, 'We are going to find Erin, aren't we, Granddad?'

There was brief but telling pause before Henry said, 'Yes.'

Biting back the tears that threatened to form, Jake followed his granddad into a waiting area. Henry pointed him to a seat and approached the receptionist. Jake's gaze skimmed over the sprinkling of people waiting to be seen. He was relieved not to recognise anyone. Word travelled fast in Middlebury. Every mouth in town was doubtless already trading gossip and speculation about Erin's disappearance. The last thing his family needed was for more fuel to be added to that raging fire.

Henry returned with a nurse, who led them to a curtained cubicle and a doctor with a stethoscope slung around his shirt collar. Henry shook his hand. 'Thanks for seeing us so quickly, Bill.'

'Don't mention it, Henry. Always glad to do a favour for a friend.' The doctor turned to Jake. 'So what have we here?'

'He's had a pretty hard fall.'

'Looks like it.' The doctor motioned for Jake to lie down on a trolley bed. Jake did so, acutely aware of the book digging into the base of his spine. The doctor cleaned the cut on his scalp with stinging antiseptic. 'It's not too deep. I don't think stitches are going to be necessary.' He shone a light into Jake's eyes. 'How do you feel, Jake? Any dizziness or nausea?'

'No. Only a headache.'

The doctor moved on to Jake's swollen wrist, feeling methodically along his bones. Jake grimaced at the probing fingers. 'Can you twist and bend your wrist for me?' asked the doctor. Jake did so with slow limited movements. The doctor nodded as if a suspicion had been confirmed. 'Do you have any pain elsewhere?'

Jake's shoulder was stiff and throbbing. But he was afraid that if he mentioned it the doctor would ask him to take off his T-shirt and they'd see the book poking out of his jeans. 'No.'

'Well, the good news is I don't see any signs of a skull fracture. We'll do an X-ray just to be sure. As for the wrist, I'm 99 per cent sure it's broken. So the next thing is to get you to radiology, young man.'

Jake was escorted to another room and asked to lie down again. A radiologist positioned the extendable white arm of an X-ray machine over his head, before retreating behind a screen. The machine whirred and clicked. The radiologist reappeared to reposition it over his wrist.

Fifteen minutes later he was sitting in yet another sterile-smelling room staring somewhat numbly at a spectral glowing negative of his arm. 'It's a good clean break,' the doctor informed him, tracing his finger along a diagonal fracture. 'It should be right as rain in six weeks.'

The doctor went into the hallway with Henry and spoke in a hushed voice. 'No one here can believe what's happened,' he said, obviously not referring to Jake's arm. 'We want you to know our thoughts are with you and your family.'

Henry thanked him again and returned to Jake. 'Well, you certainly won't be climbing any trees for a while.'

'I don't climb trees any more, Granddad,' said Jake. 'I'm too old for that.'

'Yes, you are,' Henry replied with a meaningful look. He took out his phone.

'Who are you calling?'

'Your mother.'

'But you said you . . .' Jake trailed off, lowering his head. 'Dad's going to kill me.'

'I think you might be surprised. But if the situation at home does become too difficult, you know where your grandma and I are. We'll always be here for you, Jake. You, Erin and your mum.'

Jake noted that his dad's name was pointedly absent from the list.

DAY 1
11.28 P.M.

Tom's mind drew a picture of the fog lying over the forest like a suffocating blanket. He saw himself wandering blindly through it, calling out, *Erin! Erin!* Silence. Hated silence. His thoughts drifted to Jake. He replayed the things he'd said, the backhanded slap. Oh, Christ, how could he have done that to him? Then he was back in the forest. The fog was gone, but everything seemed distorted, pulled out of shape like a child's plasticine creation. He emerged from the trees by the pool of impenetrably black water. His heart throbbed in his ears at the sight of it. The throbbing intensified as a small hand broke the water's surface. A willow-thin arm followed. Then dripping-wet long russet hair, eyes as dark as his own, a button nose, dimpled cheeks. *Erin!* Had he said her name or just thought it? He didn't know. But she seemed to hear, because she lowered her hand and pointed expressionlessly at him. *I'm coming, sweetie!* He waded into the water, gasping as it wrapped cold arms around his chest. He swam desperately towards Erin. She was only a few metres away, but it seemed to take a long time to reach her. *Daddy's here!* He caught hold of her hand and gasped again. Her fingers made the water seem warm. They closed tightly on his and began to pull him down, deeper and deeper into breathless blackness.

He opened his eyes with a jerk of his head. A sandwich and a mug of tea swirled into focus on the coffee table, surely put there by Amanda. *I must have drifted off,* he thought, reaching for the tea. It was cold. *How long was I asleep?* He glanced at the clock, recalling simultaneously that he'd removed the battery. He shuddered. The dream had seemed so real. He could still feel the touch of Erin's fingers, as cold as . . . He shook the memory from his mind, took a bite of the sandwich, chewed without tasting and forced it down with a sip of tea. He flinched so hard tea slopped over his hand when the phone rang in the hallway. He sprang up and ran to answer it. Amanda beat him to it. He looked at her in anxious expectation as she held the handset to her ear, barely able to restrain himself from snatching it away.

Her forehead squeezed into furrows. 'What? How?' There was a pause, then, 'OK, we'll be there asap.'

'What's happened?' Tom asked fearfully.

'That was my dad. He's with Jake at the hospital.'

Tom's chest constricted. 'Is Jake—'

Amanda raised her hands in a *calm down* gesture. 'Jake's fine. Well, not exactly fine, but it's nothing life threatening. He's broken his wrist.'

'Broken his wrist? How?'

'I don't know. Dad said he'd explain when we get to the hospital.'

They rushed to the car. As he drove, Tom shook his head and muttered, 'What a fucking idiot I am.'

'Please, Tom, save the guilt for later. Let's just concentrate on dealing with Jake.'

They parked up and dashed into A&E where Henry was waiting. 'He fell. Don't ask me where or how because I don't know,' he explained as he led them to Jake.

A nurse was applying the finishing touches to Jake's plaster cast. Jake looked sheepishly at his mum and avoided his dad's eyes altogether.

Tom hung back as Amanda approached Jake. 'Oh, sweetheart, does it hurt much?'

'They've given me some painkillers.'

She gently parted the hair around the scabbed cut. 'What happened?'

Jake's gaze dropped away from hers. She ran her fingers over his dusty T-shirt, a frown of realisation gathering. 'Have you been back to *that* house?'

His silence was as good as a yes. Huffing through her nose, Amanda opened her mouth to say more. Before she could, Tom put in, 'We can talk about all that later. Let's just get him home for now.' He smiled at Jake, a silent plea for forgiveness in his eyes. A twitch pulled his smile out of shape as Jake looked past him at Henry.

'Granddad said I—' Jake began, but he broke off with a quick look at his mum's worry-worn face.

Tom threw an almost suspicious glance at his father-in-law. 'What did he say?'

'It doesn't matter.' The cast dangling heavily at his side, Jake got off the trolley bed. His granddad winked at him as if to say, *Good boy.*

'Any word from the forest?' asked Henry as they made their way to the car park.

'No,' Amanda replied in a voice of toneless exhaustion.

'Well, I suppose no news is good news,' Henry said, failing pitifully to sound as if he believed his words.

When they reached the cars, Jake turned suddenly and hugged his uninjured arm around his granddad. Tom couldn't help but feel a flash of jealousy. He couldn't remember the last time Jake had hugged him like that.

'Remember what I said about your mother,' Henry murmured in Jake's ear, before drawing away. As Jake ducked into the Volvo, Henry's eyes slid across to Tom. 'He's a great lad, you know.'

Tom thought he detected a gleam of something in Henry's eyes. Was it disapproval? Had Jake told him about the slap? He found himself blinking guilty. 'I know. Thanks for sorting him out.'

He got behind the steering wheel. The journey back to the house passed in silence. The events of the previous couple of hours hung heavily in the air. Jake broke the silence as they pulled into the driveway. 'You don't have to worry about me, Mum. I won't go back to that house again.'

Amanda twisted to look at him, frowning as if she doubted his word. But when she saw the sincerity in his eyes, she said, 'Then we'll speak no more of it.'

Amanda headed straight for the living room. The clink of glass on glass told Tom she was pouring herself another drink. Jake and he stood awkwardly in the hallway. Tom almost seemed to hear the slap echoing in the silence between them. For want of something to say, he asked, 'Are you hungry?

Jake shook his head. 'I'm really sleepy. Is it all right if I go to my room?'

Tom's eyebrows lifted slightly. Jake didn't normally ask permission to go to his room. 'Of course.' He left his mouth open, wanting to say more, but unsure if now was the right time. As Jake started up the stairs, Tom added with a sort of hopeful lift in his voice, 'Just shout if you need anything.'

Jake nodded without glancing back. Tom stared despondently after him, then turned towards the living room. Amanda was in the armchair, sipping gin. Tom looked at her, but she didn't look at him.

DAY 2
1.46 A.M.

Jake was relieved to get upstairs. When his dad had hit him, two possible responses had flashed through his mind – hit him back or run. Instinct had chosen the latter option for him. He was less sure how to deal with the shame he'd seen in his dad's eyes. He was surprised to find himself feeling as if he should be the one apologising. After all, he'd been pushing his dad for months, not listening to or outright disobeying him. Was it any wonder he'd finally snapped?

He yawned as he closed his bedroom door. His limbs felt like rocks. There was only one thing he wanted to do more than throw himself on his bed and sleep. He propped his desk chair against the door – a trick he'd learned from the movies. Then he removed the book from his jeans and studied the cracked leather strap and rusty lock. It would be simple enough to cut the strap, but he was loath to damage the book. He switched on his laptop and navigated to a website that demonstrated how to pick a diary lock. He rummaged through his desk drawers until he found what he needed – a couple of paper clips. He bent one into a straight line and the other into an 'L' shape. He inserted the straight paper clip into the top of the keyhole and its L-shaped accomplice into the bottom. Then he eased out the straight paper clip, feeling it tickle the lock pins. Simultaneously, he twisted the second pick. To his surprise – he hadn't really expected it to work – the lock turned with a satisfying click.

A musty smell of old paper feathered his nostrils as he eagerly opened the book. Excitement tingled through him when he saw what was written on the first page in neatly printed black-inked letters. 'The diary of Rachel Ingham. Aged 12.' Childishly simple drawings of flowers sprouted from the words. Careful not to damage the damp-crinkled paper, he turned the page. The first entry was dated 'Sunday, 2 January 1972'. Almost eight months before the murders. He resisted an impulse to flip forwards and see if there was an entry for the 26th of July. Lauren had a bad habit of always reading the last page of a book first. To him that was like peeking inside wrapping paper – it ruined the surprise. He took the diary to his bed. Careful not to disturb the chicks, he propped the book against his plaster cast and continued reading.

> This is the first time I have kept a diary. I'm not really sure what to write so I will just write what I have done today. This morning Daddy and me went to church. Mummy stayed home with Mary because Mary was not feeling well. It was a very cold day and I could not stop shivering in the church. Reverend Douglas spoke about new beginnings. He said the New Year is a time to renew faith and come to know our Lord Jesus Christ better. I have not read my Bible for a while but tonight I will read it for ten minutes and I will read it every night from now on. When we got home Mary was playing with her dolls. She said she was feeling better.

At this point a sentence had been scribbled out so that it was almost illegible. Jake held the page up to the light and managed to make out the words, 'I don't think she was really ill in the first place.'

The entry continued with more mundane details about Rachel's day – helping Mummy prepare Sunday dinner, saying grace, an after-dinner walk along the river, Bible reading, more praying before bed. Jake sucked in a deep breath and popped his eyes wide to stave off encroaching sleep. This stuff was every bit as dull as you'd expect a twelve-year-old girl's diary to be.

The next entry was dated 'Wednesday, 5 January' and began 'First day back at school.' There was a little outline drawing of a sad face with a teardrop hanging from one eye, then

> I was sick twice this morning. I told Mummy I felt too ill to go to school but she said it was just my nerves again. Mary was really happy because she was allowed to take one of her Christmas presents to school. She took her doll Rebecca. I spoke to Christine in the playground. She went to her grandparents in Newcastle for Christmas. She said her mum wants to move to Newcastle. If Christine leaves I will have no one to speak to at school. Lessons I had today: maths, English, RE, biology. In biology I was supposed to be taught about sexual reproduction but I had to leave the class because Daddy thinks I should not learn about those things. After school Tina Dixon and her mates laughed at me and said I would never get a boyfriend if I didn't know how to do it.

The significance of 'it' had been highlighted with a red ring. Jake sighed. Some shit never changed. Kids like Rachel would always be an easy target.

> Mary was there and she thought it was really funny even though she did not know what Tina was talking about. She

told Mummy what happened and Mummy said they have a word for girls like Tina.

The next word was written in red capitals 'WHORE'.

This is more promising, thought Jake. But once again the remainder of the entry was a humdrum catalogue of chores, homework and prayers. As too were the next few entries, which were scattered haphazardly over a period of several weeks. Jake yawned again. He was on the verge of putting down the book and giving in to sleep, when the first sentence of an entry dated 'Thursday, 24 February' caught his eye.

Today is the worst day ever! Christine is moving to Newcastle. She is my only friend. Now I will be completely alone. When she told me I had to run to the toilets to be sick. Christine promised to write to me and said I could come and visit her in Newcastle. But I know Daddy will not let me go to Newcastle. He says cities are places of sin. In maths I started crying and Tina Dixon made baby boo hoo noises. I know Jesus says we should love our enemies and I do try to but sometimes I really really HATE Tina.

The word hate was ringed in red and a line was drawn from it to what looked like a Bible quotation in the margin: 'If we confess our sins He is faithful and just to forgive our sins and to cleanse us from all unrighteousness.' Next to the words was a drawing of a crucifix inside a heart.

After that there were no entries until 'Saturday, 18 March':

Christine moved to Newcastle today. I went to her house to say goodbye and we gave each other a present. I gave her a Saint Christopher pendant to look after her on her travels

> and she gave me a silver four-leaf-clover pendant with 'luck' written on it. We put on our presents and said that we would never take them off. After waving off Christine I went home and cried in my bedroom. Mary came in and said she wished I wasn't so sad. She said I could come to her dolls' tea party and be friends with her friends if I wanted. I said I'm too old to be friends with dolls and that she would be too in a few years. She said no she would not and that she would always love her dolls and they would always love her. I asked her to leave me alone but she wouldn't. In the end I gave in and went to her dolls' tea party and it did actually make me feel a bit better. Mary said it was the best dolls' tea party ever and asked if I wanted to know a secret. I said yes and she told me that she sometimes pretends to be ill so she doesn't have to go to church. I asked if she was afraid God would punish her and she stuck her tongue out and blew a raspberry. I was so shocked that I did not know what to say. Tonight I will pray for her.

Jake thought of how until two or three years ago Erin had used to pester him to play dolls' tea party with her. She'd stopped asking him long before she'd grown out of the game because he always gave the same answer, *No way. Dolls are for girls.* As he read on, he made a silent vow that he would never say no to her again. The next entry was dated 'Sunday, 19 March'. It had another eye-catching opening sentence:

> I have been crying all day. Daddy took away my four-leaf-clover pendant this morning. He saw it around my neck as we were getting ready to go to church. He said that luck is a blasphemy against God and that God has a preordained destiny for us all. I said I didn't wear the pendant because

> it was lucky but because it reminded me of Christine. I pleaded with him to let me keep it but he said no. I got angry and shouted at him that Christine was my only friend and he said that I will always have a friend so long as I am with God. After church Daddy told Reverend Douglas about the pendant and Reverend Douglas said luck is for pagans. He showed me a passage from Proverbs that said the lot is cast into the lap but the whole disposing thereof is of the Lord. We knelt together and prayed for His forgiveness for our sins. I know Daddy was right to take the pendant away but I cannot help but be angry with him for it. I do not think I will say my prayers tonight. I am too tired from crying.

In the margin was a drawing of a four-leaf clover and a crucifix. *Was that a sign of some inner turmoil?* wondered Jake. *Was Rachel doubting her faith?* He turned to an entry dated 'Wednesday, 22 March' whose margins were filled with doodles of dogs and smiling faces. Its first sentence seemed to answer his question. 'Thank you Lord for listening to my prayers.' His stinging eyes skimmed over the rest of the entry.

> I have a new friend! Mummy and Daddy bought me a puppy today. He is a beautiful nine-week-old brown labrador. We went to see him at a farm after school where he was in a barn with his 3 brothers and 2 sisters. I chose him because he was the smallest and looked sad. Daddy said I could have him as long as I feed and walk him every day. I promised I would do and Mary said she would help me but I do not want her help. Micah is my dog not hers. I know it is wrong to feel that way but she has her dolls and I have Micah. I decided to call him Micah because it

> means poor and humble. He slept all afternoon in the box we brought him home in. When he woke up I fed him and played with him. He's not allowed outside until he has had his vaccinations. I told Daddy this was the first time I had felt happy since Christine left and he said that made him happy too. I'm going to say my prayers now and go to sleep. Tomorrow I have to be up early to feed Micah.

For the next few weeks everything was all right in Rachel's little world of home, school and church. She no longer felt lonely, she stopped being sick before school and she never missed her prayers. Then on Saturday, 6 May, fate played a terrible trick on her. Jake was warned something was amiss by a drawing above the entry of a dog with angel's wings. The writing was uneven as if Rachel's hand had trembled.

> How could you do this to me, God? I thought you were a loving God. I thought you were my friend. But you are not. You are a HORRIBLE God. Micah was my only true friend and now he is dead. YOU took him from me and I will never forgive YOU.

At this point the writing became smudged as if tears had fallen on it. The next readable words were

> It is not my fault. I told Daddy that Micah's collar was too big for him but Daddy said it would be OK. But it was not OK. The collar slipped off Micah's head and he ran away. I chased him through the trees by the river but I lost sight of him. I ran to the road and shouted his name. A boy came up to me carrying Micah. Micah's eyes were closed and there was blood coming out of his mouth. The

> boy said he had seen a brown car run over Micah and drive away without stopping. He said that he did not see who was driving it. I tried to get Micah to open his eyes but he would not. The boy said he thought Micah was dead. That was when I became dizzy and had to sit down on the road. The boy helped me stand back up and took me to a bench. He asked my name and where I lived and I told him. He said his name was Hank like the American singer Hank Williams. He was wearing a white cowboy hat and spoke like a cowboy from a film.

A cowboy from a film. Jake pursed his lips dubiously. Even in these days of mass tourism, you didn't get many standard Americans visiting Middlebury, let alone cowboys.

The entry continued,

> Hank offered to carry Micah home. I was cold all over and I could not stop shaking. Hank gave me his jacket to wear and I said thank you. Hank told me that Micah had died quickly without any pain and that made me feel a tiny bit better. I don't really know why I said it but I told him I don't like cowboy films very much. He asked what I did like and I said I like *The Persuaders*. He said he liked *The Persuaders* too and asked who my favourite character was and I said Danny Wilde. When we got to the garden gate Hank said he had to go and meet someone. He gave me Micah. Micah was still warm. I gave him back his jacket and thanked him again. He said he was sorry about Micah and that he hoped I would be OK. I took Micah to Daddy and told him about the brown car and about Hank helping me. Daddy asked why Hank did not come to the house and I told him what Hank told me. We buried Micah

> by an apple tree in the garden. Daddy carved a cross into the tree and said a prayer. I closed my eyes and pretended to pray. Goodbye Micah my ONLY friend in the whole world. I almost wish I could have died with you. I WILL NOT say my prayers tonight.

Underneath the final sentence, Rachel had drawn a crucifix with 'RIP Micah' on it. And underneath that she'd written, 'Is it my destiny to be alone?'

Jake wrinkled his forehead in thought. There was no doubt this time that Rachel's faith had been shaken, if not completely crushed. He wondered, too, about Hank. Why hadn't Hank gone to the house? His line about having to meet someone seemed faintly suspect. The fog of encroaching sleep blown away by the entry, Jake read on. The next was dated 'Sunday, 7 May'.

> I did not go to church today. I lied and said that I had a headache and was too ill to get out of bed. Daddy and Mary went to church but Mummy stayed at home and looked after me. Next Sunday I will lie again. God hates me so I will hate Him right back. I wonder why He hates me? What have I done? I have followed His word and tried to be good so why am I being punished? Daddy says we are all tested in life and that we have to prove ourselves worthy of God's love. If he is right and this is a test I don't think I am going to pass it. No more prayers.

'We are all tested in life,' Jake murmured. Wasn't that the truth, he reflected, his thoughts returning to Erin.

The next entry came hot on the heels of the previous two. 'Monday, 8 May':

> Today was a strange day really bad but also kind of good. I was sick three times before school but Daddy would not let me have the day off. In history we were told that we are going on a field trip to the 5 Women stone circle. Mr Harrison gave us a form for our parents to sign so we are allowed to go. I already know that Daddy will not give me permission to go and that I will be teased by that WHORE Tina Dixon because of it. I almost cried just thinking about it. I thought it was going to be another absolutely horrible day but when I was walking home from school I saw Hank. He wasn't wearing a cowboy hat any more and his hair was combed like Danny Wilde's hair. Hank asked if I was OK and I lied and said I was. I had thought he was an American but today he spoke with an English accent.

Jake lifted his eyebrows, amused and curious. An English boy dressing like a cowboy and putting on an American accent. If Hank was nine or ten, there would be nothing unusual about that. But Jake got the impression that Hank was a good few years older, which marked him out as a bit of an oddball.

'Hank asked if he could walk me home and I said yes,' continued the entry.

> He didn't want to walk by the road so we walked through the woods by the river where it is nice and quiet. I asked why he talked like an American the other day and he said he just does it for fun sometimes. He asked how old I was and I said I was almost thirteen. He said he was sixteen and I said he looked older. He said people always said that. I asked where he went to school and he said he went to Silverton boarding school near Rothbury. I asked why he wasn't there now and he said there had been a fire and the

> school was closed for repairs. I asked where he lives and he said Netherwitton. He said he had a present for me. It was a silver bracelet with a little dog on it. He asked if I liked it and I said yes and he put it on my wrist. When we got to the back gate he said something funny. He said I was really pretty and it is a shame I am not fourteen because then I could be his girlfriend. I said I didn't want to be his girlfriend and he asked why not did I think he was ugly? I said no he was not ugly at all but that Daddy does not allow me to have boyfriends. I asked if he wanted to come in and say hello to Mummy and he said no. He asked if it would be OK if I did not tell Mummy and Daddy about him coming to see me because he did not want them to get the wrong idea. I said I would not tell them and he asked if it was OK if he walked me home again tomorrow. I said I would really like that and I thanked him for my present. He said he would meet me in the same place and we said goodbye and I went into the house. I am hiding the bracelet from Mummy and Daddy so that they don't take it away like they did my four-leaf-clover pendant.

Jake thought about the twelve-year-old girls at his school. Most of them were giggling nonentities his classmates wouldn't be seen dead hanging around with. The boys in his year fantasised about screwing big-titted teachers and celebrities, not flat-chested little girls. Hank clearly felt the same about the not wanting to be seen part. As for the other part . . . Jake didn't want to judge Hank. But it seemed to him that rather than not wanting Rachel's parents to get the wrong idea, Hank didn't want them to get the right idea.

'Tuesday, 9 May' brought another entry. The couple of dozen hearts floating around the margins gave a clue as to its contents.

> I asked Daddy about the 5 Women field trip this morning and he said no like I knew he would. He got angry and said the school shouldn't be taking children to a place like that. I said Mr Harrison said it was a very important historical monument and Daddy said Mr Harrison was a very foolish man. Daddy said the people who worshipped at that place were a cult of whores who glorified Satan. He said he was going to talk to Reverend Douglas and try to stop the field trip from happening. When he said that it made me feel really sick and I had to run to the toilet. I locked the door and refused to come out even when Daddy banged on the door. Daddy broke the lock and pulled me downstairs. He hurt my arm and I told him I hate him. I have never said anything like that before and he said hate is a sin against God and he made me kneel down and pray. I closed my eyes and put my hands together and said the prayer but in my mind I kept saying I HATE YOU I HATE YOU I HATE YOU. School was horrible as usual. At lunchtime Tina Dixon knocked me over and I cut my knee. She said it was an accident but she was lying. I wanted to hit her and keep on hitting her until she promised to leave me alone.

The entry was interrupted by the word 'HATE' written in bubble letters with devilish horns sprouting out of the H and E. After it there was an equals sign, then 'Daddy and Tina Dixon'. The entry resumed with

> After school Hank was waiting for me in the woods. He saw the cut on my knee and asked how it happened. I told him about Tina Dixon and he said he knows the Dixons and that they are all horrible people. He said Tina Dixon is probably jealous and I asked him what she is jealous of. He

> said she is jealous because she is so ugly and I am so pretty. We sat by the river and Hank asked if I was wearing his bracelet. I showed him it on my wrist. He asked if he could hold my hand and I said I would think about it. I told him about the 5 Women field trip and what Daddy said. Hank said I should not be angry with Daddy because he is only trying to protect me. I asked Hank if he is religious and he said he does not go to church but he believes in God and the Devil. We sat for a bit longer and I said I had to go home or Mummy would start to wonder where I was. When we got to the back gate I said that he could hold my hand just for a minute. He held both my hands and his hands were warm and soft like Micah. Hank said he wished we could stay there holding hands for the rest of the day. He said he would see me tomorrow and now all I can think about is how many hours there are until we can hold hands again.

Underneath this Rachel had written 'LOVE?' in bubble writing. Instead of horns, wings sprouted from the first and last letter. Jake tried to picture Rachel and Hank holding hands by the gate. But instead of Rachel's pale cheeks and big round eyes, he saw Erin's tanned face with its button nose and smiling dark-chocolate eyes. It gave him a crawling feeling to imagine her with Hank. He felt a sudden strong dislike for him. The dude wasn't merely an oddball, he was a creep.

At a soft knock on the door, Jake snapped shut the diary and slid it under his pillow. He padded across to move the chair away from the handle, then returned to bed and said, 'Come in.'

DAY 2
2.17 A.M.

Tom watched Amanda pour herself a second drink, then a third, her eyes growing ever blearier. She sat staring at a photo from a holiday the previous year. They were in a Greek taverna. Amanda had asked the waiter to take a photo. Erin was sitting on Tom's knee. Amanda's arms were wrapped around Jake's shoulders. They were all smiling, even Jake. Would they ever be together like that again? He could see the question written over and over in the tears running from Amanda's eyes.

'Why don't you try to get some rest?'

His suggestion met with frosty silence – a silence that built as the minutes slipped agonisingly by. Tom stared at the phone. He got up and stared out of the window. Silence. Everywhere silence, suffocating as a wet flannel. 'Christ, this waiting's worse than anything.'

Again, Amanda made no reply. Tom felt panic welling up. It was all falling apart. He was losing his grip on everything he loved. He dropped to his knees at Amanda's side. 'Please don't do this. We can't let this drive us apart. I love you, Amanda. Do you hear me? I love you.'

She lifted her bloodshot eyes to his. Her voice trembled out. 'Love can't bring back Erin.'

'Love gives us the strength to believe. And if we believe, then anything's possible.'

'Where did you get that crap from? One of your self-help books?'

'You said yourself earlier, we can get through this.'

'Maybe I was wrong.'

Amanda hugged her arms across herself, her eyes heavy-lidded. She looked exhausted, yet in some strange way more beautiful than ever. Tom wanted to wrap his arms around her, hold her tight and, if only for a few seconds, shut out everything except the feel of her hair and the smell of her skin. But he could tell that she didn't want to be touched. Heaving a sigh, he straightened. 'I'm going to check on Jake.'

Amanda shot him a suspicious glance. 'What for?'

'I just want to make sure he's OK. Don't worry – I won't disturb him if he's sleeping.'

You'd better not, her eyes warned. Tom wearily climbed to the attic door. He reached for the handle, but hesitated. It was time to stop walking in without knocking. How could he expect Jake to behave like an adult if he didn't treat him like one? He knocked loudly enough to be heard, but quietly enough not to wake Jake. He caught the sound of soft footsteps approaching then retreating from the door. Several times recently he'd found the door barred by a chair. He'd told Jake to stop doing it, but as usual his words had met a brick wall. Had Jake just removed a chair? If so, what was he up to that he didn't want anyone to walk in on? Tom pushed the questions to the back of his mind. Whatever Jake was up to, this was hardly the moment to burst in and question him about it.

'Come in,' said Jake.

Tom opened the door and saw the surprise in Jake's eyes. He guessed Jake had been expecting his mum. She was usually the only one who bothered to knock. Jake was in bed with his plaster cast resting on the duvet. Tom's gaze came to rest curiously on a bundle of rags with the reading lamp aimed at it. He tried to smile reassuringly, but it felt more like a grimace. 'I thought you'd be asleep.'

'I can't sleep. I keep thinking about Erin.'

A shudder ran through Tom as he thought of the watery apparition that had invaded his brief sleep. 'Can I sit down?'

Again, Jake's eyebrows rose slightly. 'Sure.'

Tom perched on the bed, struggling to think of something he could say to persuade Jake everything was going to be OK. But he knew any words would be as hollow as the ones he'd uttered downstairs. A faint movement among the rags caught his eye. He peeled back a layer of grubby material.

'Careful,' cautioned Jake as the chicks were exposed. One of the pair gave a tiny flutter of a minuscule wing.

'Where did these come from?'

Jake told his dad what had happened in the attic of the Ingham house, adding, 'I couldn't just leave them there to die. I thought I could look after them until they're old enough to survive on their own.'

Tom gave him a look as if he was seeing something new. He smiled again and this time it felt easy. The chick stretched open its beak. 'It's hungry.'

'I found some dead flies, but they haven't eaten them.'

'You need to feed them by hand when they're this age. We had chickens on the farm. I used to feed their chicks oatmeal.' Tom laid his hand on the unmoving chick. 'This one's dead.'

Jake jerked up from his pillow. 'Are you sure?'

'I'm afraid so.'

Jake screwed up his face, tears springing into his eyes. The diary had partially distracted him from what was going on. But this . . . somehow this brought it all into unbearably sharp focus. 'I promised I'd take care of them.'

'And you will take care of the one that's still alive. I'll show you how.' Tom gathered up the nest of rags.

'Where are we going?'

'This light bulb isn't hot enough. We need to get this chick warm.'

They headed downstairs to the kitchen. Amanda threw them a glazed glance as they passed the living room.

Tom knew he had to act quickly if the chick was to have any chance of survival. He grabbed a cardboard box from the pantry and emptied its contents onto the floor. 'Lucky we've got a gas oven,' he said, sliding a hand under the chick's tummy and lifting it into the box. 'We used this trick sometimes if the chicks got too cold.' He put the box in the oven and turned on the pilot light. 'That'll warm it up in no time.'

'What's going on?' asked Amanda, walking a touch unsteadily into the room.

As Jake told her, Tom rummaged through the drawers until he found what he was looking for – a plastic medicine syringe from Erin's baby days. Amanda ruckled her face as if she couldn't make sense of what she was hearing. 'It's just a baby bird,' she said to Jake. 'You don't even like animals. Why do you care if it lives or dies?'

Jake replied with a nervous shrug, uncertain how to react to the slur of anger in his mum's voice.

'Your sister's out there somewhere and *this*', Amanda jabbed a finger at the chick, 'is what you're worrying about.'

'He made a promise to look after it,' said Tom, his eyes pleading with Amanda to lay off.

With a sharp exhalation, she turned and wobbled back into the living room.

'She's struggling to cope,' Tom said to Jake in a lowered voice. A look of apology entered his eyes. 'Both of us are.'

Momentarily, neither of them seemed to know what to say. Then Tom said, 'Right, let's get this chick fed.' He mixed and warmed some porridge oats into a smooth paste and drew them into the syringe. He checked the temperature of the paste on the underside of his wrist, then tickled the tip of the syringe against the chick's beak. The chick reflexively opened up and he squirted a small blob into its mouth. 'Now you have a go.' He handed Jake the syringe. 'Not too much,' he cautioned as, emitting a tiny squeak, the chick stretched its beak wide for more food. 'That's it. A little bit at a time. He'll stop opening his beak when he's had enough.'

Jake stroked his thumb against the fuzzy underside of the chick's throat. 'Do you think he'll survive?'

'If you keep a close enough eye on him.' Tom dug another box out of the pantry, lined it with shreds of newspaper and punched holes in its sides with a knife. He lifted the chick into the box and closed the flaps. 'We'll put him in the airing cupboard until we can get our hands on a heat lamp.'

Jake glanced at the bundle of rags. 'What about the other one?'

'We can bury it in the garden if you like.'

Jake nodded. They took the surviving chick back upstairs. 'He'll like it in here,' said Tom, shifting some towels to make space in the airing cupboard for the box. 'Nice and warm and quiet. He should sleep for a few hours now.'

'Thanks, Dad.'

There was no edge in Jake's voice, only gratitude. Tom looked at his son and, for the first time, he saw beyond the awkward teenager to the man he might one day become. There was a vulnerability that he himself had never possessed – life on the farm hadn't allowed it – but there was also a stubbornness that he recognised only too well. He felt a sudden uprush of love so powerful it clogged his throat. A shrill noise rang out. The phone! He darted into the master bedroom and snatched up a handset. 'Yes?'

'The fog's clearing,' Sergeant Dyer informed him. 'We're resuming the search.'

'I'm on my way.'

Tom flew down the stairs. 'Did you hear that, Amanda? It's back on. I'm—' He stuck his head around the living room door and fell silent. Amanda was asleep – or, more accurately, passed out – in an armchair. Her head was slumped to one side. Even unconscious, there was a line like a scar between her eyebrows. A glass rested at an angle in her lap, threatening to spill its contents. He gently extricated it from her hand and turned to see Jake coming up behind him.

'Don't worry, Dad. I'll look after her.'

Tom's gaze rested on him a moment. Then he nodded as if to say, *I know you will,* and ran for the front door.

DAY 2
3.11 A.M.

The knocking brought Seth out of his dreams. He squinted at the alarm clock. He'd barely had three hours' sleep. His head felt as foggy as the forest. 'Who is it?'

'Holly. The search is back on.'

He switched on a bedside lamp, pulled on his cords and shuffled to the door.

The scrapbook! yelled the voice in his mind.

The book was open on his bed displaying a teenage girl with a pretty smile and a perm. The photo stared out of a newspaper clipping dated 'Monday, 22 May 1972'. A headline shouted 'Local Girl Falls to Her Death at Beauty Spot'. Red horns had been drawn on the girl's head. A pitchfork had been inserted into her hand.

'Won't be a minute.' Seth quickly put the book in his bag.

Get your head together. Moron!

Wincing at the shrillness of his grandma's voice, Seth sucked in a head-clearing breath. He opened the door, forcing himself to confidently meet Holly's eyes. With a mixture of arousal and resentment, he noted that she looked as fresh as when he'd first seen her outside the Town Hall. Even after a good sleep, he always woke up baggy-eyed. But then he'd been brought up – or rather, brought himself up – on fast food and exhaust fumes, not fresh eggs and fresher air.

'How are you feeling?' she asked.

'Much better.'

'Good. I thought you might need this.' Holly handed Seth a polystyrene cup of steaming tea.

'Thanks.'

'You'd better drink it quickly. The buses are leaving in five.'

They looked at each other for several awkward seconds. Seth's arousal threatened to become embarrassingly apparent as he wondered what would happen if he tried to kiss her. Would she fight him off? Or would she kiss him back, shove him onto the bed, move her lips down his neck—

Stop thinking with your cock, cut in his grandma.

'OK.'

'OK what?' asked Holly.

Seth's heart jumped. He hadn't meant to reply out loud. 'OK, I'll be quick. I've just got to get a few things together.'

'I'll wait for you in reception.'

You're pathetic. Weak and pathetic like all men, berated his grandma.

Seth took slow breaths until her voice faded to a background hum like white noise. He gathered together the few things he needed – pay-as-you-go phone, voice modifier, lock-knife – before heading downstairs.

The bus was full of the same faces as earlier. Several nodded hello. Seth mirrored their nods and their expressions. The atmosphere was subtly different from before, more apprehensive. The engine grumbled into life, the noise accentuated by the funereal hush.

Three buses headed out of Middlebury, a convoy of unspoken hope and fear. When they were a quarter of a mile or so beyond the town, instead of taking the turn for Fontburn Reservoir, they continued along the main road. 'We're heading into the forest from the other side,' said Holly.

The bus passed through a corridor of pines into a long stretch of grassy fields strung with tatters of mist. Then the road descended gently past a handful of houses into a small wood of oak and birch with a winding lake at its centre. Everything – the fields, the trees, the lake's surface – was serenely still.

'I love it out here at night,' murmured Holly.

'Me too,' Seth said reflexively, although to him the scene seemed as distant and alien as the fading stars. He wished he'd kept his gob shut when he noticed Holly looking at him as if she wasn't sure she believed him.

The bus climbed out of the wood to a crossroads. It took the right turn signposted CAMO 4, HEXHAM 22. After a few hundred metres, it turned right again through a farm gate into a mixed wood of deciduous and coniferous trees. The other two buses continued along the main road.

'This is Gallows Hill Wood,' said Holly as the bus juddered along an overgrown gravel track. 'They used to hang criminals here.'

The bus stopped behind a cluster of police vehicles and, to Seth's delight, Tom Jackson's Volvo. Police and other emergency service personnel were milling around, their jackets shining like cats' eyes in the crisscrossing confusion of torches and headlights. Seth spotted Tom and Henry peering at a map, their downturned faces half hidden in steel-blue darkness. Graham Jackson was standing with his collie, Bob, a few metres behind them, his face as unreadable as a concrete slab.

As the volunteers filed off the bus, constables handed out torches and long sticks. Seth worked his way towards Tom and Henry, eager to get close. Holly was telling him how hanged criminals used to be left to rot in their nooses as a warning to others. He made as if he was interested, but his attention was hungrily focused on the two men.

Tom and Henry lifted their heads as Sergeant Dyer addressed the volunteers. Something was missing from Henry's face, some spark of vitality. He had the look of someone contemplating the possibility of failure for the first time. Tom held himself as rigid as iron, his eyes bright with nerves.

'Two teams will make their way to the north end of Gallows Hill Wood,' said Sergeant Dyer. 'The rest of us will follow Harwood Burn towards the forest. Please take it slowly. We don't want to miss anything in the dark.'

Seth stayed close to Tom and Henry as the volunteers were divided up. As he'd hoped would happen, Henry spotted him. 'Seth, Holly, you're with us. You two have got sharp eyes.'

The search team gathered around Henry for instructions, but Tom took the lead. 'We're going to be searching the eastern half of the wood. Our search grid is narrower than before. Obviously with it being dark, we need to stay closer . . .' His voice faltered. He briefly struggled with his emotions, then jerked a nod. 'Let's get started.'

Seth's gaze lingered furtively on Tom as they spaced themselves among the trees at roughly ten-metre intervals. He took up a position to Tom's left. Graham lined up to the right of Tom, with Henry beyond him. 'Poor guy,' Holly remarked quietly. 'He looks like he's ready to fall apart.'

Seth wasn't so sure. Beneath Tom's brittle surface, he sensed a deep core of strength, an ability to endure like the rocks of the nearby hills.

'Wait up!' Eddie came running through the trees and inserted himself into the line. 'Sorry I'm late.'

The searchers swept the steadily rising ground with their torches, prodding the undergrowth with their sticks. Pines gathered thickly towards the top of the slope, squeezing out the birch and oak. The hoot of an owl echoed through the night. Another rang out in reply.

'Barn owls,' said Holly. 'That's their mating call. We've got a pair nesting on our farm. I think they're the most beautiful of all owls.'

'Me too,' agreed Seth.

'Really? What do you like so much about them?'

Seth tensed at the note of challenge in Holly's voice. Unthinkingly agreeing with everything people said was an old habit of his. Experience had taught him it was a bad habit too. Sooner or later, people saw the superficiality it concealed. As one girl he'd been briefly infatuated with had said, *What's your problem? Haven't you got any opinions of your own?* He'd struggled to come up with an answer and the girl had never spoken to him again. He'd tried to kick – or at least moderate – the habit but he had a tendency to lapse back into it when his mind was distracted.

'I just think they're nice,' he answered unconvincingly. Mocking laughter escaped from the darkness of his mind.

They searched on in silence. The wood's top end was bounded by a stream, beyond which a grassy field faded away into the darkness. Tom called everyone together. 'We're going to cross the stream and head for the forest.'

As the searchers hopped over the stream, Holly said to Seth, 'You know you don't have to say you like something just because I do.'

'Yeah, I know,' he replied defensively. Seeing Holly frown, he realised he had to give a morsel of something real to feed her feelings. 'It's just that . . . well, you make me nervous because I . . .' He trailed off awkwardly. *I like you.* Why was it so difficult to say? He'd said it to other girls.

'You don't need to be nervous.' Her voice was as soft as the air. It set his head reeling with the urge to kiss her.

Go on, do it, his grandma taunted. *Throw it all away like I knew you would.*

Seth felt the conflicting voices pulling his features out of shape, distorting his carefully composed mask. He was saved from having to decide which one to listen to by Henry calling, 'Come on you two. Keep up.'

They crossed the stream and took up their places again. The ground rose steadily, passing beyond the north-western tip of the woods after a couple of hundred metres. Yellow sheep eyes gleamed in the beams of their torches. The dim, bulky shapes behind the eyes scattered and thudded away into the distance. A spear's throw to the south dozens of torches swayed their way across the fields. Maybe a mile to the west more pinpricks of light blinked like SOS signals.

Imperceptibly, then noticeably, like paint being mixed, the sky lightened – black to blue to red to pink. They turned off their torches and quickened their pace. Seth glanced across at a swishing, thwacking sound. Tom was wielding his stick like a sword, his face fixed in a clench-toothed grimace. Beyond him, his brother was quietly and methodically working his way forwards. Seth's gaze passed over Graham's barren face to Henry. In the sun's first pale rays, Henry looked slightly deflated, like a slow-punctured balloon.

'Seth,' said Holly.

He pretended not to hear. She repeated his name, but still he didn't look at her. He wasn't ready to face up to the voices again.

DAY 2
3.36 A.M.

Jake watched his mum from the sofa. She was shivering even though he'd draped a blanket over her. Occasionally she jerked her head as if she'd been slapped. Once she'd sat up so suddenly he jumped. Her eyes had been filmy and vacant, not seeming to recognise where she was. After a few seconds, she'd closed them and slumped back into unconsciousness.

There was a knock at the front door. Jake sprang up and ran to it. He let out a relieved breath at the sight of his grandma. 'Jake, I thought you'd be in bed,' she said, running her gaze over his tired face.

'I've been keeping an eye on Mum.'

'Why would you need to keep an eye on her?'

'She's been drinking.'

Cathy cocked an eyebrow as if to say, *Who can blame her?* She followed Jake to the living room and bent to examine her daughter. 'Do you think we should try and get her to bed?' asked Jake.

'Best let her sleep it off here. You should get to bed though.'

Jake hesitated to leave. He'd seen his mum laughing drunk plenty of times, but he'd never seen her unconscious drunk. She'd always seemed invincibly full of life. But standing there looking at her, it hit him *blam* in the chest – she wasn't invincible, one day she would die. And if Erin wasn't found safe, that day might come sooner rather than later. The thought gave him the frightening feeling that if he took his eyes off her she, too, might vanish into thin air.

Cathy cupped his chin in her soft, manicured hand. 'Go on, darling. I'll look after your mum. You need your sleep if you want that arm to heal.' She tapped her cheek. 'But before you go give me a kiss.'

Jake pecked her cheek, inhaling the familiar floral scent of her perfume. She smiled. 'I needed that.'

He trudged upstairs, flopped onto his bed and closed his eyes. Instantly, his agitated mind bombarded him with a stream of fragmented images – Erin playing with her dolls; no not Erin, Mary Ingham; his dad hitting him; Rachel and Hank holding hands; his mum's booze-slackened face; the rook attacking him; the rook dead; Erin dead . . . His eyes popped open. He reached for the diary and flipped to the next unread entry, which was dated 'Wednesday, 10 May'. After a row of alternating red and black hearts, it began,

> I met Hank at the usual place after school. We sat by the river again and held hands. We talked and talked. Hank said he likes to go walking at night when the moon is out and especially if it is a full moon like tonight. He said he loves the full moon because it makes him feel as if he can do anything he wants. He asked if I can sneak out of the house and go for a walk with him. I said I'm scared Daddy will catch me. He said that if he could find a way for me to sneak out without being caught would I come? And I said yes. When I got home Mummy asked where I had been and I lied that I went to the library.

Jake blinked and rubbed his watering eyes. He was too tired to read, the words kept sliding out of focus. But neither did he want to shut his eyes. He stared at the ceiling for a while, then got out of bed and made his way to the airing cupboard. As quietly as possible, he peered into the box. The chick was asleep. Watching the barely visible rise and fall of its chest gave him a calming feeling. He stroked his forefinger over its silky fluff, wishing he could somehow climb into the box and snuggle down beside it. He returned to bed. This time when he closed his eyes he held the chick in his mind's eye, using it to fend off the images.

Sleep came fast. But just as suddenly, it seemed, he was awake again. Pale light pressed against his window. His arm throbbed within its cast. Had the pain woken him? He wasn't sure. A vague echo of something else – some piercing sound – seemed to bounce around his mind. As he reached for his painkillers, it came again. A scream. His mum's scream! He leapt out of bed and sprinted downstairs, almost tripping in his heart-pounding haste. His mum and grandma were standing with their backs to him at the open front door. His grandma had a hand pressed to her mouth.

'What is it?' he anxiously enquired.

His mum turned. The first thing he saw was her face – sickly as the morning light. Then he saw what she was holding and his breath caught in his throat. It was a doll. But no normal doll. It had a stuffed felt body maybe twenty-five centimetres long and an oversized head made from what appeared to be papier-mâché. It was wearing knitted brown boots, blue denim shorts and a white T-shirt with a pink butterfly design stitched into it. The same outfit Erin had been wearing when she disappeared. It had long wavy auburn hair, brown eyelashes and matching eyes, a button nose and dimpled rosy cheeks. But whoever had made it hadn't simply used Erin's features, they'd captured her mischievous smile too.

Normally Jake would have thought it quite cute. But right then it seemed as sinister as a voodoo effigy.

'What is this?' wondered Amanda, her voice clogged with dread.

'It's just a sick joke,' said Cathy. As if trying to convince herself, she repeated, 'A sick joke.'

Amanda's bloodshot eyes goggled at Jake like he might have an answer for her. He stared wordlessly back, although a voice was ringing out in his mind – a voice he'd never heard but instantly recognised as Rachel Ingham's – *She would always love her dolls and they would always love her.*

'Put it back where it was,' urged Cathy. 'It might have fingerprints or something on it.'

Amanda quickly set the doll down on the doorstep beside two bottles of milk. She continued to stare at it, shuddering with repulsion, yet seemingly unable to tear her eyes away. 'What kind of person would do something like this?'

'An evil person, that's who,' said Cathy. She flicked Jake a *keep an eye on her* look. 'I'm going to phone Inspector Shields.'

Amanda leaned heavily against the wall as if to stop herself from keeling over. Jake rushed to her side. 'It's OK,' she said, holding him at arm's length. 'I'll be OK in a moment. You go back to bed.'

'But Mum—'

'Just do as I say,' snapped Amanda, her voice quivering with nerves. She added more softly, 'I'm sorry, sweetie', ushering him towards the stairs with an exhausted waft of her hand.

Jake had that same feeling as in the living room, but even more strongly. It was as if everything he'd believed to be as permanent as rock had suddenly revealed itself to be as insubstantial as mist. He wrenched his eyes from her and ran back to his room. He snatched up the diary and scanned through it until he found the passage about the dolls' tea party. Was there a connection? He read the lines over and over as if searching for some hidden meaning. But the more he looked, the more his head spun with uncertainty. He needed a fresh pair of eyes.

He grabbed his iPad and FaceTimed Lauren. It rang for a long time before her sleep-rumpled face appeared on the screen. 'Have they found Erin?' Her voice was eager with concern and morbid interest.

'No.'

She irritably picked sleep from her eyes. 'What did you wake me up for then? It'd better be something—' She broke off, her mouth forming a shocked 'O'. 'What happened to your hair?'

'It doesn't matter.'

'Yeah, it does. I loved your hair.'

Jake felt a twinge of regret for impetuously cutting his hair. 'Just listen. Something's happened.' He told Lauren about the doll.

Her eyebrows arched. 'Freaky. Sounds like some voodoo shit.'

'Yeah, that's what I thought. And I also think it might have something to do with Mary Ingham.'

'Really? Why?'

'I went back to the Ingham house last night and—'

'Hang on,' Lauren cut in. 'You went back without me. I thought we were a team. Why didn't you call me?'

'I didn't want you to get in any more trouble.'

'Fuck off. You know I don't give a toss about trouble.' Lauren smiled crookedly. 'I like a bit of trouble.'

That's the problem, thought Jake. Lauren liked to play with 'trouble', but this wasn't a game. 'I found something at the house.' He held up the book. 'It's Rachel Ingham's diary.'

Lauren's eyes sprang wide. 'No way! Have you read it?'

'Some of it.'

'Shit, I'd have read it all straight away.'

'Yeah, well, there's a lot of stuff going on here. But listen, there's this one bit about Mary Ingham's dolls.' He read the passage aloud, then asked, 'So what do you reckon? Do you think Mary could have left that doll here?'

'Sounds a bit far-fetched to me.'

'What? You mean far-fetched like Satanists performing Black Masses at the Ingham house?'

Lauren pulled a *ha-ha* face at Jake's sarcastic tone. 'Eight-year-old girls like dolls. Even I liked dolls when I was that age.'

'It doesn't say Mary liked her dolls, it says she loved them.'

'Yeah, but that's just the way girls her age talk. They love butterflies and rainbows and princesses and all that crap.'

Jake lowered his frowning face. The mention of butterflies had brought a vivid image of Erin to his mind.

'What are you going to do with the diary?' asked Lauren.

'I don't know. Maybe I should ask my mum what she thinks.'

Lauren screwed her face up. 'That's a really bad idea.'

Jake gave her a narrow, knowing look. 'You're just worried she'll take it away from me and you won't get a chance to read it.'

'I admit it. I want to read it more than anything. It might solve the mystery of who killed Elijah and Rachel Ingham.'

'Or it might just be a load of crap about teenage romance.'

'Even if it is, there are still people who'd pay a tonne of money to get their hands on it. I'm talking thousands of pounds.'

Jake's frown turned into a scowl. 'Fuck that and fuck you, Lauren. All I care about is finding Erin.'

The depth of his anger took him off guard. The balance of power in their relationship had always been firmly in Lauren's favour. Basically he followed wherever she led – or at least he had until now. Lauren looked taken aback too. She seemed uncertain how to respond. Jake expected her to give him a mouthful back, but to his surprise she said, 'I'm sorry. That was a really shitty thing to say.'

'It's all right. Forget about it.'

There was a brief awkward silence. As if feeling her way into a new language, Lauren said, 'Look, Jake, you do what you need to do. I mean, like, you're right, nothing matters besides finding Erin. But here's the thing. If Mary Ingham really has got something to do with your sister's disappearance, why would she risk leaving that doll on your doorstep? Think about it. It doesn't make any sense.' An uncharacteristic wobble of emotion came into her voice. 'And think about this too. She was so traumatised by the murder of her parents that she hasn't spoken a word since. And how do the small-minded tossers around here treat her? Like a freak. An outcast. If your mum takes that diary to the police, they'll probably question Mary.'

'Yeah, so?'

'So you know what this town's like. It'll be around the whole place in five minutes. And five minutes after that, all those same small-minded tossers will have decided Crazy Mary's guilty. They'll make her life even worse than the pile of shit it already is. And all because she liked dolls when she was eight. Do you want that on your conscience?'

No, came the resounding answer in Jake's head. Lauren was right. Mary Ingham had been through so much in her life. If she was wrongly implicated in Erin's disappearance, maybe it would be the final straw, the thing that finished her off. Middlebury's inhabitants drove him mad with their narrow-minded, judgemental views. He'd always told himself he was different. But if he ruined what little life Mary had for no good reason, wouldn't that make him the same as them? Or, even worse, the very thing he claimed to hate most – a hypocrite? Of course it would. And yet, his thoughts kept looping back to the same impossible-to-ignore question. 'What if she is involved somehow?'

'She's not.'

'How do you know?'

'You've only got to look at her to know that. Tell you what. I know where she lives. Let's check her house out. And if we see anything dodgy I'll go to the police myself. Deal?'

Jake mulled Lauren's words over. 'All right, but on one condition. We do it my way. If I say no or run or whatever, you do it without argument.'

'OK, boss.' There was amusement in Lauren's voice.

'I'm not fucking around, Lauren. I mean it.'

'Chill. No arguing, I promise. So what's the plan?'

'I dunno. It's going to be difficult to get out of the house. I'll let you know when I think of something.'

Jake tapped the disconnect icon. Engine noise drew him to the window. A police car pulled into the driveway. Inspector Shields and a constable got out. There was no way he could sneak out while they were here. Not that he would have left straight away even if he had the opportunity. There was something he needed to do first. He headed to the airing cupboard. The chick opened its beak and emitted a tiny squeak. Jake tickled its throat. 'Are you hungry? Let's get you something to eat.'

When he got downstairs, his mum, grandma and Inspector Shields were gathered around the doll. 'What made you open the door?' the inspector asked Amanda.

'I heard the milkman.'

'Who's your milkman?'

Inspector Shields jotted down Amanda's reply, then looked at Jake. 'You haven't touched the doll, have you?'

Jake shook his head.

'He was in bed when I found this', Amanda's mouth curled with revulsion, '*thing.*'

'Can you think of any reason someone might have left it here?'

'No.'

'I think it's just a sick joke,' said Cathy.

'Could be,' agreed Inspector Shields. His disconcertingly probing eyes focused on Jake again. 'What do you think, Jake?'

Keeping his mouth shut for fear his nervousness would give him away, Jake shrugged. Inspector Shields squinted at the doll as if scrutinising a suspect. He gave a shake of his head. 'Can't say I've ever come across anything like it before.'

'There are some strange people out there,' said Cathy.

'No disagreement here.' Inspector Shields beckoned to a plastic-gloved constable, who came forward and slid the doll into an evidence bag. 'I'll have to ask you all to stay away from the porch until Forensics has looked it over. Like you said, Mrs Brooks, it's probably some idiot's idea of a joke. But it's always best to err on the side of caution.' The inspector's phone rang. 'Excuse me a moment.' He moved away to answer it.

Relieved for the chance to continue on his way before Inspector Shields could ask him anything else, Jake went into the kitchen. As he mixed up some porridge for the chick, he heard his grandma ask, 'Why? What for?' There was a challenge in her voice that drew him back to the hallway. She was facing Inspector Shields, one hand resting protectively on Amanda's shoulder. 'Has something happened?'

'All I can tell you is there are some questions that need answering,' replied the inspector.

'What questions? And why can't she answer them here? Why does she need to go to the station?'

'It's OK, Mum,' Amanda said with a sigh. 'I'll go.'

'But you're so tired, darling. You shouldn't have to—'

'Please, Mum. I haven't got the energy to argue. Just stay here and look after Jake. I won't be long.' She glanced at Inspector Shields as if seeking confirmation of this last statement. The inspector's face gave nothing away.

Amanda looked at Jake, her eyes sad, almost apologetic. Then she followed Inspector Shields to the police car.

DAY 2
6.41 A.M.

'Erin! Where are you?' There was no reply. But Tom kept calling out, his voice cracking like the twigs under his feet. The searchers had left the open fields behind. All they could see now were trees, trees and more trees. On and on, row after row, straight slim trunks, curving bushy branches, glimpses of brightening sky. It was going to be another beautiful day. Beautiful and awful beyond words. 'Erin! Erin!'

Tom's eyes scoured every tree, every undulation in the needle-blanketed forest floor. His temples pounded with the fear that he might miss some vital detail – a shred of clothing, a sweetie wrapper, a hair . . . For the first time in years, he silently prayed. *Oh, God, please let me find something. Anything! No, not anything*, he corrected himself. *Not blood. Not a body.* He stabbed his stick at the ground as if trying to bully it into giving up a secret. A branch scratched his face. And suddenly he was beating the tree it was attached to, senselessly spitting expletives. 'Fucking bastard! Fucking, sodding . . .'

He whirled around at a touch on his shoulder, lost in unreasoning rage, ready to lash out. He found himself glaring into eyes as regular and steady as the seasons – Graham's eyes. Tom heaved a breath. Glancing at the other searchers' sympathetic faces, he made a sharp forward motion. 'Keep going. Keep going.'

As they continued their painfully slow progress, Henry gestured for Tom to hang back. He produced a fat brown envelope. 'I didn't want to give you this in front of everyone.'

Tom frowned at the envelope as if unsure whether to take it. With a begrudging nod of thanks, he accepted it and thrust it into his pocket.

'We can discuss the terms of repayment after this is over,' said Henry.

Tom looked at him as if he couldn't quite believe his ears. 'You don't have to worry, Henry. I'll pay back every penny, plus interest.'

'I don't want the money back.'

'Then what do you want?'

'Like I said, we can come to an agreement on that later.'

Henry turned away and resumed the search. Tom stared after him with an expression that seemed to suggest he'd just sold his soul. He could guess all too easily what Henry wanted – more control over the lives of Amanda and the kids.

Sergeant Dyer and several constables approached and gestured for everyone to halt. 'Can I have a word, Mr Jackson?'

Tom's heart was suddenly beating so fast it almost snatched his breath away. 'Have you found something?'

'No. Inspector Shields needs to talk to you.'

'Where is he?'

'At the station.'

Tom shook his head. 'If he wants to talk, he can get his arse out here this time.'

'What's going on, Sergeant?' asked Henry, approaching with Eddie at his heels.

Sergeant Dyer raised his hand, palm outward. 'Please, if I could just speak to Mr Jackson alone for a moment.'

'They want me to go to the station again,' said Tom. 'But I'm not going. Not unless there's a bloody good reason.'

'I assure you there is a good reason, Mr Jackson.'

'Which is?'

'Inspector Shields will explain when you get to the station. Look, we're wasting time and that's the most precious thing we've got right now.'

Tom chewed on Sergeant Dyer's words. For an instant he seemed to hear the ticking of the living-room clock echoing in his head, relentless, taunting. 'All right.' He jerked his head for the sergeant to lead the way.

Sergeant Dyer indicated one of his constables. 'Constable Hutton will take you.'

Tom followed the constable in the direction of the Hexham Road. Behind him a dog barked. Glancing back, he saw something that stopped him dead. Sergeant Dyer was drawing Graham out of the line. The other constables were standing at his brother's shoulders. Bob barked again, disturbed by their proximity. Graham reached down to shush the sheepdog. Tom's face knotted. 'What do they want to talk to my brother for?'

'No idea,' replied Constable Hutton.

Tom darted her a dubious look. He knew bullshit when he smelled it. He started back in the direction he'd come from.

'Mr Jackson,' Constable Hutton called after him, 'we don't have time for this.'

He ignored her. The question was pounding against his head like a fist. He repeated it as he neared Sergeant Dyer. 'What do you want to talk to my brother for?'

'This isn't the place for this conversation, Mr Jackson. As I said, Inspector Shields will explain—'

'No,' Tom cut in. 'I want to know right now.' His gaze moved to his brother. 'What's going on, Graham?'

'I don't know.' As Graham spoke, his eyes fell away from Tom's. It was only for a fleeting instant, but it was enough.

'Bollocks, you don't!'

Bob bared his teeth and growled at Tom's raised voice. Graham patted his head and shushed him again.

'Tell me the truth, Graham.' Tom's hand shot out to grab his brother's shirt collar. Bob snapped at Tom's ankle, catching the hem of his jeans and dragging him off balance. Tom twisted his hand into the collar as his brother tried to yank himself free. Both men staggered and struggled to keep their balance.

The constables seized Tom, forcibly separating him from Graham and the sheepdog. He tried to elbow them away, but they twisted his arms up behind his back and thrust him to the ground.

Eddie ran over, fists clenched. 'Get your hands off him.'

'Leave it, Eddie,' gasped Tom, ceasing to struggle.

The constables lifted him to his feet. 'If they let go, are you going to behave yourself?' asked Sergeant Dyer.

Tom nodded. The constables stepped away just far enough that they could easily grab him if he went for his brother again. Tom stared at Graham, his eyes hard with promise. 'You and I are going to talk later.' He turned and stalked back to Constable Hutton. Looking over his shoulder, he saw Graham being escorted in the same direction about a hundred metres behind. After the best part of a mile, they emerged from the trees at the Hexham Road. The verges were lined with emergency service vehicles. A slow-moving single line of traffic passed between them. Constable Hutton guided Tom to the back seat of a police car. Another constable held up the traffic and waved them through. Journalists peered curiously into the car as it passed. The local news camera crew had been joined by a gaggle of reporters from national organisations. As cameras flashed, Tom resisted an urge to lower his head as if he'd done something wrong.

Once they'd run the gauntlet of journalists, Constable Hutton switched on the sirens and put her foot down. Tom stared restlessly out of the window. Graham had lied to him. He felt certain of it. But why? What possible reason could he have? They'd barely spoken for months. Their relationship was almost non-existent. He took a slow breath, trying to quieten his mind. But the questions continued to loop round and round. One possibility occurred to him – a possibility so ridiculous, so far-fetched that he immediately tried to dismiss it. But the thought lingered like the bitter aftertaste of vomit.

When they reached the police station, Tom jumped out of the car and rushed into the reception area. 'Tell Inspector Shields that Tom Jackson's here,' he said impatiently to the receptionist.

A second police car pulled up. Graham got out, but didn't enter the station. The brothers locked eyes through the glass doors. 'Mr Jackson.' Tom turned at Inspector Shields's voice. 'This way, please.' The inspector gestured for the constables to bring Graham too.

Following Inspector Shields along a corridor, Tom began, 'Just what the hell—' His throat closed on the words as he saw something – or rather, someone – through an open door. Amanda was sitting in an interview room, her eyes lowered, her shoulders slumped. She looked up and her face came alive with uncertainty. 'Tom.' She rose and stepped hesitantly towards him. 'What are you doing here?'

'They haven't told me yet.' Tom's voice vibrated with the possibility – the ridiculous, far-fetched possibility. 'Graham's here too.'

'Graham,' Amanda echoed hollowly, her eyes flitting past Tom.

Tom twisted to look at his brother too. His eyes swam back and forth between Graham and Amanda like a panicked fish. Graham was staring at Amanda as if Tom didn't exist. Amanda had paled right down to her lips. *Oh, Christ,* thought Tom, sweat breaking out all over his body, *it can't be true. Can it?*

'I don't feel . . .' said Amanda, fading off hoarsely. Her eyes rolled back, her knees buckled and she collapsed like an accordion.

'Amanda!' Tom dropped to his knees and cradled her head.

Graham rushed forward and stooped over her. Tom thrust a hand at him. 'Get away from my wife.' Voice rising with emphasis, he repeated, '*My wife!*'

Inspector Shields gestured at Graham, then the interview room. 'Get him in there.'

A constable hustled Graham into the room and shut the door. Constable Hutton felt for Amanda's pulse and listened to her breathing. 'I think she's fainted.'

'Let's get her to a sofa.'

Amanda was carried into an office. Perching beside her on a hard sofa, Tom squeezed her hands and said her name. Her eyelids fluttered but didn't open. A constable appeared with a first-aid box, dug out smelling salts and wafted them under her nose. This time her eyes popped open. She looked around as if she didn't remember what had happened or where she was. Seeing Tom, it all seemed to come rushing back. Her features crumpled and she twisted away from him.

'Look at me, Amanda.' Tom's voice was a whirlpool of conflicting emotions – concern, anger, bewilderment. She pressed her face into the sofa. 'Look at me,' he repeated, anger gaining the upper hand.

'I think it would be best if you gave your wife some breathing room,' said Inspector Shields.

'And I think you should stay out of this,' retorted Tom. 'It's none of your business.'

'I disagree. It's very much my business. Now please move away from your wife.' The inspector's voice was calm as always, but there was a warning in it.

Tom reluctantly stood and paced across the room. Inspector Shields took his place. 'Amanda, can you hear me?'

She nodded without turning to look at the inspector.

'You're at the police station. We think you fainted. But we're going to have you taken across to the hospital to be on the safe side.'

'I'm going with her. You can't stop me. She's my wife.' The insecurity was almost palpable in Tom's voice, like a man desperately clinging on to something even as it was slipping away.

'No one's trying to stop you. You have every right to go with Amanda as long as that's what she wants. Is that what you want, Amanda?'

Amanda gave a small shake of her head.

Tom's eyes widened with dismay. 'You don't mean that, Amanda.'

'Your wife's made up her mind.' Inspector Shields rose to usher Tom towards the door.

He stood his ground. 'This isn't right. Tell them, Amanda. Tell them you want me with you.'

Amanda's shoulders began to quake with sobs. The inspector took hold of Tom's arm and firmly guided him into a room across the hallway. He pointed to a chair. 'Sit down, Mr Jackson.'

Tom remained standing. 'Am I under arrest?'

'No.'

'Then what's to stop me from leaving right now?'

'Nothing, except that your daughter's missing and that what you do right now, right this second, could make the difference between her living and dying.'

Inspector Shields's matter-of-fact tone knocked all the fight out of Tom. He dropped onto the chair. 'You orchestrated that little scene in the corridor, didn't you?'

'Yes,' admitted the inspector, pulling up a chair. 'I wanted to see how you all reacted.'

'And did you see what you hoped to see?'

'No.' Inspector Shields's voice was tinged with the sadness of a life spent dealing with the darker side of humanity.

'How did you know?'

'Amanda lied to me. I've seen her phone records. At the time Erin went missing, Amanda was on the phone to your brother.' Inspector Shields consulted his notepad. 'The call lasted from 9.51 until 10.01.'

Tom squeezed his eyes shut, putting a hand to his chest as if there was a pain there. He'd known it was true the instant he saw the way Amanda and Graham looked at each other, but some small part of him had still refused to believe it. Here, though, was surely the final proof. *How could this have happened?* The question led to another, even more disturbing one. He asked haltingly, 'You . . . you don't think this has got anything to do with Erin's disappearance, do you?'

'That's what I'm trying to find out.'

Tom swayed back in his chair, shaking his head and pinching his hand over his mouth. He could just about accept the possibility of Amanda and Graham having an affair. But not this. Not fucking this!

Inspector Shields watched him steadily. 'Did you have any suspicions about your wife and brother?'

'None.'

'Are you sure?'

'One hundred per cent. Amanda and Graham hardly ever talk. Not that they dislike each other. They've just got nothing in common.' A grimace distorted Tom's mouth. 'Or at least that was always the way it seemed to me. Obviously I was wrong.'

'Does Amanda ever go to your brother's house?'

'As far as I'm aware, the last time they saw each other was back in April when Graham came round with a birthday present for her. I remember being a bit surprised because he doesn't usually bother with presents.' *April.* Could it have been going on that long? Or maybe even longer? Perhaps they'd been screwing right under his nose for years. Since even before Erin was born. Tom's stomach made like it was trying to climb up his throat. *Oh, Jesus Christ! What if Erin wasn't—* He silenced his thoughts with a vehement shake of his head.

'I'm going to ask your permission for something, Tom.' Inspector Shields's tone was suddenly less impersonal. 'Initial test results show the blood found by the stream isn't animal blood. It's human AB positive, the same as Erin's blood. Only around 3 per cent of Caucasians have that blood group. So that goes a long way towards proving it's her blood. To make absolutely certain, we'd like to take a sample of your blood so we can see if the DNA profiles match.'

'Go ahead.' Tom's voice was almost slurred. He felt as if he'd been dazed by a flurry of punches from impossible angles. He didn't know what hurt more – knowing the blood was almost certainly Erin's or the unspoken knowledge that this was about more than simply confirming the blood's provenance, it was about whether or not he was her father.

'There's another thing I need your permission for. I think it's time we made a full search of your house.'

Tom thought about the house. All the years he'd lived there, first as part of a couple, then as part of a family. All the happy moments. All the lies. But which were which? 'You can tear the place apart for all I care.'

'Wait here. I won't be a minute.'

Inspector Shields left the room. Tom clutched his head. Nothing made sense any more. It was as if the world had gone insane. The inspector returned with a sheaf of paper. 'These are consent forms for the DNA sample and the property search.' He put a pen in Tom's hand and pointed out where he needed to sign and date. Without bothering to read the forms, Tom scribbled his signature as many times as was necessary. A Forensics officer entered the room, pricked Tom's thumb and collected a drop of blood.

'Anything else?' Tom asked numbly. The pain of discovery was being displaced by the blankness of shock.

'A word of caution. Right now you might feel like doing something foolish. Don't. Go home to your son.'

'My son,' murmured Tom. That was one certainty in all this chaos. Jake was his son. Wasn't he? As if unsure his legs would carry him, he stood and approached the door. The doubt echoed mercilessly in his mind. Wasn't he?

'One more thing before you go, Mr Jackson,' said Inspector Shields. 'Where did you sneak off to yesterday afternoon when you were supposed to be getting a lift back to the forest?'

'Amanda and I went to see Carl Wright. We offered to give up the quarry if he returned Erin to us.'

'And what did he say?'

'He claimed he doesn't have anything to do with Erin's disappearance. I was certain he was lying, but now . . .' Tom trailed off into disoriented silence. He looked pleadingly at the inspector. 'What do you think?'

'Like I said, you should go home and look after your son.' Inspector Shields had his poker face back on.

'You don't give much away, do you?'

'In my job you have to consider all possibilities, no matter how unpalatable. Do you understand?' Tom nodded and the inspector continued, 'Please don't pull any more disappearing acts or I might start to think you're hiding something else from me.'

His eyes dragging along the floor, Tom followed Constable Hutton out of the station. He heard an ambulance from the neighbouring hospital and a thought cut through his shock, *What else is being hidden from me? What else don't I know?*

DAY 2
8.03 A.M.

A doctor measured Amanda's blood pressure and shone a torch into her eyes. 'How are you feeling, Mrs Jackson?'

It was the second time the question had been asked, and again it went unanswered. As Inspector Shields joined the doctor, Amanda turned on the trolley bed to face the wall and squeezed her eyes shut. When she'd fainted, it had been like falling into a black hole devoid of thoughts and feelings, worries and fears. Waking up had brought reality crashing back in like a tidal wave. Now all she wanted to do was return to that place, wrap herself in its emptiness.

'How long before we can take her back to the station?' asked Inspector Shields.

'Difficult to say,' replied the doctor. 'Her blood pressure's low. She may well have another collapse if she's put under stress.'

'Well, can I at least talk to her here?'

'You can try.'

'Mrs Jackson, can you hear me?' Receiving no answer, Inspector Shields persisted, 'I know how you feel, Amanda. I know you just want to shut yourself off and not think about anything. But I'm asking you, I'm begging you, for your daughter's sake, please talk to me.'

As if she was dredging her voice up from the bottom of the North Sea, Amanda said, 'I was on the phone to Graham when Erin disappeared.'

'You're having an affair with him.' It was a statement, not a question.

'I was.'

'How long has it been going on for?'

'Six, maybe seven months.'

'When you say "was" does that mean it's over?'

'It's been over for weeks.'

'So why did Graham phone you yesterday?'

'Because he won't accept it. I keep telling him it was a mistake, I don't love him, I love Tom. But he just carries on phoning and texting, saying how much he loves me, how we're going to live together, get married, start a family of our own.' Amanda's voice shook. 'Oh, Christ, how did I let it get so far?'

'Has Graham ever threatened you in any way?'

'No.'

'So he's never threatened to speak to Tom?'

Amanda twisted towards Inspector Shields, scrutinising his face as if searching for signs of judgement. Suddenly her words were spilling out like a pent-up confession. 'I know how this must look. You must think I'm a heartless bitch. And maybe I am. I was bored, frustrated, looking for . . . for someone to make me feel *that* feeling again. You know, that feeling when you first get together with someone, like you're the only thing in the world that matters to them. This isn't Graham's fault. I made this happen. He resisted but I wore him down. I used him to get back at Tom for making me feel so . . . invisible. I realise that sounds stupid because Tom didn't even know what was going on. But it made me feel like I had some kind of power over him, like if he ever pushed me to it I could turn round and say to him, *I fucked your brother*.'

Amanda covered her face with both hands as if to hide her shame. After an extended silence, she hauled in a breath and continued, 'Graham doesn't want to hurt Tom. Or at least he wants to hurt him as little as possible. In his mind, Tom and I will get divorced. Then, after enough time has passed to make it if not respectable then at least acceptable, Graham and I will move in together. That way Tom would never have to know about the affair.' She smiled pitifully. 'Ridiculous, isn't it? That a grown man could be so naive. But that's the way Graham thinks. To him everything's as simple as . . . as his sheep. Tom's different. Even if Graham and I left it ten years before going public, Tom would guess the truth. When Graham told me what he was thinking, I realised what a terrible mistake I'd made. I broke it off. Graham was devastated. He wouldn't stop crying. You can't imagine what it takes to make a man like him cry. I don't think he even cried when his mother died. He said he'd do anything to make us work. Sell his farm, move away, whatever it took. That's when I knew I was in serious trouble. That farm is all he's ever known. Giving that place up would be like giving up his identity.'

'He sounds like a desperate man,' remarked Inspector Shields.

'He is,' agreed Amanda. Catching the implication behind the words, she added, 'But he's also a good man. He'd never do anything to harm me or my children.'

'Are you certain of that?'

'Yes.'

'How can you be absolutely certain without even the slightest doubt that Graham wouldn't use Erin to try and force you to do what he wants?'

'I can't but . . . well, he'd have to be crazy to think that hurting my daughter would make me get together with him.'

'How do you know he isn't crazy? Working that farm all alone, year after year. Loneliness can do strange things to people.'

'Except he's not lonely. His animals are his family.'

Inspector Shields accepted Amanda's words without further argument. He'd worked in rural communities long enough to know they were true. 'How often did you meet up with Graham?'

'I don't see why that's relevant.'

'It's impossible to say what's relevant and what isn't. The more information we gather, the more likely we are to unearth some significant detail.'

'We didn't have a regular *thing*. We met whenever we had the chance. I'm not sure exactly how often. Maybe once every fortnight.'

'Where did you meet up?'

'The first time was at my house, but that was much too risky. So after that I went to the farm.'

'And what about your children? Were they ever around when you met up?'

Amanda looked horrified. 'No, of course not.'

'So they had no idea what was going on?'

'If for one second I'd thought they did, I would have broken it off with Graham instantly.'

'You say Graham's been sending texts.'

'Yes, but I've deleted them.'

'We may be able to recover them. I can't force you to hand over your phone at this moment, but I'd appreciate it if you would do so voluntarily.'

Amanda gave her phone to Inspector Shields. 'I'll do anything I can to help, Inspector.' Tears trembled in her eyes. 'I don't care what happens to me. All I want is my little girl back where she belongs.'

'That's good, because it makes what I'm about to say easier.' The inspector leaned in closer, his voice dropping confidentially. 'Is there anything else you haven't told me? This is your chance, Amanda. If you've done something you didn't mean to do, made some sort of mistake,' he swayed his hand back and forth between them, 'together we can make it right. But if you don't speak to me now, I can't help you.'

Amanda recoiled as if a snake had hissed at her. 'What are you saying? Do you think I'm some kind of monster?'

'I don't presume to think anything. And I'm not judging you. I'm simply doing my job.'

'There's nothing else.'

'If that's what you're telling me, then that's what I have to believe.'

Inspector Shields looked at Amanda as if waiting for a reply to a question. She blinked away from his gaze. 'Am I under arrest?'

'No, but it would be best if you remained either here or at the station for now. Thank you for talking to me, Mrs Jackson.'

Without replying, Amanda rolled to face the wall again.

DAY 2
8.04 A.M.

Jake spooned cereal into his mouth at the kitchen table. He glanced at his grandma, who was busying herself with the washing-up. There'd been no chance to sneak out and meet Lauren. His grandma hadn't taken her eyes off him since his mum had left with Inspector Shields. Even when he'd gone to his bedroom, she trailed after him, asking how he was feeling and a dozen other questions that didn't matter right then. He'd told her he was tired, but she hadn't taken the hint. She hadn't even really seemed to hear. She'd kept cocking her head as if listening for something. She was doing the same thing now, dishcloth hovering in her hand, soapsuds dripping on the floor.

Cathy's eyes slid across to Jake's empty bowl. 'Would you like anything else, darling?'

'No, thanks.'

'I'll make you some toast.'

'I'm not hu—' Jake started to say but broke off. Although the last thing he needed was her fussing over him, he didn't have the heart to stop her. She clearly needed to keep herself busy, keep from thinking too much.

At the sound of tyres crunching gravel, a plate clattered from Cathy's hand and she ran to the front door, closely followed by

Jake. Her face dropped when she saw Tom getting out of a police car. 'Where's Amanda?'

Tom looked past her as if she didn't exist. There was a strange intensity in his eyes. They seemed to be searching Jake's face for something.

Jake blinked uneasily 'What is it, Dad?'

'The police are coming to search the house. They're going to be taking away anything they think might help find your sister. So if you don't want them to see what's on your laptop, I suggest you take it with you when you leave.'

Jake darted a nervous glance at the street. He wasn't thinking about his laptop. He was thinking about the diary. 'Leave? Where am I going?'

'To your grandparents' house. I want you to stay there until this is over. Go get your stuff together.'

As Jake turned to head upstairs, Cathy asked again more insistently, 'Where's Amanda?'

Tom's reply stopped Jake in his tracks. 'In hospital.'

'Why?' gasped Cathy. A confrontational note edged her voice. 'And why aren't you there with her?'

'She fainted.' Tom's mouth thinned bitterly. 'And you can ask her yourself why I'm not there.' His features softened as he clocked Jake looking at him anxiously. 'Your mum's OK, Jake. Like I said, she just fainted. Now go on.'

With a knot like a fist in his stomach, Jake rushed up to his room. Almost as unsettling as the thought of his mum fainting was the way his dad had spoken about her. It was as if he hated her. Thrusting the diary, his laptop and iPad into a rucksack, he wondered what had happened. What had she done? As he hurried to retrieve the nest box, the sound of raised voices came from downstairs. He caught a few words of his grandma's: '. . . to God she'd never married you!' Then the back end of his dad's reply: '. . . yourself, you stuck-up old bitch.' His dad's and grandma's dislike of each other had only ever been hidden under a thin veneer of civility. But even when it occasionally pushed its way to the surface, they would argue through gritted smiles. He'd never heard them at each other's throats with such open animosity before.

He descended the stairs, banging his feet so they'd hear. Tom and Cathy fell silent, looking daggers at each other. 'I need to talk to *my son* alone,' Tom said, almost as if he was daring Cathy to challenge his words.

'I'll wait for you in the car, Jake,' said Cathy. Pointedly avoiding Tom's eyes, she left the house with her chin in the air.

Jake found himself tensing up as his dad turned to him. There was that strange intensity again. Tom motioned for Jake to put down the box. He caught hold of his arm and pulled him into an uncomfortably tight hug. Jake could feel tremors running through his dad. 'I love you so much,' said Tom, his voice constricted. 'You and your sister are the best thing that ever happened to me.'

'What about Mum?' asked Jake. 'You still love Mum, don't you?'

'I . . .' Tom faltered. 'I'll always love her for giving me you.' Reluctantly, he released Jake. He stared at him for a moment as if waiting for him to say something. Lips compressing into a white line, he gestured for him to get going.

Jake picked up the box and headed to the Mini. 'Are you OK?' Cathy asked as if she suspected Tom might have hurt him in some way.

Jake nodded. Suddenly it occurred to him what his dad had been waiting for him to say – *I love you too*. He felt a pang of regret. His dad was always saying it to him, but he never said it back. He just took it for granted, like everything else. Why did he do that? Why couldn't he ever just say what his dad needed to hear? He reached for the door handle, but it was too late. His grandma was already reversing out of the driveway. He twisted in his seat, not breaking eye contact with his dad until they turned a corner.

As Cathy drove, she kept jabbing at her mobile phone. 'Bloody forest,' she muttered.

'Who are you phoning?' asked Jake.

'Your granddad, but there's no reception out—' She broke off as Henry's voice came through on loudspeaker, low and crackly.

'What is it, Cathy?'

'Henry, at last! I thought I'd never get through. It's Amanda. She's—'

'You'll have to speak up,' interrupted Henry. 'The line's bad.'

Cathy's voice rose almost to a shout. 'Amanda's in hospital. She's had some kind of collapse.'

'Did you say Amanda's in hospital?'

'Yes. Tom says she fainted, but I don't—' Cathy broke off with a sidelong glance at Jake, as if she'd been about to say something she didn't want him to hear.

'Don't what?'

'I don't know what's going on. Tom's in an absolute rage. Something's obviously happened between them.'

There was a silence as if Henry was mulling over what that 'something' might be. 'Where are you now?'

'I'm on my way home. Jake's with me.'

'OK, good. Drop him off and head over to the hospital. I'll meet you there.'

'Can't I come with you?' asked Jake.

'No, Jake, I think it's best if your grandma and I speak to your mum first,' said Henry.

It was on the tip of Jake's tongue to protest, but it occurred to him that this was the perfect opportunity to meet up with Lauren.

'I'll see you soon, Cathy,' said Henry. 'And try not to worry too—' The line broke up and went dead.

'Try not to worry,' Cathy parroted with a shake of her head. 'How am I supposed not to worry? This is . . . It's . . .' she trailed off, lost for words. Tears traced a path through the fine lines beneath her eyes. She wiped them away and squeezed Jake's hand. 'Take no notice of me, darling. Your granddad's right. We have to stay positive.' She nodded as if to reinforce her words, but there was little conviction behind it.

When they arrived at Ritton Hall, Cathy entered a code into a keypad and the gates swung inwards. She pulled up to the house, removed a key from a keyring and gave it to Jake. 'That's for the front door. If you're hungry, there's plenty of food. I'll try not to be too long.'

She leaned across to peck Jake's cheek. He watched her drive off, before going inside. He silenced the beeping alarm pad and headed upstairs past portraits of previous owners of the house dating all the way back to its builder, Mayhew Ritton – a grim-faced man with brown pageboy hair. Being alone in the house usually gave him the jitters. It was easy to imagine the portraits' eyes following you along the gloomy, echoing hallways. But right then he had other things to worry about. Real things.

He put the nest box in the airing cupboard and took a quick peek to make sure the chick was OK. Then he went to the bedroom he always used when he stayed over – a smallish room in the oldest part of the house with uneven oak floorboards and a low crooked-beamed ceiling. There was a stone fireplace, a mahogany dressing table and an antique bed. A lead-lattice window overlooked a cascading fountain in the middle of the rear lawn. Erin had loved to play in the fountain as a toddler. On hot days she used to splash about naked and laughing with him chasing her.

He took out the diary and iPad. He slid the diary under the mattress and FaceTimed Lauren. She answered on the first ring. Her eyes were pasted in their customary black mascara. Her lips glistened with black gloss. She was kitted out in her camo jacket and, Jake noticed with a twinge of irritation, her blue-eye charm necklace that supposedly warded off evil spirits.

Jake pointed at the necklace. 'Why are you wearing that bullshit?'

'I don't think it's bullshit. And neither did you until now.'

'Take it off.' When Lauren hesitated to do so, he added, 'Remember what we agreed. I'm calling the shots.'

Rolling her eyes, Lauren removed the necklace. With a suggestive lift of her eyebrows, she asked, 'Satisfied, or do you want me to take anything else off?'

'Yes . . . No . . . You know what I mean,' said Jake, stumbling back into his usual awkwardness. Annoyed with himself for letting her wind him up, he snapped, 'Look, just meet me at the park in ten minutes.'

He hung up and arranged the pillows beneath the sheets so it looked as if someone was sleeping in the bed. It wouldn't fool anyone on closer examination, but it might do the trick at a glance. As he approached the window, he caught sight of the fountain again. His eyes lingered on it for a few seconds. He yanked the curtains shut and hurried from the room.

DAY 2
8.23 A.M.

The searchers passed flasks of coffee among themselves in the shade at the edge of a football-pitch-sized clearing. Henry was on the phone out of their earshot. Seth watched him, his legs jigging. The altercation between Tom and Graham had left him so charged with energy he couldn't sit still.

'Something's going down,' remarked Holly. 'You don't think—' She broke off with a shake of her head, as if angry for allowing herself to entertain whatever thought was going through her mind.

Seth knew what she couldn't bring herself to ask. It was the same unspoken question that had hung like a black cloud over the searchers since Tom and Graham were taken away – did Graham have something to do with Erin's disappearance? The possibility was all too real. Turn on the news any day of the week and there were stories about family members abducting, abusing and murdering their 'loved ones'. Seth had once read an article that pointed out that statistically kids were far more likely to be killed by their parents than by a stranger. But the statistics didn't make it any easier to face up to. If anything, they seemed to make people bury their heads deeper in the sand. As if by ignoring the truth about themselves – that they were all just one misstep or piece of bad luck away from being monsters – it would go away.

Henry returned to the group grave-faced. 'I'm sorry, everybody, I have to leave. Hopefully I should be back before too long. In the meantime I'll put you in the hands of Eddie . . .' He frowned. 'Oh, we seem to be missing another member of our team.'

Seth quickly glanced all around. Eddie was nowhere to be seen. He remembered seeing him lighting a cigarette when the team stopped for a break. Then his attention had been taken up by Henry's phone call. Eddie must have slipped away some time after that.

'Did anyone see where he went?' asked Henry. There was a general shaking of heads. 'Well, then, someone else will have to take the lead.' Before anyone could volunteer, Henry's gaze landed on Seth. 'What about you, Seth? Are you up to the challenge?'

Part of Seth – the part most comfortable observing from the fringes – felt like making some excuse about not knowing the forest well enough. But another part – the part desperate for validation and acceptance – wanted to jump up and shout, *Yes!* Acutely aware that all eyes were on him, he did what he was best at – imitating Henry's expression, he nodded.

'Good lad.' Henry pressed a map, compass and walkie-talkie into Seth's hands. 'I've marked out the next search grid in red.' He gave Seth an almost fatherly pat on the shoulder. 'Good luck.'

Henry hurried away into the trees. Seth looked at all the eyes looking back at him. He'd gone through most of his life feeling disconnected from the people around him and, sometimes, even the ground he walked on. But the expectation in their eyes gave him a strange solid sensation, like a ghost made real.

They took up their positions. With the coming of daylight, they'd reverted to twenty-five-metre spacings. What's more, the search grid centred on a particularly dense stretch of forest. That suited Seth perfectly. He was going to need some privacy.

They headed into the trees to the north of the clearing. The ground climbed steadily with occasional dips into weed-choked runnels. Seth kept furtively checking his phone. The reception flickered between zero and one bar. There was no point attempting a call if the line was too poor for the friendly chat he had in mind. He picked his way through a patch of gorse to a pimple of grass topped by more bushes. As he climbed, the reception jumped to two bars. This was his chance. 'I'm just going to answer a call of nature,' he told his fellow searchers. He waited until they were out of sight, then dropped to his knees and crawled under the bushes. Nestling into a hollow formed by several sandy burrows, he took out the voice-changer box and placed it against his phone. He dialled but after several rings his call went through to a generic voicemail. Twitching with annoyance, he tried again. This time his call was answered on the second ring.

His robotically distorted voice demanded to know, 'Why didn't you pick up the first time?'

'I'm busy,' replied the man.

'Doing what?'

'What do you bloody think? Getting your money together.'

'You'd better be careful how you talk to me,' warned Seth.

A heavy sigh filled the line. 'Sorry. As you can imagine, I'm under a lot of stress. It's not easy to come up with a million in cash in twenty-four hours.'

'I have every confidence in you. If anyone can do it, you can.' Seth's voice was full of mocking encouragement. 'If the money's not in my hands in twelve hours you know what happens.'

'You'll get it, so long as I get all the letters in return.'

'You will.'

'I'd better.' There was a warning in the man's voice now.

'I told you to watch your mouth. One more remark like that and I might decide there are more important things in life than money.' Seth's tone was both flippant and threatening. But there was something else in it, too, something that might have been the faintest nervous tremor.

'You mean like love?' The same sick yearning that Seth had noticed during their previous conversation was back in the man's voice. 'You know, she's the only thing I've ever truly loved. I'd give every last penny I have to see her again. To touch her, to run my fingers over her milk-white skin, but most of all, to look in her eyes—'

'Shut up,' snapped Seth. His voice was thick with repulsion, but there was a deep throbbing in his groin. 'Love is a lie.'

The man chuckled softly. 'If only you were right. Then we wouldn't be having this conversation. But love isn't a lie. It's a sickness. An addiction. Once it's got its hooks into you, you'll do anything for it.'

Seth flinched at the sound of twigs crunching outside the bushes. He hung up just before Holly called out, 'Seth, where are you?'

He puffed his cheeks. Shit, that was close. A heartbeat later and the whole game would have been up. He wormed his way out of the bushes.

Holly's eyebrows drew together. 'What are you doing down there?'

'I thought Erin might have crawled in here.'

As Seth stood up, Holly brushed his fringe out of his eyes. 'Your hair's a mess.'

At her touch, the throbbing intensified irresistibly. Before Seth even knew what he was doing, his arms were around Holly and he was pulling her to him, mashing his mouth against hers. His heart soared as her lips parted in reciprocation. But an instant later it plunged back to earth. 'Whoa, whoa, stop,' she said, drawing away as he thrust a hand up inside her shirt.

He didn't want to stop. He wanted to run his hands all over her. Trembling with the effort of not giving in to his desire, he said, 'I thought this was what you wanted.'

'We're here to find a missing girl, not—'

'I understand,' Seth cut in, the burning in his face turning from arousal to humiliation. He pivoted away from Holly and stalked towards the search line.

'Wait, Seth,' she called after him.

But he didn't wait. He quickened his pace, muttering, 'A lie. A big fat fucking lie.'

DAY 2
8.30 A.M.

As the police car passed beyond the outskirts of Middlebury, Tom re-sent the same text to Eddie for the tenth time in as many minutes. 'On my way to Gallows Hill Wood. Meet me at my car asap.' There was the ping of a return text. 'Will do.' It had been sent at 8.20. 'How long do you think Inspector Shields will hold my wife and brother for?' he asked Constable Hutton.

'They can be held for up to twenty-four hours without charge,' she replied non-committally.

'That's not what I asked.'

'It really depends on them. If they cooperate fully, they may only be held for a short time.' The constable glanced knowingly at Tom. 'It would be advisable for you to stay away from both of them for now.'

Tom stared darkly out of the window. He had no intention of following Constable Hutton's advice. A couple of TV news vans passed by, heading in the opposite direction. He wondered whether they'd got wind of what was happening at the station. Five or so minutes later, Constable Hutton turned into Gallows Hill Wood. It was deserted now, except for a lone constable watching over the assemblage of emergency service and volunteers' vehicles.

'Are you sure you don't want me to take you to the main forest?' Constable Hutton asked as Tom opened the passenger door.

'This'll do just fine.'

The constable treated Tom to another cautioning look, before putting the car into reverse. He approached his Volvo. There was a conspicuous space behind it where Graham's Land Rover had been parked. Had it been taken away for examination? Eddie jogged into view, sweaty and breathless. 'I got here as fast as I could. What the hell's going on?'

Tom motioned for him to get in the car so they could talk without being overheard. 'I need you to go back to Middlebury and park yourself between the hospital and the police station.'

'Why?'

'Because Amanda's in the hospital and Graham's at the station. I want to know about it the second either of them leaves.'

Eddie frowned. 'The hospital. What's Amanda doing there?'

'She pulled a little fainting stunt.'

Eddie's concern turned to surprise at Tom's scathing tone. 'Why would she do that? And what's with the attitude?'

Tom sucked in his breath, gathering himself to say what he could still barely believe was true. 'Her and Graham. They're fucking.'

Eddie's jaw slackened. 'Are you sure?'

Tom knew what he was thinking. It wasn't simply the fact Graham was his brother that made it so difficult to believe. Graham was such a dour, humourless man. A joyless sheep-shagger was how Eddie had once described him. And Amanda was . . . well, she was everything he wasn't – beautiful, vivacious. What could she possibly see in someone like him? 'Yes, I'm sure.' Tom gripped the steering wheel as if he wanted to tear it out. 'It gets worse.'

'How can it possibly get any worse?'

'They were on the phone to each other when Erin went missing. What if Erin overheard? What if . . .' Tom trailed off. He couldn't bring himself to voice any more of the *what ifs* in his mind.

'Hold on. Just hold on a sodding minute. You can't be suggesting they've got anything to do with all this.'

'I don't know what I'm suggesting. All I know is Amanda lied to the police and I'm going to find out why.'

'Isn't it obvious why? To keep you from finding out what they were up to.'

Tom stared at Eddie, his eyes desperate to believe but swimming with doubt.

'Now you listen to me,' Eddie continued firmly. 'I've known Amanda as long as you have. And I'm telling you she'd rather die than let any harm come to her children. And as for Graham, well, I have to admit the bastard's surprised me. I didn't think he had it in him.' There was a kind of perverse respect in his voice. 'But him hurt your Erin?' He shook his head. 'I'll tell you who's behind this. Carl Wright and the rest of them fanatics. And when we roll into their camp a few hours from now, they're gonna give us the truth, the whole truth and nothing but the fucking truth. Or we're gonna decorate the quarry with their teeth. What do you say, Tom? Are you with me?'

Tom was motionless for a moment. Then he nodded.

'And once we're done with those eco-pricks, we'll deal with Graham,' added Eddie.

'No. I'll deal with him alone. First chance I get.' Tom's voice was heavy with hostile intent.

'Just so long as you're ready when the Geordies get here.'

'You don't have to worry about that.'

Eddie scrunched his features as if an unpleasant image had popped into his mind. 'Amanda and Graham. I just can't wrap my brain around it.'

'You and me both.' Tom's gaze strayed beyond Eddie. 'Well, well, look who it is.'

Henry was hurrying through the woods, head down, lost in frowning thought. He passed Tom's car without looking up and climbed into his Range Rover.

'I bet he's going to the hospital,' said Eddie as Henry reversed towards the main road.

'It's time we got going too.'

Eddie got out of the car, then ducked his head back in. 'What are you going to do?'

'I'm going to find out what else that joyless sheep-shagger's been up to.'

'I'll head back via Netherwitton. See if I can beat the old fart to town.' Eddie darted to a souped-up BMW. The wheels kicked up dirt as he accelerated away. Tom struggled to keep up in his Volvo.

Eddie raced straight on at the crossroads. Tom turned left, flooring the accelerator on the straight descent to Rothley Lakes. A few minutes later he was juddering along the rutted track to Graham's farm. He jerked to a stop at the gate, sprang out and ran towards the pebble-dash house. A restless baaing of hungry sheep came from the barn. The flock should have been put out to pasture hours ago. Tom's nose wrinkled at the smell of wool and dung. It didn't end, he knew, at the house's front door. The whole place was saturated in it. As a teenager he used to spend hours in the bathroom, scrubbing himself until his skin was red raw, paranoid that the stink would become permanently ingrained in his pores.

He inserted a key into the door. His father – a doggedly fair man – had left half the flock to him. He'd insisted Tom hold onto the key in the forlorn hope that one day he would change his mind about his inheritance. Tom had never asked Graham to buy him out or for a share in the meagre profits. But all that was going to change. He stepped into a stone-flagged hallway. A flight of stairs carpeted in threadbare green led upwards. To the left and at the far end of the hallway were chipped and scuffed white doors. The walls were papered in cream Anaglypta that Tom could vaguely remember their dad pasting up. Several pairs of mud-encrusted wellies were lined up beneath some pegs with a jumble of wax jackets, scarves and hats hanging on them. Tom spotted their dad's favourite flat cap. He peered into a living room furnished with a well-worn three-piece suite, an old TV and bookshelves stuffed with their dad's sheep-breeding and fly-fishing books and their mum's cheap romance novels. Tom shook his head. Why couldn't his brother let go of all this junk? Perhaps if he had he would have been able to make a life for himself without trying to steal someone else's.

A grey-tiled mantelpiece was crowded with photographs, some in frames, others merely balanced against the wall. There were faded photos of his parents – his dad straight-backed, broad-shouldered, craggy-faced, inexpressive; his mum almost equally heavy set, short dark hair, round placid face. His gaze passed quickly over them to photos of himself, Amanda, Jake and Erin. There was a photo of them all in front of a Christmas tree, which Amanda had sent out to relatives a few years before. And there were photos of the kids dating back to when they were in nappies. There was also a recent-looking photo of Amanda standing in front of some pine trees, her face lit up by the sparkly-eyed smile he'd fallen in love with.

His jaw twitching, Tom pocketed the photos of himself and his family. He moved through to the dining room. Four mismatched chairs were pushed under an oak table in the middle of a purple swirled rug. A pendulum clock ticked on the wall above a glass-doored cabinet filled with the china his mum had reserved for special occasions. Everything neat and tidy. Nothing out of place. It was the same in the kitchen with its ancient gas cooker, Welsh dresser stacked with crockery, walls hung with pans, deep ceramic sink, and Bob's food and water bowls next to the grubby duvet he slept on.

Tom headed upstairs. He stuck his head into what had once been his parents' bedroom. To all intents and purposes, it still was their bedroom – same iron-framed double bed, same crucifix on the wall above it, same floral eiderdown, same faded yellow curtains. It was as if twenty minutes not twenty years had passed since he'd last been in there. He looked in Graham's bedroom next – neatly made single bed, a chest of bedside drawers. Tom opened the top drawer. His jaw squeezed so tight it felt as if his teeth would shatter. Amanda stared up at him from a photo. She was stretched out on Graham's bed wearing only skimpy underwear – underwear Tom had never seen before. In a second photo her mouth was wide with laughter and her hands were raised as if to hide her face.

Tom thrust the photos into his pocket. He wrenched out the other drawers and upended their contents – socks, boxer shorts, unopened condoms, lube. Sweet strawberry flavoured lube! It made him want to retch with rage. He stalked from the room to a shabby little bathroom. There were no photos waiting to torture him in there. He punched open the door to his old bedroom. Unlike the rest of the house, it bore no resemblance to when he'd lived there. Where his bed had been there was a cheap-looking MDF desk with a computer and printer on it. Somehow he wasn't surprised that his were the only belongings Graham could bear to part with.

He took out the photos of Amanda. Her laughing face, the underwear. Oh, Christ, it was too much. He squeezed his eyes shut, but the images were branded onto his retinas. A thought gouged its way into his mind. An idea. Graham had taken what he loved. And now he would return the favour.

Tom descended to the kitchen. The box of rat poison was in the same place it had always been – the highest shelf of the walk-in pantry. He snatched it down and stalked to the barn. The sheep were penned in behind a rusty gate. They milled about nervously as he climbed up to the hayloft. He toppled a bale of hay over the edge of the loft, scattering the sheep. He jumped down and broke up the bale. He opened the box of rat poison, but hesitated to upend it. The flock of white-faced Cheviots was relatively small compared to some in the area, but his dad had been immensely proud of it. The lineage of many of the breeding ewes could be traced back through generations of Jacksons to the late 1800s. That entire heritage, all the countless hours of caring and nurturing would be lost in a moment if he did this. He stood, caught between this thought and the image of Amanda on the bed. His mind returned to the photos of his parents. Their eyes seemed to stare at him, not judging, just sad. He couldn't do it to them, no matter how much he wanted to hurt Graham. Grinding his teeth in frustration, he flung the box aside. The sound of engines drew him outside.

Several police vehicles were pulling up behind his car. Among them was a van marked FORENSIC INVESTIGATION. A constable got out of it and asked, 'Mr Jackson, what are you doing here?'

'Same thing as you.'

'Have you been in the house?'

'Yes. I have a key.'

'And have you moved anything inside?'

Tom shook his head. There was no way Graham was getting back the photos. Just the thought of him looking at them made Tom want to pound his fists into something. 'Did my brother give you permission to search the farm?'

'Yes.'

Tom wondered whether he should be relieved. Surely that meant Graham had nothing more to hide.

'You're going to have to leave,' continued the constable. 'We're sealing off this property until our investigation is complete.'

Tom returned to his car. He didn't glance at the farm in the rear-view mirror. He never wanted to see the place again. When he reached the main road, he braked and sat motionless behind the wheel. He suddenly felt utterly lost. He stared at a landscape he'd known all his life as if he was seeing it for the first time. *Where now?* he wondered. *Where do I go from here?*

DAY 2
9.11 A.M.

One of Cathy's hands rested on Amanda's shoulder, the other was pressed anxiously to her own mouth. When the curtain swished open and Henry entered the cubicle, she exclaimed, 'Thank God you're here, Henry. I don't know what to do. She won't talk to me. She just keeps staring at the wall.'

Henry made a calming motion. He stooped to kiss Amanda's temple, murmuring, 'It's all right, darling. Daddy's here now.'

'Daddy.' Amanda's voice was a tremulous whisper. Her eyes slid round to his, almost lost in tears. 'I've ruined everything. I'm a terrible, terrible person.'

'That's not true.'

'Yes, it is. I've betrayed Tom. I've done something . . .' A sob swallowed her words.

'It doesn't matter what you've done, darling. You're my daughter and I'll always love you.'

Amanda closed her eyes, shaking her head as if she didn't deserve such unconditional love.

Henry stroked her hair. 'You're too good for him.'

'Am I?' Amanda's tone suggested she thought it was the other way around.

'Yes, you are. When Tom asked my permission for your hand in marriage, I gave it because I knew saying no wouldn't stop you. You're a Brooks. And when we want something, nothing stands in our way. But I always knew it would come to this one day. How can a man like him expect to keep a woman like you?'

'A woman like me? You mean a selfish bitch.'

'You're a Brooks,' Henry said again, as if the name raised her above criticism. 'And now it's time for you to come back to where you belong.'

'What do you mean?'

'I want you and the children to come and live with us.'

'Children,' Amanda said like an empty echo.

Henry took her hand, his grip firm with resolve. 'We're going to find Erin. And we're going to put this behind us.' He added meaningfully, 'All of it.'

'But Tom—'

'Forget Tom. I don't want to hear his name any more. As far as I'm concerned, you're no longer a Jackson. And neither are the children.'

Amanda gave a hard shake of her head. 'I may be a bitch but I could never do that to him.'

'We'll discuss this later. Now come on. On your feet. This is no place for you to be. You need to be with Jake.'

Pushing her exhaustion aside with a deep breath, Amanda swung her feet off the bed. Henry handed Cathy his car keys. 'I'm parked at the main entrance. Bring my car around the back. Be careful no one follows you. There are a few journalist types hanging about reception.'

She nodded and hurried from the cubicle. Henry and Amanda made to follow. With an apologetic look, Constable Foster barred their path. 'Sorry, Mr Brooks, but Inspector Shields requests that Mrs Jackson remain here.'

Henry's bushy eyebrows drew together. 'You know that nothing happens around here without my say-so, Mike. Houses don't get built, business licences aren't granted, constables don't become sergeants.'

Constable Foster shifted uneasily, but held his ground.

'Inspector Shields only said it would be best if I remained here,' put in Amanda.

'In that case my daughter is within her rights to leave,' said Henry. 'Now if you'd please step aside.'

Constable Foster hesitated a moment longer, then turned his body to let them by.

'Thank you, Mike. We Middlebury men don't forget our friends.'

Henry extended his hand and Constable Foster shook it. 'I have to inform Inspector Shields that Mrs Jackson left.'

'Of course you do. And you can also let him know my daughter will be staying at my house from now on.'

As they headed for the rear entrance, Amanda said with a contemptuous lift of her lips, 'Some things never change in this town.'

'That's very true,' agreed Henry. 'Never forget that.'

Cathy shifted over to allow Henry to take the Range Rover's steering wheel. 'What about my car?' she asked as they pulled around the front.

'We'll fetch it later when there are less of them around.' Henry motioned to the news crews thronging the police station car park. 'Better keep your head down, Amanda.'

She lay herself flat on the back seat.

'Look at them,' Cathy said with a shudder. 'Like flies on muck.'

Henry met the gaze of a stocky, bearded man leaning against the bonnet of a BMW. The man rose onto his tiptoes to peer into the Range Rover. Henry pushed harder on the accelerator. When the station was out of sight, he said, 'You can sit up now, Amanda.'

Amanda remained lying on the seat. 'The kids are going to need their clothes and . . . and . . .' She faded off. The haunted blankness was back in her eyes.

'Don't you worry about any of that. Your mother and I will sort it all out.'

'Please, darling, try to pull yourself together,' said Cathy. 'We don't want Jake to see you like this, do we now? He's worried enough about you as it is.'

With seeming great effort, Amanda raised herself into a sitting position. She rubbed her hands vigorously over her face as if washing something away.

'Here we are,' said Henry when the tall gates and golden-stoned walls of Ritton Hall came into view. 'Home.'

'Home,' Amanda parroted as if she was trying to work out what the word meant.

The gates swung inwards and the Range Rover crunched along the driveway. Henry and Cathy got out. Amanda remained seated, staring at the house with a kind of disbelief, like someone returning to a place they'd thought they would never see again. 'Come on, darling,' said Henry, coaxing her out as if she was a nervous dog.

Cathy entered the house. 'Jake, we're home. Your mum's with us.' There was no reply. She turned to Henry and Amanda. 'He must be sleeping. The poor darling's absolutely wiped out. I'll go up and look in on him.'

'It's OK, Mum,' said Amanda. 'I'll go.'

She wearily climbed the stairs and cracked open the door to Jake's room. A shape was dimly visible beneath the bedsheets. She felt a need to see Jake's face, but the covers were pulled up over his head. She didn't want to risk disturbing him by lifting them. Not after what he'd been through last night, and what he was going to have to face when he woke. Tears were suddenly rushing to her eyes. She barely had time to close the door before her sobs broke free. She sank to the floor, burying her face in her hands.

DAY 2
9.12 A.M.

A familiar wisp of smoke curled from the wooden playground house. Jake climbed the ladder awkwardly, hopping his good hand up the rungs. Lauren blew a surprised puff of smoke at the sight of him. 'What happened to your arm?'

'I fell through the floor at the Ingham house.'

'Shit. You're lucky you didn't die. Does it hurt?'

'Not much.'

Jake sat down next to Lauren and accepted the half-smoked cigarette. It tasted of her lipstick. Lauren eyed his hair. 'It looks like you were attacked by some seriously pissed-off scissors.'

'Can we not talk about my hair?'

'So what do you want to talk about?'

'My mum's in hospital. She fainted or something.'

'This whole situation's so messed up.' Lauren took back the cigarette, sucked in a drag and flicked the stub out of the playhouse. 'So let's see the diary.'

'I haven't got it with me.'

Her face fell. 'Why not?'

'In case we get picked up by the police again. I didn't want to risk having it taken away.'

'I suppose that makes sense,' Lauren begrudgingly conceded. 'But I get to read it straight after we've checked out Mary's house, right?'

Jake nodded, although he'd already decided Lauren would only get her hands on the diary once he'd finished reading it.

She jumped to her feet. 'So let's go see what the old witch has been up to.'

They made their way across town, sticking to quiet streets. Pretty little cottages gave way to an estate of pebble-dashed council houses – mostly semis, postage-stamp front gardens, no driveways.

'That's Mary's place.' Lauren pointed to a little bungalow backing onto woods. The garden was so overgrown that bushes masked the windows. Several cats were stretched out in splotches of sun on the mossy garden path. Others were prowling lazily around. Jake counted twelve at a glance.

'She definitely likes cats,' he observed.

'Especially black ones,' Lauren added meaningfully.

Jake gave her an irritated look. 'Why do you keep making out like she's some kind of witch? You were the one mouthing off about all the small-minded pricks around here treating her like a freak.'

'Witches aren't freaks. I think they're pretty cool, so long as they're not casting spells on me.'

Jake rolled his eyes. 'We need to get around the back.'

Lauren led him along a footpath shadowed by oak trees. A sagging fence bearded with ivy just barely divided the bungalow's back garden from the woods. A path had been hacked through bushes to a glass-doored porch. Newspaper was taped to the inside of the glass. A fat ginger tomcat lounged on the porch roof, like a lookout ready to pounce on any unwanted visitors.

'How are we supposed to know if she's in?' wondered Jake.

Lauren pointed out a thread of pale smoke coming from the chimney. 'I guess that means she's probably in. So what now?'

'We wait for her to go out.'

'What if she doesn't leave the house today?'

Jake thought for a moment, then shrugged.

'I'll tell you what we should do,' continued Lauren. 'We should knock and run.'

'Knock and run. What are you, like ten years old or something?'

'Screw you.'

Jake stared at the bungalow. Several minutes crawled by. The ginger tom stretched, padded over the roof and jumped into a bush. A black cat took its place. 'Changing of the guard,' commented Jake.

Lauren crossed her arms, lips compressed in moody silence.

Nothing moved except the smoke curling from the chimney and the shadows shortening as the sun inched up the sky. 'What time is it?' asked Jake.

'Look for yourself,' muttered Lauren.

'My mum took away my phone, remember?'

Lauren glanced at her mobile. 'It's nearly ten.'

'Ten o'clock,' Jake said quietly. It had been twenty-four hours since Erin went missing. Had she had anything to eat or drink? How long could a person survive without food and water? He heaved a sigh. 'OK.'

'OK what?'

'OK, let's knock and run.'

DAY 2
9.21 A.M.

Tom flinched at the ringtone like someone jerked out of a trance. He pressed his phone to his ear. 'What is it, Eddie?'

'Amanda just left the hospital with her parents. From the direction they went in, I'd say they're taking her to their house. Graham's still in the cop shop. And if you ask me he'd be better off staying there. This place is crawling with journos.'

'Thanks, mate.'

Tom hung up and shoved his foot down on the accelerator. Ritton Hall was on the south side of town, closer to the station than him. But if he moved fast he might just beat them there. Some five minutes later he pulled up at the gates and swore to himself. Henry's Range Rover was already in the drive. He pressed the intercom button. Henry's voice came over the line. 'Who is it?'

'It's Tom. I want to speak to Amanda.'

'She's not here.'

The lie didn't surprise Tom one bit. Henry and Cathy had been waiting for this chance for years. 'Bullshit. Put her on.'

'She's not here,' repeated Henry, his voice hard and final. 'And even if she was, I don't think she'd want to speak to you.'

'I couldn't give a toss whether or not she wants to speak to me. I think I've earned the right to ask her a few questions, don't you?'

Tom waited for a reply, but the intercom was silent. Fury pounded in his face. If Amanda thought she could simply remove him from her life like a pet she'd grown bored of, she was very wrong. He reversed a few feet then accelerated into the gates. They clanged and vibrated, but held firm. He reversed again and accelerated harder. The left-hand gate bowed inwards. Ritton Hall's front door flew open and Henry came running out, purpling at the sight of the damaged gates.

'What the hell do you think you're doing!' he yelled.

'Either you let me talk to Amanda or I'm going to batter your gates down,' retorted Tom.

Cathy emerged from the house and called to her husband. 'Shall I phone the police?'

Henry held up a staying hand. 'You've got a choice,' he said to Tom. 'You can either leave or I can have you slung in jail.'

Tom smiled disdainfully. He didn't believe for one second that Henry would follow through on his threat. The whiff of scandal swirling around his family was already strong enough. He revved his engine and charged again, tearing the left-hand gate off its lower hinge. The driver-side airbag exploded into his face. Thrusting it aside, he saw a gap between the gates large enough to squeeze through. He got out, crunching shards of shattered headlight underfoot.

'You're out of your mind,' roared Henry. 'Do you know what? It wouldn't surprise me one little bit if you had something to do with Erin's disappearance.'

Tom's eyes swelled like storm clouds. He thrust himself between the gates and advanced on Henry, fists clenched.

Henry retreated several quick steps, his well-padded cheeks quivering. 'Call them, Cathy!'

'No.' Amanda thrust her head out of an upstairs window. 'I want to talk to him.'

She threw Tom a look that stopped him dead. He uncurled his fists, blinking away from her. Those green eyes always had a way of making him feel guilty, regardless of whether or not he was. From the first moment he'd looked into them, they'd made him feel all sorts of things – desire, nervousness, elation, love. But most of all they'd made him want to rise above who he was, become a better man, husband and father. Even now, with their marriage as broken as the gates, the thought ran through his mind, *Can I get us through this? Can I fix it somehow, if only for the kids?*

As they waited for Amanda to make her way downstairs, Cathy said haughtily to Tom, 'You should consider yourself lucky. You've had some of the best years of my daughter's life. But now it's over.'

Tom bit down on a retort. One thing was over for sure – his relationship with Henry and Cathy. No matter how things turned out, he was finished with them.

Amanda emerged from the house, looking as if she'd just stopped crying. 'I'd like to talk to my husband alone.'

'I really don't think you should be alone with this man,' said Henry.

'I've been married to this man for sixteen years, Dad. I think I'm a better judge than you as to whether it's safe for me to be alone with him.'

Henry's narrowed gaze returned to Tom. 'If you lay a single finger on my—'

'Dad,' Amanda broke in exasperatedly. 'Just go inside will you.'

Henry put his arm around Cathy and they went into the house. Amanda motioned for Tom to follow her. They crossed the lawn to a bench encircled by rose bushes. Amanda sat down. Tom remained standing.

'What do you want, Tom?' There was a contradictory mixture of shame and challenge in Amanda's eyes.

As he looked at her, one image twisted like a knife in his brain – an image of her and Graham thrusting against each other, slick with strawberry lube. 'How long has it been going on?'

'Not long. It started in January and I ended it a few weeks ago.'

'So the kids are mine.'

'Of course they're yours. If you don't believe me, we can do a DNA test or whatever to prove it.'

'The police are already doing one.'

Tom scoured Amanda's face for signs of intensified anxiety, but she merely heaved a sigh. 'Good.'

He knew then that she wasn't lying. Tom and Erin *were* his children. He might have wept with relief if there hadn't been another question clamouring to be asked. 'Why did you do this?'

Amanda struggled to maintain eye contact. 'What do you want me to say? I was lonely. I wanted to feel—'

'That's not what I'm asking. What I want to know is why it had to be with my fucking brother!' Tom snatched out Graham's photos and hurled them at Amanda's feet. Her eyes flashed with embarrassment.

'This is pointless. Nothing I can say is going to make you feel any better.'

'Maybe, but try anyway.'

'No. I don't think I want to.' There was a trace of her mother's haughtiness in Amanda's voice. 'I think it would be best for both of us if we just went our separate ways.'

She started to rise, but Tom caught hold of her arm. 'You don't get off that easy.'

The embarrassment transformed in a blink to anger. She spoke slowly through her teeth. 'Let go.'

'Or what? What could you possibly do that would hurt me any more than you already have.'

'I could tell you the truth about why I did what I did. Is that what you really want?'

Tom hesitated to reply. Did he really want to have to live with that particular truth? Maybe it would be better to say no. He knew, though, that if he did he would always be stuck in this moment. 'Yes.'

'The truth is I wanted to hurt you as badly as possible for turning out to be just another little man. You may hate my father, but you and he are the same. All you care about is getting what you want. That's why he made sure you got planning permission. He knew the quarry would bring us nothing but grief.'

Tom's face wrinkled doubtfully. He found it difficult to believe even Henry was that cynical.

Amanda continued with a despairing edge, 'You just can't see it, can you? Your brother does. He may not have your ambition, but he knows what's really important. He'd never treat someone like a trophy to be put in a cabinet and only brought out when you need something to show off.'

'Neither would I.'

Amanda arched an eyebrow. 'I'm being truthful here, Tom. It's about time you did the same.'

'I fell in love with you before I knew who your father was. Remember?'

'Yes, but you've always used me to remind yourself how far you've come and to push yourself to go further. At least with Graham I'm a . . .' Amanda sought for the right words, 'a real person. Not a symbol.'

'Then why did you break it off with him?'

'Because I don't love him. I love you.' Amanda shook her head sardonically. 'What does that say about me, eh?'

They stared at each other for a long moment. *Oh, Christ, those eyes*, thought Tom. He could hardly bear to look into them, but neither could he bring himself to look away. The emerald irises were suddenly glistening with tears. Amanda yanked her arm free and turned away, saying, 'Anyway, none of this really matters right now, does it? The only thing that matters is finding Erin.'

'Maybe Graham can help with that.'

'He's your brother. You can't possibly think he's capable of hurting Erin.'

'It seems I don't know what either of you are capable of.'

Amanda darted Tom a horrified look. 'Are you insinuating I've got something to do with Erin's disappearance?'

'No, of course not,' he said quickly. 'Not directly.' All the *what ifs* forced their way up his throat again. 'But what if Erin cottoned on to what you've been up to and ran away because of it? Or what if Graham's using her to get back at you?'

Amanda came back at him with one of her own. 'What if we were right about Carl Wright? What if this is indirectly your fault?'

The *what ifs* hung between them like accusing fingers. 'It's impossible to know what to think,' conceded Tom. What I do know is that yesterday morning I had a wife and a family and today—' Emotions strangled his words. Now it was his turn to look away and hide his tears.

'You still do have a family.' There was a pained tenderness in Amanda's voice. 'No matter what happens between us, I'd never take the kids away from you. You'll always be able to see them whenever you want.'

Tom jerked his unshaven chin at the house. 'Not if they have their way.'

'That's not going to happen, because the kids aren't going to be brought up here.' Amanda made a sweeping motion. 'This isn't what I want for them. I know that's as difficult for you to understand as it is for my parents.'

Tom took in the sprawling gardens and imposing house. He thought of everything he'd had and everything he'd lost. 'No, it's not.' His voice was thick with regret. 'Not any more.' Without letting his eyes return to Amanda, he started towards the gates.

'Where are you going?'

'Back to the forest. Where else is there for me to go?'

'Tom.'

Something in her voice – something almost pleading – made him look over his shoulder.

'I know I have no right to ask, but do you still love me?'

A silence passed. Then Tom said, 'Yes', and continued walking, his pace quickening, his face creased with confusion as if he wasn't sure whether he was hurrying towards or away from something.

DAY 2
9.57 A.M.

'So how do you want to do this?' asked Lauren.

'I'll knock,' said Jake. 'You stay here and keep lookout.'

'See you in a minute. Unless she turns you into a toad or something.'

Jake frowned at Lauren and she wiggled her eyebrows provocatively.

The neighbouring bungalow was screened from sight by overgrown buddleias that made Jake think of the Ingham house. His gaze fell to a crude little gate of sticks tied together with frayed string and wire. He had to admit there was definitely something witchy about it. He opened the gate and furtively approached the back door. Soft rustlings came from the bushes. Peering into them, he glimpsed slanted luminous eyes staring back. He recalled something he'd read about witches. How some had the power to change into animal form and others could see through the eyes of their familiars. *Screw all that bullshit,* he thought. Mary was simply a messed-up little girl who'd grown into a messed-up woman. The question was – how messed up?

He pulled back a branch from the windows. Faded curtains were drawn across them. The black cat eyeballed him from the flat roof that sheltered the back door. Half expecting the cat to pounce on him, he hammered on the back door. He sprinted for the gate and ducked down beside Lauren.

'So what do you reckon?' he asked after a minute or so.

'She's either not in or she's not answering her door.'

'Do you think we should try again?'

'What for? If she doesn't want to answer the door, it won't matter how hard you knock. There's only one way we're going to find out what's in there.'

'If we get caught we'll be in deep shit. I think you should stay out here.'

Lauren's eyebrows angled into a V. 'We're best mates, right?'

'Yeah, so?'

'So best mates always have each other's back. No way am I letting you go in there alone. Besides, you haven't got a clue how to break into somewhere.'

'Neither have you.'

'Yeah, I do. The first thing you need is one of these.' Lauren produced a screwdriver from her pocket.

Jake couldn't help but smile. He felt a flicker of guilt at how harsh he'd been about the diary.

'Wipe that dopey look off your face and let's go see what we can see,' she said.

They slunk to the back door. Lauren wiggled her hand at the cat, palm down, little finger and index finger extended like horns, the other fingers folded under her thumb – a gesture Jake knew was supposed to ward off the evil eye. The cat slitted its eyes at them, seemingly unconcerned.

Lauren turned her attention to the door. 'It said online that it's easier to remove a window than break a lock.' She pushed the tip of the screwdriver into the flaking putty at the bottom of the window pane. 'Now you just jimmy it around until the glass comes loose.'

She waggled the screwdriver up and down, shimmying it along the pane.

'It's working,' said Jake.

'Don't sound so surprised.'

A diagonal crack suddenly appeared in the pane. A triangle of glass toppled loose, pushing aside the newspaper and shattering on the floor inside the door. The cat darted nimbly away across the roof. Jake and Lauren listened for any indication that anyone else had heard the glass break. 'Whoops,' Lauren whispered after several breathless seconds. 'That wasn't supposed to happen.'

'No way is Mary in,' said Jake. 'Unless she's deaf.'

Lauren reached through the broken pane. There was the click of a key turning in a lock. With a triumphant glance at Jake, she opened the door.

Their noses ruckled at the fishy stench that wafted out to greet them. 'Urgh,' said Lauren, 'it smells worse than my nan's knickers.'

Jake would have laughed if his heart hadn't been beating so fast. Raising a finger to his lips, he padded into a small gloomy kitchen. Every available surface was stacked high with tinned cat food. Wherever there was a gap in the ranks of tins, it was filled by plates glistening with little mounds of jellied meat. Flies buzzed around the cat turds strewn over everything.

They picked their way to a dingy hallway carpeted with cat hair. More jumbles of tins climbed the dirty white walls. A path as thin as an animal track led to three doors. The nearest opened into a bathroom whose toilet was brown with welded-on shit. In place of loo roll, strips of torn newspaper were piled on the cistern. The bath was full of tatty towels and bundles of twigs. An ancient-looking cat was nested among them, pawing at a dead mouse.

'I'd rather sleep in the woods than live like this,' remarked Lauren.

'At least she doesn't have mice,' said Jake, turning to the next door. Beyond it was a room that stretched from the front to the back of the bungalow. The glow given off by embers in the fireplace revealed more of the same – cat food, cat hair, cat turds, furry forms sleeping and stalking in the shadows. The only furniture was an armchair that looked as if it had been dragged out of a skip. A dog-eared photo of the Ingham family was propped on the dusty mantelpiece – the same photo Jake had seen on the website of the Northumberland Society for Paranormal Investigation.

He pictured Mary Ingham sitting in the armchair night after night, staring at the photo of her family. The thought gave him a sad ache in his heart.

'Let's check out that other door,' said Lauren.

'Mary's Room. NO CATS ALLOWED!' warned spidery letters on the door. His nerves doing a jig, Jake opened it. The room was too dark to see more than a shadowy suggestion of its contents. A smell like musty cloth tickled their nostrils. He flipped a light switch. They were both silent for several stunned breaths. Then Lauren murmured, 'Fuck me, the whole town's here.'

An iron-framed single bed was made up with a lacy duvet and pillow, grey with age. Next to it was a table with an electric sewing machine on it. Sewing tools were neatly laid out on a cutting mat. Rolls of different coloured fabric were stacked beneath the table. Apart from the space it and the bed occupied, every bit of wall was covered with shelves of dolls. A few of the dolls had wide-eyed, rosebud-mouthed china faces, soft-pink and baby-blue frilly lace dresses and bonnets. They looked like the kind of thing you might see in an antique store or a wealthy child's nursery. The rest of the dolls – of which there must have been hundreds – were definitely not collectors' items. Like the effigy of Erin, they had stuffed bodies and oversized heads. There was a vicar and a postwoman. There were policemen, firemen, nurses and doctors. In addition to the uniformed dolls, there was a vast cast of characters in run-of-the-mill clothing of every kind. Their faces were even more detailed than their outfits. Mary Ingham – assuming she was their maker – had recreated with uncanny accuracy everything from her subjects' hair and eye colour, right down to birthmarks, blemishes, scars and dimples. Their features were exaggerated, but not to the point of caricature. It was more reminiscent of the work of a talented portrait painter. They ranged in age from babies to pensioners.

'Look, there's Mr Turnbull, the butcher.' Jake pointed to a stout doll in a red-and-white-striped pinafore. 'And that's definitely Zoe Parr from Year Ten. And isn't that Mrs Wardle, the geography teacher?'

'It's like a screwed up episode of *Postman Pat*.' Lauren looked at a little wooden table surrounded by six toddler-sized chairs. A doll was sitting on each of the chairs in front of a china tea cup and saucer. In the centre of the table was a teapot and a plate piled with plastic cupcakes. 'Do they remind you of anyone?'

One of the dolls was wearing a navy-blue suit and tie. He had short, centre-parted hair, a thick black moustache and a thin white face. Another was wearing a flowery dress with frills at the neck and sleeves. Her lips were set in a straight line that matched her cheerless eyes. Between these was a plumpish, pigtailed doll in a green dress. To either side of them were two even more familiar dolls. One was wearing a charcoal grey business suit with a light-pink pinstriped shirt and a blue tie. He had short black hair, dark eyes and, except for a bump on the bridge of his nose, good-looking, even features. The other was wearing cut-off blue jeans and a red vest top. Tousled auburn hair framed a face a little too angular to be pretty and eyes as green as a cat's.

A shudder crawled through Jake. He wasn't sure what disturbed him more – the image of his parents having tea with the Inghams or that their effigies were dressed identically to his actual parents on the morning Erin disappeared.

The sixth doll had its back to him, but its hair sticking up in punkish tufts, black T-shirt and skinny jeans were all the clues he needed to guess its identity. He moved around the table to look at its face – sullen eyes, sulky mouth, a few zits, a hint of bumfluff above the upper lip. *Do I really look like that?* he thought. *What an arsehole.*

'She must be watching you. She knows you've cut your hair,' pointed out Lauren.

Jake peered under the bed – more rolls of fabric, boxes of cotton thread, sewing needles, cotton wool, tins of model paint, paintbrushes, glue and myriad other craft items. All stored with an orderliness that seemed profoundly out of place compared to the rest of the bungalow. He saw Lauren pulling down the waistband of his doll lookalike's jeans. She grinned stupidly. 'Sorry, I couldn't resist.'

Jake sighed. 'So what now? Do I go to the police?'

'And say what? This is all weird as fuck, but there's no law against that or you'd have been arrested years ago.'

'This is more than just weird, Lauren. I want to know why I'm having tea with dead people.'

'Why does it have to mean something bad? You wouldn't invite someone you didn't like to a tea party, would you?'

'Not unless you wanted to poison them.'

'Fair point.' Lauren pushed out her lips. 'Hey, something just occurred to me. If Mary's watching you then—'

Jake finished her sentence for her, his voice quick with realisation. 'Then maybe she knows we're here!'

As one, they turned to the doorway. As one, their eyes flew wide and they gasped. Mary Ingham was staring at them from the hallway, dead-eyed, gaunt, twigs of matted hair sticking out in all directions, like something from one of the Grimms' Tales Jake's parents used to read him. She was wearing the tatty army-surplus jacket he'd seen her collecting berries in. A frayed floral dress showed off shins covered in scratches and a fuzz of hair. Her bare feet were black with dirt. A pair of cats wound their way between her legs, purring loudly.

Jake's first thought was to shove Mary aside and make for the back door. But her unblinking eyes held him rooted to the spot. They seemed to be looking right into him. He could almost feel them rummaging through the fear and confusion in his head. Lauren's voice broke the spell. 'The window,' she yelled, springing onto the bed.

Jake spun to follow her, but tripped over the little chairs. Scattering cups and saucers, he sprawled across the table. He scrambled to his feet, trampling the dolls. Lauren had opened the curtains only to reveal a wooden board. He jerked towards the doorway as Mary let out a strangled howl. She was rushing at him, goggle-eyed, arms outstretched. He flung up his hands to defend himself, but she scooped up the fallen dolls. Clutching all six to herself, she retreated to a corner, her eyes dancing between the intruders.

Jake and Lauren exchanged a glance. Mary didn't look angry. She looked scared. Lauren reached for a doll. Mary let out a low, plaintive moan. Lauren pulled back her hand. 'It's OK,' she said. 'We won't hurt them.' Motioning at the upended chairs, she said to Jake, 'Tidy that up.'

Keeping one eye on Mary, he stood the chairs up and arranged the tea set on the table. Mary moaned again as he collected the shards of a broken cup, her expression so pitiful that he found himself saying, 'Sorry.'

With a hand that looked as if it spent a lot of time digging in dirt, Mary made a quick *give them here* motion. He held out the shards. She snatched them from his palm and, tongue poking out of the corner of her mouth, began working out which piece fitted where. Lauren and Jake glanced at each other again. Mary's fear had given way to intense preoccupation. Lauren flicked her eyes towards the door. Jake shook his head. His fear had given way, too. He no longer wanted to make a run for it. He wanted to stay and discover what, if any, secrets Mary possessed.

Mary turned her attention back to the dolls, examining them like an over-anxious mother. Satisfied they hadn't been damaged, she suddenly seemed to remember she wasn't alone and her wariness returned.

'You don't need to be scared,' said Jake.

Mary stared at him uncertainly. She inched forward and set up the dolls of her parents and sister at the table, taking great care to position them just so. She returned the other three dolls to a shelf, seated herself on one of the unoccupied chairs and motioned for Jake and Lauren to do the same.

'I think we're invited to the tea party,' said Lauren.

Jake sank onto a chair. It was so low his knees poked in front of his chest. Lauren sat down beside him. Mary briefly closed her eyes and put her hands together in silent prayer. Then, as if undertaking some sacred ritual, she delicately poured invisible tea through a silver strainer into the cups, starting with her father and working clockwise around the table. Using cake tongs, she placed a cupcake in front of each guest. Like an attentive host anxious to please, she looked expectantly at Jake and Lauren. Lauren picked up her cup and pretended to take a sip, followed by a bite of cake. Trying not to feel too much of an idiot, Jake followed suit.

'This is lovely, Mary,' said Lauren, prompting Jake with a nudge in the ribs.

'Yes, the cakes are really delicious,' he agreed.

Mary broke into a gap-toothed smile, her eyes sparkling with the unaffected joy of an eight-year-old girl. She fed her parents and sister tea and cake, before taking a sip and nibble herself.

Jake cleared his throat nervously. 'Mary, I er . . . There's something I want to ask you. Why did you put that doll of my sister on our doorstep?'

Mary's smile faded and the leathery wrinkles on her forehead grew even deeper. She touched a hand to her chest, then gestured to Jake.

'It was a gift from her heart,' interpreted Lauren.

'Yes, but why?' persisted Jake.

'Excuse us a second, Mary,' said Lauren. She addressed the dolls. 'Excuse us, Mr and Mrs Ingham, Rachel.' She drew Jake away from the table to the hallway and whispered, 'Don't you get it? To her these dolls are as alive as you and me. So giving you Erin's doll was the same as giving you Erin.'

Jake had to admit Lauren's words made perfect sense in an insane kind of way. 'Where did you pull that one from?'

She grinned, pleased with herself. 'I guess I'm just a clever bitch.'

They returned to the table. Mary smiled again, the same sweet, innocent sparkle in her eyes that made it seem as if they occupied the wrong sockets. As she poured more tea, Jake asked, 'Mary, do you know where my sister is?'

She gave him a quizzical look and nodded.

Jake's voice quickened in time to his pulse. 'Where is she?'

Mary motioned at the effigies of Jake's parents. His heart sank in comprehension.

'I think she's saying Erin's with your parents,' said Lauren.

'Yeah, I get it,' sighed Jake. He looked at Mary. 'You've got to stop it. Do you understand? You've got to stop watching my family or you're going to get in big trouble.'

Mary stared blankly back like she didn't know what he was talking about. She turned to the doll of Elijah Ingham as if it had spoken to her, then her gaze returned to Jake and she nodded.

'Thanks. We've got to go now. I'm sorry we broke into your house. I promise I'll pay to fix your window.' Jake made to stand, but Lauren nudged him and indicated the dolls. Taking the hint, he said, 'Goodbye, Mr and Mrs Ingham.' His gaze lingered on the Rachel doll. It stared back with wide eyes that seemed to be looking to him for answers to unasked questions. 'Bye, Rachel.'

Lauren waved to the room. 'Bye, everyone.'

Mary followed them as far as the back door. Jake emerged blinking into the bright day. He took a deep breath, feeling as if he'd just emerged from a surreal daydream. He glanced at Mary as if to confirm she actually existed. That distant, dead look was back in her eyes. A cat nuzzled her legs, but she didn't seem to notice.

'Well, that was a trip,' said Lauren as they walked in the dappled shadows of the woods. 'Poor cow. Whoever did that to her deserves something really nasty to happen to them.'

Jake made a muted noise of agreement.

'What's up?' asked Lauren. 'I'd say that was a pretty successful bit of investigating, wouldn't you?'

He shrugged. They'd found out where the doll came from, but they hadn't got any closer to what he really wanted to know. He quickened his pace. 'I'd better get back before someone realises I'm gone.'

When they came within sight of Ritton Hall, Jake's eyes widened and he broke into a run. He poked at the bent gates and splinters of glass, a disturbing train of thought racing through his mind. Had someone broken into his grandparents' house? If so, what were they looking for? The diary? Did Mary know he had it? Had she told anyone—

Lauren interrupted his thoughts. 'Looks like your grandparents are home.'

His gaze darted along the driveway. He was more relieved than troubled to see the Range Rover. Surely that meant there hadn't been a break-in, otherwise there would be police all over the place.

There was a good chance his pillows-under-the-bedsheets routine had been rumbled, but he'd rather that than lose the diary. There was another reason for his relief too – he'd been dreading telling Lauren she couldn't read the diary until he'd finished with it. Now he had a legitimate reason for fobbing her off.

'Should I come in with you?' she asked.

'I'll bring you the diary later.'

Lauren rumpled her face as if his words hurt. 'I wasn't thinking about the diary. I was thinking some heavy shit might be going down. I know I can be a total bitch from hell, but I . . . Well, I . . .' She looked at him from under her dark eyebrows. 'Shit, you know what I'm trying to say.'

Jake nodded. 'Best mates.'

Crossing her index fingers and curving her thumbs to touch their opposing tips, Lauren made the infinity symbol she'd so often taken the piss out of other kids for using. Jake smiled despite his anxiety. She found it almost impossible to take anything seriously. That was a big part of why he liked her so much.

'Thanks for helping me out,' he said.

'No problem. It's been the most fun I've had in ages, apart from all this shit with your sister.'

Wincing at the mention of Erin, Jake turned to squeeze through the gates.

'I'll wait for you to give me a thumbs up,' said Lauren.

When Jake reached the house, he peeked over a windowsill into a large, beam-ceilinged room. His granddad was sitting in a studded-leather armchair by a tall stone fireplace where a fire was kept burning even on warm days. Henry's troubled gaze was fixed on the flames. On a coffee table there were several monogrammed leather photo albums. Jake couldn't read the monograms, but he could guess what they said – Erin 2007, 2008, 2009, etc. There was an album for each year of her life. As there was for his, too.

An entire room downstairs was devoted to albums documenting the Brooks family history. There were photos dating back to the late 1800s. Some of Jake's earliest memories involved poring over them while his granddad regaled him with tales about their subjects. *This is William Brooks who used the money he made as a textile manufacturer to purchase Ritton Hall. This is Alfred Brooks who died aged nineteen in the First World War. This is Edith Brooks who paid for the war memorial in the market square.* And so it went on, right up to the present day. Jake's favourite photos were from the sixties and seventies. He used to laugh at the flared suits, bad hair and oversized moustaches.

Jake gave Lauren the thumbs up. She blew him a kiss and turned to leave. Two days ago that kiss would have completely thrown him. But things had changed since then, for better and for much, much worse. He slunk along the wall to the front door. As quietly as possible, he turned the thick brass handle.

DAY 2
10.01 A.M.

The image of Amanda and Graham clawed mercilessly at Tom's mind. His jaw muscles pulsed, his fingers convulsively clenched the steering wheel. Amanda had always been able to twist him around her little finger, make him feel whatever she wanted him to, be it lust or love, sadness or guilt. Guilt! He'd come away from their encounter feeling as if he was somehow the villain. How the hell was that possible? How was wanting to give your family a better life wrong?

Amanda had accused him of being just like Henry. And maybe in some ways she was right. He was driven, single-minded, willing to make sacrifices to his ambition. But, unlike Henry, he hadn't been born with a silver spoon so far up his arse it was practically sticking out of his mouth. Getting what he wanted was all Henry had ever known – that is until Tom met Amanda. For Tom the reverse was true. Amanda had been his first taste of what life could be. She'd given him a glimpse of a larger world beyond the grinding drudgery of the farm, a world of laughter and parties, of beauty and freedom. She'd made everything seem possible. And now he was losing – had already as good as lost – her. Henry had waited twenty-one years for this moment, biding his time as patiently as only a wealthy man could afford to. Despite what Amanda said, he wouldn't let her wriggle off the hook again. He would move heaven and earth to match her with the right man, trampling any chance of happiness she had in order to fulfil his social ambitions.

Just to spite Henry, Tom was tempted to return to Ritton Hall, tell Amanda everything was forgiven, plead with her not to leave him. But he knew she'd see through the lie. Even if she didn't, sooner or later all the anger and resentment would come bursting out and she'd realise that he could never truly forgive her. He could hear himself bellowing at her, *You're nothing but a spoiled rich bitch! You're not fit to be a mother!* He stared at the tree-lined horizon. No, his future – if he had one – wasn't at Ritton Hall, it was out there somewhere.

His phone rang. He answered it. 'What is it, Eddie?'

'They've released Graham.'

Tom frowned with surprise. 'How's that possible?'

'All I can think is he must have an alibi.'

'Where is he?'

'The coppers gave him a lift out towards the farm with half a dozen TV vans in tow. He got out just beyond the reservoir turning and went into the woods. The coppers are stopping anyone from following him.'

Tom knew exactly where Graham was going – a footpath through the woods led to the farm. He turned the car back the way he'd come.

'Are you going to talk to him?' asked Eddie.

'Yes.' Tom's tone suggested he intended to do his talking with more than just his mouth.

A cautioning note entered Eddie's voice. 'Do me a favour. Don't go losing that temper of yours.'

Tom smiled cynically. 'Why? You worried I'll end up in prison and scupper your plans for the quarry?'

'Partly,' admitted Eddie. 'But that's not all it is. I know what's going through your head, Tom. You're thinking about putting your fists in Graham's face until he's got no face left. I'd be thinking the same if it was me, and I'd probably do it too. But I haven't got any kids to worry about.'

Tom's forehead squeezed into furrows as images of Jake and Erin vied for ascendancy with those of Graham and Amanda. 'He fucked my wife. What am I supposed to do?'

Eddie blew a resigned breath. 'You do what you have to do. I'm with you whatever.'

'I know. You always have been. Don't worry, Eddie, I'll make sure the quarry goes ahead even if it means giving you my half of the business.'

'I don't want your half. I want us to get rich together like we've been dreaming about since we were kids.'

Tom thought of the contempt in which Amanda held their ambitions. Her words echoed back to him, *No matter how much money you make, you'll never be anything but a pathetic little man.* How easy it was for her to say that. Patronising bitch. She'd never known what it was like to be poor, and she never would. She could afford to play around with a bit of rough, knowing Daddy would always be there to bail her out.

He knew the thought was unfair. You didn't marry and have children with the bit of rough, you used them and tossed them aside. But then again, he was in no mood to be fair. He was in the mood to let rip with all his rage on the person who deserved it most – the one person who truly understood where he came from and what it had meant to him to break free of it.

He pulled over by a dry-stone wall, beyond which a grassy field climbed towards a pine plantation. 'The Geordies will be here soon,' Eddie reminded him.

'Good. Speak to you then.'

Tom hurdled the wall and sprinted towards the plantation, scanning the landscape as he did so. There was no sign of Graham. That meant he was still in the woods. Tom dropped down behind a gorse bush at the side of a footpath, his heart hammering. He didn't have to wait long. Graham and Bob emerged from the pines. Graham's head was lowered. His usually impassive face wore heavy lines of strain.

Tom rose and stepped into his path. Graham showed no surprise. Bob bared his teeth and growled. 'Stay,' Graham commanded the collie. Bob lay down tensely with his front paws extended.

His voice quiet with rage, Tom said, 'I ought to kill you.'

'Do it if you want.' Graham got down on his knees, arms dangling at his sides. 'I won't stop you.'

As Tom loomed over him, Graham closed his eyes. Tom raised a fist. It trembled in the air for a few seconds, then dropped harmlessly. With an exasperated, 'Gahh!' Tom spun away from his brother. 'You always do this!'

'I'm not doing anything.'

'Fuck you, Graham. You know what I'm talking about. Ever since we were kids, no matter what I do, I'm always the bad guy. Well, not this time! This time it's you. You and that slut wife of mine.'

Graham opened his eyes, an uncharacteristic tremor edging his voice. 'Amanda's not a slut.'

Tom stabbed a finger at him. 'You don't tell me what my wife is or isn't. If I say she's a slut, then she's a slut. Do you hear?'

Graham held Tom's gaze and said nothing.

Tom laughed grimly. 'Christ, you and she have got more in common than I ever realised. There's no one better than you two at laying on the guilt. What did I do to make you hate me so much, Graham? You wanted the farm, you got it. Half the flock was mine by rights, but I never asked for a penny. So why? Why did you do this to me? And don't you dare say it just happened.'

'We make our own decisions and our decisions make us. Dad used to say that to us when we were naughty, remember?'

'Yeah, so what's that got to do with anything?'

'So you decided to leave the farm, even though you knew Mum and Dad couldn't manage without you.'

Tom's eyes glimmered. 'Now we get down to it. You've always blamed me for their deaths.'

Graham shook his head. 'You blame yourself. I knew how much you hated the farm. I thought you did the right thing by leaving. What's happening between Amanda and me has got nothing to do with you. I love her. I think I've always loved her, but I only allowed myself to acknowledge it when I saw how unhappy she was. I made the decision to be with her even though I knew it was wrong. I'm not sorry for what I've done, but I accept that I deserve whatever you do to me.'

'Oh, how noble,' Tom retorted sarcastically. 'What a pity for you Amanda doesn't feel the same way. You see, Graham, you may not have fucked her to get at me, but that's the only reason she fucked you.'

Graham shook his head again, but the truth was written in the grimace that twitched at his face – he knew Tom was right.

An ugly smile lifted Tom's mouth. 'That's the joke of it. She didn't do this because she hates me, she did it because she loves me. Can you believe that? Sick, isn't it?'

Like an animal wanting to be put out of its misery, Graham lowered his eyes. 'Giving you a good kicking would be letting you off too easy,' continued Tom. 'I need you fit and healthy. You're going to have to work twice as hard from now on to keep the farm going.'

'What do you mean?'

'Like I said, half the flock's mine.'

'You know I can't afford to buy you out.'

'That's not my problem. Now tell me why the police released you so quickly.'

'Eric Parke was at the farm yesterday morning. I spoke on the phone to Amanda after he left.'

Eric was a vet who'd been looking after the Jackson flock for close to forty years. There was no one more respected than him in Middlebury. If he could vouch for Graham's whereabouts at the time of Erin's disappearance, then Graham had a cast-iron alibi. Conflicting emotions swirled through Tom. Relief that Graham didn't have anything to do with what went down at the forest. Despair that it meant the solution to the mystery remained out of his grasp. He quickly turned his back on Graham and started walking. With Graham out of the picture, all he wanted was to put his eyes – and, if necessary, various other parts of his body – on Carl 'Greenie' Wright.

'Wait, Tom,' Graham called after him. 'If you do this, you'll bankrupt me. Think about Dad—'

Tom felt no triumph at the anxiety in Graham's voice. There was nothing left to feel about him. 'I have thought about him,' he cut in flatly. 'He's the only reason I'm giving you any chance at all. And don't call me Tom. Don't call me brother. In fact, don't call me anything. From now on you're dead to me.'

DAY 2
10.51 A.M.

All morning Seth had avoided Holly's eyes. He didn't want her to see his longing and confusion. He didn't want her to know she had that kind of power over him. Life had taught him to rely on no one but himself, to trust no one but himself. To let people see what was inside of you was an invitation for them to exploit your weaknesses. Not that he was sure what was truly inside of him. Sometimes it seemed that he was nothing more than a hollow container for other peoples' thoughts and feelings. He wasn't even sure that what he felt for Holly was real. Perhaps his desire was just the residue of emotions leached from someone else.

He realised he'd made a huge mistake getting involved in the search. He'd thought it would be fun, but now Tom and Henry were gone it was just as tedious as the factory job he'd walked out on to come to Middlebury. In fact, working ten-hour shifts packing food products had been more interesting. At least in the factory he'd been able to amuse himself by slipping an occasional pubic hair into a microwave meal. Out here, among the never-ending pine trees, there was no chance for any mischief. Especially not now he was leading this bunch of do-fucking-gooders.

He fought to keep his oh-so-grave expression in place. If he never saw another pine tree after this was over it would suit him just fine. But when exactly would it be over? He glanced at his watch. In nine or so hours he would have to make his excuses – feign illness or some such bullshit – and leave, no matter what. The only thing stopping him from doing so right away was his reluctance to draw attention to himself. At least that was what he told himself. But his eyes told another story as they stole a glance at Holly, tracing the soft curve of her waist and breasts up to her sun-kissed face.

He wrenched his gaze away. Nine hours. After that he could wave goodbye to this arsewipe of a country for ever. He could go wherever he wanted in the whole world, become a new person with a new identity. And the past could go fuck itself. Nine more hours of wearing someone else's expression. That wasn't so long. After all, he'd been doing it his entire life.

'Seth!' called Holly. 'Come and have a look at this. I think I've found something.'

His face giving away nothing except dutiful interest, Seth approached her. She pointed to a tiny scrap of white material dangling from the sharp tip of a broken branch. 'Erin was wearing a white T-shirt, wasn't she?'

Seth nodded and got on the walkie-talkie to Sergeant Dyer. 'Keep the area clear,' came the policeman's response. 'I'm on my way.'

'I'd say we're about three miles from where Erin went missing,' Holly said as they waited for the sergeant. 'I wonder what she was doing all the way over here, assuming that came from her T-shirt?'

Seth could think of several possibilities – none of them good – but he made no reply. Holly sighed. 'Look, about what happened before, it just didn't feel right.'

'I told you, I understand.' Seth's voice was tightly controlled, devoid of emotion.

'No, I don't think you do.' Holly caught his gaze. 'I wanted you to kiss me.'

His heart began to beat faster. 'You did?'

'Yes, just not right then.'

'Well, when, then?'

'I don't know.'

Seth's brow wrinkled. He felt like he was groping his way blindly through a maze with dead ends at every turn.

Holly smiled perceptively. 'You've not had much experience with girls, have you?'

'I've had my fair share.' Seth was irritated by the defensive note in his voice. He'd told himself he would keep her at the same distance as everyone else, but she seemed to have the ability to slip past his guard without even trying. Three words was all it had taken to knock him so far out of his comfort zone his head was spinning. *I wanted you.* No one had ever wanted him before. His grandma had needed him to bring in the rent money. But she hadn't wanted him in her flat. Not really. He'd always been a burden. 'It's just that I've never met a girl like you before.'

'Isn't that a song title?' Holly joked.

Seth felt a blush rising to his cheeks. He started to turn away, but Holly put her hand on his arm. 'I'm sorry,' she said. 'You're not the only one who says dumb things when you're nervous. I've never met anyone like you before either. Most of the lads I know look at me as if they're eyeing up breeding stock or something. But when you look at me it's like . . . like you're looking past the surface.' Holly's mouth tilted knowingly. 'Oh, I realise you're not *that* different. I saw the way you looked at me when we first met. And to be honest, I thought you were just another idiot with his brain in his underpants. But since then, well, I realised I was wrong. There's a lot more to you. You do a good job of hiding it, but I see it.'

Seth moved from awkwardness to uneasy curiosity. 'What do you see?'

'I see someone who doesn't like talking about himself.'

Seth's eyes sought refuge in the trees. 'Maybe that's because there's nothing worth saying.'

'I don't believe that's true.'

'What if what I say makes you hate me?'

'Then it makes me hate you. But even that's better than feeling nothing, isn't it?'

'Is it?' Seth had lived with hatred all his life. He knew how it could eat away at you like acid. It was better to exist inside other people's feelings than deal with that kind of pain. He turned at the sound of footsteps. Sergeant Dyer, several constables and forensics officers were approaching.

Squinting at the fragment of material, the sergeant said, 'I want a cordon around this entire grid. And let's get some dogs over here asap.' As the constables carried out his orders, he wagged an approving finger at Seth and Holly. 'You two have a real knack for spotting things others might miss.' He unfurled a map that looked like an oversized noughts and crosses grid minus the noughts. The north-eastern and southern areas of the forest were almost entirely filled in with red crosses. He pointed to an area bordering the moors. 'I want your team to search this grid. If that material is from Erin's T-shirt, it seems to me that's the direction in which she was going or being taken.'

As they made their way to the new search area, Seth put a little distance between Holly and himself. From the looks she kept giving him, he could tell she was waiting for an opportunity to continue their conversation.

His grandma's voice sniped at him again: *Idiot! How many times have I told you? Don't trust girls, especially the ones with innocent eyes. They're the worst of all.*

He'd never questioned the sense of those words – until now. He'd been telling the truth when he said he'd never met anyone like Holly before. She was the first person who'd made him want to risk opening himself up. There was a high probability that all he was opening himself up to was her contempt. But what if she accepted him for who he was? Maybe she was his chance for something he'd begun to think happened only to other people – happiness. Surely it was worth the risk. Wasn't it?

No, it's not worth it! She'll stab you in the back the first chance she gets.

'Shut up, you old bitch,' he muttered.

But she wouldn't shut up. She kept hurling the same old insults at him over and over again. *You're an idiot, a retard, a moron.* He pressed his fingers to a splitting pain in his temples.

'Are you OK, Seth? You've gone really pale.'

He saw Holly had caught him up. This was the perfect opportunity to duck out of the search, he realised. All he had to say was, *I don't feel well.* But looking at her concerned face, he couldn't bring himself to. From the recesses of his mind came more words his grandma had said to him loud and often: *Why do I waste my time on you?*

Seth forced his lips into a thin smile. 'I'm fine. Do you mind if we don't talk for a while? What you said before . . .' He cleared a tightness in his throat. How did people ever get used to talking like this? 'It kind of shook me up.'

He half expected Holly to be upset, but instead she smiled sympathetically. 'Sure, Seth.'

She dropped back into the group, leaving him alone with the sneering echo of his grandma's voice. *Why do I waste my time on you? Why . . .*

DAY 2
11.02 A.M.

Tom pulled over out of sight of the tree-house lookout. He got out and slunk along the hedge that enclosed the lower slopes of Maglin Hill. He studied the protest camp through a hole in the foliage. Life was going on much the same as the last time he'd been there. Several people were clearing the trestle table from a late breakfast. Tom spotted Greenie sunning his chicken chest in a deckchair. The eco-activists' leader puffed on a cigarette, gazing around himself like a king surveying his little realm. Three hundred metres above the camp the Five Women wobbled in the sun, as if indeed swaying to some music only they could hear.

Tom wondered what would have happened if instead of stopping Amanda from attacking Greenie, he'd helped her. Maybe Greenie would have fessed up. Maybe Erin would be at home now. And maybe he'd be none the wiser to Amanda and Graham's betrayal. Would it have been better not to know? The question was pointless. The genie was out of the bottle and there was no putting it back in.

His phone rang. He quickly silenced it and put it to his ear. 'Have you seen Graham?' asked Eddie.

'Yes,' whispered Tom. 'And before you ask, he's still walking around with all his teeth.'

'Why are you whispering?'

'I'm at Maglin Hill. How far away are the Geordies?'

'That's the other reason I'm phoning. They just arrived. Where are you parked?'

'About a quarter of a mile before the quarry turn-off.'

'We'll meet you there.'

As Tom returned to his car, Eddie's BMW climbed into view followed by a minibus. Eddie parked up and jumped out. 'This is it, Tom. This is fucking it.' His voice was ramped up with nervous excitement.

Fifteen figures filed off the minibus, looking like a bouncer's convention on a day trip. A skinhead with a neck indistinguishable from his shoulders approached them. Eddie made the introductions. 'Tom, this is Dave Simpson. Dave, this is my business partner, Tom Jackson.'

Dave held out a knuckle-scarred hand. 'Sorry to hear about your daughter,' he said in a heavy Geordie accent. Tom gave him the brown envelope. It burnt worse than ever to use Henry's money. He would rather have pawned everything he owned if there was time. But there wasn't.

Dave glanced at the wad of banknotes the envelope contained and nodded approvingly. 'How many protesters are there?'

'Maybe twenty-odd. I think a couple more arrived today.'

'I reckon we can deal with twenty-odd lentil-eaters. We can do this one of two ways. We either give them fair warning to clear out. Or we just roll in there and flatten the place.'

'No way are they clearing out without a fight,' said Eddie.

'The lads will be pleased to hear that. They didn't come all this way to twiddle their thumbs.'

'What are we going to do about the lookout tree?' asked Tom.

Motioning for Tom and Eddie to follow, Dave headed around the back of the minibus. He opened the rear door, revealing an arsenal of baseball bats, axes, crowbars and bolt cutters. He patted a chainsaw. 'I reckon that'll do the job nicely.'

Tom thumbed an axe. 'Jesus Christ, we want to scare them, not kill them.'

'Relax. We know what we're doing,' Dave reassured him. He took out a pair of plastic zip-cuffs. 'We'll slap these on them before they even know what's happening.' He turned to his men. 'Reet, lads, let's tool up.'

Dave handed out the tools cum weapons, along with luminous tabards. 'Saves any confusion about who's on what side.'

Tom slapped a baseball bat into his palm. Frowning, he put it down. He didn't trust what he might do with it if Greenie refused to cooperate.

'If you're not comfortable with this, feel free to wait here until the fun's over,' said Dave.

Eddie hefted a crowbar. 'Bollocks to that. We've waited long enough to get our hands on these cunts.'

'Don't go hitting anyone with that,' cautioned Dave. 'Unless you want a GBH charge.'

Eddie pulled a face like a child warned away from a sweet jar.

Dave and his men got back on the minibus. Eddie ducked into the BMW, saying, 'Bring it on.'

Tom sat silent next to him, lips compressed, eyes fixed on their target.

The minibus crept past them. When the quarry came into view, it put on a surge of speed. Its tyres spat stones as it skidded onto the quarry track. From up ahead came the clanging of the lookout alarm. For an instant, as if in suspended motion, the activists gawped at the vehicles charging towards them. Then, frantically directed by Greenie, they burst into action, dousing the cooking fire, ducking into tents, running for the barricade of tyres and tree trunks.

The minibus screeched to a halt in a cloud of dust. Dave and his men piled out. 'Come on, lads!' Dave brandished a baseball bat like a warrior leading his troops into battle. 'Let's show these dirty hippies we mean business.'

Several dogs hurdled the barricade, barking furiously. There was a dull crunch as Dave's bat landed on the skull of the lead animal. It collapsed, yelping in agony. The rest skittered away. A young man with 'NO QUARRY' scrawled on his torso ran towards the Geordies, shouting, 'You can't do that.'

'We can do what we fucking like, pal,' retorted Dave. 'We're not the police.'

A couple of his men jumped on the activist, expertly wrestling him to the ground and cuffing his wrists and ankles. The rest charged the barricade, where more activists were in the process of chaining themselves to tree trunks. 'Shame on you! Shame on you!' chanted the activists as they were cut loose and dragged away.

By the time Tom and Eddie reached the barricade, they were confronted by a confusion of flailing limbs and swearing voices. A woman pushed her filth-caked palms into Eddie's face, yelling, 'If you shit on the earth, the earth will shit on you.'

'The dirty cow's got shit on her hands,' he choked. 'Help me grab her.'

Tom began clambering over the barricade.

'Where are you going?' Eddie shouted after him.

Tom's eyes were locked on Greenie. A hand grabbed his ankle. He wrenched himself free and jumped down to the ground. A couple of activists had chained themselves to the base of the lookout tree. One tracksuited heavy was in the process of cuffing them, while another applied bolt cutters to their chains. The heavies ran for cover as a man in the treehouse tipped a bucket of liquid on their heads. Tom blinked as it splashed his face. The sour tang of urine invaded his nostrils. He didn't stop to wipe his eyes.

The Geordies were upending, tearing down and smashing everything in their way. Shouts rang back and forth. *Earth rapists! Fucking hippy! You're hurting my arm! Give me any more shit and I'll break it!* Tom paid no attention to any of it, homing in on Greenie like a hawk after its prey.

Greenie's arms were outstretched as if he was calling to some great spirit in the sky. 'None of you will escape cosmic justice,' he cried.

'Where's my daughter?' Tom demanded to know through clenched teeth.

Greenie took one look at his enraged face and fled. Tom pursued him up the footpath towards the Five Women. He made a wild grab for Greenie, knocking him off balance. Greenie tumbled down a steep grassy bank above the quarry. Tom lurched to catch his hand and found himself falling towards the edge too. He ploughed his free hand into the turf, snagging a root. Every muscle quivering, he fought to hold onto Greenie. For a second both men stared at each other. Then Greenie's mouth formed an 'O' of terror as he plummeted from view. There was a thud as he hit the ground ten metres below. Tom peered wide-eyed after him. Greenie was sprawled out on his back, one leg at an unnatural angle, eyes closed. With a sick feeling of horror, Tom saw that the activist's blond hair was rapidly turning red.

Eddie dropped to his knees at Greenie's side and felt for a pulse. 'Christ, I think he's dead,' he shouted to Tom.

'Murderer!' yelled an activist cuffed on the ground nearby.

Dave looked over Eddie's shoulder at the ashen-faced Greenie. 'Fuck. This is really bad. Sorry, but we didn't sign up for this.' He made a retreat gesture. 'Come on, lads, we're out of here!'

As the Geordies ran for the minibus, Eddie said, 'We have to go too, Tom.'

Tom didn't hear him. The activist's shout seemed to reverberate in his ears, each echo louder than the one before. *Murderer,*

murderer, murderer . . . He knew he'd tried to save Greenie. But what if no one else did?

Eddie yelled at him again. This time a word got through. *Erin.* It jerked him back to himself. He couldn't stay here. He had to find Erin. He clambered back to the path and ran for the BMW. A torrent of furious voices pursued him. 'Coward! Murderer! You're gonna burn for this!'

As Eddie slammed the car into reverse, Tom clutched his arm and pointed. 'Look!'

On the summit of Maglin Hill a white-robed figure was holding a staff aloft.

'Do you see that?' Tom asked as if doubting his eyes.

'I see the bastard,' growled Eddie.

The last two lines of the poem the priestess had pressed into Tom's hand came back to him like a parting shot. 'We take the consequences of our actions,' he murmured hollowly. 'And so must you.'

DAY 2
11.24 A.M.

On feet as soft as the paws of Mary's cats, Jake padded up the stairs. He paused, stomach clenching, at the creak of a floorboard, then continued to his bedroom. The pillows were still in place. The trick had worked. He quickly pulled down the sheets and started to rearrange the pillows.

'I thought I heard movement up here.'

Jake jerked around guiltily at his mum's voice. He was so shocked by how she looked – sunken cheeks, dark-ringed, lustreless eyes – that he almost forgot his dismay at being caught out. Everything about her – even her usually thick, wavy hair – was lifelessly flat. It was as if a vampire had been at her.

'How are you feel—' Amanda started to ask. She fell silent, looking at the pillows and the boots on Jake's feet. She gave a little shake of her head. 'You promised you wouldn't go back to that house.' Her voice was wearily disappointed rather than angry.

'I haven't been.'

'So where have you been? Actually, you know what, don't bother telling me. I'm too tired to listen to your lies right now.'

Cathy came up behind Amanda. 'Jake, you're awake.'

'He's not been to sleep,' said Amanda.

'Poor darling. Mind you, it's hardly surprising considering—'

'No, Mum. He's not been to sleep because he wasn't in bed.'

'What do you mean he wasn't—' Cathy broke off. Then her voice rose in realisation. 'Oh.' She sighed. 'Jake, I know you're frantic with worry. We all are. But you can't keep doing—'

'Save your breath, Mum,' Amanda interrupted again. 'He doesn't care what we say. He'll just do as he pleases regardless.'

Jake's eyes appealed to his grandma to come to his defence. She shook her head as if to say, *Sorry, darling, not this time.* His remorseful gaze returned to his mum. She looked at him sadly, then turned to walk away. Cathy gave him a faint sympathetic smile, before following her.

Jake heaved a sigh. Self-pity turned to concern as he remembered the chick. He hurried to the airing cupboard. The baby rook was very much alive. At the touch of his fingertip, it opened its beak and squeaked hungrily. He squirted a few blobs of oat paste onto its tongue. Sated, the chick settled down among the shreds of newspaper. The tension faded from Jake's face as he watched it sleep. He quietly closed the box and returned to his room.

He pushed the dressing table against the door, then retrieved the diary from its hiding place and sank back against the pillows. He flipped through the yellowed pages to where he'd left off – 'Thursday, 11 May' – and began reading.

> Something amazing happened last night. I couldn't sleep because I kept thinking about what Hank said about going for a walk. I looked out of my window at the moon which was like a big bowl of milk and I saw something that made my heart beat really fast. Hank was in the garden. He looked at me and I looked back at him. We stayed like that for what felt like ages and then Hank waved for me to come outside. I shook my head but he kept waving so I put

> on some clothes and tiptoed downstairs. I was really scared that Mummy or Daddy would hear but they didn't. Hank was waiting at the back door. I was amazed to see that the door was open. I asked Hank how he opened it and he said he had learned how to do it at boarding school. He said his dorm was locked at night so he had to pick the lock when he sneaked out for a walk. I asked if he could lock it again and he said yes. He said he had something to show me and that it wouldn't take long. I put my shoes on and we ran across the garden holding hands. I had never been in the woods at night before and they looked different. I told Hank and he said that was why he liked the moon so much because it made it seem like you were in a new world. He said that when he was out on his own at night it felt like the whole world belonged to him. We walked along the river to a field and Hank pointed at something on the ground. I thought at first it was a sleeping sheep but then I saw that it wasn't sleeping it was dead. There was something black on its wool. I asked what it was and Hank said it was blood.

The entry was interrupted by a pencil drawing of a sheep with a halo and wings, before continuing,

> I asked Hank if he thought the sheep had been killed by a fox and he said no. He said it looked like someone had stabbed it and cut its throat. I said why would anyone do something so horrible? He said he was not sure if he should tell me. I said why not and he said because he didn't want to scare me. I promised not to be scared and he said the sheep was killed by devil worshippers. I asked how he knew that and he told me about an article in the *Gazette* about a local farmer whose sheep keep being killed. The article

> said police are investigating but haven't been able to find out who is killing them. The worst attack was on the 6th of June last year when 6 sheep were killed in one night. Hank said this proved it was devil worshippers because 6 sheep were killed on the 6th night of the 6th month which makes 666 which is the number of the Devil. I put my hand on the sheep and it was warm. Hank said it wasn't killed long ago which meant the devil worshippers could be close by. He asked if I was scared and I said no which was true I was not scared. I said it would be fun to go looking for the devil worshippers and Hank said I was very brave but it was time for me to go home. We ran back through the woods to the house. Hank asked if I'd enjoyed our walk and I said yes I enjoyed it a lot and then he kissed me on the mouth. I was surprised and he asked me if I minded being kissed. I said not by him and then I said goodnight and went to my bedroom. I feel really strange. My head is dizzy and I still can't sleep. I keep wondering if I feel like this because I am in love

Instead of a full stop, the entry concluded with a heart drawn around a question mark.

Jake thought about the sheep. Was it possible that Hank was right? No doubt, Lauren would say yes. And Elijah Ingham might well agree. But surely Rachel had suggested the most likely explanation – the sheep was simply killed by a fox. Another possibility occurred to Jake. What if Hank had killed it? But why would he do such a thing? Was he trying to impress Rachel in some twisted way? Or was he playing some kind of game?

The next entry was dated 'Tuesday, 16 May'. It began somewhat hysterically.

> Hank where are you? I have gone to our secret meeting place every day since our kiss but you are never there. Where are you? I need to see you and tell you about what happened at school today. Tina Dixon is not just a bully and a whore she is EVIL.

The word was triple-ringed in red.

> When she heard that I was not going on the field trip to the 5 Women she said what's wrong are your mum and dad scared of some stones? I stupidly told her what Daddy told me. I said you should be scared of that place because it's used by a cult of whores who glorify Satan. I thought that might scare her but she just laughed and called me a retarded idiot and then her friends laughed too and they danced around me singing Rachel is an idiot Rachel is a retard Rachel is a moron. That was bad enough but something even worse happened later. I stayed behind while everyone else went to the 5 Women. It was lunchtime when the bus got back. Tina and her friends came over to me in the playground. I knew something had happened because Tina was smiling. She said my dad and some other people from church had been at the 5 Women. She said Daddy told Mr Harrison he should be ashamed of himself for polluting children's minds with Pagan filth. And Mr Harrison said it was Daddy who should be ashamed for trying to stop children from learning about their heritage. And then Daddy got angry and shouted that Mr Harrison was no better than a Satanist. Mr Harrison asked Daddy and the other people to leave but they said it was their duty to stay and pray for the children. And then Tina put her hands together and said you know what I pray to God

> for? I pray that you and your family all drop dead so that I never have to look at your retarded faces again. I told her to take that back and she said make me. Then I got really angry and pushed her. She pushed me back and I fell over and hit my head really hard. Mrs Hedley saw and took us to Mr Turnbull for fighting. When I touched my head I found it was bleeding. Mr Turnbull gave us both detention and said that he would be phoning our parents. After we left his office Tina said that she is going to kill me and she gave me a piece of paper with this on it.

The sentence ended with a drawing of a gravestone with 'R.I.H. Rachel Ingham' on it. 'I think R.I.H. means Rot in Hell,' continued the entry.

> But Tina is the one going to Hell not me. After detention Daddy came to pick me up. I told him what had happened and he said and unto him that smiteth thee on the one cheek offer also the other and him that taketh away thy cloak forbid not to take thy coat also. I started to cry and I yelled at him that this was all his fault and he said I was right because he had allowed me to neglect my Bible. When we got home he made me sit and read Luke but when he wasn't looking I read Exodus instead. An eye for an eye, a tooth for a tooth, a hand for a hand, a foot for a foot. And I prayed that Tina Dixon gets what she deserves but I did not pray to God like Tina did because God doesn't listen.

Jake flipped the page, thinking, *If she didn't pray to God, who did she pray to?* The next entry was dated to the following day.

> Today started off really horribly but ended really nicely. I was sick before school for the first time in a few weeks and when I got to school Tina gave a throat cut sign. I hid at playtime so that Tina could not get me. At the end of school Tina and her gang were waiting at the gates. I stayed in the foyer for ages until they left. On the way home I went into a phone box and asked the operator for the number of Silverton boarding school. I thought I might be able to phone the school and speak to Hank and tell him what is going on. The operator said there was no number for a Silverton school. I felt really confused and angry. Why did Hank lie to me? I went to our secret place and Hank was there. I was happy to see him but I tried not to let him see that. I asked where he had been and he said he had to go back to school. I said there is no such place as Silverton boarding school. I asked why he had lied. He said because he was afraid that if he told me the truth I would not want to be his girlfriend. I asked what the truth is. He said the truth is that he is not sixteen he is nineteen.

Jake wrinkled his nose. Sixteen was bad enough, but nineteen . . . The dude wasn't merely a creep, he needed locking up.

> Hank said he would understand if I told him to get lost. I thought about it then I said it didn't bother me that he was nineteen but that I didn't want him to lie to me any more. He promised that he wouldn't.

Jake raised a dubious eyebrow. Hank obviously didn't know how to do anything but lie. Why couldn't Rachel see that? Was it naivety? Or did she just not give a shit?

> Hank asked why I was so late coming home from school and I told him what had happened at the 5 Women. He said my dad was right the 5 Women is a dangerous place. I asked why it was dangerous and he said he wasn't sure if he should say. He said I might laugh at him. I promised not to laugh and he told me how he went to the 5 Women once on one of his night walks and saw something really strange. He said that he was standing inside the stone circle when a figure appeared to him. I asked what he meant by appeared and he said it appeared out of nowhere like a ghost. He said it was a naked man. I asked what the man looked like and he said he looked perfect like a Hollywood movie star. He said the man didn't say anything. They just looked at each other then Hank ran away. I asked who the man was and Hank said he was certain that the man was a demon. I asked why he thought that and he said because he felt a pure evil coming from him. He said that devil worshippers had summoned the demon and now it inhabits the 5 Women. He asked if I believed him and I said yes. I also said that I think Tina Dixon is a devil worshipper. I showed him the cut on my head and said Tina is going to kill me. I said that I prayed Tina got killed before she could kill me. Hank said I do not need to worry because he will protect me from her even if she is a devil worshipper. We held hands and kissed for ages then he walked me home. Tonight I will say my prayers again but not to God. I will say thank you for sending me Hank. Thank you, thank you, thank you.

Jake shook his head. He didn't know what was nuttier – Hank's story or Rachel's unquestioning acceptance of it. He couldn't help but smile crookedly as he thought about Lauren. She'd cream her knickers when she read this stuff. He could just imagine her at the Five Women trying to summon up the demon.

The margins of the next page were cluttered with a jumble of suns, moons, stars, hearts, dogs, cats, birds, smiling and sad faces. The entry was dated 'Monday, 22 May'. It began in block capitals

> TINA DIXON IS DEAD! When I got to school her friends were all crying in the playground. Some of the teachers were crying too. I asked someone what was wrong and they said Tina was dead. My heart began to beat really fast and I had to run to the toilets because I thought I was going to be sick. There was a special assembly and Mr Turnbull told us that Tina had been found at the quarry on Maglin Hill on Sunday night. She had fallen from the top of it. He said that the whole school was in shock and that it was hard to know what to say about such a tragedy. A policeman came into class and spoke to us. He asked if anyone had seen Tina on Sunday. I said I had not which was true. Everyone kept talking about how they couldn't believe it and how sad they were. I didn't say anything because I didn't feel sad at all. I felt happier than I had done since Micah died. Tina was right I will go to Hell. At playtime there was a rumour going round that Tina fell because she was drunk on vodka. After school I ran all the way to the meeting place and told Hank what had happened. He said he already knew and that gave me a strange feeling inside. Not a scared feeling but a feeling of butterflies in my stomach. I asked how do you know and he showed me the *Gazette* which had a photo of Tina on its cover underneath the headline 'Local Girl Falls to Her Death at Beauty Spot'. The article said Tina had gone out with friends on Sunday

> lunchtime and not come home for her tea. Her parents had got worried and called the police. But it wasn't the police who found Tina it was a man walking his dog. The police say that Tina's death appears to have been a tragic accident. Hank asked if I was pleased Tina was dead and I said yes although I know I shouldn't be. He said yes I should be because Tina was a real bitch. I asked if he thought she was dead because I prayed for it. Hank said he supposed it depended on who I prayed to.

There was that question again. Who had Rachel prayed to? It jabbed its way into Jake's mind along with a whole lot of others. Foremost was: had Hank played a role in Tina's death? There was no mention of anything suspicious. But surely it couldn't just be a crazy coincidence. And why hadn't Rachel asked if he had anything to do with it? Jake had been willing to give her the benefit of the doubt before, but he struggled to believe that even a twelve-year-old from a strict religious background could be that naive. He thought about that 'feeling of butterflies'. He got the same feeling himself when doing something wrong but exciting. He nodded to himself. Yeah, she had her suspicions all right. She didn't ask because it suited her not to know the answer.

Resisting the urge to skip chunks of writing in his desire to know where all this was leading, Jake read on.

> Hank walked me home and we kissed at the back gate. Then he said three words that I will never forget. I love you. And I told him I loved him back. He said we should seal our love with blood. He had a penknife and we each cut our thumb and pressed them together. He said that now we are as good as man and wife.

The entry finished with bubble writing that proclaimed, 'RACHEL AND HANK TOGETHER 4 EVER.'

The next entry was dated almost a month later. 'Saturday, 17 June'.

> I am sorry for having neglected my diary for so long. I think I have not needed to write anything because I have been so happy. Since Tina's death everyone leaves me alone at school. I still have no friends there but I don't care. All I think about all day is seeing Hank. We only have half an hour together but it easily makes up for all the time I spend on my own. We kiss and hug and talk about everything and anything. Hank is thinking about becoming a vet because of what happened to Micah. He says that I can be his assistant if I want to. He really wants to go on another night walk but I am too scared to sneak out of the house again. I think my parents are getting suspicious. Yesterday Mummy asked me again why I keep being late home from school. I told her I'm at the library working on a project about the English Civil War which we are learning about in history class. Also later on Daddy asked me something odd. He asked if any boys at school were bothering me. I said no and he made me promise to tell him if any of them did. I told Hank what Daddy said and Hank said we should be more careful for a while. So today he walked me straight home and now I feel really sad because I only had a few minutes with my beloved.

Again there was a big gap between entries. 'Tuesday, 11 July' was preceded by an 'R.I.H. Tina Dixon' headstone. Then came a couple of brief sentences: 'There was an article in the *Gazette* today about Tina. The coroner decided her death was an accident.'

The next day brought another entry.

> Only 6 days before school breaks up for the summer holidays! I am counting down the hours. 6 more days and then Hank and I can spend as much time together as we want for 6 whole weeks. I'm so excited that I feel like bursting. But I am also a bit nervous. Hank asked me today if I am a virgin. I said yes and he said he is too. He said he would like to lose his virginity with me. He asked if I felt the same and I said yes but that I don't want to get pregnant. He said he will make sure I don't get pregnant and he asked me when I want to do it. I said in the holidays when we have the whole day together. He asked if I was scared and I said no but that I do not want to end up a whore like Tina Dixon. He said I am not a whore because we love each other. He said that is all that matters. He is right. I do not care what God thinks about me any more. All I care about is Hank.

Jake snorted through his nostrils. He'd wondered when Hank would get around to wanting more than hugs and kisses. He doubted that the slimy creep was a virgin. Or maybe he was. Maybe he couldn't get it up with girls his own age. The next entry was dated 'Monday, 17 July' and framed in ominous black like a funeral notice.

> I hate my parents. I HATE THEM I HATE THEM. They have ruined my EVERYTHING! When I got home today Mummy asked why I was late and I said I had been to the library. She said she had phoned the library and I wasn't there. She asked again where I had been and I said I was telling the truth. She said I am a liar and sent me to my room and locked me in. Mary whispered through

> the keyhole Rachel's been a naughty girl Rachel's been a naughty girl. I told her to get lost. When Daddy got home from work he came to my room. He was really angry. He asked me if I was seeing a boy and I said no. He said lying lips are an abomination to the Lord and that I would remain in my room until I told the truth. But I will never tell them about Hank. NEVER NEVER NEVER. I would rather die.

Raised voices from downstairs prodded their way into Jake's consciousness. He jumped up, shifted the dresser away from the door and padded along the landing to the top of the stairs. His mum was pulling on her shoes by the front door, watched worriedly by his grandma.

'They probably won't let you anywhere near the search,' said Cathy.

'I don't care,' replied Amanda. 'They found a piece of Erin's T-shirt. They might find her next. I have to be there if they do.'

'You don't know that it came from Erin's T-shirt.'

Henry stepped into the hallway from the living room. 'And you don't know that it doesn't, Cathy. Amanda's right. She should be there. I'll take her.'

'No, you won't, Henry,' said Cathy. 'Look at you. You're absolutely dead on your feet.'

Amanda held out her palm. 'Give me your car keys. I'll go alone.'

'Alone.' Cathy sounded hurt. 'Do you really think I'd let you go alone? You're in an even worse state than your father. If you must go, I'll take you. Henry will stay here with Jake.'

'Fine. Let's just get going.'

There was such heart-rending urgency in his mum's voice that Jake wanted to rush downstairs and ask if he could go too. He knew she'd say no, though. Not because she was angry with him, but because she wanted to protect him. Besides, the lure of the diary was too strong. He couldn't bear the thought of leaving it when he was so close to the end. As his mum and grandma headed out the door, he returned to his bedroom and resumed reading.

'Wednesday, 19 July'. Once again, the entry was bordered by black.

> I was sick this morning for the first time since Tina Dixon died. Mummy brought my breakfast up to my bedroom because I am not allowed downstairs. I could not stomach a mouthful. Mummy said she was sorry to have to do this to me but it was for my own good. I asked how keeping me prisoner in my room is good for me. She said that we must live to please God and those who live by the sinful nature cannot please God. But I do not want to please God because God does nothing to please me. Hank does lots of things to please me. Mummy said that although what I have been doing may feel right it is wrong. She said that is how Satan seduces us. He disguises himself as an Angel and by the time we realise who he is it is too late. When she left my room I started crying. Later on Daddy came to see me. He read to me from the Bible for over an hour. As he was reading I started to feel sick. I tried to hold it back but I couldn't and I was sick on the carpet. Daddy called Mummy to clean it up. He said that I was sick because of my sin and that he will read to me every day until the Devil is purged from my body.

The following couple of entries were in the same vein. Day by day, Rachel seemed to be sliding deeper into despondency. Jake skimmed over them, his gaze lingering on sentences such as 'I can't stand it any more', and 'I wish I was dead', and 'I don't know who I hate more

God or my parents.' Then on 'Sunday, 23 July' instead of black the entry was bordered by the usual doodles of stick figures, animals, flowers, moons and stars. 'I have seen my beloved!' it began.

> I was not able to speak to him but just looking at him lifted my heart up into the clouds. I was allowed out of my room today to go to church. I did not listen to anything Reverend Douglas said. As we left the church I saw Hank sitting at the end of a pew near the back. He didn't look at me but as I passed he stood up and brushed against me. In the car I found a note in my coat pocket. My heart began to beat so fast I thought it would burst! Later on in my room I read the note which said I will come and see you tonight. It is dark now and everyone is asleep except me. As I write this I am waiting at my window for my beloved. The sky is clear and I can see a smiling face in the moon.

'Tuesday, 25 July', the day before the murders. The entry started breathlessly:

> Last night my whole world changed! I waited up for ages but Hank did not come to the garden. Eventually I fell asleep by the window. I do not know how long I was asleep for but I woke with a start and as if by magic Hank was there in my bedroom. At first I thought I was dreaming but then Hank kissed me and I knew I was awake. We held each other close and spoke in whispers. I said Daddy will kill you if he finds you here and he said he is not afraid of him. I told him why I was being kept in my room and he said they could not keep us apart forever. I said they would do everything they could to try. My whole body was shaking from stopping myself from crying and I said I . . .

Jake read the rest of the sentence out loud, '. . . wish they were dead.' His heart beating almost as fast as he imagined Rachel's must have been, he read on.

> Hank went quiet when I said that. After what seemed like ages he said do you really mean that? And I said yes if it meant I could be with him. Then he said there was something about the demon at the 5 Women that he hadn't told me. He said the demon had spoken to him. It said Hank has a great power inside him that means he will get everything he ever wants but that he will go to Hell for it. Hank said he asked why he was going to Hell and the demon said because of love. Hank asked what was so bad about love and the demon just laughed. Hank asked the demon what its name is and the demon said you will find out on the day you die. Then the demon disappeared. Hank said to me so you see I knew you were going to ask me to do this. I said I have not asked you to do anything. Hank said I thought you wanted me to kill your parents. When he said that I could not speak. It was like there was something inside me holding on to my words. All I could do was nod. Hank said so you do want me to kill them and I nodded. Hank said OK I'll do it the night after tomorrow night when the moon is full and we'll blame it on devil worshippers. I managed to say I love you. He said I love you too more than my own life and after Wednesday night nothing will keep us apart. We kissed for a long time and then I said you should go. Hank did not want to risk sneaking through the house again so we tied the bedsheets to the radiator and he climbed out of the window. I lay awake for the rest of the night and all I could think about was how much I love Hank and how wonderful things will

> be after Wednesday night. Tina was right I am going to Hell but I do not care.

A shiver ran through Jake. So this was it. Finally, after over four decades, the secret was revealed. He tried to imagine killing his own parents and failed. It was too fucked up. It almost made the idea of it being devil worshippers seem quaint. All the way through the diary he'd thought Hank was the one manipulating Rachel, but now he found himself wondering whether it was the other way around. He got the feeling she'd known exactly what she was doing when she wished her parents dead, despite her stunned silence after Hank offered to do the deed.

Trembling with anticipation, he turned the page. 'Wednesday, 26 July'. The entry started off as if it was a perfectly normal day.

> I took a nap this afternoon. I was tired because I did not sleep well last night. Mummy brought me my tea. It was lamb chop, boiled potatoes and cabbage. I ate every last bit because I know I will need all my strength. Daddy came to see me and we read the Bible together. Afterwards he said you may hate us for this now but when you are older you will thank us. He kissed my forehead before leaving. I can still feel where his moustache tickled me. It is 8 p.m. now. Mary has just gone to bed. She said goodnight through my keyhole. It is not dark yet but the ghost of the full moon is outside my window. Not long now. I thought I would feel nervous but I don't. I feel really calm. It is almost 11 p.m. now and dark outside. Mummy and Daddy will be going to bed soon. I think I heard a noise downstairs just a minute ago like a glass falling to the floor. Someone is coming up the stairs. They are unlocking my door.

There were a couple of blank lines, then the entry resumed: 'It is all over.' Jake assumed Rachel was referring to the murders, but the next sentence proved him wrong.

> I never want to see Hank again. It was him. He killed my beautiful Micah. He came to my room and said my parents were dead. He was dressed all in black with black gloves on. There was blood on his face. I asked if he was hurt and he said it wasn't his blood. He said he needed my help with something downstairs. We went quietly downstairs so as not to wake Mary. Mummy was on the kitchen floor. Daddy was in the living room. There was loads of blood. I didn't realise a body had so much blood in it. They didn't even look like my parents any more. They looked like dolls whose heads had been smashed to pieces. Hank gave me some gloves and we used the blood to draw all sorts of strange symbols on the walls. I asked Hank to bring Mummy into the living room so that she could be with Daddy. I don't want them to be lonely even if they tried to make me lonely. After he'd done that Hank said he was going to steal some things to confuse the police and make them think it might be a burglary. We put all the silverware and ornaments into bin liners and took them to Hank's car. I had never seen his car before and when I did I felt sick. It was a brown Cortina with red stripes.

A nauseous feeling of his own rose inside Jake. Cold with sudden sweat, he reread the sentence several times. Then his gaze raced onwards, hardly taking in the words any more.

> I remembered Hank saying Micah was run over by a brown car. I got on my knees and looked at the bumper and I

> found a dent and some bits of hair the same colour brown as Micah. Hank asked what I was doing and I asked him did you kill my dog? He said no. I said we promised not to lie to each other. He said I'm not lying. But I knew he was. He kissed me and said he would see me in a few days when all the fuss over my parents has died down. I said OK. But I won't see him in a few days. He took my Micah from me and I will never EVER forgive him for it. I am finished with this diary as well. Before I call the police I will hide it somewhere where no one will find it

Instead of a full stop, the diary ended with a little heart cracked in two. The fact Rachel was more concerned about Micah than her parents didn't even enter Jake's thoughts. There was no room in his mind for anything other than that one sentence – *It was a brown Cortina with red stripes.* He set the diary aside and rose from the bed. On the balls of his feet, he returned to the top of the stairs. The house was silent. He crept downstairs, remembering to avoid the creaky floorboard that had given him away before. The living-room door was slightly ajar. As he dodged past it, he glimpsed his granddad in the armchair. He slunk into a room lined by bookshelves full of red-leather photo albums. Each album had a year embossed in gold lettering on its spine. He picked out several ranging from 1970 to 1973 and flipped rapidly through them.

He found what he was looking for towards the back of the 1972 album – a photo of his granddad wearing a kipper-collared shirt and flares. Dark-brown hair was swept back from his tanned forehead. He was smiling and resting one hand proudly on a brown Cortina with a red stripe running along its side. Jake swallowed queasily. Was it possible? Were Hank and his granddad the same person? He did a quick mental calculation. His granddad would have been twenty-two not nineteen in 1972, but that proved nothing. He shook himself as if trying to dislodge the question, but it was embedded like a nail in his mind.

He teetered on the brink of phoning his mum and spilling the whole sordid tale, but his thoughts flashed through the times he'd spent with his granddad – playing chess, watching old films, fishing, talking, laughing. His granddad couldn't be Hank. He just couldn't be. Could he? It suddenly occurred to him that there might be a way to find out for certain. With a steadying breath, he tucked the album under his arm and headed for the living room. His granddad was staring solemnly into the fire. His watery blue eyes slid around to Jake. 'What have you got there?'

'I've been looking through old photos.'

'Of your sister?'

'No. I was trying not to think about Erin.' Jake realised there was a grain of truth in his words. 'Is that wrong?'

Henry gave an understanding shake of his head, holding out his hand for the album. Jake gave it to him. Henry looked through the photos, smiling faintly at his younger self. 'People used to say I looked like Tony Curtis.'

'Who?'

'He was a popular actor at the time.'

Henry came to the car photo. Trying to sound casual although his heart was galloping, Jake said, 'I really like that car.'

'I do too. It was my pride and joy.'

'When did you get it?'

Something that might have been a frown touched Henry's face. 'Why do you ask?'

'No reason,' Jake said quickly. 'I just wondered.'

Henry pursed his lips in thought. 'I think it was December '72. I bought it off a chap I knew from school.'

Jake could have hugged the breath out of his granddad. December! More than four months after the murders. So Hank and Henry weren't the same person. 'What was the name of the man you bought it off?'

'He had an unusual name for these parts. Hank. He lived over at Netherwitton. I don't know if he still lives there. I haven't been in contact with him for years. He was a queer sort of chap.'

'That's him!' cried Jake. 'He's the one.'

'What one?'

Jake's words tumbled out. 'The one I've been reading about, Granddad. The one who killed the Inghams.'

Henry held up his hands. 'Slow down, Jake. You've lost me. Do you mean Joanna and Elijah Ingham?'

Jake nodded. 'I found Rachel's diary. She was in love with someone called Hank. Her parents tried to keep them apart. That's why Hank killed them.'

'Where did you find this diary?'

'Under Rachel's bedroom floor.'

'And where is it now?'

'Upstairs. I'll show you.'

Catching hold of his granddad's hand, Jake pulled him up to his bedroom. Henry scrutinised the diary for a long moment. He puffed out his breath and shook his head. 'This is incredible. For forty-odd years people have been blaming it on burglars, devil worshippers, even little green men. But no one ever suspected for a second that it could be anything to do with their own daughter. I remember her. Rachel Ingham. She seemed so . . . so sweet and innocent.' He shook his head again, repeating, 'Incredible.'

'Do you think we should tell the police?'

'There's no question about it, but . . .' Henry hesitated as if unsure whether he should say anything more.

'But what, Granddad?'

'I really don't want to speak to the police right now. You see, Jake, something . . . well, let's just say something's happening.'

'What's happening?'

Henry was silent, his face puckered with uncertainty.

'Please, Granddad, you can tell me. I'll keep it secret if you want, I promise.'

Henry looked intently at Jake, then nodded as if satisfied by what he saw. 'No one else knows what I'm about to tell you, and, for now, it has to stay that way. Your sister's life depends on it.'

Jake's eyes sprang wide. 'Do you know where Erin is?'

'No, but I know what's happened to her. She's been kidnapped.'

'By who?'

'I've no idea. But the kidnapper is demanding a ransom of one million pounds.'

'One million,' Jake repeated in astonishment. 'Are you going to pay?'

'I'd give every penny I have and more to protect my grandchildren.'

Images from kidnap movies reeled through Jake's brain. He saw Erin tied up and blindfolded in a darkened room. He saw her being spoon-fed by a masked figure. Her kidnapper needed to keep her alive to get the ransom. But if the police got involved she would have to die. That was how it always worked. 'So you're going to meet the kidnapper.'

'Once I've got the money together I'm to call and arrange a time and place to exchange it for Erin. I was about to make the call when you came into the room. I was trying to think of somewhere nearby and private to meet.' Henry tapped the diary. 'Now this has given me an idea.'

'The Ingham house,' Jake gasped, as if answering a life-or-death question.

Henry nodded. 'I think it fits the bill perfectly. How did you get inside?'

Jake told him about the gap under the fence and the loose window plate. Henry steeled himself with a deep breath. 'Right, I'm going to make the call. You stay here and don't move a muscle. I don't want to risk a single sound that might spook the kidnapper.' His lips thinned into a tense smile. 'Wish me luck.'

'Good luck, Granddad.' Looking at his granddad's exhausted but determined face, Jake felt compelled to add, 'I love you.'

'I love you too,' replied Henry. 'More than my own life.'

DAY 2
12.06 P.M.

The search was reaching fever pitch as the prodding figures, snuffling dogs and circling helicopters were compressed into a smaller and smaller area. Seth emerged from the trees onto moorland dotted with dark pools and bisected by meandering streams. He marked off another completed grid on the map.

'Where to now?' asked Holly.

He pointed south-west along the straight edge of the man-made forest. 'Sergeant Dyer says we're to take a break first.'

'We need it. Everyone's knackered.'

The searchers gathered in the shade. No one had the energy for conversation. The mood had been buoyed by the discovery of the scrap of material, but tiredness had soon crept back in to sap their spirits. Seth shook his head when someone offered him a sandwich. He wandered away from the group onto the moor, half hoping Holly would follow, half hoping she wouldn't. He sat down amid the heather, closed his eyes and lifted his face to the sun. He could still faintly hear his grandma: *Little whore . . . Waste my time . . . Little whore . . .*

'Seth.'

His eyes snapped open and squinted up at Holly.

'Do you mind if I sit with you?' she asked.

He shook his head. They sat in silence for what seemed to him like a very long moment. He could sense her want, her desire to know him emotionally, mentally and physically. He realised now that she would never fully give in to the last of those desires until she'd satisfied the first two. He opened his mouth. He wasn't even sure what he was going to say until the words came out. 'I didn't come here for a holiday.' His voice was low, like he was confessing his sins.

Holly looked at him curiously, but didn't press him to go on.

His grandma's voice rose up louder than ever: *Don't you dare! Don't you dare!*

'This is difficult for me.' Seth's blank face seemed to contradict his words. He didn't possess an expression that made sense of the emotions competing for space inside him. 'My grandma died last week.'

Idiot. Retard. Unspeakable moron!

'I'm sorry to hear that.'

'You wouldn't be if you'd known her. She . . .' *was a fucking bitch.* Seth's mouth adjusted the thought to, 'She wasn't a very nice person. She took me in after my mother abandoned me. I sometimes think she only did it so she'd have someone around to yell at and call names. Every day it was idiot this, retard that.'

'That's horrible.'

That's nothing, thought Seth, his mind spooling back over the times his grandma had beaten him black and blue, the times she'd locked him under the stairs until he was faint with thirst and hunger.

'She kicked me out when I was fifteen. I spent the next few years sleeping rough.' At Holly's horrified expression, he added, 'It wasn't so bad really. In some ways it was a lot better than being at home. I could do my own thing. I got beaten up a few times, but mostly no one messed with me. Last year I managed to get a job.

Nothing special, just a factory job. But I saved up enough to rent a bedsit. I decided to go see Grandma for the first time in a couple of years. I don't really know why. I think I just wanted to show her that I wasn't the total waste of a life she'd made me out to be. She was sick. Too weak to work or even look after herself. The landlord was going to kick her out. I couldn't let that happen. Even with all the crap she'd done to me, she was still the only family I had. So I stayed and looked after her.'

Seth fought an urge to drop his gaze at the undeserved admiration and sympathy in Holly's eyes. His grandma had had a way of twisting people to her own ends. She'd had nothing except contempt for men – or anyone else for that matter – but she'd used them for money and protection. She would make these eyes at them. Wide, scared eyes. Like she was a deer in the headlights and they were the only ones who could save her. And they would fall for it time and again. But Seth had seen the trick too many times for it to work on him. He would have abandoned her to her fate if she hadn't pulled another trick out of her sleeve. She'd promised to tell him a secret that would make him rich. He'd been sceptical; after all, she told lies like other people ate bread. But she'd shown him her scrapbook of articles about the Ingham murders. Pointing at a black-and-white photo, she'd said, 'That's me with your great-grandma and granddad. Their killer was never caught. But I know who did it. It was someone rich. And they'll make you rich too, if you play your cards right.'

Seth had known at once what she was suggesting – blackmail. He'd known, too, that she was telling the truth about the photo. Rachel Ingham might have had a different name to his grandma, but she had the same big brown eyes. The realisation had led to a swirl of questions. How did she know who the killer was? Why hadn't she told the police? Why hadn't she blackmailed the killer herself? In reply, his grandma had cackled and said, 'All in good time.'

'What was wrong with her?' asked Holly.

Seth shrugged. 'She wouldn't see a doctor. She was terrified of them.' That was true, but only in a loose sense. His grandma had been terrified of doctors, along with anyone else she considered to be snooping official types. He'd thought this was down to her professed hatred of authority, until he learned she was living under an assumed identity. 'I did the best I could, but she went downhill fast. Last Monday she started having difficulty breathing. I begged her to let me phone an ambulance, but she refused. What could I do? It was her life, right?'

'I suppose,' Holly said a touch uncertainly. 'Wasn't she afraid of dying?'

'She didn't seem to be. I stayed with her all night. She got worse and worse until her lips turned blue. Before she died, she asked me to bring her ashes back to where she was born and scatter them on her parents' graves.'

Holly's eyebrows lifted in understanding. 'She was born in Middlebury.'

Seth nodded. 'That's why I came here.'

This was an outright lie. His grandma couldn't have cared less what happened to her corpse. He'd left her to rot in the shitty little flat where she died. He thought about the final minutes of her life – her bony, liver-spotted hand pointing him to the love letters; her barely there voice laying out the truth about the murders. 'Hank was clever,' she'd said, 'but not as clever as me. He tried to make me forgive him for killing Micah by sending love letters signed with his real name. He kept it up for years, even after he got some whore pregnant and had to marry her. But I'll never forgive him. Not even when I'm in Hell.' A smile had flickered on her lips, as if manipulating some psycho into killing her parents was her proudest achievement. But Seth had sensed the hollowness behind it. Not even she'd been able to fully conceal that.

'What was your grandma's name?' asked Holly.

'Tina Dixon.' Seth heard again the chuckle of twisted glee that had sputtered through his grandma as she told him about the real Tina Dixon.

'Dixon,' mused Holly. 'That's quite a common name in these parts. You might still have family around here.'

'Grandma said they were all dead. Which suits me fine. I don't want anything more to do with my family.'

'What about your dad?'

'I've never met him. I don't even know his name, and I don't want to.'

Holly wrinkled her forehead. 'I just can't wrap my head around the thought of having no family.'

'You get used to it.'

'I don't think I could get used to it. I think I'd go mad.'

'When I lived with Grandma, I often used to feel like I was going mad. Even now she's dead, I . . .' Seth dropped into clumsy silence, struggling to find the words to express himself. His head felt woozy. He'd held back most of the truth. But even so, the last ten minutes had exhausted him more than the previous two days.

Wait for it. Here it comes, sneered his grandma. *This is where she runs a mile. Why would she want anything to do with a pathetic failure like you?*

Holly gave Seth a tentative look. 'When this is over we should do something. Go for a meal or a drink or whatever.'

You were wrong! You were wrong! The realisation rang in Seth's head like church bells. Another realisation pierced him. Wrong or right, it made no difference. When this was over, when his business here was complete, there would be no going out for drinks with Holly. He would have to put as much distance as fast as possible between himself and Middlebury. He wondered desolately whether he would ever meet anyone like her again or whether he was doomed to always be alone.

Poor baby. His grandma made sarcastic *boo hoo* noises. *Forget her. If by some miracle you pull this thing off, you'll be able to buy all the little whores you ever need.*

As if to reinforce her words, Seth's phone rang and a familiar number flashed up. 'Excuse me,' he said, jumping to his feet and moving quickly away. Descending into a gully with a stony stream trickling through it, he answered the call and opened his mouth to speak.

The voice box! As he placed the little box against the phone's mouthpiece, his grandma jeered, *You really are the biggest idiot I've ever known.*

'You don't call me, I call you,' he snapped into the phone, reddening with anger at himself.

'I've got the money,' came the unruffled reply.

'You've got the money,' Seth said like a distorted echo, a rise of surprise in his voice. He felt an almost hysterical urge to laugh. *See I can do it,* he triumphantly told his grandma. *I can! I can!*

You're not home and dry yet, she cautioned.

'Yes, that's what I said. We need to meet right away.'

There was something condescending in the speaker's tone that irritated Seth. He felt as if the strings of control were being subtly prised out of his hands. He tried to grab them back. 'I decide when and where we meet.'

'Fine, but I'm alone now. Later there'll be other people here and it'll be impossible for me to slip away without being noticed.'

Seth frowned in thought. He'd already decided where they would meet – an isolated stretch of road outside Middlebury. He'd gone through the scenario in his mind a thousand times. He would be wearing a balaclava and – in case anything funny went down – carrying a replica handgun. The exchange would happen quickly and silently, then both men would go their separate ways. He did a quick calculation. If he feigned illness, someone would doubtless give him a lift back to town. But first he would have to walk out of the forest. That would take the best part of an hour. Then say fifteen or twenty minutes to drive to the hotel, five minutes to pick up the letters, another ten to drive to the meeting place. And, of course, he wanted to be there first to make sure he wasn't heading into an ambush or anything. 'We'll meet in two hours. There's a road about three miles north of Middlebury—'

'My wife has my car. It has to be somewhere I can walk to. I was thinking we could meet at the Ingham house. I assume you know where that is.'

There was that condescendingly superior tone again. But this time it aroused curiosity rather than irritation. Yes, Seth knew where the house was. He'd been debating whether to pay it a visit ever since arriving in town, torn between a fascination to see where his grandma grew up and the thought, *What does it matter? All you need to know about her is that she can't hurt you any more.*

Perhaps I can't hurt you, but he can, pointed out his grandma.

'What are you trying to pull?' asked Seth.

'Nothing, I promise you on my family's life.'

'We both know what your promises are worth.'

The voice on the other end of the line took on a note of offence. 'I promised to protect my Rachel and that's what I did.'

In a twisted way, there was no denying the truth of those words. But that didn't make Seth any more comfortable with the idea of meeting a murderer on his former killing ground.

'Look, do you want this money today or not?' continued the man. 'Because this is the only way it's going to happen.'

Seth's head turned as he heard his name being called in the distance. He peered over the lip of the gully. Holly was wading through the heather in his direction. Did he want the money today? He had to make a decision fast. 'OK, the Ingham house it is.' He knew he was being manipulated, but what other choice did he have?

He hung up as Holly shouted, 'Seth, we're continuing the search.'

'I'll be there in a minute.' Squatting by the stream, Seth slapped his cheeks and splashed a little water over his face to make it look as if he was clammy with fever. It was a trick he'd used before to bunk off work early. He glimpsed something on the far side of the stream – something shiny. He balanced across the water on stones and squatted to get a closer look. It was a broken silver bracelet with a heart on it. He looked along the stream in both directions. To his right it curved around a grassy bend. To his left an overhanging boulder jutted out of the gully bank. He squinted at the dark shadows and even darker peaty earth beneath it. His eyes widened.

DAY 2
12.27 P.M.

Jake resisted the urge to pace around as he waited for his granddad. He didn't want to risk even a single creak of the floorboards. He kept directing frowning glances at the diary. Something was niggling at him but he couldn't quite put his finger on it. Not with his mind spinning with thoughts of Erin. The door opened and his granddad entered.

'It's all arranged,' Henry said tensely. 'The exchange will take place in an hour's time at the Ingham house.'

'Did you speak to Erin?' In the movies, the cops or whoever always asked to speak to the kidnapped person.

'No.'

'Then how do you know she's still alive?'

'I don't.' Henry patted the brown leather briefcase he was carrying. 'But the kidnapper isn't getting this until I see Erin.'

'There's a million pounds in there? It doesn't look big enough.'

'A million pounds takes up less space than you'd think. Now I'd better get going. I want to get to the house well before the kidnapper.'

'I'm coming with you.'

Henry shook his head firmly. 'No, no, no. That's not happening.'

'But I can help,' protested Jake. 'What if the kidnapper tries to hurt you?'

'I don't want you any more involved than you already are, Jake.'

'Please, Granddad! Erin's my sister. I have to be there. I'll stay out of sight. I promise.'

Henry looked at Jake pensively. 'Regardless of what I say, you'd follow me anyway. Wouldn't you?'

Jake nodded.

Henry heaved a sigh. 'All right, but you stay out of sight no matter what. And I mean no matter what. Deal?'

'Deal.'

With a grave smile, Henry rested a hand on Jake's shoulder. 'You're a good boy, Jake. I'm proud you're my grandson. I want you to know that.'

Despite his anxiety, Jake felt a flush of pleasure.

'Right, let's go get your sister back.' As if it was an afterthought, Henry pointed to the diary. 'Oh, and you'd better put that somewhere out of sight. We don't want your mum or grandma finding it.'

'Why? What does it matter if they do? We're giving it to the police anyway.'

'I know that's what I said, but perhaps we should do some investigating of our own first. We don't know if Hank's even still alive. If he isn't, and if he's survived by a family, it's worth considering what sort of impact this diary would have on them. We don't want to needlessly ruin anyone's life, do we now?'

'I suppose not.' Jake returned the diary to its hiding place.

'No one else has read the diary, have they?'

'No. My friend Lauren knows about it, but she hasn't seen it.'

'Good. Now let's forget about the diary for the moment and focus on the task ahead of us.' They headed downstairs. 'I want you to wait here for five minutes after I leave. We can't risk being seen together in case the kidnapper is watching. I'll go into the Ingham house and when I'm sure it's safe I'll signal for you to follow. OK?'

Jake nodded. 'Do you think I should take a weapon? A knife or something?'

'Absolutely not. Remember your promise.' Indicating for Jake to stand well back, Henry opened the front door. They exchanged a final glance, then Henry closed the door behind him.

Jake darted to the living-room window, throwing a glance at the grandfather clock. Peeping around the curtains, he watched his granddad disappear through the gates. His gaze shifted back to the clock. Less than a minute had ticked by. He headed into the kitchen and slid a carving knife out of a block. He stared at it uncertainly, before returning it to the block. He looked at the time again. Still another three minutes to go. This was the longest five minutes of his life! His heart was beating so hard it made him want to puke. He futilely tried to calm himself with deep breaths. He thought about the chick and ran upstairs to the nest box. The chick appeared to be sleeping. Watching the rise and fall of its breathing had its usual, almost magical, calming effect. 'See you soon,' he murmured. He returned downstairs and checked the clock again. It was time.

As he left the house and made his way along the lane, his eyes scoured the trees, hedges, fields and gardens for anything suspicious. There was a woman pushing a pram, a man mowing a lawn, a car passed by. All perfectly normal. Jake tried to appear normal too, resisting the urge to walk faster than usual until he reached the woods that fringed the river. Reasoning that if the kidnapper was watching it would be obvious where he was going, he allowed his nervous excitement to get the better of him. He ran to the flaking green gate. His gaze lingered for a heartbeat on the pentagram, before he skirted along the hedge. He crawled into the garden, peering through the long grass at the house. The sun beating on his back and the nerves churning in his stomach brought prickles of sweat to the surface all over his body.

Once again, the minutes seemed to stretch out like melted plastic. Finally, his granddad poked his head out from behind the loose metal plate. Henry gave a quick thumbs up and drew back into the house. That was the signal! Jake sprang to his feet and sprinted to the boarded-up French doors. He slid into the echoingly bare room. 'Granddad,' he whispered, struggling to see anything in the gloom.

His squinting eyes travelled over the dusty floorboards to the gaping fireplace, then along the graffiti-daubed walls. The room appeared to be empty. Goosebumps crawled up his arms. The house felt cold, colder even than when he'd gone there at night. 'Granddad,' he whispered again. 'Where are you?'

Still, there was no reply. That niggling feeling returned more strongly, a sense that he'd seen or heard something significant but couldn't think what. He crossed the room and peered into the hallway. Dead leaves rustled as a breeze blew from somewhere. Suddenly, in a voice that seemed to be both inside and outside his head, it came to him. *I love you too, more than my own life.* That was what Hank had said to Rachel. And that was what his granddad had said to him. Gasping in horrified realisation, he turned to run for the French doors. At that instant he felt an intense pressure in his left side, like someone had punched all the air out of him. Eyes bulging, he looked down. A knife was sticking out from just below his armpit. His gaze moved from the hand gripping its handle up to a familiar pair of teary eyes. His mouth opened. All that emerged was a strangled whimper. He tried to reach for the knife, but his arms wouldn't obey. His legs gave way as his granddad pushed the blade deeper.

Henry caught Jake and lowered him to the floorboards as gently as he used to tuck him into bed. 'That's it, my sweet boy,' he murmured. 'Sleep now, sleep now.'

As Jake spiralled down towards unconsciousness, a final thought flashed through his mind: *What about the chick? Who will look after it?* Then, like fingers snuffing out a candle, his eyelids came together.

DAY 2
12.28 P.M.

The overhang was about half a metre high. Seth peered into its cool gloom. He made out a leg and arm covered with mud and scratches, grimy denim shorts and a once-white T-shirt, a face partly hidden by a tangle of auburn hair. Erin was lying on her belly with her arms at her sides. The hair above her forehead was matted with what appeared to be dried blood. There were reddish-brown streaks on her face and clothes too. Her eyes were open, but unfocused.

She's dead, thought Seth. Then she blinked and fear flooded her eyes.

'It's OK,' he said, squirming towards her. 'I'm here to help.'

Erin showed no sign of understanding. She weakly tried to push Seth away as he slid his arms under her. As he manoeuvred her out from the overhang, she trembled like a terrified rabbit. Her hair fell away from her face, revealing sunburnt cheeks and cracked lips. A congealed gash jutted out of her hairline. The skin around it was swollen and discoloured. Seth attempted a reassuring smile, repeating, 'It's OK, it's OK.' She felt as light as a doll in his arms. He waded across the stream and climbed the opposite bank. He glanced down at Erin. She stared back, her bleary chocolate-button eyes no longer scared, but not at ease, just sort of watching. 'Everybody's been looking for you, Erin,' he said. 'Your parents, your grandparents, the whole of—'

'Erin,' she interrupted in a tiny hoarse voice that seemed to suggest the name was unfamiliar.

'They'll all be so happy to see you.' Seth lifted his gaze. The other searchers were fanned out by the treeline. Holly was looking in his direction, shielding her eyes from the sun. Then they were all turning to look, and then shouts were ringing out and they were running towards him.

'Oh my God, please tell us she's alive,' said someone.

'She's alive,' replied Seth.

'An air ambulance is on its way,' Holly informed him. 'Sergeant Dyer says to move Erin as little as possible.'

Seth gently lowered Erin onto a blanket. Another blanket was placed over her. Holly tried to give Erin some water, but she pressed her lips together and looked at Seth. Holly pushed the bottle into his hand. 'You try.'

Cupping Erin's head, Seth upended the bottle against her lips. She allowed some water to pass between them.

'She likes you,' Holly said with a little smile.

He looked down as Erin's fingers curled around his. Then, suddenly, it was like something warm was rushing into him, filling him up to overflowing. Tears spilled uncontrollably down his cheeks. He fought an urge to hide his face and was relieved when his fellow searchers turned their heads at the *whump-whump* of a helicopter. A fat-bellied, yellow mountain-rescue helicopter descended a hundred metres or so away, flattening the heather, stirring up swirls of pollen. Seth shielded Erin's eyes.

Two paramedics in red jumpsuits emerged from the helicopter, carrying a medical kit and a collapsible stretcher. The searchers moved back to give them space. They worked on Erin quickly and methodically, checking her vitals, cleaning and bandaging her head, encasing her neck in a brace. Sergeant Dyer and several constables joined the onlookers. The paramedics lifted Erin onto the stretcher and carried her to the helicopter. Seth felt a strong reluctance to let her out of his sight. His gaze followed the helicopter into the sky. He flinched at a pat on his shoulder.

'Bloody good job,' Sergeant Dyer congratulated him. 'You found Erin just in the nick of time. She wouldn't have survived much longer.'

'How does it feel to know you saved her life?' asked Holly.

'I . . .' Seth faded into uncertainty. All he knew was that for the first time in as long as he could remember, he felt something pure and true. And he wanted to hold onto that feeling even more than he had done Erin's hand.

'I think that means he's a bit overwhelmed,' said the sergeant. 'Now, Seth, I need you to show me where you found Erin.'

Seth led him to the boulder. 'At approximately what time did you find her?' asked the sergeant.

Seth glanced at his watch. The sight of it gave him a jolt. He should have been well on his way to the Ingham house by now. There was no way he'd be able to make it by the agreed time. He'd have to rearrange the exchange. He felt himself going cold at the thought. After answering Sergeant Dyer's question and those that followed it and promising to attend the station to make an official statement, he headed off in search of a suitably secluded spot to make the call.

Holly homed in on him. 'Do you fancy going for that drink? I think we've earned it.'

Sorry but I can't, his grandma's voice rang out. *Go on, retard, say it.*

He started to put on a carefully self-schooled apologetic expression. It felt so easy, like slipping into old clothes. But then, as if he'd touched something slimy, his features creased. 'No.'

Taken aback, Holly said, 'But I thought . . .' She shook her head in an *oh, forget it* gesture and turned away from him.

'Wait. It . . .' It wasn't you I was saying no to – that's what Seth had started to say. But realising how crazy it would sound, he continued, 'It's not that I don't want to go for a drink. I just can't go right away. I have to make a statement at the police station. But after that we can meet up and do whatever.'

He reached for Holly's hand. She laced her fingers into his, a mischievous glint in her eyes. 'I could go for a bit of whatever.'

Seth's cheeks grew warm at her suggestive reply. She smiled and tugged at his hand. 'We'd better start walking or the bus will go without us.'

'You go ahead. I have to make a quick call.'

'OK, but first I just need to—' Holly leaned in and stole a kiss, before whirling away.

Seth stared after her in a momentary daze. He took out the pay-as-you-go phone and opened the contacts list. There were only two numbers on it – Henry Brooks's landline and mobile. He deleted them both. It wouldn't be difficult to find them again if he wanted to. But he didn't want to. Not ever. He stood basking in the silence of his mind for several deep breaths. Then he started after Holly.

DAY 2
1.04 P.M.

Henry felt for a pulse in Jake's throat and couldn't find one. He tenderly kissed Jake's forehead. Hooking his hands under Jake's armpits, he dragged him out of sight of the French doors. He gripped the knife again. Steel grated on bone as he pulled it free. He retrieved the briefcase and placed it in the centre of the living room, before returning to his hiding place in the deep darkness to the side of the French doors. Holding the knife ready, he leaned against the wall to wait.

His tongue moved slowly over his lips. He hadn't been inside the house since the night of the murders. Before the last two days, he'd barely even thought about all that in years. But now waves of memory broke over him, threatening to overwhelm his consciousness. He saw himself creeping up behind Elijah Ingham. He saw the hammer crashing down. He heard the dry, then increasingly wet crunch of Elijah's skull as he hit him again and again. Blood was everywhere – so intensely red it almost seemed to glow. He saw Rachel – her eyes so luminous they made the blood seem dull by comparison. It was a sweet agony to remember her so vividly, to know that the moment he'd thought she became truly his was instead the moment he lost her for ever.

Or was it for ever? Was he about to see her in the flesh again for the first time in forty years? Or had she passed the letters on to someone else? Logic suggested the latter possibility. If Rachel was going to blackmail him, why would she have waited so long? But then again, there'd never been anything logical about their relationship. It had been doomed from the start. That was obvious to him now. Back then, though, it was as if they'd been possessed by something primordial, something beyond reason or rationality. Part of him hoped logic was right. He didn't want to see what the passing years had done to Rachel. He wanted to preserve her as she'd looked the last time he saw her – perfect porcelain skin, hair like brown silk.

Not that it had ever simply been about her looks. Really she'd been quite a plain girl – chubby-cheeked and snub-nosed. But her eyes! Such vulnerability. Such innocence. It had been almost hypnotic. He'd had to find out what was behind them. How deep did the innocence go? At first he'd seen her as a plaything. It had amused him to fill her head with nonsense about devil worshippers and demons and watch her turn against her parents. Then he'd learned what was beneath her surface and his world had shifted on its axis. He'd become the vulnerable one. That part of him yearned to look in those eyes again and feel that connection, that sense of twin souls coming together – even if it was only for an instant as he thrust the knife into her.

Henry stopped leaning against the wall. Cold was seeping from the plaster through his shirt. How much longer was he going to have to wait in this damp old hole of a house? He squinted at his watch: 12.40. That couldn't possibly be right. He put it to his ear. The damn thing had stopped ticking. He took out his phone. The screen cast a pale glow, highlighting the creases of his pinched jowls. It was almost two o'clock. Not too much longer to wait, especially if the blackmailer was shrewd enough to arrive early and check out the house – which Rachel most certainly was.

As more minutes slipped by, Henry began to shiver. He silently swore at himself for not bringing his jacket. He was going to end up catching a chill at this rate. Eventually, judging that more than enough time had passed, he glanced at his phone again: 2.36. Where the hell was this bastard? What kind of idiot turned up late to collect their blackmail money? Surely not Rachel.

Ten more minutes passed. He ground his teeth in irritation. This was ridiculous! Either this bastard was playing some kind of game or they'd lost their nerve. He'd give them five more minutes then . . . Then what? His brow wrinkled, but only briefly. The 'then what' was obvious. It would be a high-risk strategy, but what else could he do? He couldn't ring the blackmailer. The police were certain to check his phone records. With all the forensics these days, they'd doubtless be able to determine he made the call after Jake died. And given the lies he intended to tell, that would be a quick route to a life sentence. Waiting around much longer doing nothing wasn't an option either. Every minute the corpse lay there getting colder left his plan more exposed to failure. As far as he could see, his freedom hinged on one thing – greed. If the blackmailer made the love letters public, it would all come crashing down no matter what he did. But he felt confident that wouldn't happen. You didn't kill the golden goose.

The allotted minutes, plus a couple more elapsed. 'Bugger you then, whoever you are,' scowled Henry, dialling 999. The call failed to connect. No bloody signal! With a snort of annoyance, he snatched up the briefcase and thrust his way out of the French doors. His phone pinged. 'Ten missed calls' – all from Cathy. Had she returned home and discovered Jake and he were gone? Whatever it was, it would have to wait. He opened the briefcase, revealing an empty interior. He tossed it into a bush and dialled 999 again. This time he got through. In a breathless, groggy voice he told the emergency operator, 'I need an ambulance. My grandson . . . He's been stabbed.'

'How long ago?' asked the operator.

'I'm not sure. I think I lost consciousness.'

'Are you injured too?'

'My head . . .' Henry faded into a groan.

'Are you still there?'

'Yes.'

'Is your grandson conscious?'

'No.'

'Is he breathing?'

'I can't tell. I'm pulling the knife out of him.'

'No, don't do that. What's your address?'

Henry told the operator, adding desperately, 'Hurry. I . . . I think I'm losing con—' He slurred off into silence.

'An ambulance is on its way. Hello, can you hear me?'

Henry didn't reply. As he re-entered the house, the signal broke up. He knelt and pulled up Jake's blood-sopped T-shirt. There was so much blood it was impossible to tell where the knife had penetrated from looking alone. He felt around until he found the straight-lipped wound. Very carefully, he slid the knife through the tear in the T-shirt and inserted it back into the wound. He planted his hands on the floorboards. As if performing a crazed prayer, he smashed his forehead against the rough wood again and again until blood streamed down his face.

DAY 2
1.42 P.M.

Tom stared blankly out of the BMW, while Eddie lit a fresh cigarette with the end of his old one. They were parked on a dirt track in a copse of oak trees. Tom's phone rang. He glanced at it, but didn't answer the call.

'Is it that inspector again?' asked Eddie.

'Yes.'

'That's the fifth or sixth time he's rung in the last hour.'

The phone rang off and Tom returned to staring out of the window. Eddie heaved a sigh. 'Look, mate, I'll sit here as long as you want, but . . . well, don't you think you should speak to him?'

'Why? So he can tell me what I already know. That Greenie's dead.'

'We don't know that for sure. I could have been wrong.'

'He's dead.' Tom's voice was as heavy as a coffin. His phone rang again. Uncertainty creased his face. 'It's Amanda's mother.'

'Answer it!' urged Eddie. 'It might be about Erin.'

Tom put the phone to his ear and waited for Cathy to speak. If she was ringing to give him more grief about Amanda, he would hang up without a word. Amanda's voice vibrated down the line, anxious and excited. 'I think they've found her, Tom! I think they've found Erin!'

The words were like a jolt of electricity restarting his heart. 'Where?' he gasped. 'Is she all right?'

'I don't know. They're not telling us anything. I'm on my way to the hospital.'

A sick feeling seized Tom. Why weren't the police saying anything? Surely that was a bad sign. 'I'll meet you there.'

They were only twenty minutes from the hospital, but to Tom the journey seemed to take hours. Reporters were clustered at the main entrance. They scattered as Eddie sped towards them, hammering the horn. Tom sprang out before the BMW had fully stopped. A constable approached him, hand outstretched in a *stop right there* gesture. Tom dodged around the constable and ran into the hospital. He spotted Amanda and Cathy standing arm in arm by the reception desk.

Amanda shrugged off her mum and hurried towards Tom. 'The doctors are examining her.'

'So she's . . .' Tom could barely bring himself to ask, 'alive?'

'Yes.'

His next words came in a rush of relief. 'Have you seen her?'

As Amanda shook her head, Eddie's voice rang out in warning. 'Tom, watch out!'

He spun and saw Eddie scuffling with a constable. Inspector Shields stalked into reception backed up by three more constables. 'Tom Jackson, I'm placing you under arrest for the attempted murder of Carl Wright.'

Constable Hutton made to grab Tom's wrist. He shoved her hand away, retreating several steps.

'Do you want to add resisting arrest to the charges?' threatened the inspector.

'I have to see my daughter.'

'You gave up that right when you attacked Carl Wright.'

'Please, Inspector. Erin might be seriously injured. For all I know this could be the last chance I have to see her. I'm begging you to just let me see her, then you can do what you want with me.'

Inspector Shields considered the plea and said, 'You'll have to be handcuffed.'

Tom eyed him warily. 'Do I have your word that you'll let me see Erin?'

'I'll speak to the doctors. It's up to them not me. That's the best I can do. And it's a lot more than you deserve.'

Tom held out his hands. Constable Hutton clicked on the cuffs. She held Tom's arm as they made their way to Intensive Care.

'You said attempted murder. Does that mean Greenie's not dead?' asked Tom.

'Not yet, but it's touch and go,' replied Inspector Shields.

Tom heaved a breath. Touch and go. It was still bad, but it was a hell of a lot better than dead. 'I tried to save him.'

'That's not what I hear.'

Tom was guided to a chair in a waiting area. Amanda and Cathy seated themselves opposite. 'I'll find out what the situation is,' said Inspector Shields, heading into Intensive Care.

Tom stared at the floor, light-headed with anticipation. He felt an almost frantic need to hold onto someone and be held. He wanted to look at Amanda, but wouldn't allow himself to.

'What's taking so long?' she said.

The fear in her voice drew his gaze like a magnet. He saw that she was looking at him with the same need. And suddenly, for that moment, all the anger was forgotten. He held her with his eyes, thinking only of his love for Erin. Inspector Shields returned with a woman in blue overalls.

'I'm Doctor Nesbitt,' she introduced herself.

'We're Erin's parents.' Amanda indicated herself and Tom. 'How's our daughter, Doctor?'

'Erin's suffering from exposure and dehydration. She has multiple minor cuts and abrasions, along with a more serious head injury.'

'But she's going to be all right?' Tom put in anxiously.

'She's stable and out of imminent danger.'

Tom and Amanda exchanged a look of pure relief. 'Thank God,' breathed Cathy.

Doctor Nesbitt continued in a cautioning tone, 'However, we are very concerned about the head injury. There's no skull fracture, but Erin is delirious and seems to be suffering from memory loss. This could be as a result of dehydration. Or it could be a symptom of a brain injury we haven't detected yet.'

Her lips wobbling with the effort of holding back tears, Amanda asked, 'Are you saying she's brain damaged?'

'No, I'm simply saying we need to run more tests to determine the cause of Erin's symptoms. As I said, there's no skull fracture. So we're hopeful that no permanent damage has been done.'

'Is she awake?' asked Tom.

'She's drifting in and out of sleep.'

'Can we see her?'

'I think that would be a good idea. It might jog her memory.'

'I'm afraid I can only allow Mr Jackson to see Erin at this time,' said Inspector Shields.

Amanda stared at him in dismay. 'You can't think I did this to my own daughter!'

'I'm sorry, Mrs Jackson, but until Erin has recovered sufficiently to tell us what happened this is how it has to be.'

'This is absolutely ludicrous,' Cathy said indignantly. 'That little girl needs her mother.'

'It's OK,' sighed Amanda. 'The inspector's only doing his job.' She looked at Tom. 'Make sure you tell her how much I love her.'

With Constable Hutton at his elbow, Tom followed the doctor and inspector into the ward. He stared at Erin through an observation window. Her head was bandaged. An IV drip was attached to one of her wrists. Her eyes were closed. She looked so calm, so peaceful, so perfect. Tears sprang into Tom's eyes. He said to Inspector Shields, 'Will you take the handcuffs off?'

'I can't do that.'

'It'll upset Erin seeing me with them on.'

The inspector removed his jacket and draped it over Tom's wrists. 'That'll have to do.'

'Thank you.' As if afraid of waking Erin, Tom padded to her bedside. With infinite gentleness, he took her hand and bent to kiss her cheek. 'Hi, beautiful,' he said, smiling as her eyes fluttered open.

She looked up at him for a long silent moment, then murmured, 'Daddy.'

'That's right, darling. It's Daddy.'

'Where's Mummy?'

'She'll be here soon. She told me to tell you how much she loves you.' Tears spilled from Tom's eyes. 'We all love you so, so much.' His lips trembled as he fought not to break down completely.

Doctor Nesbitt shone a light into Erin's eyes. 'How are you feeling, Erin?'

'My head hurts.'

'May I speak to Erin?' Inspector Shields asked when the doctor had finished examining her.

Doctor Nesbitt gestured for him to go ahead.

'Hello, Erin. My name's Glenn Shields. I'm a policeman. We spoke earlier. I asked how you hurt your head, but you couldn't remember. Can you remember now?'

'I . . .' Erin's face scrunched as if the question made her headache worse.

'It's OK, sweetie,' soothed Tom. 'Don't worry if you can't remember.'

The inspector showed Erin a photo of the forest clearing where she went missing. 'Do you know this place, Erin?'

'I think so.' Her eyes suddenly lit up as if someone had flipped a switch. 'I fell over and banged my head really hard.'

'How did you fall?'

'I tripped.'

'Then what happened?'

The light went back out. Erin looked at Tom as if hoping he would answer for her. 'I can't remember. I'm sorry.'

'Thank you, Erin,' said Inspector Shields. 'You've been a big help.'

Tom drew the inspector aside and said quietly, 'I think my wife can come in now.'

Inspector Shields instructed Constable Hutton to fetch Mrs Jackson. A moment later, Amanda dashed into the room. 'Oh, my baby. My poor darling,' she exclaimed, grasping Erin's hand. 'I'm so sorry. I should have been watching you. I promise I'll never take my eyes off you again.'

'I've lost my bracelet,' said Erin.

Amanda laughed tearfully, feathering her thumb over Erin's wrist. 'I'll buy you a new one. We'll go shopping and you can choose any bracelet you want.'

Watching his wife and daughter, the achingly hopeful thought came to Tom, *It's all going to be OK. Erin's going to be fine. Greenie's going to survive. Maybe even Amanda and I can somehow find a way past our troubles. We can still be a real family. The four of us together, happy . . .*

The thought dissolved as Inspector Shields said, 'Mr Jackson, it's time.'

Tom's heart squeezed, but he kept his feelings from his face. 'I've got to go now, sweetheart.'

Erin's hand tightened on his. 'Don't go, Daddy.'

He gave Inspector Shields a look of appeal. The inspector sighed. 'You've got five more minutes. I'll be waiting in the corridor.'

'Please try to keep talking to a minimum,' said Doctor Nesbitt. 'Erin needs rest.'

The inspector and doctor left the room. The doctor's cautioning was needless. Erin was dropping back into sleep even before the door was closed. 'Will you be here when I wake up, Daddy?' she managed to murmur.

Tom fought back a wince. 'I don't know.' As her eyelids fluttered down, he said, 'I love you.'

'And I . . .' Erin faded off before she could say the words. Tom didn't mind. It was enough to look at her face, to hear her breathing.

He murmured to Amanda, 'She's asleep.'

Tears glistened in Amanda's eyes. 'What's going to happen to you?'

'I don't know.'

'And what about us?'

Tom shook his head. Tentatively, his hands moved across the bed. Amanda took them in hers and said, 'I've been such an idiot.'

'We both have.'

Inspector Shields poked his head into the room. Tom and Amanda drew apart as if they'd been doing something they shouldn't. 'I need to talk to you both,' said the inspector, urgently motioning them into the corridor.

Exchanging an uneasy glance, Tom and Amanda left the bedside. 'There's been a report of an incident involving your son and Henry Brooks,' the inspector informed them. 'An ambulance is on its way here.'

Amanda automatically clutched Tom's arm. 'Have they been hurt?'

'That's all the information I've got. We can meet the ambulance at A&E.'

Constable Hutton took hold of Tom again. He threw a final glance at Erin as if trying to fix her face in his memory, before allowing himself to be pulled after Amanda and Inspector Shields.

'What's going on?' Cathy asked when they reached the waiting room.

'It's Dad and Jake,' Amanda said without breaking her stride. 'We have to go to A&E.'

Cathy anxiously scurried after her. 'Why are they in A&E?'

'That's what we're going to find out.'

Their footfalls echoing through the corridors, they raced to the ambulance drop-off area. A pair of doors flapped open as a paramedic guided a stretcher trolley through them, closely followed by a constable. The figure on the stretcher had butterfly stiches on his forehead and nose. He appeared to be unconscious.

'Henry!' cried Cathy, rushing to her husband's side.

'Cathy, is that you?' Henry weakly lifted his head. His eyes rolled glassily from Cathy to Amanda. 'I did everything I could to get Erin back, but the kidnapper . . .' He squeezed his eyes shut. 'Oh, Jesus. Oh, God.'

'What are you talking about?' asked Tom. 'What kidnapper?'

'Please move out of the way,' said the paramedic. 'This man needs urgent medical attention.'

Tom stood his ground, repeating, 'What kidnapper?'

The paramedic turned to the police. 'Are you going to do something about this?'

'Are Mr Brooks's injuries life threatening?' enquired Inspector Shields.

'They don't appear to be, but—'

The inspector cut off the paramedic. 'Then let's hear what he has to say.'

Tears streamed from beneath Henry's eyelids. 'I went to pay the kidnapper. Jake . . . he must have followed me. The kidnapper stabbed him.'

Cathy let out a shriek and clasped her hands to her mouth.

Her eyes horrified saucers, Amanda exclaimed, 'Jake's been stabbed. Where is he?'

'I tried to stop the kidnapper from getting away, but I was knocked unconscious and . . . and when I came round Jake was . . . Oh, God, he was gone.' Henry choked off into body-racking sobs.

Amanda swayed as if she might faint. Tom caught hold of her, although the floor seemed to be wobbling beneath his own feet.

'My colleagues were working on the stab victim when we left,' put in the paramedic.

Henry's eyes snapped open. The fogginess had been replaced by a sudden sharp focus. 'Are you saying Jake's alive?'

'He was fifteen minutes ago.'

'Can you please find out how he is?' asked Amanda, her voice as thin as a violin string.

The paramedic put in an earpiece and got on his radio. 'They're bringing him in,' he informed her. 'They'll arrive here in about five minutes. He'll be going straight into surgery.'

Amanda and Cathy gave simultaneous sobs of relief. Henry was silent. Tom stared at his father-in-law as if trying to bore a hole into him with his eyes.

Inspector Shields was looking hard at Henry too. 'At what time did the meeting with the kidnapper take place?'

'I'm not sure,' said Henry.

'Surely you arranged a time?'

'Yes, but I was kept waiting.'

'OK, then how long ago did the meeting take place?'

'Maybe an hour. It's so hard to think.'

'Did you see Erin?'

'How could he have when she's here?' said Cathy.

Henry's eyes grew even wider. 'Erin's here?'

'She was found on the moors about two hours ago,' said Inspector Shields.

Henry's face clouded with bewilderment 'But . . . But that means . . .'

'It means she was never kidnapped. It would seem someone's taken advantage of her disappearance to make some money.'

'And I fell for it. God forgive me, what a fool I've—'

'Liar!' The word burst from Tom like a bullet. His face disfigured with rage, he dove at Henry. His hands clamped on the injured man's throat and shook him. 'What have you done? What the fuck have you done?'

Henry's eyes bugged out of his head. His pulse pounded against Tom's hands.

'Get him off my husband!' screeched Cathy.

Constable Hutton sprang forward and attempted to prise Tom's fingers away, but he held on like someone clinging to the edge of a bottomless pit. Inspector Shields grabbed him in a choke hold and wrestled him to the floor.

'He's lying!' Tom roared. 'You saw the look in his eyes when he heard that Jake's alive.'

'Calm down!' commanded the inspector. 'And I'll try to find out if you're right.'

Tom subsided into breathless, trembling submission.

'I'm going to stand up,' continued Inspector Shields. 'If you move or speak, I'll have you dragged out of here. Is that clear?'

Tom nodded. The inspector got to his feet, motioning for the constables to keep an eye on Tom. Cathy draped herself protectively over her husband. 'Please stand aside, Mrs Brooks,' said Inspector Shields.

His face an ugly shade of purple, Henry wheezed, 'Do as he says, Cathy.'

She reluctantly moved away, glaring with undisguised hatred at Tom.

'Now, Mr Brooks, what can you tell me about the supposed kidnapper?' asked the inspector.

'It was a man.'

'Did you see his face?'

'He had a mask on.'

'What about his height and build?'

'I'm not sure. It all happened so fast.'

'Is there anything else you can tell me? Did this man say anything that might help us track him down?'

'I can't think of anything right now. Maybe something will come back to me when my head's clearer.'

'Fucking liar,' hissed Tom.

'Right, get him out of here,' commanded Inspector Shields. The constables grabbed Tom and hauled him along the floor.

'He's lying! Can't you see that?' Tom appealed desperately to Amanda.

Her gaze wavered between him and Henry as if she was struggling with an impossible choice. The double doors swung shut, muffling Tom's shouts.

DAY 2
3.15 P.M.

Henry's eyes rolled and flickered again. 'I feel dizzy.'

'I insist that you allow this man to be attended to,' said the paramedic.

Inspector Shields stepped aside and the paramedic resumed pushing the stretcher. 'Cathy . . . Amanda,' slurred Henry.

'We're both here, darling,' replied Cathy. She looked across the stretcher at Amanda. 'Aren't we?'

Amanda made no reply. The doors flapped open and another trolley bed was rushed into the corridor. A blood bag dangled above the limp form strapped to the stretcher. Jake's face was like a sheet of white paper. The sight of it made Amanda's legs go weak again. She fought back the sensation. When this nightmare was over – one way or another – then she could collapse. She rushed to Jake's side.

Cathy's gaze was torn between her husband and grandson.

'Go with them,' said Henry.

'No.' said Amanda. She jerked her chin at Henry, 'Stay with . . . him.' There was a slight hesitation, as if she was trying to work out who 'him' was.

She followed the stretcher as far as the operating theatre. She caught a glimpse of several figures in surgical smocks. Then a nurse shut the theatre door and all that was left for her to do was wait. And wait. And wait. She paced around, sat down, stood back up and resumed pacing.

Cathy came into the waiting area. Her face was streaked with tears of mascara. She looked every one of her years and more. 'Your father has a concussion, but they tell me he should be OK.'

Amanda said nothing, showed no sign of relief.

Cathy took her daughter's hand with an imploring look in her eyes. 'He's not a liar.'

She made to say something else, but Amanda cut in, 'Please don't, Mum. Not now.'

They waited together in silence. Finally, a doctor emerged from the operating theatre. Amanda and Cathy's hands tightened against each other as he said gravely, 'We've managed to stop the bleeding, but the loss of blood caused a cardiac arrest. Jake responded to resuscitation and is breathing for himself. However, the sudden cut-off of oxygen to the brain has left him in a coma.'

'Will he come out of it?' asked Amanda, trembling on the edge of control.

'I'm afraid only time will tell.'

'Can I see him?'

The doctor led them to Jake's bedside. He was hooked up to a bewildering array of tubes and monitors. His chest was heavily bandaged. He looked as if he was in a deep sleep. Amanda removed her hand from Cathy's and rested it lightly on his. Tears ran down her cheeks, but she somehow managed to keep them from her voice. 'Hello, sweetheart. I've got some good news. We found Erin. She's going to be fine. Everything's going to be fine now. When you wake up, we'll all go home together. You, Erin, me and . . .' She couldn't bring herself to say 'your dad'. Enough lies had been told already. She watched desperately to see if her words had any visible effect. They didn't.

'And I've got more good news, darling,' said Cathy. 'Your granddad is—' She broke off as Amanda shot her a look that could freeze blood.

Amanda's troubled eyes returned to Jake. She couldn't be sure she hadn't imagined it, but it seemed to her she'd felt a tiny flicker of movement from him. 'Jake can you hear me?' she asked. But once again, it was as if she was talking to a statue.

ONE WEEK LATER

Henry stared at Jake from the end of the bed. Jake's vital signs had been stable for several days. An MRI had shown signs of brain activity, which the neurologist described as encouraging, while cautioning that it was difficult to say what it meant in terms of the prognosis for regaining consciousness. Everything was uncertainty. Henry's insides were churning with it – for the opposite reason to everyone else's. All the decades of building his fortune. All the generations it had taken to raise up the family name. All of it hung on a thread as fragile as Jake's grip on life.

The worst of it was the loss of control. If Rachel had taught him one thing, it was that without control there was chaos. And once you were caught in that whirlpool it was a downward spiral into madness. He had to wrest back control. The question was: how? A few minutes alone with Jake and a pillow would be a good start. But Amanda was barely ever away from Jake's side. And when she was, her place was taken by the strange creature who was Jake's best friend. His mind was in such turmoil it couldn't seem to hold on to her name. She was the one who'd told the police about Rachel's diary. That had thrown up some awkward questions. But considering he'd burnt the bastard thing, the questions amounted to nothing but speculation. The girl had complicated matters further when, after keeping it to herself for a couple of days, she told the police about Mary Ingham. That had given him a bit of a shock. He'd always wondered if leaving Mary alive would come back to haunt him. His worry had proved groundless. When the police forced entry to her bungalow, Mary had suffered some sort of fit and lapsed into a catatonic state. Word had it she'd been sectioned. A forensic sweep of the bungalow had, of course, turned up no evidence linking her to Jake's stabbing. So once again all the police were left with was speculation. But that was where the good news began and ended.

The girl had been at Jake's bedside when Henry and Amanda arrived at the hospital. She'd sat with him all night so Amanda could get some sleep. Not that Amanda had done much sleeping from the looks of her.

Amanda's eyes were bloodshot and sunken. She was brushing Jake's hair over and over again – a ritual she went through every morning. The girl was reading a novel to Jake. The neurologist had stressed how important it was to keep his brain stimulated. When she lowered the novel and yawned, Amanda filled in the silence. 'Erin's getting better every day,' she softly told Jake. 'More and more of what happened is coming back to her. Last night she remembered how she followed a stream out of the forest. She says you once told her to do that if she ever got lost. So you helped save her life. She's made you a card to say thanks. There's a mountain of other cards for you to read when you wake up too. A bagful has been arriving every day from people who've read about you in the papers. Oh, and your little chick's doing well. Erin's been taking care of it. I think it's really helping her get over what happened to her. She wants to give it a name, but I said that's up to you. I'm taking her to see your dad this afternoon.'

'Amanda,' Henry said in a cautioning tone. 'I don't think Jake needs to hear about that.'

'Well, I think he does. I want him to know exactly how things stand. Anyway, it's not as though Tom will be in there for long now.'

That had been another dollop of shit on the cake, reflected Henry. Carl Wright had pulled through his injuries and corroborated that Tom tried to save him. Tom was still on remand, but only for the illegal eviction, not attempted murder. He would be out in a matter of months, if not weeks.

The girl yawned again. 'Is it all right if I head off, Mrs Jackson? I'm totally knackered.'

'Of course, Lauren,' smiled Amanda. 'You go home and get some rest.'

Lauren, that was her name. She would be pretty if she got rid of the make-up. She obviously fancied herself a bad girl, but Henry could see through her. Rachel would have eaten her for breakfast.

'See you later, Jake,' said Lauren, standing to leave. 'I'll bring a new book. Any requests?' She looked hopefully at Jake's comatose face. Her gaze moved to Henry. 'Bye, Mr Brooks.'

He mustered a smile. 'Bye, Lauren.' His eyes followed her to the door. She darted him a glance. His smile broadened. Oh yes, he could see through her all right. She didn't believe his story about the kidnapper. Or at least she suspected it was a lie. Not that he cared what a silly little girl like her thought. He turned to Amanda. She was a different matter altogether. He wanted so badly to know what was going on in her mind. Her face had always been an open book to him. But now it was as if that book had been closed and locked. She hadn't questioned his story. Maybe that was because she believed it. Or maybe, like himself, she was biding her time to see how things turned out with Jake.

'We should be going too,' he said.

'It's only half an hour's drive to the prison,' said Amanda. 'We've got plenty of time.'

Henry expelled a disapproving breath. 'Do you really think a prison's a fit place to take a nine-year-old girl?'

'We've been through this already, Dad. I'm taking her. End of story.'

Fucking Tom Jackson! Henry wanted to explode at Amanda. *Will I never be rid of him?* 'Well, who's going to sit with Jake?'

'Graham.'

'Graham!' Henry repeated incredulously. 'I thought you wanted nothing more to do with him.'

'This isn't about me. Jake loves his uncle.'

Amanda returned to brushing Jake's hair and chattering on inanely to him. Henry was no longer listening. His mind was back in that whirlpool, spiralling downwards. *Loves his uncle. Nonsense! She could have asked me to stay with Jake, but instead she asked the idiot who caused all this in the first place. Surely that means she doesn't trust me . . .* He almost flinched when Graham entered the room. He smiled to conceal his distaste at the faint smell of sheep.

Graham nodded a silent hello to him. His features were as stoically inexpressive as ever, but a flicker of pain passed over them as he looked at Amanda.

She quickly blinked away from his gaze and pointed out some magazines. 'If you could read these to Jake that would be great. There's a TV guide. I've circled programmes Jake enjoys. There's an iPad here too with his favourite songs on it. I think that's everything.' She looked at Henry as if for confirmation and he found himself thinking, *Maybe I'm wrong, maybe she does trust me.*

'I shouldn't be gone more than two or three hours,' continued Amanda. She bent in to kiss Jake's forehead. 'See you soon, beautiful.'

Henry gave one of Jake's feet a squeeze. 'Bye bye for now, sweet boy.'

On the way out of the room, Amanda paused and met Graham's eyes. 'Thanks for this.'

'Glad to help,' he said. This time he was the one who looked away.

As if she'd been released, Amanda hurried from the hospital. Henry's Range Rover was parked outside. Dark clouds gathered on the horizon as they drove to Ritton Hall. They seemed like a manifestation of the bruises on Henry's face. As the Range Rover pulled up to the house, Cathy came out onto the doorstep.

'How is he?' she asked.

'No change,' replied Henry.

Amanda glanced about anxiously. 'Where's Erin?'

'In the back garden,' said Cathy.

'I asked you not to leave her alone outside.'

'Oh, Amanda, what could possibly—' Cathy broke off. Amanda was already hurrying around the side of the house. Cathy heaved a sigh, turning to Henry. 'She'll have a nervous breakdown if she carries on like this much longer.'

Henry headed inside without replying. He was thinking about the final dollop of shit – the question that was tormenting him almost as much as Jake's stubborn refusal to die. Why hadn't the blackmailer called? *One million or the letters will be all over the Internet by this time next week.* That was what the blackmailer had threatened. It was 'this time next week' now. He'd spent much of the past few days scouring the Internet for new information about the Ingham murders, his heart skipping whenever he came across a previously unseen link. Every minute the blackmailer remained silent chipped away at his certainty that greed would prevail.

'Would you like a cup of tea?' asked Cathy. She had to repeat the question three times before it got through.

Henry gave her a little smile and a nod. Cathy rubbed his shoulder. 'Poor darling, you're still not right, are you?'

'I don't think the concussion has quite cleared up.'

She tenderly touched the bruises on his face that were fading from black to yellow. 'Well, you look a lot better today.'

Henry patted Cathy's hand. 'Another day or two and I'm sure I'll be back to my old self.'

As she headed to the kitchen, he entered the living room and opened his laptop. The 'new email' icon pinged up. Blood began to pound in his ears when he saw the sender's name – 'Hank'. The email's subject was entitled simply 'Love'. He opened it and scanned the message: 'You were right, I would do anything for it.' Underneath was a link for 'www.thetruthabouttheinghammurders.com'. He followed it and was confronted by a photo of a letter he'd written in what, before the events of the past week, had been his darkest moment.

'Dearest Rachel,' it began,

> I'm writing this to prove beyond doubt that I love you. This is not simply a letter it's a confession. I told you my name is Hank, but that was a lie. My real name is Henry Brooks. Until recently I was studying law at King's College London. I was forced to defer my studies after my father fell seriously ill. I had been impatient to return to London, but you made me want to stay in Middlebury. You are my everything and I want to give you everything, even the power to send me to prison for the rest of my life. Here then is my confession: on the night of Wednesday July 26th 1972 I murdered Elijah and Joanna Ingham. I did this for one reason alone: love. I buried the things I stole from the Inghams at the Five Women. I acted on my own without anyone's knowledge. There it is, my darling sweetheart, the final proof of my feelings towards you. Use it to destroy me if you wish or accept the truth and make me the happiest man in the world.

The letter was signed, 'Yours for ever and always, Henry Brooks.'

As Henry read the letter, he felt as if he was falling. Spinning down . . . down . . . down . . . At the sound of footsteps, he flipped the laptop shut. 'Henry, what is it?' Cathy asked as he stalked past her, his face like granite.

He made his way outside and grabbed a spade. Cathy worriedly trailed after him. 'What's wrong? Why won't you talk to me?'

Henry flung the spade into his Range Rover's boot and climbed behind the wheel. Cathy put her hand on his arm, but he shook her off and slammed the door. Eyes dead ahead, he accelerated sharply away.

THE LAST DANCE...

Amanda's features relaxed a little at the sight of Erin. The little girl was sitting on the rim of the fountain, absently swishing her hand in the water. There were patches of peeling skin on her face and faded crisscrosses of scratches on her arms and legs. The dark scab on her hairline was the only outward sign of her ordeal that would leave a lasting scar. Amanda knew there were other less visible, but possibly even longer lasting scars. Every night Erin suffered nightmares in which she was lost in a forest with no hope of ever finding her way out.

At the sound of an engine flaring and tyres biting gravel, Amanda quickly reached for Erin's hand and drew her towards the front of the house. 'What's wrong, Mummy?' asked Erin.

'Nothing, darling.'

When they reached the driveway, the Range Rover was already speeding out of the gates. Cathy was staring after it with troubled eyes.

'Where's Dad going?' asked Amanda.

'I don't know. He was looking at his laptop one minute. The next minute he stormed off without a word. I'm worried, Amanda. It's not like him at all. What if it's something to do with his concussion? He might not even realise what he's doing.'

Amanda frowned doubtfully. From the way her dad was driving, it looked as if he had a definite urgent purpose on his mind. She hastened into the house. Cathy stood with her arms around Erin's shoulders as Amanda looked at the laptop. Amanda's face pinched into sharper and sharper lines. Her lips trembled as if she'd been touched by a sudden chill.

'What's on there?' Cathy asked fearfully.

'I'll tell you later,' Amanda replied with a meaningful glance at Erin. 'I'm going after Dad.'

'But you don't know where he's gone.'

'I've got a good idea.'

'Can I come with you, Mummy?' asked Erin, looking up at her, wide-eyed.

Amanda's voice softened. 'No, sweetheart. You need to stay here with Grandma.' She kissed Erin's head. 'I won't be long.'

'I really think I should be the one going—' Cathy started to say. She broke off as Amanda gave her a look that was both hard and pleading.

Amanda's gaze fell to Erin again. With a physical wrench, she turned and hurried to her car. She put the laptop on the back seat and pulled out of the driveway. A savage agony burnt in her eyes as she thought about Jake's face when he'd been brought into the hospital. It had looked as dead as dead could be. The sight of it had torn a hole right through her. She'd thought no other pain could come close to that. She'd been wrong.

She slammed on the brakes as an eerie scarecrow of a figure stepped into the lane. Frizzy greying hair framed a face as wrinkly as the tree the woman had materialised from behind. An ankle-length white gown hung loosely on her bony, barefooted frame. Her eyes were the only thing alive in an expressionless mask. They stared at Amanda in a pitifully imploring way.

'Mary,' breathed Amanda. What was she doing here? Had she run away from hospital? All kinds of rumours concerning Mary were swirling around Middlebury. The most outlandish one was that she was involved in a Satanic conspiracy led by whoever killed her parents. Amanda had treated the rumours with the contempt they deserved. From what Lauren had said, it was clear Mary believed she was doing a good deed when she left the doll of Erin on the doorstep.

Amanda waved for Mary to move out of the way, but she merely stood there as if waiting for something. As Amanda started to get out of the car, Mary darted to open the passenger door and ducked in.

'Get out,' demanded Amanda. Mary sat staring rigidly out the window. She cut such a pathetic figure that Amanda couldn't bring herself to put much force into her voice as she threatened, 'I'll call the police.'

No response. Amanda eyed Mary narrowly. Did she know who killed her parents? If so, she had as much right as anyone to confront the murderer. And if not, it was time she found out. 'OK,' said Amanda, nodding as much to herself as Mary. She restarted the engine.

She drove fast to the quarry, skidding to a stop behind Henry's Range Rover. Broken wood, tyres and scraps of tarp piled up ready to be burnt were all that was left of the protest camp. There was a thick, round stump where the old oak had guarded the quarry's entrance.

Amanda ran up the footpath towards the Five Women, with Mary following a short distance behind. Mary stopped suddenly as if she'd hit an invisible barrier. She was trembling violently. Although Mary was the older woman, Amanda felt a motherly pang of sympathy. She held out a hand, but Mary didn't take it.

The sound of a spade slicing into earth drew Amanda's attention. Warily now she passed through the opening in the grass bank that ringed the standing stones. Her dad was frenziedly digging at the centre of the circle, his face purple with exertion, his shirt dark with sweat. The spade struck something metallic. Dropping to his knees, he began clawing up handfuls of earth.

'Tom was right,' Amanda said in a voice of breathless hatred. 'You lied.'

Henry jerked towards her, but didn't seem to see her. His eyes were somehow there but not there, as if he was dreaming with them open. He turned back to the hole, thrust his hands into it and pulled out a bulging black bin-liner. A glimpse of something rusty showed through a tear.

'How could you do it?' The words were like hooks being dragged out of Amanda's throat. 'How could you do that to your own grandson?'

Henry reeled backwards suddenly, his eyes gaping at an empty space between the standing stones. 'Who are you?' he cried. He shook his head frantically. 'No. You don't exist. I made you up.'

'What is this?' scowled Amanda. 'Are you going to pretend to be insane now? Well, it won't work. You're not going to worm your way out of this.'

Henry dropped the bag and a claw hammer fell out of the tear. 'Don't tell me.' He clapped his hands over his ears. 'I don't want to hear it!' He made for the circle's entrance in a staggering run.

As he passed Amanda, she spat in his face. He didn't wipe it away or even seem to notice. Gown billowing, Mary sprang from behind a standing stone. Hissing like a feral cat, she clawed Henry's face with long fingernails. He staggered backwards and fell with her on top. His hands latched onto her scrawny throat and he rolled to straddle her. She raked his skin again, drawing blood.

'Let go of her!' screamed Amanda, grabbing his arm. He elbowed her in the chest, knocking her to the ground. Her hand landed on the hammer.

Henry gouged his thumbs into Mary's windpipe. Her hands dropped limply to her sides. Her eyes rolled white.

Winded, Amanda struggled to her feet. She raised the hammer and brought it down. It sank with a crunch into Henry's skull. He didn't cry out, but rose stiffly, took several faltering steps and keeled over like a felled tree. Blood leaked out of his nostrils. Crimson tears spilled from his eyes as he rasped, 'I know his name. I know his name.'

Amanda stared at her father emotionlessly. All she could feel was the void left by Jake's face. She turned at a sound from Mary. Mary's lips formed two words so faint as to be hardly heard. 'Henry Brooks.'

Amanda held out her hand again. This time Mary took it. Henry's breath was winding down like a dying clock. Before it could stop, they walked away. As they descended the hill, the Five Women danced silently behind them.

ABOUT THE AUTHOR

Ben Cheetham is an award-winning writer and Pushcart Prize nominee. His writing spans the genres, from horror and sci-fi to literary fiction, but he has a passion for dark, gritty crime fiction. His short stories have been widely published in magazines in the UK, US and Australia.

Ben lives in Sheffield, UK, where – when he's not chasing around after his young son – he spends most of his time locked away in his study racking his brain for the next paragraph, the next sentence, the next word.

If you want to learn more about Ben, or get in touch, you can look him up at www.bencheetham.com or www.bencheetham.blogspot.com. Find him on Twitter @ben_cheethamUK and on Facebook at www.facebook.com/BenCheethamBooks.

Printed in Great Britain
by Amazon

27490702R00209